Acclaim for Am... and Her E...

HIGHLAND PRINCESS

"[A] captivating . . . mix of romance, adventure, humor, courage, and passion. . . . A MUST-read."
—*The Best Reviews*

"A dynamic story . . . Those who desire a lusty battle of wills will thrill to the lovers' personal feud."
—*Romantic Times BOOKclub Magazine*

"Powerful . . . Exciting . . . Loved it."
—*Romantic Review*

"Five stars! Grips the audience from the onset and never lets go . . . Delightful."
—*Affaire de Coeur*

"A fabulous medieval Scottish romance . . . a unique heroine who is more than just feisty."
—*Midwest Book Review*

THE REIVER'S BRIDE

"Features the same intriguing mix of romance, adventure, and a sprinkling of magic as the 'wee folk' continue to play matchmaker with mortals."
—*Booklist*

more . . .

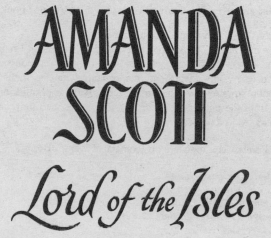

AMANDA SCOTT

Lord of the Isles

WARNER
FOREVER

NEW YORK   BOSTON

Cover design by Diane Luger
Cover art by Franco Accornero
Typography by David Gatti
Book design by Giorgetta Bell McRee

Warner Books

Time Warner Book Group
1271 Avenue of the Americas
New York, NY 10020
Visit our Web site at www.twbookmark.com

Printed in the United States of America

First Paperback Printing: May 2005

10 9 8 7 6 5 4 3 2 1

During the fourteenth century, the surname Stewart was in transition from an occupational term to a surname. Robert the Steward assumed the throne in 1371 as Robert II, progenitor of the Stewart dynasty of Scotland and England. Robert's daughter, the princess Margaret, went by the name of Lady Margaret Stewart.

For readers curious about canonical hours mentioned in the text, in winter the hour of None, at one-thirty, was a time of prayers for relatives and friends, followed at two by the midday meal. Vespers, at four-thirty, was evening prayer, and supper came afterward.

For those who like to know how to pronounce the names and places mentioned in *Lord of the Isles,* please note the following:

Ardtornish = Ard-TOR-nish
Chalamine = HAH-la-meen
Creag na Corps = Craig nah core
Duart = DOO-art
Eilean Mòr = EE-lee-an MORE
Gillean = Jill-ANE
Hebrides = HEH-bri-deez
Isla (or its present-day spelling, Islay) = EE-lah
Lochbuie = Lock-BOO-ee
Lubanach = LOO-ban-och
Maclean = Mac-LANE
Macleod = Mac-LOUD
Reaganach = RAY-gan-och

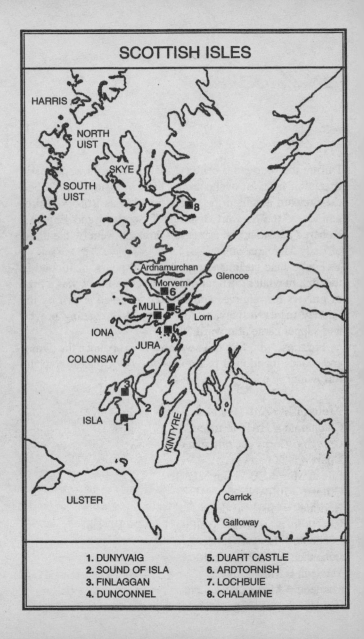

SCOTTISH ISLES

HARRIS

NORTH
UIST

SKYE

SOUTH
UIST

Ardnamurchan

Morvern   Glencoe
■ 6

MULL
■ 5
7 ■ ■ ■ 4   Lorn

IONA

JURA

COLONSAY

■ 3
2

ISLA
■ 1

KINTYRE

ULSTER

Carrick

Galloway

1. DUNYVAIG	5. DUART CASTLE
2. SOUND OF ISLA	6. ARDTORNISH
3. FINLAGGAN	7. LOCHBUIE
4. DUNCONNEL	8. CHALAMINE

Chapter 1 —————————

Scotland, the Highlands & Western Isles,
Spring 1370

The unruly night turned suddenly terrifying when a lightning bolt ripped across the black heavens, followed instantly by a deafening crack of thunder that all but muted the pelting din of the rain. The storm that had muttered, growled, and spat at the lone, miserable rider throughout the afternoon and evening, attacked with a vengeance, startling him and his horse so much that it nearly unseated him.

Struggling to keep his own fear from further terrifying the poor beast, he forced calm into his voice and firm steadiness into the hand that held the reins, only to be nearly unseated again when great flickering branches of fresh lightning, one after another, clawed and stabbed the world around him, slashing sky and land amidst cracks of thunder so loud it was as if the gods beat drums inside his head.

His horse, mad now with terror, reared and plunged, in grave danger of hurting itself or hurling him into oblivion, because the narrow track, although serviceable enough in daylight with rain spattering him in irregular bursts, now boiled and rushed beneath them like a snowmelt river in spring spate. With footing precarious, he fought to bring the frightened animal under control, succeeding only when a lull occurred as suddenly as the onslaught had. The rain eased to a drizzle.

Knowing that the storm was as likely as not to renew its fury, he knew, too, that the longer he stayed in the open, the greater the risk to his safety. More than once during the past four hours, he had berated himself for pressing on from Glen Shiel in the face of such strong storm warnings. But he had wanted to reach Kyle Rhea and the ferry crossing to the Isle of Skye before nightfall so that he could return his borrowed horse and sail home to Lochbuie.

However, much as he wanted to feel his own boat beneath him again, no man of sense would risk oarsmen or vessel, not to mention himself, by trying to pole a ferry or row a longboat anywhere tonight. He needed to find shelter, and quickly.

By noon that day, the clouds had hung so low over nearby hills as to make him wonder idly if, by standing atop his saddle, he might touch them with his whip. Then darkness had drawn nearer, the clouds had turned purple-black, and the winds had attacked, roiling them into frenzied harbingers of what he presently endured.

The wind chose that moment to pick up again, and the rain, too, slanting sheets of it that threatened to drown both him and the horse. Lightning flashed again but more distantly, and the crack and roll that followed took time to reach him. The worst of the storm, at least this part of it, was moving on.

He had complete sympathy with the horse, for if the truth were known, the crackling bolts frightened him witless and had done so since his childhood, when he had feared that such a bolt might crack open the sky and drop God right out of heaven to smash headlong into the ground or the sea. And even if the lightning failed to get God, it could certainly get him.

Maturity had eventually persuaded him that an all-powerful God could survive lightning, but it had not yet persuaded him that his own mortal body was any match for it. He had fought to conquer his fear, and he certainly did not admit its existence to anyone but himself, because he had his reputation to maintain. A fierce, battle-seasoned soldier who stood six feet five inches in his bare feet did not admit to a bairn's terror of nature's flaming arrows.

With gust-driven rain beating down on him again and increasingly distant sheets of lightning providing the only light ahead, he bent his thoughts sternly toward finding shelter. He knew of only one landowner nearby who might provide acceptable hospitality on demand, and although he might find a crofter sooner, a croft would provide few amenities for himself and his horse. Therefore, albeit with reluctance, he would seek out Murdoch Macleod of Glenelg.

In the darkness, he was not certain of his exact location, but he knew that the castle he sought lay nearby, most likely just beyond the steep ridge to his left. The ridge was itself something of an obstacle with the storm's threat still hovering, but time mattered more now than risk, so he turned the pony uphill and murmured a polite request to God that He hold His fire at bay until they had crested the ridge.

The rain stopped as he wended his way upward, and shortly after he reached the crest, a full moon broke suddenly through flying black clouds overhead, lighting the storm-blown landscape and revealing a long, narrow loch glimmering in the glen below, with a great castle perched formidably atop a promontory jutting into it from its rugged northern shore.

The moon dipped back behind the clouds as abruptly as it had revealed itself, and darkness enveloped the world again, albeit not for long. A few minutes later, silvery moonlight pierced the curtain of flying clouds again. The wind still howled, sweeping up the narrow glen, hurling gusts at him that nearly buffeted him from his horse and whipping the dark loch into foam-crested waves. But with moonlight glinting on its dark, rumpled surface, and lights burning in the upper windows of the castle, he could see his way now and could almost feel the warmth of welcoming fire, food, and drink that he knew he would find inside its great hall.

That he would also find the love of his life there never crossed his mind.

∞

The wind raged around Castle Chalamine. Lightning flashed and thunder roared, terrifying at least four of the castle's youngest inhabitants into shrieks, but that only added to already existing pandemonium, because supper was sadly late in making its appearance.

"We're hungry, Cristina," ten-year-old Sidony lamented for the third time.

Nine-year-old Sorcha echoed her, adding, "'Tis very late, is it not?"

With their fine white-blond hair, thin faces, and pale blue eyes, the two youngest Macleod sisters looked almost like twins, for they were nearly the same height, and presently their frowns were exactly alike as they faced their eldest sister.

"They'll bring your supper soon," eighteen-year-old

Lady Cristina Macleod reassured them. "I've sent Adela to hurry them. Mariota, love," she added, "pray do not stand so near the fire. Your skirt is almost in the flames."

"But I'm cold! Can you not tell someone to build this puny fire larger?"

Before Cristina could reply that the fire in the huge fireplace was large enough, seventeen-year-old Mariota added querulously, "Where is Father?"

The laird himself answered that question by striding into the hall through the buttery door at the north end of the great hall, bellowing, "Blast those knaves below, Cristina! I've told them the dogs must not be let into the kitchens, and here is Adela telling me that my supper's been put back because two of the lads got into a snarling fight over a roast they'd put on the carver's tray."

Bewildered, Cristina turned nonetheless calmly to meet this new crisis. "Two of the cook's lads were fighting over a roast, sir?"

"Not cook's lads! Did I no just say they'd let the damned dogs into the kitchen again? I dinna ken what manner o' household ye run here, but—"

"Indeed, and you are right to be vexed with me, for I am sure you must have said that about the dogs straightaway, but with everyone complaining at once and that storm outside crashing thunder about our ears as it is, I simply did not hear you. What is it, Tam?" she asked, turning to meet the lanky gillie hurrying toward her from the stairway entrance. "Pray do not tell me 'tis yet another crisis."

"Nay, mistress. Least I dinna think he be a crisis, only that there be a gentleman rode up t' the door t' request hospitality."

"God bless me, Cristina," bellowed his lordship. "What

sort o' fool rides his horse through a storm as bad as this one?"

"The sort who finds himself caught unawares, I'd expect."

"Och, aye, indeed, and if he didna note that the sky has been threatening a deluge all day, then he is a very great fool, as I said from the outset!"

"Would you have us deny him the shelter he seeks, sir? It must be as you command, of course. Tam is but awaiting your instructions."

"Faugh! Deny him? I said nae such thing, lass, and well d'ye ken that. Am I a barbarian?"

"No, sir, certainly not."

"Is it no a matter o' Highland law and custom to admit anyone requesting shelter and to guarantee his safety whilst he accepts our hospitality?"

"You are perfectly right, sir, as always," Cristina said, gesturing to the gillie to admit the gentleman. "Oh, and Tam, do see that someone looks after his poor horse, too," she added. "With all this thunder, it must be terrified."

"Aye, my lady. I'll see to it."

"One moment, lad," Macleod barked. "Did our visitor tell ye his name?"

"Aye, laird. He did call himself Hector Reaganach, Laird o' Lochbuie."

Cristina's breath caught in her throat.

"The devil he did!" Macleod exclaimed. "Calls himself Hector the Ferocious, does he? Well, no matter. I ken who he is—a Maclean. Upstarts, every one of them!"

The gillie hesitated, but recovering her wits, Cristina motioned again to him to go and fetch their visitor up to the hall.

When Tam had gone, she took swift stock of the scene

before her. Her three youngest sisters had been playing a game, the rules of which apparently demanded that they chase each other from one end of the hall to the other, scattering any number of articles across the room as they did. To add to the mess, her father had spread documents out on the high table despite its having long since been laid for supper.

"Isobel," she said to the twelve-year-old organizer of the game, "pray—"

But although she had intended to issue a string of commands to her several siblings and two menservants presently in the hall, a new voice interrupted from the doorway of the inner chamber behind the dais, demanding in shrill tones to know if she had any notion when they were going to take their supper.

"For I fear that I'm nigh starving, and I do believe that we ought to have had our supper more than an hour ago, so if you do not want to have to nourish me back to health or, worse, to bury me, pray send for sustenance, my love."

Lady Euphemia Macleod looked as if she were starving, for she was rail thin. Although approaching the end of her middle years, she had never embraced the marital state. Instead, she had lived with her younger brother, Macleod of Glenelg, since his marriage some twenty years before, serving as little more than a cipher in his household until eight years before when Anna, Lady Macleod, had died suddenly while fighting to give birth to a ninth daughter.

Sadly, the babe had also perished in the struggle, but Lady Euphemia proved overnight to be an undiscovered asset, taking swift charge of the family in the chaos of shock and grief that threatened to engulf them all. For three long months she had dealt capably with every child, adult, and crisis, right up to the day she had looked at then-eleven-year-old Cristina and said mildly, "You have a capable nature, my dear, and a natural air of command. 'Tis your right and duty, rather than mine, to act as mistress of your father's household and hostess to his guests until such time as he is kind enough to provide you with a husband. At that time, naturally, you will pass the candle to our dearest Mariota."

With those chilling words, Lady Euphemia had cheerfully returned to her position as cipher, and Cristina had picked up the reins of the household.

"Leave it to a blasted Maclean to show himself at such an inconvenient hour," Macleod snapped. "Where's the jug, Cristina? I've a raging thirst on me."

Nodding to one of the menservants to attend to the laird's thirst, Cristina was moving to help the children put their things away when a resounding crash of thunder rattled the shutters, black smoke billowed from the fireplace as if the devil himself were about to enter the chamber, and someone shrieked, "Fire! Oh, help!"

"Bless me, what now!" Macleod snapped.

The shrieking continued, but blinded by the swiftly growing cloud of smoke, Cristina could not see what had happened although she easily recognized the voice.

Apparently, Lady Euphemia did as well, because she said, "Mariota, what is it? For mercy's sake, child, stop that screeching." But her words had no effect.

"Calm yourself, Mariota," Cristina said firmly, feeling her way as rapidly as she could past the high table toward the fireplace and her shrieking sister, only to be abruptly shoved aside as a huge figure swept past her.

Having turned his weary horse over to one lad, Hector followed a second one into the central tower of Castle Chalamine. The entry opened onto a winding stone stairway, and as the wind blew the door out of his guide's grasp and slammed it against the wall, the lad shouted, "I'll take your damp cloak and battle-axe, sir, an it please ye."

Removing the ancestral axe he nearly always carried with him in its sling, and shrugging off his sodden cloak, Hector handed over both and was shutting the door as the lad hung them on pegs in the wall, when they heard a great crack of thunder followed by feminine screams from above. The gillie reacted quickly, leaping up the twisting stairway with Hector taking time only to bar the door before following. But at the doorway into the hall, the lad paused, apparently stunned by the smoke billowing past him as the shrieking continued.

Hector pushed the lad aside, took in the smoky scene at a glance, and strode toward the screams, scarcely noting as he did the one or two obstacles he swept from his path.

As he had expected, he found a lass amidst the still-billowing smoke, trying ineffectively and without missing a screech, to beat out flames that had ignited one side of her long overskirt and now shot up to threaten her arms and face if not her life. With smoke blinding him to any nearby bucket or jug, he grabbed the fabric below her hips and, ignoring her screams, ripped it free and flung it into the fireplace.

When she continued to shriek, he caught her by the shoulders and gave her a rough shake. "Stop that screeching," he commanded. "Tell me if you're burnt."

Instead, she burst into tears and collapsed in his arms.

Startled, he held her as he snapped, "Someone get over here, shift these logs, and stir up that fire. It is the only way I know to clear out this smoke."

A calm female voice nearby said, "Pray attend to that,

Tam, and add another log whilst you are about it. Mariota, stop that noise now and tell us if you are hurt."

The face buried against his chest shifted slightly, and a tearful voice said fretfully, "I don't think so, but how horrid! It was as if the wind had turned into some demon, Cristina, breathing fire all over me! It was killing me!"

"Don't talk drivel," Hector said sternly. "You should certainly know better than to . . . to . . ."

She looked up at him, and the words he had been about to speak died in his throat as he stared into the face so close to his own, revealed now in all its splendid glory as the smoke began at last to clear.

She was stunningly beautiful with eyes as clear green as new spring grass, and hair like the spun gold one heard about in seanachies' tales. Her figure, as his hands could attest, was slim and pliable, her still-heaving breasts soft and plump, her waist so tiny that he was sure his two hands could span it, her hips flaring voluptuously below. Her lips were so soft-looking and full that had he not been burdened with years of training in courtesy, he'd have tasted them immediately. Never in his life had he seen such a beauty, and that despite his own vast experience with the gender and the fact that his brother had married a woman touted by all as the most beautiful in the Isles. Raven-haired Mairi was glorious, to be sure, but no man of sense would say she held a candle to the beauty he held in his arms.

"You can let her go now, my lord," said the same matter-of-fact voice he had heard moments before.

Startled, he turned his head and found the source of that voice standing right beside him. Noting her plain russet gown and the simple linen caul that concealed her hair, he nearly decided that she must be the beauty's maidservant before he recalled the way she had commanded the lass to calm herself and opted instead for a poor relation or paid companion.

The amusement in her eyes was another matter. She was looking at him as if she knew him, but he was nearly certain he had never seen her before. With a polite nod, he looked again at the delectable morsel he still held, determined that she did indeed seem steady enough to stand on her own, and released her.

The matter-of-fact voice went on, "You were right to scold her, sir. I had warned her only moments before that she was standing too near the flames."

"Indeed, she did," the beauty said with a tremulous smile that nearly bowled him over with its brilliance. "But I was so very cold, you see, and I never expected the fire to attack me like that. I cannot think how it came to do such a horrid thing."

"I wager 'twas the lad opening the door below for me to enter," Hector said. "It blew out of his grasp, and doubtless with the wind as it is, it created a powerful draft that pulled smoke and flames into this room." Much more gently than before, he added, "You must take greater care in future not to stand so near, mistress."

"By heaven's grace, sir," she said, wide-eyed, as she clasped her slender little hands beneath her round little chin, "how very wise you are!"

❧

Cristina knew Hector Reaganach. She had seen him and his twin brother, Lachlan the Wily, Lord High Admiral of the Isles, on three separate occasions when her father had taken her to court at Ardtornish Castle for the Lord of the

Isles' grand annual Easter hunt and the splendid feast that always followed.

Macleod had hoped that Cristina would attract the attention of some suitable nobleman's son, so that he could marry her off at last. Her next youngest sisters, Mariota and Adela, had mixed emotions about her lack of success, she knew. Mariota wanted her to marry but did not want to assume her responsibilities, and Adela knew who would have to shoulder them. Adela knew, too, for all of them did, that once Cristina was married, Mariota would quickly follow. All of the Macleod sisters were fair and graceful, but Mariota's beauty stopped men in their tracks.

It had certainly stunned Hector Reaganach, Cristina thought with amusement as she watched them.

He had attracted her the first time she laid eyes on him, because although men had labeled him "ferocious" or, at the very least, "stern," his laughter was infectious, his stories and songs amusing, and as big, strong, and handsome as he was, he looked like a man who could easily take care of himself and anyone else he chose to look after.

Feeling deep relief and gratitude that his quick action had saved Mariota, she said quietly, "Thank you, sir," before adding, "Mariota, love, do you not think that perhaps you should put on a fresh skirt?"

"Indeed I should," Mariota exclaimed. "I hope you are not scandalized by seeing my underskirt, sir, but if you are, you have only yourself to blame."

"Mariota," Cristina said gently, "his lordship has done you a signal service. You should thank him prettily, then go and put on a fresh skirt."

"But it *is* his fault," her sister insisted, looking impishly up into his eyes. "He ripped my best overskirt right off me!"

Hector Reaganach chuckled and shook his head at her.

His eyes were the deepest, bluest blue that Cristina had ever seen. Even now, in the smoky, flickering light from the hall's torches, cressets, candles, and fireplace, she could see how blue they were. But Mariota did not care about the color of his eyes. The saucy girl was still laughing—nay, flirting outrageously with him—and the wretched man did not seem to mind a bit.

"Here now, Mariota," Macleod said suddenly, reminding Cristina that he was still in the hall, "run along and make yourself presentable, lass. Ye're making a right fool o' yourself."

With another twinkling look at Hector, Mariota obeyed, and since Tam was still looking after the now brightly burning fire, Cristina signed to one of the other lads to clear Macleod's documents off the table and lay another place.

As she did, Hector Reaganach strode to her father with his hand outstretched, saying, "Forgive me, sir. In all the bustle, I did not see you standing there."

"Aye, sure, but I must thank ye for your quick action," Macleod said gruffly, shaking hands with a sour expression. "The brainless chit might well ha' gone up in smoke whilst we scurried about trying to find her. I expect, as tall as ye are, ye could see right over the smoke."

"I just followed her shrieking," Hector said with a disarming smile. "'Tis I who am beholden to you though, sir. That storm out there is raging, and I am grateful to have a roof over my head again."

"Aye, well, ye were a right fool and all to be out in such a muck."

"I was, indeed," Hector agreed. "I have no doubt my father would be as wroth with me as you are, sir, so I'm thinking you must be a man of sense. 'Tis a lucky man you are, too, with such beautiful daughters."

Although he spoke tactfully, Cristina knew from experience that he, like every other man who cast eyes on Mariota, had noted the beauty of only one daughter. Nevertheless, she appreciated his tact and decided he was considerate.

Her father, however, only snorted. Brusquely and without any tact whatsoever, he said, "Aye, sure, I ken fine which daughter ye've been staring at like a lovesick owl, but ye'll ha' the goodness to keep your hands off the lass, and ye'll no flirt wi' her under me own roof, sithee."

"Flirt with her? Faith, sir, I believe I want to marry her. I cannot think of a better life than one spent gazing at her beautiful face day in and day out."

"'Tis a fool ye are then, just as I said," Macleod said frankly. "Ye'd do a sight better to wed a wench who can run a household as cleverly as our Cristina can—aye, and look after the sick and the gardens as well. Nobbut what I doubt I'd let ye have her either," he added with a narrow look.

Cristina sighed, recognizing her father's tactic at once.

Macleod believed that a man always desired a thing more if he feared it might be beyond his reach. But with Mariota in the mix, that tactic made no impression on Hector Reaganach.

He smiled and nodded kindly to Cristina as he said, "I am sure that Mistress Cristina—nay, 'tis Lady Cristina, I'm sure. I beg your pardon, lass."

She said nothing, merely fixing her steady gaze on him, knowing what he would say next as well as if she had put the words in his mouth herself.

He held her gaze for a moment before turning away to say to Macleod, "I'm sure she is everything a wife should be, sir. But 'tis your younger daughter that has taken my fancy, and surely she, too, is of marriageable age."

"Aye, she is, but I've five daughters o' marriageable

age," Macleod said testily. "Mariota's seventeen, Adela six-teen, Maura fifteen, and our Kate has turned fourteen. Since any lass can marry at thirteen, that makes five o' them."

"Then, doubtless, you'd be pleased if I were to take one off your hands."

"I would, but Cristina must be first as she's the eldest."

Tam had filled the laver, and Cristina was motioning the younger girls to wash their hands, but she turned back at these words and saw both consternation and stubbornness written large on Hector Reaganach's face.

To divert him from blurting out something that would stir Macleod's anger and doubtless befoul their supper table with unpleasantness, she said, "My father believes it is un-lucky for a younger daughter to marry before her elder sis-ter, sir. Surely, you can understand that. Many Islesmen believe as he does."

"Sakes, Macleod," Hector said, "I'd never have thought you superstitious."

"Oh, but you need think no such thing, sir; indeed, no," Lady Euphemia said with a swift, measuring glance at Macleod. "My brother prides himself on knowing what is what, you see, and very wise he is, too, so you won't sway him from it. If he declares that you must offer for our Cristina, you had very much better do so. Indeed, she is a grand good lass, is Cristina, and kind, so pray do heed my brother, sir, for Mariota's rather too fond of herself, and tem-peramental into the bargain."

"Enough, Euphemia," Macleod snapped. "Ye've nae call to criticize the lass."

"No, Murdo, certainly not. I am sure I never meant to do any such thing."

Casting a glance at Hector, Cristina saw his gaze narrow and believed he understood that her aunt would now support

Macleod's position. Surely, he had known enough dependent women in his life to recognize one and comprehend that she believed that her peace and security depended on pleasing her host.

But even as Cristina reassured herself, she saw that look of resolve settle over his handsome features again. She was certain from what she had seen of the man that he had not thought of marrying anyone before he had entered the great hall. But all it would take now for him to press this sudden yearning of his, would be Mariota's reentrance into the room.

In the hope of explaining before then that Macleod would reject his offer, and thus avoid grievous insult, she said, "I believe it is not so much superstition that drives my father's belief, sir, as his concern that if he does let one of his younger daughters marry first, bad luck may fall upon the Macleods."

"Sakes, lass, that is precisely what makes it superstition!"

"I disagree, sir. To be superstitious, one must *believe* that ill luck will follow. My father merely wishes to take care that if ill luck should chance to befall our clan, the others will not blame him for it."

Hector gave her a measuring look. "I think you should have the privilege of meeting my brother, lass. He, too, enjoys quibbling. I do not."

Macleod's temper was short. Frowning, he said, "As your brother is already married, ye ha' nae reason to present him to Cristina. Nor be there reason to continue talking on the subject if ye've nae wish to marry her yourself."

"Perhaps you and Hector Reaganach would prefer to take supper in the inner chamber, where you may discuss the matter as you choose," Cristina said. "I promised the children that we'd sup in the hall tonight, because of the storm."

As if to punctuate that promise, another great crack of thunder shook the stone walls, and Sidony shrieked.

"We'll all eat in here," Macleod said. "We've nae need to speak privately, for I've made up my mind, and nae man will change it."

Hector Reaganach smiled. "With respect, sir, we'll see about that. The sons of Gillean are not noted for patience or for turning away with the goal in sight."

"Aye, well, we Macleods ken our own minds, lad. Remember that."

Cristina sighed again, foreseeing a long and fractious meal.

Chapter 2

The storm outside picked up fury again as they moved to take places at the high table. Startled by a particularly loud crash of thunder, young Sorcha tripped. She caught herself but in the process banged a knee at one of the table's corner legs.

"Kiss your thumb, lass," Maclcod commanded. "'Twill ease the pain."

As she obeyed, Cristina saw Hector hide a smile and knew he thought that Macleod's superstitions were foolish. Suppressing a jolt of annoyance, she glanced down the table to be sure her sisters were standing quietly, waiting for their father to speak the grace before meat.

The storm grew even fiercer, with lightning flashes changing the light in the vaulted chamber from moment to moment as cracks and rolling, thunderous booms battered against the castle's stone walls, making it doubtful that anyone heard more than an odd word here and there as Macleod spoke the words of the prayer.

Finishing with a brusque "Amen," he gestured for them all to sit.

As they obeyed, Isobel shook back her flaxen plaits and

said clearly to Hector Reaganach, "Why were you out in such dreadful weather, sir, if you agree with my father that it was dangerous?"

Cristina, who had wondered the same thing but would never have put herself forward in such an unbecoming way, waited for an intervening roll of thunder to fade before she said, "Civilized people do not ask such questions of their guests, Isobel. Pray, attend to your supper and allow him to enjoy his in peace."

"But how am I to learn things if I may not ask questions?"

"Dinna be impertinent, lassie," Macleod said.

Conscious of Hector Reaganach's amused eye upon her, Cristina said, "We can discuss that later if you like, Isobel. Presently, you must tell Tam what you would like him to serve you from that platter he is holding."

With a sigh, Isobel obeyed.

Shooting a stern look at her, Macleod said, "We dinna want to hear your voice again, nor any o' the rest o' ye either. Nobbut what the child put a good question to ye," he added, shooting a sharp look at Hector. "Just listen to it roar out there. 'Twere a daft thing to be riding through such a din and deluge, so I trust ye had good reason for subjecting yourself to the experience."

"I did," Hector said as Isobel shot a resentful look at Cristina.

Cristina did not respond to the look, deciding that if her outspoken little sister had not yet learned that their father considered himself above deferring to the rules of civility, she soon would.

The look of amusement in Hector's eyes deepened when her gaze met his again, but instead of annoying her further, this time the look warmed her to her toes, and she felt an odd inclination to smile at him. She told herself she was merely pleased that he had retained his civility despite her father's prying questions, but she knew she was attracted to the man and wished with all her heart that she were not. She also noted that although his gaze drifted once or twice in Mariota's direction, he did not allow it to linger. Her sister's frown indicated that she had also noted that fact and did not admire his good manners as much as Cristina did.

Macleod was still gazing at him, clearly waiting for him to say more. When Hector turned instead to help himself from a dish of stewed mutton, Macleod said testily, "Well, what was your reason then for being out in yon storm?"

Hector continued to help himself to the mutton, but Cristina saw a muscle twitch in his jaw. She did not know him well enough to guess what he was thinking, but she could tell that Macleod's cross-questioning had begun to annoy him.

Having taken as much stew as he wanted, he turned to his host and said mildly, "As it is his grace's business to which I attend, sir, I'm certain you must understand that I cannot divulge the details to you here at the table."

"Sakes, lad, lest ye've forgotten, I serve as a member o' his grace's Council o' the Isles. Therefore, I've every right to ken his business if it has aught to do wi' the Isles, as I suppose it must."

"I have not forgotten your position," Hector said. "I will be happy to discuss it privately with you at your convenience, but 'tis not a topic for bairns' ears."

"Och, aye, then," Macleod said, glancing up and down the table as if he had just remembered that his daughters were present.

"But that's not fair," Mariota protested. "I'm not a child, and I want to hear your adventures, sir. I'm sure you must have had exciting ones, and I shall die if I cannot hear them. Can you not send the children off with Aunt Euphemia, Father?"

Much as she would have liked to call Mariota to order as she had Isobel, Cristina held her tongue, knowing that scolding her would serve no purpose since Mariota would ignore her. However, seeing Isobel open her mouth to protest, she shot that young lady a minatory look that kept her silent, then turned back as Hector said with a smile to Mariota, "Anyone with half an eye can see that you are not a child, my lady."

"Well, you need not say that as if you want only to placate me, my lord," Mariota said archly, fluttering her ridiculously long, dark lashes.

"I was agreeing with you, lass," he said.

Mariota tossed her head. "You said you want to marry me, but surely you do not think I'd marry a common messenger, even if he rides for the Lord of the Isles."

"Mariota!" Cristina exclaimed, unable to restrain herself this time. Shooting a hasty glance at their father, to attempt to gauge his temper, she added, "My dear, truly, you should not speak so to a guest."

Macleod gnawed a mutton bone, apparently undisturbed by Mariota's impertinence. Hector seemed unperturbed as well, for he said only, "Is that what you think, that I am but his grace's messenger?"

Mariota gave a dismissive shrug. "I'm sure it is nothing to me what your position is or whom you serve. Your clan is a sadly unknown one—to me, at least—and therefore most likely not a suitable one with which to ally myself."

"Sakes, lass, I'd think that being laden with eight daughters for whom he must find husbands—even as beautiful as you all are—your father would not be so hard to please."

" 'Tis I, not he, who is hard to please, sir," she said, tossing her head. "After Cristina marries, I shall have dozens of offers from which to choose—offers from the very best families, too, I promise you."

" 'Tis true," Macleod said complacently. "The lass will ha' her pick o' the Highlands and Isles, so she needna take the first upstart son of Gillean that wants her. She'll take a man what kens his history, one as *has* a history farther back than a few odd generations or so."

"With respect, sir, I warrant that our Clan Gillean history is as ancient as your own," Hector said.

"Nay, now that canna be," Macleod said, "for we Macleods ha' been in existence since the beginning o' the world. I warrant ye'll no be telling me that any Maclean lived afore the Flood now, will ye?"

"Which flood would that be?" Hector asked.

"Aye, sure, I'm no surprised ye dinna ken the Bible as well as I do, for all that yon Macleans claim to be one o' the learned clans. Still, I expect I ken that good book well enough for us both. I'm speaking o' the great Flood that drowned the entire world, save that lad Noah, and his family and flocks," Macleod said.

"That Flood, eh?" Hector said. "But I'm thinking there were Macleans aplenty before that Flood, and afterward as well."

"So ye say," Macleod said. "However, I ha' never heard that any Maclean walked aboard Noah's Ark."

"Noah's Ark?" Hector said, raising his eyebrows. "Faith, we'd no need of Noah's Ark. Whoever heard of a Maclean that had not a good boat of his own?"

A heavy silence fell, as if everyone in the chamber had stopped breathing. Then Macleod uttered a bark of laughter, and Hector grinned at him.

"Truly, sir," he said, "I meant no disrespect, but you ken my history well enough, and my present position in the Isles as well. Surely, you must agree that an alliance betwixt our two families would serve us both well."

"'Tis true ye've acquired a deal o' power," Macleod admitted. "Leastways, that wily brother o' yours has, and ye've acquired a respectable amount o' land, too, thanks to his canny ways."

"Is it true they call your brother Lachlan the Wily?" Isobel asked.

"Aye, lass," Hector said, smiling at her. "He is Lord High Admiral of the Isles and also serves as master of his grace's household."

"I've heard of him," she said. "Is it true that he abducted his grace and—?"

"That will do, Isobel," Macleod said harshly. "I dinna want to hear your voice again, or things will go very unpleasantly for ye."

Grimacing, the little girl muttered, "Yes, sir."

Macleod glowered next at his guest. "We see what the world has come to when bairns ken as much about the doings o' the powerful as that wee one does. Your brother— aye, and ye, too—should be ashamed o' some of the things ye've done to gain your positions."

"My brother would respectfully disagree with you, sir, for he believes that in a good cause, even wrongdoing can be virtuous."

"But no man should serve as judge in his own case," Lady Euphemia said.

Clearly startled, Hector said with his charming smile, "You have read the Maxims of Publilius Syrus, madam?"

"Oh, goodness no," Lady Euphemia said, shooting a nervous look at her brother, who was frowning again. "Mercy me, sir, how very strange that you should mistake me for a Latin scholar, when I promise you I am no such thing. Why, everyone knows that only the sterner sex can benefit from education, and so it doubtless astonishes you that I, a mere female, should have had any at all, but my father, although not as learned a man as your own, was generous with his daughters and allowed us to sit with our brothers if we liked, whilst they took lessons with their tutors. You, I am sure, have a far greater acquaintance with the Roman masters than I, but I do find some of their notions quite fascinating. I confess, though, that I admire Sextus Propertius more than Publilius Syrus, for it was Sextus, was it not, who said, 'There is something beyond the grave; death does not end all, and the pale ghost escapes from the vanquished pyre.' So comforting, don't you agree?"

"I own, madam, that I am not familiar with that particular quotation," he said with what Cristina believed was commendable, and extremely civil, restraint.

"Oh, but one cannot be surprised at that, can one?" Lady Euphemia said. "For like many educated gentlemen, you have doubtless acquired much learning, sir, so one cannot wonder at your having forgotten a few things, whilst it must astonish you that I should have dared to speak so forwardly as I did. But to be telling the children, particularly such an outspoken child as our Isobel, that doing wrong can ever be virtuous—"

"Be silent, woman," Macleod snapped. "He doesna want to hear it. Nor do I."

"Oh, certainly, Murdo . . . That is, certainly not! Pray forgive me, my lord," she added to Hector. "I cannot imagine what prompted me to speak so to you."

"That rattling tongue o' yours needs nae prompting," Macleod said sourly.

"Her ladyship clearly has a curious nature," Hector said, smiling again.

Cristina smiled, too, in approval of his chivalrous attempt to soothe Macleod's temper, although he might as well have saved his breath.

"Aye, Euphemia's a curious woman," Macleod said. "Listened at doors as a child, and may still do so, since Isobel has apparently picked up the habit."

"She did not learn such habits from me," Lady Euphemia said, indignantly. Catching her brother's eye, she modulated her tone, saying earnestly, "Truly, you must know I would never do such a thing in your house, Murdo. I only listened as a child because I thought the stories your tutors told were as good as the seanachies' tales. And even when they were not, they still fascinated me."

"Foolishness," Macleod declared. "A man doesna build estates and wealth by studying. That takes hard work, a strong sword arm, and powerful friends."

"You have certainly accomplished much, sir," Hector said. "The Macleods have grown to be one of the most powerful clans in the Isles."

"'Tis true," Macleod agreed, nodding. "Ye'll ken fine that Macleod o' Lewis be me kinsman, and he's done well for himself, aye. He's wedded to his grace's eldest daughter, Marjory, ye ken, by his first wife, Amy Macruari."

"Just as my brother Lachlan married his eldest daughter by the Princess Margaret Stewart," Hector said gently.

"Ah, bah, she's nae princess yet, me lad, and may never be, regardless o' what them fools in Edinburgh did say. I'm thinking Robert the Steward be a poor choice to replace the present King o' Scots."

"I know many who agree with you, sir," Hector said

equably. "I cannot deny that there are men in Scotland from older families who—"

"Aye, well, if the sons o' Gillean be upstarts, only think what that makes a man who produces bairns like a rabbit, calls them all Stewart after the position he holds, and claims the throne through his kinship to Robert the Bruce's sister, without possessing half o' Bruce's brains or skill wi' a sword."

"You may be right, but Robert the Steward is nonetheless the man the Scottish Parliament has designated heir to the throne, and we cannot alter that unless you mean to incite civil war," Hector said.

When his host frowned, he added, "I would submit, sir, that an alliance with Clan Gillean, such as the one I propose, would vastly increase your power after Robert does succeed, by binding you and your kinsmen even closer to the throne of Scotland and to the Lordship of the Isles."

To Cristina's surprise, her father did not reject the notion outright this time.

As the unexpected silence lengthened, Mariota said curiously, "How would our marriage do that, my lord?"

"Because my brother and I are trusted henchmen of the Lord of the Isles," he said. "Doubtless, you would become friends with my brother's wife, Mairi, who is his grace's daughter."

Mariota looked thoughtful before she said, "But as one of his grace's councilors, my father is well acquainted with the Steward, are you not, sir?"

Macleod gave a curt nod, saying to Hector, "As I said afore, once Cristina's off me hands, Mariota can look as high as she chooses for her husband, so I've nae need for closer connection to MacDonald or the Steward. Indeed, the Steward might add to his consequence an he allies himself wi' the Macleods. If he ever does come to wear the crown, I'd no turn down his offer to make our Mariota a princess."

Cristina glanced at Mariota, who looked thoughtful again.

"Oh, how exciting that would be!" Lady Euphemia exclaimed. "Would it not, my dear? Only think of seeing all the other ladies bow before you—well, except for the Queen, of course. But that would mean Alasdair Stewart, would it not, Murdo? I own, I have heard disturbing things about that young man. Do they not call him by some horrid name—Wolf, or some such? But the others are all either married already or are far too young to suit our Mariota, are they not?"

"I don't want to marry a bad man or a child, Father," Mariota said quickly.

Ignoring both of them, Macleod said to Hector, "I mentioned that possibility only to point out how high the lass may look. She is no for ye, Hector Reaganach, but I admit I'd let ye ha' Cristina in a twink, not only to reinforce me connection to MacDonald, but to see the lass wedded so the others may be so as well."

Hector met Cristina's steady gaze and said quietly, "As I said before, sir, I've no wish to offend Lady Cristina—"

"Oh, you won't do that," Lady Euphemia interjected. "Our Cristina never takes offense, do you, love? Why, Cristina is our rock. Nothing disturbs her."

"That is true," Sidony agreed, speaking for the first time and smiling at her eldest sister. "Cristina never has moods like Mariota or Adela. She is just Cristina."

Cristina thanked the little girl, adding matter-of-factly, "I know you mean that as a compliment, Sidony. But now, if you girls have finished eating, we will excuse ourselves to the gentlemen. It is time you were all getting ready for bed."

Not even Isobel argued with her, so she excused herself to the two men and ushered her sisters from the hall.

⸏⸏⸎

Impressed despite himself at the ease with which Lady Cristina shepherded her seven sisters from the chamber, Hector deduced nonetheless that, despite her words to little Sidony, she had not taken her aunt's comment as a compliment.

Had anyone asked what had stirred this deduction, he could not have explained, but he knew as well as if she had told him herself that she did not enjoy hearing her aunt describe her as the "rock" on whom everyone else depended.

Perhaps it had been the glint in her golden eyes or the slight tension in her jaw that had given her thoughts away, perhaps the stiff way she held her body.

He found himself wondering what manner of men her father had introduced to her that none had yet offered for her. Her figure was quite pleasing and her lips eminently kissable. Of course, once any man clapped his eyes on Mariota... But surely, Macleod had had better sense than to parade his prize about while he attempted to marry off her sister. In truth, all eight of the Macleod sisters were beautiful, and despite his earlier comment to Mariota, he could not imagine that Macleod would have difficulty finding husbands for any of them.

He was vaguely aware that Lady Euphemia was dithering on again about something, but he paid her no heed until she said, "Really, my lord, Cristina would make you much happier in the years to come."

"I beg your pardon, my lady," he said. "My wits must have wandered."

"And nae wonder, either," Macleod growled. "Should ye no be helping Cristina wi' the bairns, Euphemia?"

"Oh, yes, of course, and so I shall at once," she said. "I was just saying that good people so rarely understand because they simply cannot imagine . . . Well, not when they wouldn't themselves, you know. And so often they simply accept things rather than questioning . . . But you need not concern yourself, sir, for I can see that my dear brother—so wise, always—will easily persuade you to marry our dearest Cristina, and she will make you ever so much happier, don't you see?"

Not having the slightest idea what she was talking about, Hector just smiled, but Macleod said indignantly, "Whatever are ye nattering about, woman? Never mind," he added hastily when she opened her mouth to explain. "We dinna want to hear it, so run along now wi' the others. We ha' important matters to discuss."

She fled, and silence settled over the two men while gillies hurriedly cleared the rest of the food away, leaving only a large jug of brogac and two pewter mugs.

Lifting his mug, Macleod said, "Here's to arranging this business betwixt us. But first ye'll tell me what MacDonald's up to, that he's sent ye out and about to see folks? It canna be simple diplomacy when he sends ye and that battle-axe they say ye always carry wi' ye."

Hector took a sip of his mug's heady contents as he gathered his thoughts, then set it down and said, "You'll recall that MacDonald traveled to Inverness several months ago to meet with the King."

"Aye, sure, they say he bent the knee to our Davy at last, for all that he swore over and over he'd never do it," Macleod said. "Always said that as a sovereign prince himself, he'd nae call to submit to David Bruce. It just shows ye."

Choosing his words with care, aware that Macleod was no strong supporter of either MacDonald or the Steward, and had as low an opinion of the reigning King of Scots as anyone in Scotland, Hector said, "MacDonald met with David at the Steward's behest, to make amends in hopes of forestalling future unpleasantness."

"In other words, the Steward wanted our Davy to ken fine that MacDonald be aligned wi' him and thereby prevent Davy's trying to shift the crown o' Scotland to an English prince's head, as he did afore. Och, well, I dinna like the man, but I never said he were stupid. Still, what has that to do wi' ye being out in yon fury tonight?"

As if to punctuate his question, another clap of thunder rattled the castle.

"The Steward means to spend Shrove Tuesday and the first week of Lent with his daughter and her family," Hector said.

"Does he, indeed? At Ardtornish or Finlaggan?"

"Ardtornish," Hector replied. "As you know, MacDonald moved the annual Council of the Isles at Finlaggan forward this year. A fortnight afterward, however, he desires everyone to meet at Ardtornish, as we usually do."

"Does the Steward intend then to take part in our Council at Finlaggan?"

"Nay, his party will travel from Stirling directly to Ardtornish. My mission is to inform as many of the great Isles' families as possible of his visit, so that any who wish to pay their respects may do so."

"And MacDonald ha' sent ye about to make this suggestion? 'Tis my understanding that both he and your brother send ye out only when they want to make plain their strong desire for compliance wi' their wishes."

"I am but one of several messengers," Hector said blandly.

"But he ha' sent ye to me."

"No, sir," Hector said. "As I explained earlier, the storm caught me returning from Glen Shiel, and I did but seek shelter here. You may be sure that his grace would not intentionally send anyone else to invite you to take part in such an important occasion. Knowing that you would certainly attend the Council, he means to invite you himself."

Macleod gave him a sharp look, but Hector met it easily. Although MacDonald had indeed sent him to make plain to many of the great families his strong desire that they send their representatives to pay respects to the Steward, Macleod's name had not been on that list because MacDonald had known the old curmudgeon would not reject a personal invitation and would resent anything less.

"I should perhaps tell you," he added, "that his grace also wants to gather a flotilla of boats to meet the Steward and protect him on his journey. Doubtless, he will ask you how many boats your Macleods can contribute."

"Aye, well," Macleod said, "I did wonder why he had moved up the date for our Council, but it presents nae difficulty for me. I dinna think the Steward's the best man, but I'll lend a boat or two, and I'll no stand against him. Indeed, 'twill provide excellent opportunity to show off my beautiful Mariota . . . That is to say, it will if her sister be safely wedded by then." He smiled meaningfully at Hector.

Hector grimaced. He was not surprised that Macleod had agreed so readily to cooperate. Like most of the others to whom he had taken his messages, Macleod doubtless looked forward to the splendid, if not yet royal, revelry that would accompany Shrove Tuesday's feasting at Ardtornish, because the winter thus far had been dreary and wet, albeit not particularly cold. Satisfied to have successfully avoided one pitfall, Hector turned the subject to a more challenging one.

"I'll assume from your agreement that I may tell his grace he can count on you, sir, but as to Mariota's attending the festivities, I hope she will attend them with me. Indeed, if all goes well, perhaps we can introduce several of your daughters to suitable families there. But first, it is my hope that we might discuss my desire to win your daughter's hand in marriage."

"I ha' already told ye, ye can ha' Cristina wi' me blessing. She'll make ye a fine wife."

"Macleod, I've no need to hide my tongue behind my teeth with just the two of us here. I don't want Cristina. I want Mariota, and well do you know it. Set your superstitions aside and think of what such a marriage will bring to you and yours."

"I ken fine that ye want Mariota. Every man that claps eyes on the lass wants her, but I've said and I'll say again that ye'll no have her until Cristina be wedded. If ye dinna ken any man who wants Cristina, ye must take her yourself or leave them both be, and I'll thank ye no to mention the matter to me again."

"Don't be a fool," Hector said, dropping his civil manner at last and not without relief. "You gain naught by antagonizing me, and I have no sympathy for your foolish superstitions. His grace and my family are pushing me to marry, so perhaps you may imagine how they will react when I tell them that I've found the woman I want, but her father won't let me have her because of his superstitious nature. You know that his grace loves a good story. Why, I warrant he'll repeat it to every Islesman he meets. Is that what you want?"

Macleod glowered, but Hector understood from his silence that the older man was at least considering the difficulty of his position. He would not want to aggravate MacDonald, and all the Isles knew that both Maclean brothers were in high favor with the Lord of the Isles. To make an enemy of Hector the Ferocious would do Macleod no good at all.

The older man maintained his silence for some moments longer. But then he sighed, nodded, and refilled both mugs.

"Ye make a good point," he said. "I'll no pretend that your proposal's to me liking, but when ye put the matter in such a manner, ye leave me nac choice but to bend me principles to suit ye. An ye promise me ye'll do all ye can to see me other lasses well married, and that ye'll stand by me if ill luck befalls Clan Macleod, I'll arrange your marriage, and we'll drink to it now, the two of us."

Smiling, but ruthlessly suppressing the surge of triumph he felt, Hector met Macleod's steady gaze, touched mug to mug, and drank to their agreement.

Chapter 3 ————

The Isle of Mull

Hector entered the great hall at Duart Castle two evenings later just as his four-year-old namesake let out a scream of fury and took a swing at his mother, who was attempting to pick him up.

Lachlan Lubanach Maclean, his namesake's fond father and Hector's twin, stepped between the two, picked up his angry son, nodded a brief welcome to Hector, and bore the still-screaming child from the room. Clearly, the pair did not go far, because the screaming stopped abruptly, then began again on a different note. A few moments later, silence fell, although Hector's quick ears picked up the sound of his brother's stern voice, and he felt a pang of sympathy for the child.

Meeting his sister-in-law's rueful gaze, he said, "I seem to time my entrances badly of late. I must try to mend my ways."

"Where else have you timed yourself badly?" she asked, raising an eyebrow.

"Glenelg," he said. "My entrance there was even more dramatic. I arrived just in time to save a lovely lass whose skirt had caught fire."

"Mercy! You must tell us all about it, but you are always welcome here, sir, as you know. As for Hector Og's temper, I expect he comes by it honestly, as does his brother. My mother has frequently said that I've simply borne the children I deserve. Indeed, I'm grateful that our wee lassie has inherited her father's temperament instead of mine."

"Then I'm thinking you'll have to watch her even more closely than the lads," he said, grinning. "Have I told you what your husband was like as a bairn?"

"I've told her all she needs to know," his twin said as he returned to the hall and strode forward to greet Hector properly. Lachlan was some inches shorter than he was, and slimmer, his hair a shade or two lighter, but otherwise the resemblance between them was strong. "I apologize for that abrupt departure," he said. "Hector Og is developing a mind of his own, not unlike some others I could mention."

"You are not referring to me, I hope," Hector said.

"Nay," Lachlan said, grinning impudently at his wife. "Not you. We did expect you back some days ago, however. What kept you?"

"A number of things."

"Indeed? I thought you were just delivering his grace's invitations to the Shrove Tuesday feast and collecting boats for my flotilla."

Mairi laughed. "You thought no such thing, and well do you know it since you had as much to do with sending him off as my father did. Do not let him tease you, sir. If the truth were known, I suspect he wishes he might have gone with you."

"Now that," Hector said with a smile for his twin, "would

definitely have stirred conjecture. Do you not think folks might have wondered why his grace had sent his Lord High Admiral to issue such invitations, not to mention asking them to provide boats? Faith, they'd have thought we had a war pending."

Lachlan shrugged. "The only war hereabouts at present is the one we are waging with a headstrong four-year-old."

Hector chuckled. "So my small namesake has his own mind, has he?"

"Aye," Lachlan said, giving him a straight look.

"You were very severe with him."

"I was. He will inherit great power one day, and with power comes responsibility. If he does not learn to rule himself, he will be a poor leader of others. Therefore, I'll thank you not to encourage his insolence, if you ple— What do *you* want?" he added in a much sterner tone, looking past Hector.

Turning, Hector beheld his nephew, standing sturdily in the narrow archway through which he had departed so ignominiously only moments before. He met his father's stern gaze, not flinching even when Lachlan folded his arms across his broad chest and narrowed his eyes.

"Please, my lord, I've come to apologize," the little boy said. He showed no fear, but spoke in a clear, firm voice, albeit with a childish lisp that gave short shrift to his l's and r's.

"To whom do you wish to direct this apology?" his father demanded.

"To you, sir," he said, "but more to my lady mother. I-I'm sorry, mam!"

Tears sparkled in his eyes then, and when Mairi opened her arms to him, he flew into them, hugging her hard.

"Take him to bed, sweetheart," Lachlan said with an indulgent smile.

"I will," she said. "But don't the two of you dare discuss anything important until I return, or I'll have something to say to both of you. Have you eaten, by the way?" she asked Hector.

"Aye," he said. "I went to Lochbuie first to clean up and have my supper."

"Good," she said. "I'll just tell them to bring brogac and a few tidbits to keep you from starving before morning. You'll spend the night with us, of course."

"I'd like that, thank you," he said.

"No need for thanks," she said. "'Tis as much your home as ours, as always, but if you tell him one thing before I return, I'll hand you your head in your lap."

He grinned at her, his fondness for her strong. With her glossy black curls, dark blue eyes, flawless skin, and magnificent figure (despite being the mother of three small children), not only was Mairi of the Isles a beautiful woman but also a strong and worthy wife for the future chief of Clan Gillean.

His own taste had always strayed to a different sort of woman, more submissive, and one that—to his way of thinking—was more feminine, although no one would ever accuse Mairi of being unfeminine. He just preferred women who admired his strength rather than those who attempted to compete against it. He hoped Mairi would not take long putting the bairn to bed. He wanted to share his news, but he knew better than to do so before she was there to hear it.

Lachlan said, "So tell me briefly what you learned and how many boats I may count on. What of MacDougall of Dunstaffnage?"

"Some forty boats," Hector said. "And MacDougall will

come, of course, if only to try to find a husband for his younger daughter, Sarah, and perhaps one who will suit Fiona as well. I did not see her, but he says that although she is once again living at home and has emerged from her mourning, she is firm in saying she does not want to marry again yet. Sarah is no match for her, of course, but Mac-Dougall should be able to find someone suitable for the lass."

"MacDougall does not support the Steward," Lachlan said.

"Nay, but he'll be respectful and won't risk offending MacDonald. He'll send two longboats, too, because I made it clear that MacDonald would take it ill if he made an issue of his distaste. 'Twas likewise with Macleod of Glenelg."

Lachlan frowned. "So you met him, too. I suppose that means you had to tell him about the reception for the Steward. MacDonald wanted to ask him personally."

"I'll explain all that, but—" He glanced toward the archway.

"Don't fear her temper. Mairi won't fly into the boughs over political details that she can guess for herself. 'Tis the more personal ones she'll want to hear. She kens, for example, that you visited Macleod of Lewis and her sister Marjory. She will want to hear all their news. MacDougall she kens well enough, and Fiona visits us. I've seen him, too, but I wanted to hear what you think of him."

Hector was not so certain that Mairi would be so discriminating. She had, after all, said not to say a word until she returned. Nevertheless, since Lachlan would one day be chief of their clan, he was as much Hector's liege as the Lord of the Isles was. He was all but acting chief already, because their father, Ian Dubh Maclean, was more interested in scholarly pursuits than in political ones. That the

Macleans were one of the ancient learned clans was a fact that he took seriously.

"How is our father?" Hector asked, more to turn the subject than because he expected any news in particular. Ian Dubh was usually involved in his studies at Bellachuan, their home on the Isle of Seil.

To his surprise, Lachlan said, "You can see for yourself. He's here."

"Here?"

"Aye, he said he wanted to visit his grandchildren. I was a bit worried about him, since such an interest seemed out of character, but it appears that he merely wants to discern if any of the three has the wit to follow in his path."

"Do you think one can tell such a thing at their tender ages? Young Finguala is not quite two years old yet, and Hector Og and Ian are but four and three."

"Father said he knew when we were still creeping on all fours that I'd be the scholar and you the warrior. He said you were protective of me from the moment I emerged from the womb, nearly twenty minutes after you did."

"I wonder how he could have thought such a thing."

"He said you squalled until the nurse picked you up and let you see me. Then you fell silent."

"And your supposed intellect?"

"I looked at you, he said, and seemed contented, as if I knew the two of us could manage anything we desired in life. You looked odd a moment ago, by the way, when I mentioned Macleod. Is there aught of him that you should tell me?"

"Not before your lady returns. I like my head right where it is, thank you."

A gillie entered then with a tray upon which stood two

pewter goblets, a jug, a basket of rolls, a platter of sliced meat, and a jam pot.

Lachlan poured the whisky while Hector helped himself to a roll, breaking it in half and slipping two thick slices of roast beef into it.

"Thought you said you'd eaten," Lachlan said with a grin.

"I did, but you eat better than I do. I don't know what your people do to the meat here, but it always has more flavor than ours at Lochbuie."

"Ask Mairi; she'll know."

"Ask Mairi what?" that lady demanded as she strode briskly back into the hall, smiling at both men.

"About meat," Hector said. "What do you do to it to give it such flavor?"

"Faith, I don't know," she said. "I enticed one of the cook's lads from Ardtornish to accompany us when we came here, and he tends to all that. I'm sure it has something to do with the spices he rubs into the roast before he puts it on the spit, but as he has never put a dry or tasteless meal in front of us, I have not troubled my head about it. You may ask him anything you like."

He nodded but knew he would not bother. The meat at Duart was delicious, but the food he ate, as long as it was plentiful, was not important enough to him to waste his time quizzing his twin's kitchen staff about their methods.

"So tell us your news," Mairi said. "What of those at Lewis?"

"All well," he said. "Your youngest nephew now has four teeth and a mop of blond curls. The eldest is to foster with Argyll after Easter. Your sister is in splendid health, and her lord is his usual stoic self, which was annoying during the time I spent with them, but which I came to recognize as an excellent character trait after I met his uncle at Chalamine."

"When you mentioned Glenelg earlier, I thought you had met him at Lewis," Lachlan said. "I own, your going to Chalamine surprises me. You knew that MacDonald intended to tell Macleod of the reception when he arrives at Finlaggan. He does not trust the man, for all that he serves on the Council of the Isles. What stirred you to approach him betimes?"

"The weather," Hector admitted, glancing from his twin to Mairi and back again. "I got caught in a storm whilst riding through Glen Shiel. My only choice for shelter seemed to be a crofter or Chalamine, so I opted for the latter."

Mairi frowned, but Lachlan said with a twinkle, "Was there lightning?"

"Aye, damn you, there was, and rain pelting down on me as if that Noah lad ought to have begun building a new Ark."

"Noah?"

Hector grimaced, then grinned. "Aye, you ken the chap. Macleod tried to tell me his kinsmen littered the world before any sons of Gillean blessed it with their presence. Insisted that he'd never heard of any Macleans on Noah's Ark."

"What an insolent man," Mairi said. "He sounds most uncivil."

"Aye, well, I told him the Macleans had no need of Noah's Ark."

With a sleepy smile, Lachlan said, "I warrant he wanted to know then how our people survived the Flood."

"Aye, and I told him that there never lived a Maclean who had need of another man's boat to take him from harm's way."

"You didn't," Mairi exclaimed, laughing. When he

nodded, she laughed even harder. "How I'd have liked to see the old rascal's face! What did he say then?"

"He laughed, and not long afterward he agreed to let me marry his daughter," Hector said casually, watching them both closely.

His news clearly stunned them, apparently rendering Mairi speechless. Even Lachlan was silent for a few moments. But he never remained so for long.

"How came this about?" he asked evenly.

Mairi glanced at him, visibly reacting to his tone of voice.

Hector recognized the warning tone, too, but he met his twin's sharp gaze easily. "If you had seen the lass, you would not ask such a foolish question."

"A beauty, eh?"

"I've never seen her equal."

"I doubt she can match my lass," Lachlan said.

Realizing that he had stepped onto thin ice, Hector hesitated.

"Faith, sir," Mairi said to her husband, "you cannot expect every man to think me as beautiful as you do, certainly not after I've borne you three bairns!"

"You are as beautiful as ever, lass," Hector said. "Men still call you the most beautiful woman in the Isles, and I'll not dispute that, because your looks are extraordinary, and motherhood has done naught to change that."

"I fear you cater to my vanity, sir. But?"

"But my lass is extraordinary, too. She does not look anything like you, yet I have never seen her equal. She took my breath away the first time I laid eyes on her, and from what her father tells me, my reaction was the same as that of every other man who has clapped eyes on her."

"As I recall," she said thoughtfully, "Macleod of Glenelg

has a host of daughters for whom he must find husbands, and he has yet to find even one."

"Aye, for he insists on marrying off his eldest lass first. He would have foisted her onto me had I allowed it."

"Foisted?"

"Aye, for she is as naught beside her sister. I tell you, I no sooner saw that lass than she stole my heart, but Macleod is a gey superstitious man. He was determined to give me his eldest instead. Feared that if he let a younger one marry first, some dire consequence would fall upon his clan."

"So your interest has fallen upon a younger daughter," Lachlan said.

"Aye, the second one, but the diamond in his collection, I promise you."

"What is she like?" Mairi asked.

"Faith, did I not just tell you? She is beautiful."

"Perhaps she meant that you might tell us something more than that," Lachlan suggested gently. "What color is her hair?"

"Golden. Like spun gold. It was loose when first I saw her, and even with clouds of smoke billowing about her, her hair looked glorious, as if sunlight shone round her beautiful face."

"Smoke?" Mairi said. "What smoke?"

"I told you earlier, her skirt caught fire, but thankfully I put it out before she suffered any harm."

"Faith, man," Lachlan said. "You sound besotted."

"And you did not? When you fell in love with your lady here?"

"I warrant I never sounded as daft as you do. Has this paragon any tocher, let alone one worthy of you and your kinsmen?"

"What can that matter? I have enough to keep her, and I

shall acquire more over time, more power, too, if what has occurred so far speaks for the future. I can support a wife, my lad, and any number of bairns as well."

"Aye, you can," his brother agreed. "But I would remind you that you have a duty to our clan as well as to yourself."

"But what is she like?" Mairi asked again.

"I told you."

"You told us she has blond hair, sir. Mayhap you have failed to notice that quite half the women in the Highlands and Isles have blond hair. I want to know what she is like."

"Very well," he said, frowning as he tried to remember something more about Mariota that would satisfy Mairi. "She has blond hair and green eyes, like new grass. Her figure is . . . good." He hesitated, wondering how much he ought to say about that. Meeting his twin's gaze, he detected a twinkle and decided that he had said enough about Mariota's figure. "She is beautiful, stunning. You'll see," he promised. "Our wedding is to be in ten days' time."

"Why such haste?" Lachlan protested. "That does not even provide time enough for the priests to call the banns."

"We've no need of banns. Macleod has his own chaplain, who will do as he bids. We decided the wedding should proceed quickly, so that I can get the lass settled in at Lochbuie before he and I must travel to Finlaggan for the Council. Also, he wants to take his eldest daughter and mayhap the next one or two to Ardtornish to meet the Steward when he comes."

"Doubtless to seek husbands for them there," Lachlan said.

Mairi was frowning. "You still have said nothing about what she is like, sir. I do not care about her hair or her eyes. I'm sure you would not fall in love with an ugly woman. But what does she think about? Is she intelligent? Does she care about important things? Does she want lots of children? Does she know anything about organizing and running a large household? Yours at Lochbuie, I need not hesitate to say, would certainly benefit from a woman well versed in such things."

"Faith, lass, I don't know what she thinks about! Do you think a man like her father gave us any time to be private with each other? No man of sense would risk letting his daughter be alone with a man before she is safely wedded to him!"

Mairi and Lachlan exchanged smiles, reminding him that they had spent many forbidden moments together before they had married. He grimaced.

Lachlan said, "I wish you well, brother, and hope she will make you happy. If she does not, I warrant you will know how to rectify the situation."

"I don't know," Mairi said. "I should feel a deal better if I thought you knew anything about her other than that she has a pretty face and enticing eyes, and that she will doubt-less look well in your bed."

Her husband choked back a laugh, but Hector ignored him, saying simply, "You will soon meet her and can judge her for yourself, because you both must certainly attend my wedding."

"Never fear, brother, we'll be there," Lachlan said. "Indeed, I think we should have another round of brogac to seal that bargain and to wish you well."

"I'll drink to that myself," Mairi said, hugging Hector. "And I'll always be here, sir, if she needs me. Pray, tell her that for me."

"I will, lass, and thank you," he said, kissing her forehead.

"Enough of that now, the both of you," Lachlan said.

Laughing, Hector told them an amusing tale about one of his visits, and with the subject safely changed, they continued to converse amiably until bedtime.

⤙⤙⥽⥽

Cristina had not returned to the great hall after shepherding her sisters upstairs to their respective bedchambers, and although she had arisen at her usual time the next morning, she learned then that, the storm having ended, their guest had already departed for Kyle Rhea to rejoin his men and set sail for home.

Not until later that day did she learn anything about what had passed between him and her father, and then only when Macleod said casually as she was directing the servants in laying the table for the midday meal that he had agreed to a wedding with Hector Reaganach.

Surprised, she said, "You agreed to allow him to wed Mariota?"

"Aye, well, 'tis true that the lad believes as much."

Staring at him, she said, "Surely he does not believe a falsehood, sir. Pray, be plain with me, for you cannot mean to make an enemy of a man so closely associated with the Lord of the Isles."

"Have I no said I mean to make him me son-in-law?"

"But if that is true, how can he believe falsely that he is to marry Mariota?"

"I ha' said from the outset that ye must be the first to wed, daughter, and I dinna tell lies—no to me own kin, that is."

"But Hector Reaganach cannot have agreed to marry me," she protested.

"Nae one can say I didna make myself plain to the lad."

That was true, she knew. Still, if Hector Reaganach had

departed in the belief that his host had agreed to let him marry Mariota, he would not agree later to marry anyone else. He had already made it plain that he did not want Cristina.

"He'll just refuse to marry anyone else," she said. "And what of Mariota? Do her feelings not matter to you?"

"Nay, why should they? She kens naught o' me conversation wi' the lad, nor will ye tell her. Ye'll no be pretending she cares for him, because I heard her myself say she doesna think him worthy o' her. Nor do I think him worthy, either. He's nobbut a Maclean, after all."

Repressing indignation that he would think a mere Maclean good enough for her but not for Mariota, Cristina said nothing for several moments. What her father had said was true, after all, in that Mariota had shown no interest in Hector Reaganach other than the usual flirtatious interest she showed in any man.

At last, forcing calm into her voice, Cristina said, "What is your plan, sir? How will you tell him that he cannot have her? For he will come here, will he not, expecting to take possession of his bride?"

"Aye, and he'll take her, too," Macleod said.

"But you have just said that he cannot have her."

"I said nowt o' the sort. I said he couldna have Mariota."

"Then—"

"Are ye daft, Cristina? Have I no said from the start who his bride must be?"

A chill shot up her spine. "Your meaning is plain enough, Father, but you cannot force the man. He has already said he will not have me."

"Never fear, lass," Macleod said cheerfully. "Ye're a good, obedient daughter, and I mean to see ye well rewarded. Just leave everything to me, and the matter will sort itself out as it should."

Knowing well the uselessness of argument, Cristina put her faith in Hector Reaganach, certain that that gentleman would not allow Macleod to dupe him into anything he did not want. She likewise said nothing to Mariota about their father's intentions, believing they would come to naught and being sure that Mariota had no interest in Hector Reaganach.

It was not long, however, before everyone at Chalamine knew that the laird was planning a wedding. He conferred with his parson, ordered a feast, and sent out invitations. To Cristina's relief the guest list had perforce to be short, including only nearby kinsmen, because while a man like Hector Reaganach might scorn to stay inside when storms descended upon the Highlands and Isles, others were not so hardy as to set out in heavy seas even for a grand occasion. And the weather continued to be unpredictable, with wind and rain one day, gray skies the next.

Mariota remained oblivious until four days before the wedding was to take place. Not being the sort of young woman who took an interest in much that did not concern her, particularly if anyone might expect her to do chores, she paid little heed to the frenzy of cleaning, the ceaseless baking, and the other preparations. But when her father told her as the family members were breaking their fast that morning, that she would be giving up her bed to a visiting cousin whose family intended to pass that night at Chalamine, she demanded to know why she should.

"Why, because o' the wedding, o' course," her father replied testily.

"What wedding?"

"Ha' ye no been paying attention, lass? We ha' been

preparing for the day nigh onto a fortnight now. Cristina is to be wedded on Saturday."

Mariota looked astonished. "To whom?"

"Why, to Hector Reaganach, o' course. D'ye no recall that the man came here looking for a bride?"

"Goodness me," Lady Euphemia said. "I know you mentioned Cristina several times, Murdo, but I thought you were simply mistaken. Indeed, I thought he intended to marry our Mariota, and moreover, I believe he thought so, too."

"Is there really going to be a wedding?" Isobel asked. "I thought we were just doing the usual spring cleaning."

Cristina grimaced at the shocked expression on Mariota's face. On many occasions over the past days, she had itched to tell Macleod that she would not be party to his scheme. The knowledge that he would ignore her arguments or, worse, that he would react physically, as he had in the past when dealing with insubordination, had kept her silent.

Had she suspected even for a moment that Mariota wanted Hector as much as he wanted her, she would have refused to have anything to do with Macleod's scheme, whatever the consequences to herself. But she had been certain Mariota had no such wish—as certain as she was that Hector Reaganach would put an end to the plot as soon as he learned of it. Now she was not sure of anything.

Mariota looked from her father to Cristina. "I don't understand," she said grimly. "How can Cristina be marrying Hector Reaganach? He wanted me."

"But you said you did not want him," Cristina reminded her. "You said he was unworthy of you, that he will never be as wealthy as his brother is. You even said his battle-axe—"

"I said it is a barbaric weapon," Mariota said, wrinkling her nose. "It is."

"Aye, well, axe or no axe, he's no worthy o' ye, lass,"

Macleod said. "Ye can have any man ye want, right up to a royal prince, as I've told ye afore."

"But if Hector wants me, why should Cristina have him?"

"Now, lassie, dinna go on about that," Macleod said coaxingly. "Ye didna want the man, and ye were wise to reject him. Recall what men call him. He'd make ye a harsh husband, I'm thinking. But the plain fact be that a marriage betwixt our family and his—being as close as they be to the Lord of the Isles—can well benefit us all. He has only to marry the right one o' ye."

Mariota's expression changed in a flash from perplexity to outrage, making Cristina's stomach clench in an all-too-familiar way. Hoping to forestall the impending scene, she said quietly, "I am sure that Hector Reaganach will have something to say about all of this. Perhaps we should all wait to see what—"

"We ha' nae need to wait," Macleod interjected. "I mean to see that all runs smoothly. Ye'll all do just as I bid ye, and it will be well."

"Am I the only one who sees how unfair this is?" Mariota demanded furiously. "Hector Reaganach loves me! He wants me! And the pair of you, the two of you who are supposed to love me most of all, are instead conspiring against me to keep him from having me. You are cruel and unnatural, both of you, and I warrant he will slash you to pieces with his battle-axe when I tell him what you mean to do! And I *shall* tell him. You know I shall!"

"I forbid ye to say one word to the man," Macleod snapped. "Ye'll suffer me gravest displeasure, Mariota, an ye do any such thing."

"Goodness me, do you think our dearest Mariota will care for that?" Lady Euphemia asked, looking agitatedly from one member of the family to another. "That is to say, I don't think she truly gives a fig for . . . I mean, she has such an independence of spirit, sithee, that she scarcely ever thinks about what anyone else wants, and I'd venture to guess . . . Oh, dear, that is not what I mean to say, certainly not, but she never will, you know. I fear that if you want this scheme of yours to succeed, Murdo, you'll simply have to lock her away until it's done."

"Faith, are you against me, too, Aunt? I should have known you would be, of course, because you always agree with Father. But you're wide of the mark if you think he would ever lock me up. He could never be so cruel to me."

"Did I say that he would?" Lady Euphemia asked. But she might as well have addressed the ambient air, for none of her audience responded.

"Nay, love, of course he would not be so cruel to you," Cristina said soothingly to Mariota. "Nor would I let him do such a thing. Mayhap you should run away, though, and lie down to rest and recover your usual cheerful temperament, whilst I talk more with him. Your eyes are all reddened now, but a little nap will soon restore their sparkle."

Lady Euphemia said nothing more until after Mariota had left the room, but when neither Cristina nor Macleod spoke, she said thoughtfully, "I do believe you will have to, you know—lock her up, that is."

"Don't talk daft, Euphemia," Macleod snapped. "The lass will come around, for she kens fine that she canna wed until her sister does. I'll no be the one who brings the Macleods' good fortune down like rubble round our ears, all for a lack o' resolution. Now, I've said all I'll say on the subject, so let there be an end to it."

Cristina exchanged a look with her aunt and sighed. He was being far more stubborn than usual, and she could see no safe path through the storm ahead, but she had to find one. That went without saying, because Mariota's happiness was at stake. That her own seemed likewise in peril was not a subject on which to dwell. She simply had to put an end to her father's mad, impossible scheme.

As a first step, she gave her aunt a slight but speaking nod, whereupon Lady Euphemia immediately invented an excuse to take herself out of the room. When she had gone, Cristina said, "Forgive me, Father, but I must protest the role you have set for me to play in this business."

"What the devil are ye saying? Speak plainly if ye must speak at all!"

"Very well, I won't do it," she said bluntly. "That should be plain enough."

Chapter 4

Macleod stared at Cristina, his face turning red with fury. "What the devil d'ye mean, ye won't? Ye'll do as I bid ye, lass, and there's an end to it."

"I won't marry a man who wants my sister, sir, nor do I believe he will agree to it. I was willing to submit to your command when I believed that Mariota had no interest in marrying him, but knowing she wants him, I cannot. You apparently agreed that he could marry her, and you must keep your word to the man."

"Bah, nae bargain's complete without ye spit on your thumbs and press them together, which we never did, so I'll have nae backchat from ye or your sister. I'm doing what's best for Clan Macleod, whilst I warrant she only wants the man because she fears ye'll get him. She'll soon see me own course will suit her better."

Although Cristina did not doubt that her sister's sudden interest in Hector was the result of her possessive nature, Mariota's reasons did not matter.

"I'm sorry, sir," she said firmly. "I simply cannot support this mad scheme."

Macleod slapped her then, but although the blow was

hard enough to bring tears to her eyes and make her stumble a step backward, she did not cry out, giving him look for look as she raised a hand to her stinging cheek. "You may do as you please to me," she said. "But I doubt that even your tame parson will help you force a union if both the bride and bridegroom refuse to take part."

"Ye were willing enough to do it afore your foolish sister took it into her head to set up a fuss."

Bluntly, Cristina said, "It would be more accurate to say that I saw no point in debating the matter, because I was and still am certain that Hector Reaganach will say all that I wanted to say and more."

"And what if he does not object, lass? What then?"

"Perhaps the notion would appeal to me more if he did want it, sir," she said honestly. "I'll not deny that I like him. But the plain fact is that he does not want me. He wants Mariota, and she wants him."

"Ah, bah, Mariota doesna ken what she wants," Macleod said. "As for Hector Reaganach, what if I tell ye he'll no speak a word in objection?"

Cristina's heart did a little jump, making her bite her lower lip to suppress the feelings that stirred instantly at the thought of a Hector Reaganach who wanted her. But still she shook her head. "I'll not help you disappoint Mariota," she said. "She wants him now, sir, whatever her reason, and I am loath to figure as a woman who stole my sister's intended husband."

"Ye'll figure as nae such thing," he snapped. "I'll sort out Mariota afore the day if I have to lay me whip about her sides. D'ye want to be responsible for that?"

"No, of course I don't, but that would be most unfair," Cristina said, knowing he was capable of doing whatever he believed was necessary to get his own way. "Punish me if you must, but do not punish her."

His eyes gleamed, and she knew she had taken a misstep in the debate and that he sensed victory. "Ye'll do as I bid ye," he said gently. "For if ye defy me further, lass, I'll ha' nae choice but to believe ye do so because Mariota has set up a fuss, and for that I will punish her, I promise ye. D'ye go now and fetch the lass. 'Tis time and more that I make her understand her duty as a daughter o' this household. By the time I've finished wi' her, she'll make nae further complaint about the matter. Go now."

Cristina sighed, knowing she had lost the battle, because once he began proving his point, none of her sisters would be safe from his temper. He would punish Mariota and then, as angry with himself as with Cristina, he would punish the slightest infraction that any of them committed, for so it had happened many times in the past.

"Very well, sir," she said, resigned. "I'll do as you bid me."

"Good lass," he said. "I thought ye would."

❧

From that point, time passed too swiftly for Cristina. The weather remained uncertain, as if the weather gods could not decide which season of the year it should be. If the sky cleared, the winds howled around Chalamine as if, Cristina thought, they were also displeased with the recent turn of events. And Mariota was as unpredictable as the weather. One moment, she refused to speak to Cristina or to anyone else. The next she behaved as if nothing untoward were happening. Lady Euphemia told Cristina as they were counting linens for wedding guests who would remain overnight that they should be grateful for Mariota's indecision.

"Because you know how it is when she goes into a rage," she said earnestly. "I tell you, my dear, 'twas what I feared most when your father told her he had decided that you were to marry Hector Reaganach."

"People do change their minds, Aunt," Cristina replied. "That Mariota changed hers about Hector is not so strange. Moreover, she feels things deeply, as you know, for she always has."

"Oh, my dear, I do know what you mean, although I should not say she feels things so much as that she dramatizes and exaggerates those emotions she chooses to display, but do you not think that our Mariota spends much more time than she should just *dwelling* upon her emotional state? Why, my mother—aye, and my grandmother, too—would have said that she ought to be thinking more about those around her than about herself, but if our dear Mariota spares a thought for anyone save herself, I do not think I have borne witness to the event. Have you?"

Cristina smiled. "Now, Aunt, I know that you enjoy her usually sunny temperament as much as the rest of us do, for when Mariota is happy, no one could be kinder or more thoughtful. I promise you, I shall miss her dreadfully when she marries and goes away to live with her husband, whoever he might prove to be."

"But, my dear, you will be going away before Mariota, for your father is utterly determined that you shall marry Hector Reaganach."

Suppressing a sigh, Cristina said, "I fear that my father has built a false scheme, and one that cannot prosper. You saw Hector Reaganach and have had plenty of time to judge his character. Do you think he is the sort of man who will let my father lead him about by the nose? I do not. Therefore, I do not believe I am going anywhere. Now, perhaps you can find a maidservant to take these linens to their proper chambers and see the beds made up. Our guests will begin arriving tomorrow, and come what may, we must proceed as if we believe that events will transpire exactly as my father intends."

"Oh, yes, my dear, for in my experience, things nearly always do come off just as he plans. I have set aside a coin for Lord Hector's shoe, because I fear he will need all the luck we can provide for him, do not you?"

Cristina did not reply, knowing that nothing she could politely say would express her feelings, particularly since she was not certain what she felt. Had the situation been normal and the marriage arrangements properly made betwixt her father and Hector Reaganach, with herself as the intended bride in both their minds, she knew she would be eagerly anticipating the ceremony. As it was, she felt anything but eager for the time to pass, because she could imagine no good coming from the inevitable clash between the two men.

Hector had spent the previous ten days in a flurry of activity. Having passed his first night on the Isle of Mull at Duart with Mairi and Lachlan, he had traveled the following day by boat from Lochbuie to Ardtornish Castle, some five miles up the Sound of Mull, to make his report to the Lord of the Isles.

MacDonald being well pleased with the news that nearly everyone he had invited to join his Shrove Tuesday feasting would attend, the two had spent an hour or so discussing other news that Hector and his men had gleaned in their travels. All in all, the Isles seemed peaceful, although Mac-Donald did express reservations with regard to certain clans that seemed particularly displeased with Robert the Steward as heir to the Scottish throne. Much had been accomplished in the nearly sixty years since the Bruce and William Wallace had united Scotland, but enmity between clans still existed and could, at any time, erupt into trouble.

Hector had not seen his father at Duart, because that gentleman had not deigned to join the others for supper. Therefore, having sat up late with Mairi and Lachlan, and risen early to make his report to MacDonald, he had expected upon his return to Duart to apprise Ian Dubh of his intention to marry. However, although he had spent only the one day at Ardtornish, he learned when he returned that his father had abruptly departed for Bellachuan.

"Did you tell him my news?" he asked his twin.

"I did not, nor should you have to ask me such a question," Lachlan said, eyes twinkling. "It is your news, after all."

"Coward," Hector muttered.

"Not at all," Lachlan retorted. "I would not steal the moment from you. He will be most interested in your chosen bride, I know, and since I have never met her, I could have told him only that she is a younger daughter of Macleod of Glenelg. That would scarcely recommend her to him, as you must know. But your enthusiasm for the connection will surely assuage any criticism he may have."

Hector frowned. He had been eager to impart his news to his twin and Mairi, expecting no more than that they would be happy for him. Lachlan's lukewarm reception of the news and Mairi's continued requests to know more about Mariota's thoughts and household skills had been somewhat daunting but had not diminished his delight in his choice. Reassuring himself that Lachlan's competitive nature made that gentleman fear that Mariota's beauty might put Mairi's in the shade, he decided he was making too much of things. Shaking his head at his twin, he said, "I'm for Seil in the morning then. I would not have him learn of this from anyone else."

"He will return here soon, if you want to put off the reckoning," Lachlan said. "He discovered a trunk stuffed with documents that apparently originated in the days of Wallace and Bruce. I had thought we had returned all such things to MacDonald after he bestowed Duart upon us, but Father says he is certain that these documents will greatly interest his grace's keeper of records. Naturally, though, he wishes to examine them carefully before he returns them."

"Naturally," Hector agreed with a smile, knowing his father's passion for all things historical. "Nonetheless, I'm for Seil. It would be most improper to delay my invitation to the wedding any longer. He rarely puts himself to the trouble of attending such events, but I am his eldest son, after all."

Lachlan only grinned and wished him Godspeed.

❧

Hector's meeting with his father passed uneventfully. If Ian Dubh did not express joy at the proposed union, neither did he condemn it. As they talked, he sifted through a pile of documents, from which he had scarcely looked away long enough to react to his news, saying only, "A Macleod, eh?"

"Aye, sir. I warrant you may have hoped for a more rewarding connection. Indeed, Lachlan said as much to me."

"Nay, lad, you and your brother have already gained much for Clan Gillean, so I wish only that you be happy. As

you have waited this long to make your choice, I warrant
you must know your own mind."

"I do indeed, and I believe you will approve of my choice
when you see her. I'm hoping you will do me the honor of
traveling to Glenelg with me for the wedding. Lachlan and
Mairi will make up the rest of the party."

"As to that, we'll have to see," Ian Dubh said, peering
closely at a document from which numerous wax seals on
gold and red ribbons dangled. "I made an interesting discovery during my recent visit to Duart and only returned to
Seil to attempt to reconcile one or two details with our mu-
niments here."

"Lachlan said you'd found a trunk with documents
belonging to his grace."

"Aye, and I mean to show them to MacDuffie of Colonsay, who is—"

"Hereditary keeper of the records to the Lord of the
Isles," Hector said. "I've met him several times, sir, whilst
Lachlan and I have served as your ambassadors to the Coun-
cil of the Isles."

He did not think it wise to mention that he and his twin
had once held MacDuffie hostage along with two or three
others, in order to clear up a potential misunderstanding. His
father already knew something of that incident, as did many
other Islesmen, but Ian Dubh most assuredly did not know
the whole story, nor did Hector intend to be the one who told
him. Just as it was his right to inform his father of his intent
to marry, so was it his twin's business to relate the details of
that interesting event, if Lachlan ever decided it would be
useful for Ian Dubh to know.

"Ah, yes, of course you've met MacDuffie," Ian Dubh
said, nodding.

"Do I take it then that you will return soon to Duart?" Hector asked.

"Aye, indeed, for I cannot long retain control of these documents, you see, and although MacDuffie is an excellent man in his way, he merely keeps the records. He does not attempt to understand them or to learn from them."

"Then I will hope you can find the time to go with us to Glenelg," Hector said. "Macleod did not suggest that he intends to invite a large company. Indeed, he said that he hoped I did not mean to stay longer than our wedding night."

"Macleod has never been a man to waste his gelt," Ian Dubh said, setting down the document he had been looking at and picking up another. "Doubtless, he looks only for you to take the lass off his hands and provide a good home for her. He has a number of marriageable daughters, I believe."

"Aye, eight of them altogether," Hector said. "She is the second."

"Indeed?" Ian Dubh looked at him. "Then I own I am surprised, for I had not heard that he had married off the first one. But doubtless, I missed hearing about it."

"Nay, for the eldest still lives at Chalamine," Hector said.

"Interesting, because I'd heard that he is a most superstitious man."

"He is, indeed. He tried to persuade me to marry the eldest, saying he feared some calamity or other would fall upon Clan Macleod if I did not, but I convinced him to let me have Mariota."

"Then your powers of persuasion have greatly improved," Ian Dubh said.

Knowing he could gain nothing useful by responding to that statement, Hector held his tongue, and they parted shortly thereafter.

Back home at Lochbuie, he found plenty to occupy his time, because he saw at once that his home, although sufficiently comfortable for him, was not nearly comfortable enough for Mariota. Setting the servants to work, he ordered them to make all tidy for his bride, then turned his attention to preparations for the annual Council of the Isles at Finlaggan.

His twin had a reputation for being the best-informed man in the western Highlands and Isles, and had gained that standing by meticulously cultivating informants, many of whom were scions of noble families who as lads had fostered with Ian Dubh at Seil. Lachlan maintained correspondence with many of them and depended on Hector to nurture their support in other ways. Therefore, every year, before the Council of the Isles, it fell to him to make contact with any member of Lachlan's network that they had not recently heard from.

He had accomplished much of this business during his recent travels, but two gentlemen remained to visit. He set out to do that as soon as everything at Lochbuie seemed to be in train, and returned two nights before he and the others were to set sail for Glenelg.

Lochbuie looked quite presentable to him by then, both inside and out, because it was still too early in the season to expect even the kitchen gardens to produce much in the way of color or even greenery. The weather had remained chilly, and the skies were still gray. Nevertheless, all looked tidy, and he set out for Duart with an eager heart.

The first setback came when he found his father deeply involved in his new discoveries and not at all interested in setting them aside to attend the wedding.

"I'll meet your lass soon enough," Ian Dubh said when pressed. "I have already met Macleod and do not need to refresh the acquaintance, especially since you mean to go and return overnight. The journey to Glenelg is long, and 'tis not a pleasant time of year to travel on the water or by any other means."

MacDonald had also declined his invitation, saying that he had much to do before everyone met at Finlaggan, and would see them there soon enough.

But the worst blow came that evening, when an urgent message arrived for Lachlan from Ardtornish, informing him that a clash had erupted between the MacDuffies and the MacKinvens of Colonsay over collection of the petrel oil used as holy oil for sacramental purposes in Scottish abbeys and elsewhere. MacDonald wanted his Lord High Admiral to go himself and settle the dispute before it affected the latest collection of that lucrative oil, which his grace sold to churches all over Europe through the powerful Hanseatic League, and which was responsible for much of the income of the Isles.

Thus it was that the following morning, although two Maclean longboats set out from Duart for Chalamine, except for the oarsmen and helmsmen, only Hector, his brother's wife, and her woman, Meg Raith, were aboard as passengers. The journey was uneventful if one discounted depressing gray skies and constant drizzle, but since the oarsmen had strung canvas over the stern of the boat for the ladies and anyone else who cared to take shelter, even the rain was bearable.

They passed that night with the Skye kinsman of MacDonald's who had lent Hector the horse he had ridden to Glen Shiel and Chalamine during his previous visit, crossed to Kyle Rhea on the mainland the next morning, and thus arrived at Chalamine well before time on Hector's wedding day.

Tam, the same lad who had greeted him on his first visit, greeted them at the castle entrance and took them up to the great hall, empty of smoke this time and prepared for the ceremony to come. But if Hector had expected that ceremony to take place at once, circumstances soon disabused him of the notion.

He saw no sign of his bride or her sisters. The only family member in the chamber was his host, who sat on a stool before the huge fireplace, draped in a large towel, while a gillie trimmed his hair and beard.

"Sit, sit," he commanded, gesturing vaguely toward a nearby settle, and assuring Hector that he knew both of his companions well. "We'll be finished here in a trice, I promise ye. Be sure to burn all the trimmings," he added in an aside to his barber. "I willna ha' them left about for anyone to pick up."

Mairi smiled. "One cannot ever be too careful, can one, sir?"

Beaming at her, Macleod said, "'Tis true, 'tis true, me lady. Such things all too often contribute to evil purposes. I see that nae one can gather hair clippings, nor yet me nail clippings, to work evil against Clan Macleod."

Hector exchanged a look with his sister-in-law but noted that she did not smile. His first inclination had been to chuckle at her comment, but his host's swift, approving response killed that impulse.

"The High Admiral didna come?" Macleod said, raising his eyebrows.

"No, sir," Hector said. "A squabble erupted over petrel oil, and his grace dispatched him to deal with it. His lady insisted on accompanying me, however."

Macleod's approval of Mairi remained clear as he said, "I

didna expect ye so early, me lady, else ye'd no ha' walked in on me like this."

"'Tis nothing, sir, I assure you," Mairi replied graciously. "Mayhap you would like me and my woman to go and assist the bride with her preparations."

"Nay, nay, thanking ye all the same," he said, waving away her offer. "The lass will be a bit shy today, and not knowing ye, she'd likely be in a dither from worrying and forget her lines and all."

"Do you not also have an older daughter, sir? One upon whom the brunt of these preparations must have fallen? Doubtless I can make myself useful to her."

"By me troth, me lady, ye be our honored guest. I'll no ha' ye doing the tasks o' a scullery maid here at Chalamine. I'd be better pleased an ye—aye, and me future son as well—will take a mug o' brogac wi' me afore I ask one o' the maidservants to show ye to the chamber where ye'll sleep tonight. Come now, I'll be that offended an ye refuse, either o' ye. Tam, pour them each a generous dram, will ye now, lad?"

There being no gracious way to refuse such an offer, they accepted the whisky, although Mairi did no more than touch her lips to her mug when Tam handed it to her. Then she said casually, "Have no other guests arrived, sir?"

"Aye, sure, a few, but they'll be out and about now, I'm thinking. We've no made much ado about this marriage, since it be happening so quick. We'd no like to start any wicked rumors, would we, lad?" He winked at Hector, who felt a sudden urge to say exactly what he thought of the man. Only the knowledge that his intended would likely disapprove of his creating a rift with her family before they had even said their vows held him silent.

Nevertheless, he shot Mairi a look of gratitude when she

said, "I cannot imagine that anyone could find fault with this wedding, sir. The Macleods are well-known to be noble folk, as are the sons of Gillean."

"Aye, sure, me lady, and I meant nowt by what I said. The fault lies wi' the short time at our disposal. Macleods be spread throughout the Isles, sithee. We'll be sending out word o' the match soon enough, but we had little time to gather folks, what with the weather and all. Had we done this in summertime, the matter would ha' been different, but sithee, our lad here were that set on great speed."

Mairi nodded, but when he offered her more of the heady brogac, she refused, saying she would prefer to retire to her room and dress for the festivities.

"Aye, ye do that then," Macleod said. "The parson will be speaking the words shortly afore Vespers. Then, after prayers we'll ha' the wedding-night feasting and proper bedding o' the bride and groom."

Surprised that the ceremony was taking place so late, Hector missed his twin sorely, for had Lachlan been with him, he might at least have discussed the unusual nature of this wedding with him. But he did not think it proper to discuss such things with the redoubtable Mairi, especially since she would doubtless expect him to do something to alter the arrangements if he did not like them.

He realized that although he was a formidable henchman, capable of carrying out the most complex and dangerous orders, and of commanding men with ease when he knew what his twin or MacDonald expected of him, he had rarely made significant decisions on his own. Neither was he in the habit of questioning other powerful men's decisions without strong cause and prior consultation with Lachlan.

And since it was Macleod's home and Macleod's daughter he was marrying, he decided the manner of the wedding was no concern of his. Doubtless, Macleod knew what he was doing, and the only thing Hector cared about was that he and Mariota would soon be husband and wife.

He heard Macleod's mention of the wedding night with mixed feelings. On one hand, he looked forward to it with unleavened eagerness. On the other, once he realized that neither his father nor Lachlan would attend the wedding, he had hoped to take her straight home to Lochbuie. That last hope was clearly impractical now, especially in view of the hour set for the ceremony. He would have to reconcile himself to spending at least the one night at Chalamine.

After Mairi departed to dress and Macleod's hair suited that gentleman's notion of what was correct, he refilled Hector's mug of brogac with his own hands, refilling his own as well.

Demurring, Hector said, "If I keep drinking that brew, sir, I'm thinking I won't be worth much as a husband tonight."

"Faith, lad, ye'll do your duty by the lass. Ye're a young, lusty fellow, so I've nae worry about that. Sakes, instinct will take over, be ye ape-drunk or no."

"I'd as lief my lady not see me ape-drunk on our wedding night," Hector said lightly. "I'm not a man who drinks heavily at any time."

"Och, now, ye've scarcely had three mugs! I'd never ha' taken ye for a lightweight wi' the whisky, lad."

"My duties keep me sober, sir. When one's right arm and battle-axe are needed, one cannot take time first to sober up."

"Aye, I expect that's true enough," Macleod agreed amiably, but Hector thought he looked disappointed nonetheless.

A twinge of guilt struck him at the knowledge that he had given Macleod yet another reason to disapprove of him, but he shrugged it off. Macleod would learn soon enough that his son-in-law was worthy of his daughter. Even so, Hector finished the whisky, wondering as he did if his host meant to feed him anything before the ceremony.

Apparently, he did not, for although Macleod agreed soon enough that the time had come to dress for the wedding, by the time Hector returned to the great hall, the other guests had arrived and were in festive humor.

The only other member of the bride's family that he recognized was Lady Euphemia, who approached him when he caught her eye. She smiled, saying, "I am delighted to see you again, sir, and before the wedding as well, for I did hope to find at least one tiny moment to speak with you before the ceremony had begun."

"Aye, well, you have found that moment, my lady, but where are my bride's sisters? I expected to see them all here."

"Oh, I expect you'll see them soon enough, sir. To my mind, the less one sees of them—or rather, hears of them, for they are generally noisy—the better. But I did not approach you to speak of the girls, did I?" Clearly not expecting a reply, she reached into her sleeve and extracted a silver coin that she handed to him. "For luck, don't you know? You must put it in your shoe—at once now, lest you forget."

He smiled, thinking the entire Macleod family was too superstitious for its own good, but obediently slipped the coin into his shoe. Nodding approval, Lady Euphemia took herself off, but she had scarcely turned away before Macleod joined him again, carrying his apparently everpresent jug of whisky.

Clearly, plenty of drink was available, but not a morsel of food had shown itself. Hector refused his host's offer of another mug, however, insisting that he preferred to recite his vows from an upright position rather than lying flat on his back, as he was sure he soon would be if he attempted to keep up with Macleod. The man seemed utterly unaffected by the heady drink.

When the priest entered the hall, Macleod called him over to introduce Hector to him, insisting that both enjoy yet one more mug of brogac with him. Hector sighed but could see no way to avoid drinking with the two, especially since the priest clearly expected him to do so.

Glancing toward Mairi, he saw that she was merrily enjoying herself amidst the Macleod kinfolk. Surprisingly, no children had come into the hall, and he still saw none of his betrothed's sisters. But although he took note of that fact, he found his brain unwilling to ponder it, and looked instead for some sign of his bride.

"Ye'll no see her till the time," Macleod said, grinning and clearly reading his thoughts. "'Tis fearful bad luck for any groom to see his bride afore the ceremony, on the day."

"Aye," the priest agreed. "'Tis true, that."

At last, however, Macleod signaled his piper, who began to play a solemn tune. At a gesture from the priest, Hector followed the piper obediently to the dais and the makeshift altar there.

As he stepped onto the platform, he misjudged his step, tripping.

"Kiss your thumb, lad, quickly," Macleod advised. "Ye'll no want bad luck during your wedding night."

Hector nearly laughed but caught himself, wondering why he seemed to have so little control over his body. On such an occasion, even the urge to laugh seemed odd, but his head felt as if a thick Scottish mist had settled in around his brain. Truly, Macleod's brogac was powerful stuff if a few mugs were enough to make him feel so disoriented, even dizzy.

The pipes skirled, and he saw her walking toward him in a cloud of gilded satin. The guests . . . There seemed to be more now, twice as many, or his eyes were making two of everyone he saw. He gave his head a shake, but that only made him dizzier. He feared briefly that he might be sick but rejected the notion as soon as it struck. He was rarely sick, and now was not the time. How Lachlan would laugh to see him brought low by three measly mugs of Isla's brogac.

His veiled bride stood beside him, although he did not recall seeing how she got there. Her sisters seemed to be attending her, but he kept losing count and could scarcely tell them apart. They were all fair and all seemed young, too. Where was the vixen? Nay, not a vixen precisely, but although he pondered for a moment, he could not find the word for what she was. His thoughts would not sort themselves.

He spoke the words the parson told him to speak, put the ring on her finger when bidden to do so, and then it was over, and they were walking to their places at the high table. Oddly, the lass sat to the left of Macleod, still veiled, and he sat to the man's right. The arrangement seemed odd for only a moment, however, before he recalled that ladies nearly always sat to their host's left, and gentlemen to his right. Or was it the other way? His mind simply refused to provide answers.

The celebration grew rowdier, with songs sung and pipes piping. Some folks got up to dance a ring dance, but Hector sat and watched, having all he could do to eat some of the food put before him and drink the many toasts offered to his health and that of his lady. The entire company seemed to have had too much to drink—even Mairi, he thought, easily able to imagine what his twin would say to him if he heard from others that his lady wife had grown tipsy at the wedding. That, however, was the last thought of any consequence that passed through his head before he heard his host announce that it was time to escort the happy couple to their bed.

His bride got up at once and went with her aunt and some other ladies, including Mairi, to prepare for bed.

What followed seemed dreamlike, as a host of Macleod kinsmen bore him off, stripped him of his clothing, and put him into bed with his bride, who remained shyly veiled. Amidst a chorus of cheering and ribald comments, the priest blessed the couple and the bed. His senses whirling, Hector's head began to ache, his dizziness to increase, and then came only a dark, swirling cloud of black.

Chapter 5

Hector awoke wincing, because some idiot had opened the curtains and a too-bright sun spilled unwelcome rays into the room. His first thought was to shout for a gillie to shut the curtains again, but even as he opened his dry mouth to do that, his headache reasserted itself, reminding him of the condition he had been in when he fell asleep—if one could so define the stupor into which he had fallen. As he tried to recall why he had drunk so much, he became conscious that someone else was in his bed, and memory swept in.

How, he wondered, could he have forgotten his wedding night? He was married now, the husband of the glorious Mariota, but he could remember next to nothing about the ceremony or what had followed it.

He turned his head on the pillow, noting that she was lying on her side about as far away from him as she could lie, facing the wall against which the bed stood. He frowned, trying to remember claiming his husbandly rights. Could he truly have been so lost to the whisky as to have forgotten such a significant event?

Her hair was a sunny cloud of curls on the pillow, paler blonde than he remembered it, but doubtless that was no more than the effect of the sun's brightness. She breathed lightly, softly, and his body stirred with lust.

∽∾

Cristina lay stiffly beside her husband, scarcely daring to breathe, let alone to sleep. She had lain so nearly the whole night, terrified that he would waken and reach for her. They were well and truly married now, just as her father had wanted them to be, but the reality was even worse than she had feared it would be.

She remembered the horror she had felt when four or five Macleod kinsmen had borne him into the room and unceremoniously dumped him onto the bed beside her. Then, with no concern for her modesty, one of them had snatched back the coverlet and draped it over him. Another had yanked off her veil, terrifying her, lest Hector see that she was not Mariota, but he was too far gone with drink to notice, and no one else was surprised to see her, since Macleod had neglected to tell anyone else that Hector had expected to marry his second daughter rather than his first. And although she had met Lady Mairi at Ardtornish, everyone knew that the Macleod sisters looked much alike, and Mairi had never laid eyes on Mariota. Moreover, the priest had hastily mumbled the words of the ceremony, so that no one had heard him say Cristina. And since nearly everyone had been indulging in her father's whisky, most of the guests were too drunk to notice anything amiss.

Hector's bearers' speech was boisterous and bawdy, clearly shocking some of the ladies, and Macleod ordered the priest to lose no time in blessing the bed and the newly wedded couple. Then, ordering his guests to depart and leave them to consummate their union, he leaned close to

Cristina and muttered, "Ye'll no defy me now, lass, or by heaven, I'll stay here myself to see the deed properly done."

"I've no wish to defy you, sir," she said honestly. "'Twould only create a scandal. But what he will do when he comes to his senses is another matter."

"Then see that ye please him well, so we'll ha' nowt to worry us."

"I will lie with him as his wife, sir. I can do no more than that."

"Aye, well, ye can and all, but I've nae doubt the man will instruct ye in your wifely duties. Here, Hector," he said loudly, giving her bridegroom a hearty shake. "Pay heed to your wife now, lad, and do your duty by her."

Hector had groaned, then turned and flopped a heavy arm over her.

Apparently satisfied, Macleod had left her to endure her husband's aimless pawing. Shortly thereafter Hector had begun to snore and she had managed, not without difficulty, to extricate herself from his clutches.

How easy it had been then to tell herself that she had simply obeyed her father and was therefore only doing her duty. It was true Macleod had left her little choice, but one always had a choice if one was willing to suffer the consequences of that choice. And the plain fact was that every choice had consequences. What those would be for her, she could only guess, but she would soon find out, because he was awake. She knew because his breathing had altered, from stertorous to steady.

The moment of discovery was so close that she could not breathe. She wanted to curl into a ball, or better yet, to disappear, to return to yesterday when she was unmarried and could still change her mind about duty and obedience.

Sensing movement next to her, she started nonetheless when his large hand grasped her shoulder.

"Look at me, lass," he murmured. "I would see you in the morning light to savor your beauty. I fear I was not as attentive as I might have been last night. I hope I did not hurt you."

Remembering for perhaps the hundredth time since the priest had united them that men called him Hector the Ferocious, Cristina wondered if she would live to see more that day than the sunrise. But she was no coward. Drawing a deep breath, she turned to face him.

Hector gasped and shoved himself up on one elbow, wincing at the pounding in his head but ignoring it otherwise as he exclaimed, "You!"

"Aye, sir, it is I," she said with calmness that he thought bordered on the perverse. By rights, she ought to have been terrified. When he gaped at her, she added in the same tone, one that reminded him of a nursemaid he and Lachlan had had when they were small, "I fear that you have been the victim of a dreadful trick. Indeed, I would not be astonished if you wanted to murder me for my part in it, but I hope you will not. You must realize that I did but obey my father's will."

"But where is your sister?"

"In her bed, I imagine, considering that the day has scarcely begun. Do not blame her, I pray you. She had as little to say about this as did I."

"But we cannot be married! At the very least, your name was misspoken!"

"Nay, it was spoken properly, but the priest has a quiet

voice, sir, and no one but Lady Mairi would have been surprised to hear my name instead of Mariota's. We were well and truly married and have now lain together as man and wife, so there is naught that either of us can do to alter things."

"The devil there isn't!" he exclaimed, sitting upright, scarcely able to contain his fury. "I will immediately demand an annulment."

She bit her lower lip, but whether from vexation or in an attempt to control her emotions, he could not tell. She still seemed much too calm, and he remembered that he had thought her composure unnatural when first they met. Surely, however, the present situation would distress any normal woman.

He moved to get out of bed.

"I pray you, sir, do nothing in haste," she said, and this time she seemed troubled, even to be pleading with him. "You would much embarrass me and yourself as well, I fear. You have a reputation, after all, for being a man who gets what he wants, who wields great power. If you leap out of bed and fly from this chamber now, demanding annulment of our marriage after sleeping with me, consider what everyone will believe."

"Don't be daft, lass. Everyone will know that your father tricked me."

"They certainly will if you tell them so," she agreed.

"Aye, and when I tell them that I woke up in bed beside you instead of your sister, it will be clear to the least intelligent amongst them that your father performed a despicable deception by foisting you on me in her place."

She caught her lower lip between her teeth again, but this time, he thought he sensed anger. Even so, her voice retained that devilish calm when she said, "You still are not thinking clearly, I fear, for they will know as much only if you tell them. No one hereabouts knew that you intended to marry Mariota, because my father told everyone he invited that you wanted to marry me. You undoubtedly told people that you were going to marry Macleod's daughter. Did you mention Mariota's name or tell anyone that you were marrying his second daughter?"

"I told my brother, Lady Mairi, and his grace that I was marrying Macleod's second daughter," he said. "I also told them that her beauty is so startling that it stops men in their tracks," he added brutally.

She seemed unfazed by either his tone or the harsh words.

"I doubt that his grace or your brother will say aught of it to anyone else, especially since neither is here," she said. "They may wonder at your taste when they see me, especially after they see Mariota, but unless you named her or told a host of people that you intended to marry Macleod's second daughter, most will think nothing of it. Your people will welcome your wife to Lochbuie, and folks here will congratulate you. Moreover," she added thoughtfully, "I believe it is not easy to gain an annulment after a man and woman have lain together as husband and wife."

He was angry with her but not nearly as angry as he was with her father or with himself for allowing Macleod to trick him, and he had already said things to her that no gentleman should say to any lady. To tell her that he did not even recall consummating their marriage seemed unnecessarily cruel, even shameful.

He had never known himself to get so drunk that he could not remember things. Yet, clearly, he had done just that, and the blame lay more with himself than with Macleod. He ought to have been firm in telling the man he did not want any more brogac, but when guests began offering toasts, he had feared it would be surly to refuse to drink them. Worse now was the thought of facing Lachlan.

How his twin would laugh at his having been so deceived, for he was coming to believe that Macleod had purposely intoxicated him. It occurred to him that perhaps the crafty old man had even put something into his mug besides the whisky, some potion or other that had increased the effects of the drink. Not that it mattered. He simply ought to have refused to drink more than he wanted.

"I know you are furious with me," she said quietly. "I do not blame you for that, not in the least. I would just ask that you not shame me in front of our guests and that if you must seek an annulment, you will do so quietly after we have left Chalamine. I will not fight it, but you should perhaps know that my father has many friends in the Kirk. The Abbot of Iona—a Mackinnon who has strong connections on Skye, as we do—is a particular friend. You will have to apply directly to the Pope, and your petition will doubtless arrive at much the same time as the abbot's does, because I know he will honor my father's wish to support our marriage."

"You speak of the Green Abbot, Fingon Mackinnon," he said, knowing that of all the priests in Scotland that one was most likely to do all he could to block any plea a Maclean made to the Pope.

"Aye, sir. Do you know him?"

"I do. Iona, the Holy Isle, is near our land on the Isle of Mull."

He saw no reason to tell her more about the relationship the Macleans endured with the abbot. If he took her to Lochbuie, she would learn of it soon enough, but he would expect her to cast off some at least of her Macleod loyalties if she accompanied him home, even if it were only for the short time they remained married before he could gain his annulment.

❧

Cristina watched him wrestle with his thoughts, having no great difficulty deducing what they must be. At least he had not instantly murdered her, although he might do so yet. He was certainly angry enough, because his jaw had clenched, and his blue eyes blazed, although he held his tongue. She could only be grateful for that, since she was certain she did not want to hear what he would say to her. But at least words would do her no great harm. Considering his reputation, he might well be capable of throwing her out the window if he grew angry enough.

Clan feuds had begun over much less than what Macleod had done to him, so she was glad he had not brought an army of friends and supporters to witness his wedding. Had he done so, he might well have taken out his anger on Chalamine and its inhabitants immediately. But he and Lady Mairi had come with a surprisingly small escort for such powerful folk. Clearly, Hector had taken Macleod at his word when he had said he did not want to house a large number of guests, and his courtesy had served her father's purpose well.

Oddly, Cristina dreaded facing Lady Mairi even more than she had dreaded facing Hector Reaganach. Her ladyship had a reputation for kindliness but also one for fiercely protecting her kinsmen, and surely, as her brother-in-law, he counted as one of those. Men said that MacDonald valued his daughter's opinions, even regarding political matters, and thus her ladyship wielded influence of her own in the highest quarters, where the deception perpetrated on Hector

Reaganach would amuse no one. The thought of what likely lay ahead of her made her shudder.

Her train of thought ended when she realized that his expression had altered from angry frustration to grim speculation. Involuntarily she shifted away from him.

Fearing that the movement, however slight, might make her seem cowardly, she stiffened, saying in the forced calm tone that she had used before, "What is it, sir? Have you decided what we must do?"

"So you mean to allow me to decide what happens next, do you?" he said with a touch of sarcasm. "If that be so, then I think your father—"

"Please, sir, consider the alternatives reasonably. You do not want to appear a fool, nor do I want to figure as a thief."

"Thief?" His eyebrows shot upward.

She shrugged. "What else? If you tell the world that my father and I tricked you, prevented your marriage to Mariota, and forced you to marry me instead, how clse shall I appear but as a woman willing to steal her sister's intended husband?"

He frowned, making her wonder if he was actually able to feel some small sympathy for her dreadfully awkward position, or if he had simply remembered that earlier she had called him a fool. In either case, she did not like that frown.

"Where is my axe?" he demanded.

"I do not know," she replied, trying to ignore the icy chill the question stirred at the base of her spine. "It will be safe though. No one would dare take it."

"They'd better not," he growled. "That axe is the one my ancestor Gillean wielded to excellent effect against the Norsemen at the Battle of Largs more than a century ago. I'd be gey wroth were aught to happen to it."

"Did you want it for any particular purpose?" she asked.

An audible quaver in her voice made her wish she had kept silent.

"Nay, lass," he said more gently than he had spoken before. "I asked because that axe is important to me and to my clansmen. I'd not want to lose it, but I do not make war on women, whatever wrong they may have done me."

She swallowed, astonished by the flood of relief that swept through her. She assured herself that she had not really been afraid of him, but she knew that some men beat their wives when they were angry, and his anger had unsettled her customary calm. More than that, it had distressed her.

"You may not make war on women," she said. "But you can certainly get angry with them."

"Aye, when they deserve my anger, but you have not yet seen me angry, lass. I'd advise you not to stir my temper more than you already have."

Another shiver shot through her at the thought that she did deserve his anger. Without thinking, she said honestly, "You are right to remind me of my guilt, sir."

He grimaced. "Nay, lass, I am but venting my spleen. I know well whose fault this business is. My own father, in his fashion, warned me that I was not paying sufficient heed to Macleod's superstitious nature. I also understand family duty, including the heavy burdens it can impose, and I ken fine that you had little power to stand against him."

She swallowed hard, believing she had had another choice but had cravenly decided it was unacceptable. Guiltily, she wondered how much of the fault lay with Macleod's threats and how much with her own desires and the attraction she had felt to Hector Reaganach from the first time she had laid eyes on him.

"What thinks your sister of this devilry?" he asked.

Feeling heat in her cheeks, Cristina said, "She is annoyed, of course. Mariota does not like being commanded, you see. She prefers to have choices offered her, as do we all, I suppose."

He pressed his lips firmly together, clearly fighting to keep from venting more of his spleen at her. He had stuffed pillows behind him, and sat now with his muscular arms folded across his muscular chest, staring straight ahead. His profile was impressive, for he was a handsome man, but she was glad she was getting only the side view. That was intimidating enough.

Hector wished his body would quit responding to the sound of her voice. He had not realized before how sultry it was. It rose and fell with her words and phrases like soft, entrancing music, and parts of him—well, one part in particular—seemed to respond to every nuance.

Only moments before, he had wanted to leap from the bed to find Macleod and strangle the sly bastard. Now, here he was, trapped for the moment, because if he got up she would see exactly how the sound of her voice and the thought of touching her affected him. And that would never do, because in his experience, women delighted in seeing how their wiles affected men. Such sights—again, in his experience—gave every woman a heady sense of power.

He barely heard what she said next, but he was instantly aware that when she stopped speaking he wanted her to go on.

That thought hung in his mind for a moment before he reminded himself that Mariota was the woman he wanted, the woman Macleod and the wee wicked witch beside him had tricked him out of marrying. Tightening his folded arms and pressing his lips together, he told himself that whatever potion Macleod had given him to drink was still addling his wits. He was generally a man who thought easily and quickly on his feet or in any other position, but he could not seem to think now of anything but her smooth-looking skin and entrancing voice.

He felt a sudden urge to chuckle as the reaction stirred what he often thought of as "twin response," because such thoughts seemed to enter his head in Lachlan's voice rather than his own: "Aye, lad, you think well enough on your feet," the voice said. "'Tis when you're on your back that that puny brain of yours quits working."

"Do you find what I just said about Mariota amusing, sir? I assure you I did not mean it so."

He turned his head to look at her, unaware that his expression had altered. In fact, he was nearly certain that it had not, and while his brain did not always obey his wishes, his body always did unless it was ailing—which had happened only twice, as far back as he could remember—or was severely intoxicated.

Sternly, he said, "You may be sure that I find nothing in this situation to amuse me."

"Then perhaps you are hungry," she said equably.

His stomach not being that part of his body upon which his attention had focused, he had not thought of food, but the mere mention of it made him realize that he was ravenous. He had not eaten much of anything—at least, not to his knowledge—since arriving at Chalamine late the previous morning.

"I am fairly peckish," he admitted.

"I, too," she said. "But before we summon food, we must—that is, you should—decide what you mean to do."

Her annoying calm made him conscious of a desire to show that he, too, could remain civil under stress, but with a strong temptation to test her mettle, he said, "What course would you suggest?"

Her eyes widened as they had before, telling him that he had surprised her again. But she did not hesitate to reply.

"If you could manage to act naturally, as if naught were amiss, and we could leave Chalamine today without causing a scene, I would be much obliged to you," she said. "I mean to honor my vows in any event, so until such time as you cast me off, I'll act as your wife in every way that you command me. I am accustomed to running a large household, and to dealing with the needs of any number of vassals and tenants, so I can be an asset to you until we must part. All I would ask in return is that you not shame or humiliate me before my kinsmen or your own."

He considered her words only briefly before nodding. "'Tis a reasonable request," he said. "I will agree. However, my agreement does not mean I will not seek at once to overturn this marriage of ours."

Her eyes seemed to change as he watched from molten gold almost to green, then back to gold again. It was doubtless no more than a trick of the changing light outside, a cloud passing over the sun or some such thing. He did not want to look away to see what caused it, however. The change fascinated him.

Her cheeks reddened, and he realized he was staring. Clearing his throat, he said, "Keep yourself well covered, lass, and I'll shout for my lad to fetch us food."

With that, he threw back the coverlet and got out of bed, striding naked to the door.

Cristina watched him for a moment before she said, "Just one thing, sir."

To her consternation, he turned to face her. She had seen naked men before, had even helped carry water and towels to the hall when male guests wanted to bathe. But this was different, very different. He was a splendid-looking man from his massive shoulders and muscular chest to his narrow waist, slim hips, and powerful thighs.

"What is it?" he asked. "'Tis damnably cold standing here."

She forced her gaze upward to meet his, swallowed, and said, "Before you call for your man, sir, we—that is, you— should tell me exactly what we are to do."

A lock of his dark hair had fallen over his left eye, and as he reached up to brush it impatiently aside, he grimaced, saying, "We'll do as you suggested. I want scandal no more than you do, and although you deserve that I should leave you here with your father, I won't inflict that humiliation on you or on myself. You were right to remind me that I'd look like a fool or worse if I treat you badly or admit that your father tricked me so easily."

She drew a deep breath and let it out again. "Thank you," she said.

"Don't thank me yet," he warned. "I'll take you to Lochbuie with me, but you'd be wise to do nothing there to try my patience further. I'll look into getting an annulment as quietly as possible though. No need to make a song about it."

"I'd be most grateful for that, sir. Will you . . . that is, will we . . ." She paused, swallowing again. Then, taking courage in hand, she said quickly, "I am, after all, your wife in every way, both legally and in the eyes of the Holy Kirk, so you have every right to use me as you will. I just wondered—"

She expected him to tell her she was a fool, that he had no interest in her whatsoever, that Mariota was the only Macleod he desired. Instead, he gave her a narrow, searching look. When she met it steadily, he said, "I don't suppose it matters one way or another now, as you are my wife in the eyes of the law and the Holy Kirk. Suppose we just see how we get on. At present, I assure you, my only desire is to put distance between ourselves and Chalamine."

With that, he turned toward the door again, yanked it open, and gave a shout for his man. Then, with a muttered exclamation, he bent over and picked up something from the floor outside the door, presenting Cristina with an excellent view of his fine, muscular backside.

Turning back into the chamber, he shut the door, and she saw that the object he had picked up was a wicker basket with a flat lid. A stubby willow peg thrust through loops in the wicker held it shut.

"With luck," he said, "this contains bread and ale for our— What the devil!"

Cristina heard mewing as he unfastened the lid and spilled two fluffy kittens—one coal black with a red ribbon around its neck, the other ash gray with a white one—onto the floor of the bedchamber. The black one promptly attacked the gray one, and they rolled right over one of Hector's feet.

"Isobel," Cristina said confidently. "I recognize her red hair ribbon on the black one. She must have decided to present them to us as wedding gifts."

Again, he surprised her, for instead of expressing anger or annoyance, he scooped up both kittens, one in each hand, and strode back across the room to hand the gray one to her.

"Cute little things," he said, tickling the black one under the chin. "They look like ashes and soot. How old do you think they are?"

"I know exactly how old they are," she said. "The kitchen cat produced six of them just two months ago. Our cook has complained ever since that he can scarcely move without tripping over them."

"So your little sister decided to help him out by giving two of them away."

"I warrant she thought I'd like to have something to remind me of home," Cristina said. "But if you do not want them, we can leave them here."

"Would you like them to go with us?"

She thought for a moment, wondering if it would annoy him if she said yes.

"Don't worry about me," he said, as if he had read her mind. "I don't care one way or the other, although it would be churlish to refuse her gift, I suppose."

"We'll keep them both then, and call them Ashes and Soot," Cristina said firmly as the gray one climbed onto her stomach, sat down, stared at her unblinkingly, and began to purr.

Chapter 6

Half the household was apparently still asleep, but Hector left Cristina with one of the women to dress and pack anything she still had to pack, while he sent his man to prepare their horses, and went to look for Macleod.

Finding that rascal in the great hall, already tucking into a large breakfast, Hector said with careful control, "We'll not strain your hospitality, sir. My wife and I will be leaving for Lochbuie as soon as she is ready to depart."

"I see ye've come to your senses then about which o' me lasses will suit ye best," Macleod said matter-of-factly. "I'd no taken ye for a man o' much sense afore now, but I dinna mind admitting that ye've surprised me, lad."

"We are not finished with this business," Hector said grimly. "You have proven yourself a most untrustworthy man and not one who is ever likely to regain my respect, but neither will I humiliate your daughters, sir. Apparently, their feelings did not enter into your scheming."

"Nay, then, why should they? They are but daughters and do as I bid. As for untrustworthy, faugh! We never spat on our thumbs to seal any bargain betwixt us, and ye got exactly what I promised ye from the outset—me firstborn daughter. Me clan's good fortune must come afore aught else, and if ye dinna understand that, me daughters do. They'll marry as daughters should, at their father's will."

"Legally, they have the right to refuse to marry," Hector pointed out.

Macleod shrugged. "I ha' raised them to be obedient, and I'm thinking ye'll be one to thank me for that afore long. A disobedient wife be nowt but trouble to a man, as ye must ha' seen for yourself a time or two. Ye should heed the lesson."

Having no wish to engage the old scoundrel in a debate about women, Hector nodded curtly and said, "I'll be thanking you for your hospitality, sir, and I'll thank you even more if you'd be kind enough to send a lass to the lady Mairi's chamber to tell her we'll be leaving shortly."

"Aye, I'll do that, and I'll see you at Finlaggan, I expect. Or will your esteemed parent deign to join us at the Council this year?"

"My brother and I will attend as we have these four years past, sir."

"Then I expect you'll be able to tell me then how well my lass adjusts herself to married life," Macleod said with a smirk.

Wanting to throttle him, Hector held his peace, waiting only long enough to be sure he did send a maidservant to warn Mairi that they would be leaving at once.

He wondered where Mariota was but was glad not to encounter her since he could not imagine any conversation they could have that would not prove both awkward and, under the circumstances, improper.

To his astonishment and satisfaction, he found Cristina ready to depart when he returned to their room. Mairi and her woman, Meg Raith, met them in the hall moments later, and their horses were waiting when they went out into the yard.

Macleod, Lady Euphemia, and all seven of Cristina's sisters hurried out to bid them farewell, and Hector smiled despite himself when twelve-year-old Isobel strode up to him and demanded to know if the kittens were safe.

He pointed to the wicker basket tied to his own saddle. "Ashes and Soot are as safe as they can be," he said.

She smiled. "Those are good names for them, I think."

"They were a thoughtful gift, lassie, sure to remind your sister of her home and all of you."

Isobel nodded, serious again. "We will miss her, sir. See that you take good care of her."

Cristina had been hugging her sisters in turn, Hector glanced her way as she moved to hug Mariota, and over her shoulder, Mariota stared at him. Her beautiful emerald eyes filled with tears as she did.

When he looked quickly away, Isobel said quietly, "You'll be glad you married Cristina, sir. She will make you a better wife than Mariota would."

Meeting her solemn gaze, he tugged one of her flaxen plaits. "You should not speak so of your sisters, lassie. Nor can you know whereof you speak."

"I know," she said. "You'll see."

He wondered how much the child knew about her father's scheming, but Cristina came then and hugged her little sister, after which he helped her mount her horse. His two gillies had already assisted Mairi and Meg Raith with theirs, and so they were soon on their way. He waited only until they had ridden onto the ridge above Chalamine before ordering the two lads to ride on ahead and warn the ferry men of their coming. As soon as they had ridden beyond earshot, he said quietly to Cristina, "We must tell Mairi the truth, lass."

"Aye, sir, I know that," she said.

Mairi glanced from one to the other. "The truth, eh?" she said. "I thought something was amiss. I have never known you to take a drop over the mark, sir, but if I am not greatly mistaken, you were far from sober long before the bridal supper ended yestereve."

"I don't remember much about the ceremony, let alone that supper," he admitted. "As to what followed . . ." He shrugged.

Mairi smiled at Cristina. "I hope he did not behave too badly, madam."

Her eyes widened. "No one has called me 'madam' before now."

"Many will now, my lady," Mairi said.

"Please, madam, I hope you will call me Cristina."

"I will, and you must call me Mairi, but you did not answer my question."

"And a damned impertinent question it was," Hector told her.

"Surely, you should not speak so to her ladyship, sir," Cristina said.

He looked at her, surprised, but Mairi said sweetly, "No, he should not. Only think what my husband would have to say to you, sir, if he heard such insolence."

He gave her a look, and Cristina said, "I see that the pair of you have become brother and sister in truth as well as in law. I have often wished for a brother, almost as much as my father wished for a son, but my mother produced only daughters."

"Your mother died in childbed, did she not?" Mairi said.

"She did," Cristina said so bleakly that Hector shot a curious look at her.

The expression on her face reminded him of his own mother's death when he was fifteen, and stirred the grief that always lay just beneath the surface of his emotions, as the memory of that dreadful day always did.

"I was eleven when it happened," Cristina added. "Mariota was nine."

"And speaking of Mariota," Hector said with a pointed look, wanting to get off the uncomfortable subject of deceased mothers as quickly as possible and also to explain matters to Mairi without further ado.

Cristina flushed. "Indeed, sir, you are quite right that I should be the one to tell her. To put it plainly, my lady, Hector Reaganach thought he was marrying my sister Mariota, but my father tricked him into marrying me instead."

"Without your consent?" Mairi asked, raising her eyebrows as she gazed shrewdly at Hector.

He met that look with a grimace, but before he could speak, Cristina said ruefully, "You strike to the heart of the matter, madam. I am as guilty of the deception as my father was."

To his surprise, Hector found himself saying, "She had little choice though, because the old scoundrel commanded her to do it. Do you think you would have defied your own father in such a case?"

Mairi looked at him again, and remembering how she and his twin had met, how quickly she had fallen under Lachlan's spell and he under hers, Hector wished he had not asked the question. But Mairi was too kind to say anything that would mock the position in which Cristina found herself.

She said evenly, "When fathers command, most daughters obey. I warrant you had no choice in the matter."

Cristina sighed. "I could have refused, but he threatened to beat not only me but also Mariota, saying that if I defied him, I would be doing so only because she wanted him and that therefore she would bear responsibility for my refusal."

"Clearly, your father is a man who knows how to get his way, but did your sister truly want Hector?"

In a tone that should have warned her his patience was wearing thinner than usual, Hector said, "Mairi."

She twinkled at him, but Cristina said, "Mariota did want him, and he wanted her. What my father did was dreadful, and I should not have helped him, whatever the consequence to me or—I suppose—to Mariota."

"Well, the deed is done now, so we must all make the best of it," Mairi said. "I, for one, am looking forward to having another woman on Mull with whom I can speak freely, or as freely as one person ever speaks to another," she added with another twinkling look at Hector.

"I begin to think that I should have a serious talk with my twin about your impertinence," Hector said.

Mairi chuckled, and when he glanced at Cristina, he saw that she was smiling. He was glad Mairi had not pursued any further the question of his treatment of his new bride on their wedding night, but the thought stirred a memory of how easily his bride's voice had stimulated his body. He realized as she smiled that he had not noticed before how small, white, and even her teeth were.

⁂

Cristina saw him looking at her and wondered if she had got something stuck between her front teeth. Unable to find anything with her tongue, she turned her thoughts to Lady Mairi, who seemed to have decided to befriend her. She certainly liked Mairi and looked forward to having a new friend, even if she lived on the Isle of Mull for only a short time before Hector procured his annulment.

They crossed to Skye on the log ferry at Kyle Rhea and rode directly to the harbor where Hector had moored his longboats. The men in the two boats cheered when they saw them coming, and she saw that besides the Clan Gillean banner each one also flew the gold banner with the little black ship symbol of the Lord of the Isles. The sight reminded her of her new husband's power, and she sighed again.

Leaving the ponies with the gillie from Skye, they boarded the lead boat and quickly took their places. The sun continued to shine, although fluffy white clouds scudded overhead, reminders that the weather could change before the day was out.

Hector left the women seated on benches facing each other near the high prow and made his way to the stern, where he sat beside his helmsman.

The sails were soon up, and the oarsmen began rowing to the helmsman's beat. Before long, a stiff sea wind filled the sails, and their speed increased, reminding Cristina that men called such longboats and their big brothers, the Isles' galleys, the greyhounds of the sea, because of their swift speed and agility.

The journey from Skye to the Sound of Mull was nearly fifty miles, she knew, and Duart Castle sat at the far end of the Sound, on the northeast tip of the Isle of Mull, with Lochbuie twenty miles beyond it on the south end of the island. So with each stroke of the oars she was leaving her family farther behind.

To divert her thoughts, she asked Mairi to tell her more

about the isle that would be her new home, and Mairi willingly complied. That she loved Duart Castle and believed Cristina would feel the same love for Lochbuie was clear. But Cristina could not help thinking that Duart's proximity to Ardtornish—the Lord of the Isles' favorite seat and a mere five miles west of Duart—might contribute a good deal to her new friend's love for Duart Castle and for the Isle of Mull.

They arrived at Duart some seven hours later, and seeing it high on its promontory, dominating the end of the Sound where it met the Firth of Lorn and Loch Linnhe, and doubtless providing spectacular views, Cristina could understand Mairi's love for the castle. She rather hoped they would spend the night there, and in fact, Mairi invited them to do so, but Hector shook his head.

"It is still some hours till darkness," he said. "I want to go home."

Mairi gave him a look that Cristina could not interpret, but he only smiled and said, "He won't be home from Colonsay yet, lass. Tell him or don't, as you choose, and send him to see me or tell him to send for me when he wants me."

Cristina looked from one to the other, catching Mairi's eye. The older woman grinned at her and said, "You'll soon learn that Lachlan, Hector, and I tend to speak in half sentences and glances, my dear, but if you are as quick as you seem to be, you'll soon learn to read the messages as easily as we do. I was but asking him if he did not intend to tell my husband your news straightaway, but he reminds me that Lachlan is doubtless still in the midst of negotiating a truce between two clans warring over petrel oil."

"Petrel oil?"

"Aye," Mairi said. "'Tis outrageously valuable oil—

much finer than whale oil—that one obtains, unfortunately, by killing young petrels. The Isles teem with the birds, though, and kirks all over Europe and Britain use the stuff as holy oil for the sacraments. My grandfather, Angus Og, arranged to collect it for use on the Holy Isle and throughout Scotland, and my father sells it on the continent of Europe through the Hanseatic League, which is—"

"A collection of eastern nations that do business together," Cristina said. "My aunt's curiosity leads her to question the mendicant friars whenever they pass our way, so she knows about such things and tells us everything she learns."

"I see," Mairi said, smiling. "She's as good as a tutor then."

"Oh, yes," Cristina said with an answering smile. "I shall miss her as much as I'll miss my sisters, for all that my father thinks her a dithery fool."

"I warrant she will come to visit you whenever she can," Mairi said.

"I'll walk up with you, lass," Hector said to Mairi, cutting their conversation short. "I don't like the look of those darkening clouds west of us."

"Winter is not over yet, is it?" Mairi said, glancing westward. "I hope you will enjoy good weather for the Council of the Isles."

"Won't you be going to Finlaggan?" he asked.

"I've not decided yet," she said. "I used to love sitting in on all the councils, but now I find myself more interested in my children. So, unless you mean to take Cristina with you . . ." She let her words trail off, raising her eyebrows as she did.

He shook his head. "She'll want to settle in at Lochbuie, and although anyone may attend who wishes to do so, few

men take wives or children to Finlaggan. Mayhap I will take
her to Ardtornish for the Shrove Tuesday feast, but until then
she'll do better to bide at home."

Cristina wondered at his using the term "home" but decided he meant it only as his home, not hers. Still, she was
curious to see it. The Isle of Mull, with its lush green forests
and soaring granite peaks, intrigued her. When Mairi invited
her to walk with them up to Duart Castle, she accepted with
alacrity, not waiting to hear what Hector might say about it.

He sighed, making it clear that he did not want to tarry,
and she wondered if he feared that his brother might return
betimes. He did not seem in any hurry to talk to that gentleman, but truly, she could not blame him for that.

Duart Castle's great hall proved homey and inviting. She
noted at once two gold pillows with embroidered black
ships on them, and following her gaze, Mairi said, "Those
were wedding gifts. My sister Elizabeth embroidered them."

At that moment, three small children dashed into the hall,
shrieking in delight at their mother's return, and Mairi soon
had her hands full.

Picking up the older of the two boys, Hector turned to
Cristina and said, "This is Hector Og. Would you like to
greet my new wife, lad?"

"Aye, sure," the little boy said. "She's a bonnie one. May
I kiss her?"

Cristina laughed and turned her cheek toward him, but he
caught both cheeks with his hands and turned her face to his,
kissing her soundly on the lips.

"As you see," Mairi said dryly, "he is Hector's namesake
in every way."

Cristina grinned at the child. "I am pleased to make your
acquaintance, sir."

"I like her, Uncle," he announced. "Bring her to see us often and often."

"If you behave yourself, mayhap I will," Hector said, putting him down. "We're off now, Mairi. I'll thank you for looking after Cristina whilst I'm away."

"Aye, sir, I'll do that," she said, adding to Cristina, "And you must come to visit me whenever you like."

"Thank you, I will," Cristina said before her husband hustled her out the door and back down to the jetty.

The rest of their journey took less than three hours, and dusk fell before they sailed into Lochbuie Bay and she got her first glimpse of the tall central tower of the castle at the head of the bay. It was not as formidable-looking as Duart, for although it sat on a knoll overlooking the bay, it commanded only the bay, but she suspected that its views included an expanse of the sea beyond.

The jetty was sheltered, the nearby water calm. They disembarked and walked up a flight of stone steps to the top of the knoll, then through a tall gateway in the curtain wall and up wooden stairs to the castle's main entrance. Inside, a winding stone stairway led up to a sprawling great hall that to Cristina, accustomed as she was to the homelike clutter of a careless father and seven active younger siblings, seemed stark and unwelcoming.

Scarcely giving her a minute to orient herself, Hector said, "What do you think of the place?"

"It's . . . it seems very large," she said, hoping that its size was the factor he had expected would impress her most.

"Aye, it is," he said. "It is also astonishingly tidy, if I do say so."

"I expect it is, sir. You do not have a houseful of rowdy children."

He grinned. "My lads are rowdy enough. You should

have seen it before I made them clean it up. The place needs a housewife's firm hand, believe me."

She nodded. "If by that you mean that I may do as I please here, I welcome the opportunity. It is a fine, spacious hall."

"I thought so," he said, nodding. "Art hungry, lass?"

"I'm nigh to starving," she admitted.

"You, there," he bellowed to a gillie who hurried in just then, "bring food for her ladyship and your master, and quickly!"

"Aye, laird. There be a roast on the spit, so we'll bring it out straightaway."

The lad was as good as his word, and food came speedily, but to Cristina's fastidious taste, the roast had been on the spit hours longer than necessary and lacked flavor. Since the sun still set by five o'clock, she doubted the dry meat had resulted from not knowing when to expect them. Resolutely, she ate what they served her, wondering why they provided no sauces and why the bread was stale. Hector had been away only a short time, after all. Realizing she had her work cut out for her, she hoped he had meant what he said about giving her free rein.

After supper, he showed her to a bedchamber across the landing from his own. She had forgotten to ask him about finding a maidservant, but she needed none to undress herself, and as tired as she was, wanted only to go to bed. Although the room was small, the bed was comfortable, and she slept well.

The following day, Hector spent the morning showing her the rest of the castle, most of which seemed sadly neglected. Their bedchambers lay on the same level as the hall but in a smaller tower that adjoined the main one, forming an L. A protective curtain wall rimmed with a plank wall walk extended from the residential towers to form a rectangle. Inside it stood the kitchen, bake house, and a spring-fed well. Ponies, sheep, and a few milk cows occupied a railed pasture outside the wall.

Hector seemed content enough to have her there and had not once mentioned Mariota. Cristina knew what her sister would have thought of Lochbuie.

Mariota would not see the possibilities suggested by the great hall, let alone by the rest of the castle. Given time, Cristina knew, she could turn it into as homey and welcoming a place as Duart was, but such a task would have irked Mariota. She would expect Hector to turn it into a rich man's dwelling without troubling her to do anything more than tell him what she liked and did not like. But Cristina knew better than to say any such thing to Hector, even if she had been willing to speak so disparagingly about her sister.

The following day, Lachlan Lubanach arrived as they were sitting down to their midday meal. She had suggested to her husband's cook that he delay putting the roast on the spit until after they had broken their fast, and that he might also provide fresh salmon if possible. Clearly eager to please her, the cook had explained that the laird preferred mutton or beef for his dinner but that he was sure someone could catch a fish for her ladyship. Satisfied that she had established some rapport with the man, Cristina looked forward to enjoying her dinner.

When a gillie announced Lachlan, she saw Hector stiffen, but he greeted his twin with evident delight nonetheless, and endured a hearty clap on the back and a demand that he introduce his bride at once.

Lachlan's greeting was all that Cristina might have wished, but she grew tense waiting to learn if Mairi had explained matters to him or not.

She did not have to wait long.

"Did she tell you?" Hector demanded before Lachlan had even sat down.

"Aye, of course she did," he said, adding with a grin, "I thought you were a gowk, but I see now that you've struck gold. Clearly, you were mistaken about which sister is the beauty."

Startled, Cristina looked sharply at him but could detect no lack of sincerity. His eyes were as deeply blue as Hector's, but they twinkled more mischievously than did even the lady Mairi's. Indeed, so much did they reveal of his delight that she could not doubt his approval.

"You are kind, sir," she said, "as kind as your lady wife. But you cannot approve of the manner in which we deceived your brother."

"Of course I can approve of it," he said, grinning at her. "Do you know how seldom it is that anyone gets the better of Hector? Why, I have been trying to do so off and on all my life, ever since he beat me into the world by twenty minutes or so, but I rarely can manage to do it."

"And nearly always suffer grievously for trying," his brother added grimly. "Have done, will you? Mairi said it best when she said, 'What's done is done.' I mean to look into the possibility of an annulment, but I don't want to make a fuss about it. Can you help me with that?"

"I don't know that I should," Lachlan said, eyeing Cristina in a more measuring way. "You may think yourself a fool for having married a lass other than the one you expected, and I always approve when you realize that you, too, can do foolish things. But I'm thinking you'd be a worse fool to cast this one back."

"I'll thank you to let me decide that, my lad, and since

I've had about enough of your sauce, you'd do well to refrain from further speculation on the matter."

"Oh, aye then, I'm mum. What have you learned to aid us at Finlaggan?"

Realizing that the two men had much to discuss before their departure for the administrative hub of the Lordship of the Isles, Cristina left them to their discussion and went in search of the housekeeper. Discovering that the castle boasted no such creature, she decided that the need to acquire one would provide the first test of her husband's suggestion that she could do as she pleased with the castle.

Waiting only until Lachlan was preparing to depart for Duart, she rejoined them and said, "I was wondering if perhaps, between the two of you, you might help me resolve a problem or two."

"What is it, lass?" Hector asked.

"As you know, sir, I brought no waiting woman with me, thinking that your housekeeper would surely know someone suitable to take up the position. But I have just discovered that—"

"That he has no housekeeper," Lachlan said, chuckling. "I am in your debt now, madam, because my lady wife charged me to discover if there be aught we can do to help you make yourself comfortable here, and she specifically mentioned the dearth of maidservants and women in general at Lochbuie. She said to assure you that betwixt Ardtornish, Duart, and various Maclean kinsmen on the island, she can help you acquire a full complement of servants for this benighted place."

"I shall be most grateful to her if she can," Cristina said. "Apparently the castle has housed only men until now."

"Aye, so my lass pointed out to me," he agreed. "And since his men are nearly all men-at-arms, Mairi feared you would find the place sadly lacking."

"Oh, no, sir," Cristina replied instantly. "The castle is magnificent, and I found it particularly clean and tidy. No one would guess that only men had lived here, let alone only fighting men. That it bears no other woman's stamp can be only an advantage. I should do my best not to tread on anyone's toes, of course, if that were necessary, but you cannot imagine how free your brother has made me feel to do as I like here. I shall certainly welcome Lady Mairi's help in finding a proper housekeeper and maidservants though, I promise you."

"Faith, I'm just glad you brought the subject up," Lachlan said. "She would have handed me my head in my lap had I forgotten to deliver her message to you."

"Might have been an improvement," Hector muttered.

Lachlan shot him a look but made no reply, taking polite leave of Cristina instead and telling her not to worry while they were away at Finlaggan, that she would be perfectly safe at Lochbuie.

When he had gone, she realized that Hector was regarding her quizzically.

"What is it, sir? Have I a smudge on my cheek—or worse?"

He smiled then, making her wish that he would do so more often, because the smile lit up his face and set twinkles dancing in his eyes.

"Nay, there is no smudge," he said. "I was just feeling neglectful for not realizing that you might be worried about staying here alone whilst we're gone."

"I shall hardly be alone," she pointed out. "Moreover, I'll have much to occupy me and Lady Mairi to bear me company when I desire it."

"As to that, lass," he said so seriously that she wondered

if he meant to forbid her to travel to Duart, "I would have you take care."

"Is the Isle of Mull not safe then?"

"'Tis safe enough in general," he said. "But you will soon note that Mairi does not travel about the isle alone, and I do not want you to either. Clan Gillean is not the only one here, and some of the others enjoy making mischief."

"What do you advise me to do?" she asked.

"Take at least two armed men when you travel about on horseback, and do so only in daylight with clear weather. When you visit Mairi, you will go by longboat and stay overnight, just as she will likely do when she visits you here. The journey can be done both ways in a day, as you have seen, but doing so at this time of year would leave you little time for visiting before nightfall."

"Very well, sir. I will do as you suggest."

"Sakes, lass, that was not a suggestion but a command."

With that, he turned and left the hall.

Cristina stood for a long moment, staring thoughtfully after him, wondering if he thought she had no common sense or if he just liked issuing orders. Her father, she had long since come to realize, was of the latter sort, with the result that few of his daughters paid much heed to his commands when his back was turned.

She had tried to teach the younger ones filial duty just as her mother had taught her, but since Macleod often issued contradictory orders and would not tolerate discussion, she had found it impossible to insist that they follow every one. In time, they had all learned to obey him while he stood over them, but otherwise they tended to ignore his commands unless he made it clear, as he had over the business of her marriage to Hector Reaganach, that he meant to be obeyed.

Hector was another matter. He would not be at Lochbuie

to enforce his commands for at least a sennight, if not longer. Still, he was not the sort of man who would issue contradictory orders or who would tolerate defiance. So far, his orders had been reasonable, even the one that had made her grit her teeth. Nevertheless, she was accustomed to making the decisions when it came to running a household, and she knew she would not relish having him constantly putting his oar in.

It occurred to her then that Lachlan was also clearly in the habit of issuing orders and seeing them instantly obeyed. Yet Mairi just as clearly had a mind of her own and might well, therefore, provide excellent advice about matters even more important than housekeepers and maidservants.

Accordingly, early the following morning, after waving good-bye to her husband, her brother-in-law, and their several longboats full of oarsmen, she summoned a gillie and gave him a message to carry to Duart, asking her ladyship if it would be more convenient for Cristina to come to her or for Mairi to journey to Lochbuie. The answer came that very afternoon in the shape of Mairi herself.

Entering the hall with a brisk step and a wide smile, Mairi exclaimed with evident delight, "Here I am, my dear. Your people are looking after my oarsmen, and I mean to stay the night, so we can get to know one another comfortably!"

Chapter 7 _____

I fear we've paid small heed to how Hector was living here," Mairi said as the two ladies sat at the high table in the hall enjoying their supper after Cristina had shown her guest over the castle. "He always comes to us at Duart, or Lachlan comes here, so I've not visited Lochbuie since I was a child first learning to ride my pony. My gillie, Ian Burk, would let me ride to the top of a hill, where we could look down on Lochbuie, which was one of my father's holdings then."

"Does not his grace own all the Isles?" Cristina asked.

"As Lord of the Isles, he controls nearly all, but some holdings are heritable, including my husband's and yours," Mairi said. "Others, such as the Mackinnons here on Mull, hold theirs at my father's pleasure. He wields power across much of the western mainland, too, including Kintail," she added, "which is why your father serves as one of his councilors."

"Lachlan Lubanach and Hector serve as councilors, too, do they not?"

"Aye."

"But is not Ian Dubh Maclean still living?" Cristina asked.

"Aye, sure, he is. In fact, he is presently with us at Duart, where he is happily studying some documents he found recently, which apparently detail events that took place whilst Robert the Bruce was beginning to unite Scotland."

"Ian Dubh is interested in such things then. My aunt told me that the Macleans are one of the learned clans."

"Aye, they are, but if you are wondering at the power Lachlan wields, I should tell you it derives primarily from his relationship with my father. However, Ian Dubh has also named him to succeed as chief of Clan Gillean, and he has assumed much of the power of that position already because of his father's lack of interest. He and Hector began to serve as his ambassadors to the annual Council of the Isles at Finlaggan some years ago. Hector now assumes that duty alone though, because Lachlan's position as Lord Admiral assures him a seat at the council table."

Cristina nodded, storing the information away for future reference. She had enjoyed showing her guest around the castle, because she quickly saw that Mairi had even more experience than she did with managing large households. They had discussed furnishings and maintenance, as well as stores and cleaning, tenant needs, gardens, the number of servants she would require, and other such important topics. At one point, Mairi had suggested that Cristina make a list of items she would like to have to furnish the barren rooms more comfortably.

"Hector will be bringing visitors home frequently now," she said. "With a wife to see to their comfort, he will doubtless want to entertain more often."

"Will he?" Cristina asked, frowning. "You know that he does not look upon me as his true wife. You were kind not to inquire about my having a separate bedchamber, but surely you noticed that I do."

"That is not unusual," Mairi said bracingly. "My sister Marjory has a separate chamber, and I've heard of others who do as well. Most husbands sleep with their wives in the great chamber, of course, except in very large establishments, where they often sleep in an inner chamber behind it. At Finlaggan, my mother sought a separate chamber long ago so she could sleep through the night, because my father carries on business at all hours in the great chamber. He sleeps with her in the inner chamber now, though, and his man fetches him to the great chamber whenever someone needs him."

Cristina knew her guest was just being polite, but she had grown fond of Mairi in the short time she had known her, and she felt comfortable enough now to dismiss the gillies who hovered about in case they required anything, and to say, "I have a question of a more personal nature I'd like to ask you, if I may."

"Faith, ask me anything that comes into your head."

"Hector issues orders as if I were a person lacking a brain. My father is also a domineering man, but he expected me to make household decisions on my own without pestering him, and when he gave an order that went against common sense, I ignored it and did as I thought best when he went away again."

"Has Hector given orders that go against common sense?"

"No," Cristina said. "They seem perfectly reasonable, but I cannot imagine that we shall always agree. I have told him I will honor my vows and obey him as any wife should obey her husband, and I mean to do so, but I own, his manner does tend to set my teeth on edge. I am not temperamental by nature—"

"That is plain to the meanest intelligence," Mairi interjected with a chuckle. "I'll warrant that he treats you exactly as he would treat one of his men-at-arms, albeit with more civility. Lachlan tends to be much the same. Faith, but most men are like that, I believe. I remember when Lachlan and I first met and became attracted to each other, he frequently told me to leave everything to him, not to bother my head about anything. Since I had been accustomed to conferring with my father and brothers about anything that concerned me in the slightest, I thought it absurd for him to tell me I should stop being involved in such decisions. I firmly believe that two heads are better than one when any thinking must be done."

"What happened?"

Mairi smiled. "He eventually came to trust me. Hector will do the same if you are patient." Her smile widened to a grin. "Not that I was in any way as patient or tolerant as you seem to be. I once pushed Lachlan into the Sound."

"You didn't!"

"I did."

Cristina tried to imagine what Hector would do if she should ever try to do such a thing to him. "What did he do?"

Mairi laughed. "Fortunately for me, I made good my escape before they pulled him out, and by the time we met again, he had other things on his mind. He has warned me, however, that I must never do such a thing again if I want to avoid serious consequences. I just said he'd better behave if he wants to stay dry."

Cristina shook her head. "I envy you your easy relationship with him. I want to make up to Hector for the wrong I did him, but part of me wishes that I could tell him to his face that I do not like having orders flung at me."

Mairi shrugged. "But you *should* tell him. I doubt that he will eat you, and as for making it up to him for your father's wrongdoing, you cannot. Although I agree that you had choices you might have made differently, I'll warrant that nothing you did would have swayed Macleod from his course. Do you honestly think you could have held out against him, as determined as he was, and as superstitious as he is?"

Cristina opened her mouth to say that of course she could have, but common sense intervened. Compared to ignoring Macleod's orders when they were contrary, standing up to him when he was truly determined, and angry, was another matter. She had no doubt that he would have beaten her and Mariota as well, and although she might have endured her own punishment without changing her mind, she knew that in the end he would have forced her submission to his will.

At last, with a grimace, she said, "I would have given in."

Mairi nodded. "My husband says that the most important thing in life is learning to recognize necessity, to understand when it exists and when it does not. I have come to see much wisdom in that philosophy."

"They do say that Lachlan Lubanach is very wise," Cristina said.

"They say wily rather than wise, but I do think he has great wisdom."

They continued to talk comfortably, and Cristina found herself confiding more in Mairi than she ever had in anyone else. Her aunt's distracted nature did not lend itself to confidences, nor did that lady encourage them. As to her sisters, Adela was a sympathetic listener, but she shared so few of Cristina's responsibilities that Cristina disliked burdening her with her worries or dreams, and Mariota had time for no one's thoughts save her own. Since she regularly laid her problems at Cristina's feet to solve for her, Cristina rarely mentioned her own.

She realized as she prepared for bed that night that, despite her large family, she had led a lonely existence before meeting Mairi of the Isles. Evidently, Mairi realized it, too, because the next afternoon, as she prepared to go, she said, "You must come to me now, and soon, but I've been thinking that perhaps you might like to invite one of your sisters or that delightful aunt of yours to visit Lochbuie. They might enjoy helping you pull the place into order, and I think you miss them. This place will be less lonely if you have some familiar folk about you for a time."

Cristina thought about that advice only briefly before deciding to follow it. Summoning Hector's steward, a worthy man who seemed to know his business well and had willingly advised her on one or two matters pertaining to Lochbuie's tenants, she asked him how she should go about extending her invitation.

"Ye've only t' tell me what ye want t' say t' them, m'lady, and I'll send a boat up t' Glenelg as soon as ye like."

She almost asked him if he did not have to request permission from Hector before sending his longboats off to other Isles or the mainland, but quickly decided she would be foolish even to bring up that subject. Instead, she said, "That is what I will do then. Can the boat also bring them here?"

"Aye, sure, if that be your will."

"It is," she said. "How long will it take?"

"A day up and a day back, plus what time it takes your kinfolk to prepare. How many guests d'ye mean to invite?"

"Only two, I think. One sister and my aunt."

"Then I need send only the one boat. If ye'll give me their names, and what message me lads should deliver t' them, I'll send it off at dawn tomorrow. They may return day after tomorrow by suppertime, but more likely the day after. I'm guessing they'll want a bit o' time t' pack their things 'n all."

The speed with which the steward could grant her wish gave her instant second thoughts. What would her aunt think? More to the point, what would Macleod think? Then she recalled that Macleod, like Hector and Lachlan, would likely be on his way to Finlaggan already. Therefore, she could not invite Adela, who had been her first choice, because that would leave Mariota in charge of Chalamine and the children, which would not do. She loved her dearly and missed her, but she knew her faults, and knew also that Mariota would loathe having so much responsibility thrust upon her, whereas Adela would accept it with ease.

Realizing that she did miss Mariota, she decided that she would let her decide if she wanted to visit Lochbuie. Her first inclination was that Mariota would be uncomfortable, as she would be herself, but a few moments' thought told her that her sister, as practical as she was about most things, would already have dismissed Hector from her thoughts. He was now, after all, Cristina's husband, and thus surely no longer of interest to Mariota. And Mariota would enjoy the journey and the chance to flirt with an entire longboat full of muscular oarsmen.

As for Hector himself, she thought he would be pleased to have Mariota at Lochbuie. Her own feelings were mixed, because she could not be certain Mariota would not flirt with Hector and speed him on his way to an annulment. But she would certainly be disappointed if Cristina invited any of the others without inviting her, and thus the decision seemed to make itself.

Her mind made up, Cristina issued her first real command as Lady Maclean to the patiently waiting steward, and the next morning at dawn, she watched the longboat sail out of the bay on its way to Kyle Rhea to fetch her aunt and sister.

Hector and Lachlan arrived at Port Askaig, the harbor nearest Finlaggan, days earlier than his grace's other councilors, because as master of his household, Lachlan was responsible for seeing all in readiness to receive the other councilors, their entourages, and anyone else who cared to attend the Council of the Isles.

The administrative hub of the Lordship occupied two islets in Loch Finlaggan, a pleasant sheet of water set amidst woodland and heathery hillsides on the Isle of Isla, fifty miles south of the Isle of Mull. The palace complex occupied Eilean Mór, the larger of the two, while the Council held its meetings on the smaller one, on which stood the massive stone table of the great Somerled, the first man to unite the Isles. That union had lasted only until shortly after Somerled's death two hundred years before, but MacDonald of the Isles had skillfully re-created it and had ruled it successfully now for forty years.

Despite Lachlan's many responsibilities, he was efficient, and Hector had journeyed to Isla in his round of the clan chiefs and others to be sure that all was in readiness, so little remained for the brothers to do other than looking over and approving the arrangements. As Lachlan's right-hand man, Hector was usually the one to implement any plan that his twin concocted.

At Port Askaig, they found men and ponies awaiting

them, and left at once for Loch Finlaggan, some five miles inland.

Until then, although the brothers had talked at length of the many things pertaining to the days and duties that lay ahead, Lachlan had remained unusually reticent with regard to Hector's marriage. Having politely expressed his hope that Cristina was well, when Hector joined him in the lead longboat after his small convoy landed in Lochbuie Bay, he had focused their subsequent conversations on matters such as the number of boats each Isles chief would send to escort Robert the Steward, the ructions that had developed over the collection and sale of petrel oil, and other problems that had arisen since the last Council of the Isles.

Hector, uncomfortably aware of his twin's relative silence on the subject of his unfortunate marriage, not to mention Lachlan's apparent approval of Cristina as his bride, had been reluctant to broach the matter. Deciding to do so now, he said, "Ride ahead with me. I would speak privately with you."

"As you wish," Lachlan said. He was staring straight ahead, but Hector thought he detected a little smile and grimaced at the sight. If the situation amused Lachlan, he would never hear the end of it.

They rode some minutes in silence until he could be certain the wind would not carry their words to the others. Then, he said, "I do mean to seek an annulment as soon as I can. As I understand the matter, I shall have to apply to the Pope."

"Aye, that is the proper course, but I'm not sure I'd advise taking it."

Anger stirred, but he continued evenly, "Surely, you do not think I should simply submit to Macleod's wicked deception!"

"I know it galls you that you let him dupe you, but since his scheme succeeded, I'm thinking that anything you do now to oppose it will make you, and therefore Clan Gillean, look like the villain in the matter. By all you have told me, Cristina was but her father's innocent pawn. Moreover, I like her."

"You are not the one married to her!"

"True, but my duty is to Clan Gillean, as is your own."

"Then I repeat, do you truly expect me to play victim to Macleod?"

"Not if his trickery were widely known, but since he is unlikely to make it so, I expect you to handle the matter deftly, so that it does not reflect badly on our clan. I likewise expect you to understand that if you do seek to annul this marriage, Macleod is going to paint your actions in the poorest light possible."

"Sakes, but you ask too much!"

"I ask more," Lachlan said, looking at him now, his eyes narrowed, his tone sterner than Hector was wont to hear from him. "I expect you to do nothing in haste but to act instead as you do when you put any idea of mine into action. Weigh the merits of whatever course you decide to take, then do the right thing by Cristina."

"You want me to keep her."

"I want exactly what I said I want," Lachlan said. "No more, no less."

Hector wished briefly that they were still twelve, so he could wrestle his twin to the ground and force him to acknowledge his point of view. But he recalled that Lachlan had occasionally prevailed even in those days, merely by relying on his wits instead of his brawn. And now, to all intents and purposes, he was acting chief of Clan Gillean, so Hector knew that if he appealed to their father, Ian Dubh would support Lachlan and order Hector to do as Lachlan bade him.

There were times that Hector felt as if he were but Lachlan's other half, much the same to his twin as an arm or leg, with no real identity of his own. Even his extensive lands and estates he owed to his twin's wits, for they had come to him at the same time that Lachlan had won his own lands and power, as an addendum.

Such thoughts caused him momentary twinges of guilt when they plagued him, because he was loyal to his twin and to Clan Gillean. Even so, he thought Lachlan was acting the chief over him unnecessarily now, and the emotion he felt resembled resentment more than guilt.

Lachlan eyed him warily, and Hector suspected that he was accurately reading his thoughts. They each had an uncanny ability in that regard.

Moments later, when Loch Finlaggan appeared below them, marked at its head by an ancient standing stone, Hector said, "Macleod will be here soon, likely gloating."

"Aye, he will, and MacDonald would keep peace with all the Macleods, because along with their Nicholson kinsmen and their close friends the Mackinnons, they litter nearly every northern isle. Moreover, Macleod of Glenelg wields power in Kintail, on Lewis, and with his cousin on Skye; and his grace needs them all, especially with the Steward's visit so near and disturbances erupting on several isles over petrel oil. He would show the Steward that he keeps a strong hand on the Isles, and that because of that strong hand, the Isles will wholly support the Steward."

"But few northern Islesmen support Robert the Steward, or have much admiration for any of the Stewarts, as his kinsmen begin to call themselves."

"Exactly," Lachlan said. "'Tis the very reason I want no

scandal or upset at present. I will inquire quietly into this matter of annulment for you, beginning with our esteemed parent, who knows much of such matters. Anyone you ask yourself will suspect at once that you mean to set aside your brand-new wife, and few Islesmen will look kindly on such an act. You must also be willing to give cause."

"She aided her father's trickery," Hector said, feeling instantly guilty at making such an accusation after assuring Cristina that he understood her dilemma. With a wry grimace, he admitted as much. "I did tell her I do not hold her at fault, so we should not use that against her."

"Nay, for we both know how difficult it is, even when one has the legal right, to go against one's parents' wishes. To accuse her of abetting his crime would be hypocritical at best, and at worst, unnecessarily cruel."

Much as he would have liked to disagree, Hector could not. In any event, he was content to hold Macleod solely responsible, although if Lachlan or his grace meant to forbid his calling the man to account for his perfidy, he would be furious. He understood that to pursue a feud in the midst of the Council would not be wise, but he could not let the man gloat over such a trick, so he would have to think on it. Usually, Lachlan did the thinking for both of them, but Hector was confident that his own wits would meet the challenge.

❦

At Lochbuie, Cristina was enjoying herself. Never before had she enjoyed such authority. Hector's servants obeyed her without question, as did the gillies and maidservants that Mairi sent to Lochbuie for her approval. As soon as Cristina had seen the longboat off to Glenelg, she had taken advantage of Mairi's invitation and had spent a full day and night at Duart, where she met her new father-in-law soon after her arrival, when he joined them for the midday meal.

He was tall, gray-haired, and slender with shrewd blue eyes and a certain elegance of manner. Having discovered that both of his sons held him in awe, she was pleasantly surprised to find him unintimidating, his conversation engaging.

"That we have not met until now is not entirely Hector's fault," he said at one point with a gentle smile. "He invited me to the wedding, but I had submerged myself in historical documents and could not tear myself away."

She smiled ruefully. "If you know the whole tale, sir, I am persuaded that you must be very glad to have missed our wedding."

He shook his head. "Arranged marriages, no matter how arranged, often answer very well, my dear."

He was so different from Macleod that she scarcely knew what to make of him at first. But he continued to make gentle conversation until the meal was over, and by the time he returned to his documents, she knew she liked him very much.

Mairi warned her that she would very likely not see him again during her visit. "He loses himself in his studies," she said. "I have to send a lad to fetch him when meals are ready, and he always says he'll be along straightaway, but nine times out of ten he forgets and I send food to him later."

Ian Dubh surprised her that evening though, for he came to supper as well, and asked Cristina if she had any requests for him.

"If memory serves me, Lochbuie is poorly furnished, but I shall be returning to Seil soon," he added. "I'll tell my people there to set aside some things for you to look at whenever you like. Doubtless, you will find something useful."

Thanking him warmly, Cristina decided that her husband was a lucky man.

After conferring about Lochbuie's immediate needs, Mairi promised her a longboat laden with furnishings, and sent it two days after their visit.

Cristina expressed astonishment at both the speed and the wide selection, but the longboat captain assured her they were odds and ends that had been cluttering rooms at Ardtornish and Duart, and that Lady Mairi had said she could use them as long as she liked. Several colorful arras cloths accompanied the furniture, and these she ordered hung on the great-hall walls to warm that chamber.

In her explorations, she had discovered an empty tower room in the smaller of the two towers, and had decided that she wanted it for herself. Since no one else used it, she chose furnishings for it now to make it her own.

She had brought a few items from Chalamine, including a small chest of her mother's with an embroidered cushion top that Lady Anna had worked with her own hands, and a knitted shawl that her ladyship had often worn. Cristina carried these to the chamber with her own hands and set them lovingly in place.

The chest contained her needlework, and she set it near a back stool, over which she draped the shawl to use for extra warmth when needed. The chamber boasted only a small open hearth and would doubtless be either unbearably smoky or chilly in winter, but for now the chamber was not uncomfortable, and she believed that with a heavy curtain over its sole window, it would serve her well.

At Chalamine, she had had no place to call her own, for she had shared a bedchamber with both Mariota and Adela, and every corner and cubby of the castle served a purpose she could not ignore. Even when she had found time to take a walk or a ride, as likely as not, one sister or several had gone with her.

For much of her life she had yearned for a corner she could call her own, a retreat or sanctuary to which she could retire when she wanted to think or just to be alone. Now she had such a place and loved it. Ashes and Soot seemed to love it, too, because they followed her whenever she went there and curled up in one gray-and-black ball, purring contentedly until she was ready to leave again.

Mairi had also managed to find her a housekeeper, a comfortable-looking woman called Alma Galbraith, who was kind and capable, and who even got along with Hector's cook, Calum. He was clearly a man who took his duties seriously and who brooked no interference, but he also served meals that, while they might do well enough for men-at-arms and servants, were insufficiently palatable to suit Cristina's notion of what was due to her husband and his guests.

Although Alma got along with Calum, Cristina soon saw that, as quiet and kind as Alma was, she would be no match for him. Moreover, the final authority in such matters fell to the lady of the household. Accordingly, knowing Mariota would complain bitterly if the food was not up to Chalamine's standard, she bearded the cook in his kitchen the day before her guests were due to arrive from Glenelg.

"Calum," she said, "I am hoping that my lady aunt and my sister will arrive in a day or two to visit, and the meals we have had until now, although sufficient, have lacked a certain variety of flavor to which they are accustomed."

"Sakes, your ladyship, I be willing t' cook up whatever ye like. Ye've only t' tell me how ye want things prepared. The laird dinna care. So long as he has beef or mutton on the table, he'll eat whatever ye put before him, so it did seem a pity t' make the lads sweat over grand meals when simple fare pleased him as well."

"Then if you like, I will give you some of the recipes from Chalamine," Cristina said. "My aunt and sister will doubtless enjoy whatever you prepare as long as you manage to include a few familiar dishes just for them."

With that matter satisfactorily resolved, she turned her attention to the bedchambers and decided that she would not try to add any more furniture until they had lived a few months with the items Mairi had sent. That would give her time to learn if Hector noted any deficiency or had particular requests.

The longboat returned the following day. Learning of its arrival as soon as it entered the bay, she rushed down to the landing to meet it, but the first person to disembark was neither Lady Euphemia nor Mariota.

"Where are Ashes and Soot?" Isobel demanded as she flung herself at Cristina and gave her a powerful hug. "How much have they grown?"

"Faith, love, they are barely ten days older than when you last saw them!"

"Cristina! How glad I am to see you again," Mariota exclaimed, hurrying to her and hugging her. "I have missed you so much! Adela does everything wrong!"

"I've missed you, too, my love. I'm so delighted that you came."

"Of course I came," Mariota said, looking surprised. "I wanted to see you, and to see the place where I was supposed to live. Is it splendid? Shall I fall into a flat despair of envy over your grand estate?"

"Oh, my dearest," Lady Euphemia exclaimed as a gillie assisted her from the longboat, "you should not say such things. Although I know you must be curious about

Cristina's new home, you should be more tactful in your questions, or better yet, you should wait for her to tell you what she wants to tell you. Not that I do not want to know the same things—Isobel, too, I'm sure. I wager you are surprised to see Isobel with us, Cristina, but if you were thinking when you sent your men to fetch us—and how very surprising *that* was, to be sure—that your father had already departed for Finlaggan, you were sadly mistaken, for he had not. Indeed—"

"That's true," Isobel interjected before Lady Euphemia could go on. "He said that if you were going to take away both Aunt Euphemia and Mariota, you might as well take me, too, because only you know how to deal with me when I get one of my starts. That's what he said, and I was very glad he did, I can tell you."

Mariota said with a sigh, "You are becoming a dreadful chatterbox, Isobel. Pray hold your tongue for five minutes so that the rest of us can speak."

Isobel tossed her plaits, but did not argue, saying only, "Where are they?"

Cristina smiled at her and said, "They are probably sleeping or playing in front of the fire in the great hall. If you run up that path yonder, it will take you directly there. I can also arrange for you to have a pony to ride whilst you are here, but I must tell you straightaway that Hector has forbidden us to go out alone, so do not expect any of the gillies to let you ride outside the wall without an escort."

Promising that she would not, Isobel ran on ahead of them.

Watching her, Lady Euphemia frowned. "Do you mean we're not safe here?"

"No, I do not mean that at all," Cristina assured her, explaining as she gently urged them up the steps to the castle.

"Then I expect that Lady Mairi also rides with an escort," Mariota said when Cristina had said such escorts were customary for noblewomen in the Isles.

"She does," Cristina said.

Mariota nodded, but Cristina noted that unlike Isobel, she did not promise to take an escort when she rode out. Knowing her sister's propensity for taking her own path, she decided to make certain that she did not defy Hector's orders, at least not until Cristina could determine for herself just how absolute those orders were.

Although it was another sennight before he returned, it seemed to her that her relatives had barely settled in. They were gathered in the great hall for supper, expecting at least another day or two to pass before his return, so when he and Lachlan strode into the hall, Cristina exclaimed in surprise.

Noting the frown on her husband's face as he gazed around the refurbished chamber, and the heavier frown when his gaze encountered first Mariota, then Isobel and Lady Euphemia, she held her breath. But he greeted his guests politely as he strode to the high table, took his customary seat, directed Lachlan to another, and ordered a gillie to carve meat for them. Then he said to Cristina, "I hope you have sufficient food for our oarsmen."

"Indeed, sir, your cook is an excellent creature. Although I did not expect you back so soon, he has been prepared for your return these two days and more."

"Cristina told him he had to be ready, no matter when you came, sir," Isobel said, smiling warmly at him.

"That was well done of her," he said. Returning his gimlet gaze to his wife, he added, "Am I correct in assuming you've made many changes here, madam?"

"Aye, sir," she admitted, watching him warily but feeling her temper stir.

"We must have a talk after supper then," he said. "You doubtless hope that I shall approve them all."

Forcing a smile, Cristina turned to welcome Lachlan back to Lochbuie and to introduce her relatives to him. His easy courtesy relieved her tension, but shortly afterward, when she caught her husband's eye again, it returned in full measure.

Chapter 8

During the previous sennight, Cristina and her guests had formed the after-supper habit of retiring to a smaller chamber off the great hall that they had made cozy with cushioned benches and back stools, where they occupied themselves with needlework or conversation. Therefore, she had made no further attempt to provide entertainment for them. She felt that lack now, however, because she could think of no suggestion to make that would induce the other ladies or her brother-in-law to linger at the table after they had finished eating.

The moment came all too soon, because when Lachlan had eaten his fill, he smiled and said, "Thank you for an excellent meal, madam, the best I have had at this place. You have done a great deal in a very short time. I'm impressed."

"Thank you, sir," she said sincerely. "I trust you mean to spend the night."

"I'm grateful for the invitation, but not tonight," he said. "I'm in a pother to get home to my lass and the bairns, because I have been away more than I like of late, and I've missed them. Doubtless we'll be seeing you at Ardtornish though, if not before, so until then, I'll bid you adieu."

Within minutes, he and his men were gone.

Mariota fluttered her lashes at Hector and said brightly, "Cristina told us you went to Finlaggan, sir, to attend the Council of the Isles. But she knew naught of their business, so I hope you mean to tell us all about what happened there."

Cristina had noted that Hector's gaze drifted to her lovely sister from time to time throughout their meal, but she could scarcely blame him, because Mariota was looking her loveliest that evening. Her emerald green gown matched her eyes, and since they had expected no company, her hair hung in loose curls held away from her face by a pair of plaits that began near her small, well-formed ears and intertwined around the top of her head to resemble a royal tiara.

Hector smiled at her comment but shook his head as he said, "'Twas men's talk, hours of it, that would bore you witless to hear, lass."

Surprised, Cristina said, "But surely women attend the council meetings, sir, for Lady Mairi told me that she frequently did so before her children were born. Even as a child, she did."

"Aye, well, Lady Mairi is his grace's daughter, and he is wont to indulge her whims," Hector said without looking away from Mariota.

"I suppose he might be," Cristina said. "Still, I thought . . ." She fell silent without finishing the sentence when she realized that he was not listening.

⚬⚬⚬

Hector was smiling at Mariota, who smiled back, sending waves of delight through him. Sakes, but she was magnificent! How cruel Fate was, he thought, to have conjured up such a mess to envelop him!

Aware of an odd silence, he wrenched his gaze from her and glanced at the others, realizing that Cristina was eyeing him with a frown that made him search his conscience in much the same way he had when his mother had gazed at him so.

The memory caught him unawares, but he heard the echo of his last words to her in his mind and realized that he might have sounded critical of MacDonald or of Mairi. He realized, too, that the usually verbose Lady Euphemia had said not a word. Meeting his wife's frown with one of his own, he said, "What is it?"

She hesitated, but Isobel said bluntly, "She was speaking to you, but you were not listening because you were gawking at Mariota."

"He was not gawking," Mariota said indignantly. "You are the most impertinent child in the Isles, Isobel, and I think you should leave the table at once if you cannot behave properly."

"I only said—"

"Hush, Isobel," Cristina said gently. "You need not leave, but you should not answer questions that are not addressed to you, love. I was merely going to say, sir, that I believe you ought to answer Mariota's questions. Surely, a woman need not be his grace's daughter to learn what goes on in the Council of the Isles."

"Aye, lass, that's true," he said, grateful that she had dealt so diplomatically with her sisters and glad to have something unexceptionable to say. Nevertheless, he felt the need to add, "I meant naught of criticism by my words, only that womenfolk usually take small interest in our business at Finlaggan."

"But Mariota is interested, and doubtless Aunt Euphemia is, too."

Irritation stirred, and had Lady Euphemia not been sitting there, watching them with birdlike interest, he might have curtly commanded his wife not to address him as she would a three-year-old.

Isobel said, "You must be very important, sir, to take part in meetings with the Lord of the Isles. Is he a nice man?"

Turning to her with relief, he said, "He is a powerful man, lass, but also a thoughtful one. I think most folks would agree that he is kind—unless they disobey the laws of the Isles, at all events," he added. "Are you enjoying your visit here?"

"Oh, yes," she exclaimed. "Cristina has arranged for me to ride every day."

He glanced at Cristina. "You do not encourage her to ride alone, I hope."

Grimacing, Isobel said, "I do not know why you think she should not, sir. I have frequently ridden alone at home."

"Does she ride alone?" he asked, meeting Cristina's gaze with ease this time.

"No, sir," she replied calmly. "We have all been mindful of your orders."

"I should hope so," he said. Then, smiling at the others, he said, "I hope you will forgive us if we leave you to entertain yourselves for the rest of the evening. As you might imagine, I have several matters I want to discuss with Cristina."

Mariota pouted. "If you were truly concerned about my welfare, sir, I should think you would know better than to leave me with no more entertainment than my aunt and little sister. A true gentleman does not abandon his lady guests with naught of interest to amuse them."

Isobel chuckled. "If you seek amusement, Mariota, you ave only to watch the kittens at play. I think they are in the itchen. Shall I fetch them for you, or would you prefer to lay a game with me?"

"Do not make me tell you again to hold your tongue, Isoel, because you will be very sorry if you do," Mariota said harply. Then, pouting prettily again as she turned back to lector, she said, "Do you see how it is, sir? Most unfair!"

He grinned at her, amused by her flirtation, but when 'ristina stood and signed to the gillies to finish clearing the igh table, he recalled that he had much to say to her. To lariota he said, "I promise I'll make it up to you, lass. No ood host should allow his guests to suffer boredom. I colect that you like to ride."

"Aye, I do, and I brought a very becoming riding dress ith me, too."

"Then mayhap I'll take you out in the morning after we reak our fast."

"Me, too?" Isobel demanded.

Much as he would have liked to refuse, he knew that he ould not do so without drawing censure for attempting to rn a simple outing into a private matter. Nor did he want disappoint her, however, because something about the hild appealed strongly to him. So he smiled and said, "Aye, ssie, you, too. And now, if you will all forgive us, we'll bid ou good night. Come, my lady."

He put a hand to her back to guide her toward the door, oting that her right hand shook as she lifted her skirts to go ith him. It was just as well, though, if she was a little afraid f him. From all he had seen so far, the chit had taken far too any liberties in his home. He needed to remind her that he as master here.

✑✑✑

Cristina fought to control the anger that had surged through her when Hector responded so flirtatiously to Mariota's blandishments, but the emotion increasingly plagued her, and she did not know why it should. She loved her sister very much, and although she had frequently noted the effect Mariota had on men, never before had it bothered her, because she had believed Mariota felt her worth too much to allow her flirtations to cross the line in any way.

Now, however, matters were different. Her own sense of guilt at depriving her sister of the husband she had apparently decided she wanted after all, added to her irritation with Hector's behavior since his return, had turned her emotions inside out, making her fear she might give way to them in a most unseemly, even dangerous way. She could vaguely remember succumbing to high emotion from time to time as a child and being roundly scolded or punished each time. The punishment for an adult would be far worse, surely, in loss of respect if nothing else.

A lady simply did not allow her emotions to overwhelm her. At least, ladies other than Mariota did not. But Mariota was different, and had always insisted on different rules for herself. She said she thought emotionally rather than logically, because that was just the way she was. In time her family had come to realize that they must not expect her to act as the rest of them had to act. Her nature was therefore freer than most women's, certainly more so than anyone had ever allowed Cristina's nature to be. Mariota had been a merry child, impulsive and into mischief all the time, a child much like Isobel, although never as intrepid as Isobel was.

Macleod doted on Mariota—spoiled her, Lady Euphemia said. If Mariota was naughty, Macleod would scold Cristina because she was older and should have watched her sister more carefully. And Cristina had accepted that responsibility. Then, as more sisters joined the family, she had accepted responsibility for them, too, especially after their mother died.

Lady Anna's death had shocked them all, but outwardly Mariota had seemed to suffer the most. For weeks, she had scarcely spoken. Then she had abruptly pulled herself out of her grief, throwing herself instead into tasks that had never interested her before. She refused to allow the maidservants to tidy the bedchamber she shared with Cristina and Adela, insisting on doing it every day herself. That phase lasted only a short time before she tired of it, but she had seemed unnaturally fragile for months, easily upset, easily hurt, easily angered, even enraged.

Such emotions were not for Cristina, however, and the fact that she wanted to scream or throw something now, preferably at her husband, disconcerted her. As she walked silently beside him toward the stairway that wound up through the thick north wall of the central tower, she dared not speak even to ask him where they were going, lest she say aloud the other words fairly shouting in her head.

Her greatest fear was that someday her mental conversations would erupt in real shouts, born of a rage to equal any of Mariota's tantrums. If that ever happened, she feared that the earth might split beneath her feet and swallow her—or that some equally cataclysmic fate would overcome her.

When they reached the stone landing outside Hector's bedchamber, he pushed the door open and indicated that she should precede him inside. Following her, he stopped at the threshold and gazed about in astonishment.

"Sakes, you've even turned my room upside down!"

Smoothing damp palms on her skirt, she faced him, fighting to keep her calm as she said, "I beg your pardon, sir, if I misunderstood you before you left for Finlaggan, but I did believe you gave me license to do as I pleased here. I merely sought to make this chamber more comfortable for you, but if the result displeases you, I can simply order it put back the way it was."

He did not reply at once but strode to the narrow, arched window and examined the shutters. "You had these polished or oiled or something. They were rough and dull before, but now they gleam."

"Aye, sir, they've been sanded and oiled. They had grown dry, you see, and if one does not oil them regularly, one must soon replace them, as you know."

"Aye, but I rarely think of such details."

"You are too busy, sir, tending to more important matters."

"'Tis true, lass, and this was well done of you. But what of those bed curtains? You scarcely had time to make them, let alone to embroider those birds and flowers all over them."

"Do they displease you?"

"Nay, though I do not think a fighting man ought to sleep in a field of daisies. I'm just wondering how you accomplished so much in so short a time, and how much all of this is costing me. In truth, I suppose I do think you should have discussed so much change with me, and sought my approval before you began."

"It has cost nothing but time and effort so far," she said. "Most of it comes from Lady Mairi, who sent things from Ardtornish and Duart for us to use until we decide exactly what we—that is, you—want to do here. She said we may keep anything we find useful and return the rest as we re-

place things. I thought it very kind of her, but if you do not
like to be beholden to your brother and his—"

"It is not that," he said.

Cristina waited, but he did not seem inclined to continue,
and she did not think she ought to mention just yet that Ian
Dubh had offered them things from Seil.

Hector pressed his tongue against the back of his teeth,
realizing that since he *had* given her permission to do as she
pleased at Lochbuie, he could not say what he was thinking
now, which was that the lovely Mariota might not approve
of all these changes once he got the marriage annulled.
Sakes, he could not even ask Cristina if Mariota liked what
she had done.

Noting guiltily that she was still waiting with her usual
patience for him to explain himself, he shrugged and said,
"You have made the place very comfortable, which is good,
because I invited several people at Finlaggan to spend a
night or two with us here before they sail on to Ardtornish
for the Shrove Tuesday celebration."

"How many?"

"I don't know," he said. "Does it matter?"

"No, I suppose not. I just wondered if we should expect
a family or two, or a hundred people."

He grinned then. "I can try to make a list, lass, but I don't
think it can have been a hundred."

"Then you need not bother with your list, sir. I know
what I must do, and I am sure that Mairi will advise me if I
need help."

"Good lass," he said. "I think I'll go out to the barn for a
time, to see if anything has gone amiss during my absence."

She nearly told him his steward had everything in order there, too, but held her tongue, deciding she would rather see him go outside than back to the hall to flirt with Mariota. Instead, recalling his invitation to her sisters, she said, "Do not forget to order horses for us all to ride in the morning after we break our fast, sir."

He looked startled, as if he had already forgotten, but then he said ruefully, "I can't do it tomorrow, lass. I promised the lads we'd begin careening the boats first thing in the morning, so they'll look their best for the Steward's visit. You'll have to make my excuses for me, but promise Mariota we'll do it another time."

Wondering again if she had been wise to invite her enticing sister to Lochbuie, she waited long enough to be sure she would not encounter her husband again, and then went to the little parlor, where she found her aunt and sisters.

"Was Hector angry with you?" Mariota asked as Cristina walked in.

"Mercy me, my dear, one must not inquire into the private affairs of married persons," Lady Euphemia scolded. "Even if one is burning to know what happened, one simply must not ask, for it is very rude to do so, particularly when the person you are asking is your hostess, not to mention your elder sister."

"Well, he looked angry," Mariota said.

Isobel chuckled. "I think he was still recovering from finding his home littered with Macleod women. I'll wager you did not tell him beforehand that you meant to invite us, did you, Cristina?"

"No, because I did not think of it until after Lady Mairi spent the night here. She said she thought I might be lonely with him away, and I knew she was right. Moreover, when I learned how easy it would be to fetch you from Chalamine,

I could not wait. But he said naught about your coming, Isobel. He was just surprised by all the changes I had wrought here in his absence."

"Well, he seems much more domineering than I thought he was," Mariota said. "I like strong men—as who does not—but he is a fool if he thinks I shall allow him to dictate to me, or if he truly thinks I need an armed escort to ride about on the Isle of Mull. I have hitherto sought to please you, Cristina, but now that I have seen for myself that it is quite safe, I would have you remember that I am accustomed to looking after myself. And if Hector thinks there is no discord in Kintail, he is much mistaken. One simply has to know where it is safe to ride and where it is not, and so I shall tell him when he takes us out riding in the morning."

Cristina suppressed a sigh, recalling many uncomfortable conversations with her father, who strongly disapproved of Mariota's habit of riding alone but blamed Cristina for not putting a stop to it. Even Macleod realized that Mariota generally did as she pleased without consulting anyone else, and if he could not stop her, Cristina did not know how he had expected her to do so. However, now Hector had given the command, and she could trust him to enforce it. Drawing on her vast experience with her sister, she decided to approach the subject tactfully.

"I am afraid he has realized that he cannot spare the time to ride with us tomorrow," she said, "but he charged me to tell you he will do so as soon as he can. I was hoping that you and Isobel would ride with me instead. We've not yet ridden north along the coast toward Duart, so we can do that if you like."

"May we visit Lady Mairi?" Isobel asked. "I should like to see her again."

"It is too far to ride unless we spend the night," Cristina

said. "But perhaps one day during your visit, we can take a longboat up the coast to visit her. Duart's location provides spectacular views of the Firth of Lorn and the Sound of Mull."

Before Isobel could reply, Mariota said, "I suppose it would be pleasant enough to ride a short distance along the shore to see more of this island, but I think I would prefer to ride west along the south coast. We've not done that either."

"That is what we will do then," Cristina said, well satisfied. "I shall tell them to have the horses ready for us directly after breakfast."

Accordingly, the following morning, she arose at her usual time and hurried down to the kitchen to be sure the cook had all in train there before she entered the hall to find her aunt and sisters awaiting her at the high table.

"Such a lovely morning," Lady Euphemia said.

"It is, indeed," Cristina agreed. "Would you like to ride with us, Aunt?"

"Oh, dear me, no," Lady Euphemia exclaimed. "I dislike bouncing about on horseback and rarely do so unless by necessity, for I never learned to ride without a saddle as you all did, you know, and to be sitting in what amounts to a basket that tilts and sways with every movement of one's horse, thinking that at any moment it will pitch one onto the ground or into a stream, is not what I call pleasure."

Cristina had known as much but had felt obliged to extend the invitation. "What will you do whilst we are gone?" she asked with a smile.

"I shall sit quietly with my tambour frame and watch dust motes dance in those sunbeams pouring through yonder windows," Lady Euphemia said with a comfortable sigh. "You cannot know what a treat it is for me, my dear, to have to do only what I wish to do. Why, I cannot remember another such time in my life, but your servants here require little assistance, and you provide me with no tasks. It is quite delightful, I promise you."

"If you should desire tasks, Aunt Euphemia, you have only to tell me so," Cristina said. "I'm sure I can think of something. Your embroidery is lovely," she added. "If that cushion cover is meant for Lochbuie, I shall be most grateful."

"Well, it is," Lady Euphemia said. "But I had meant to surprise you."

Cristina moved to give her a hug. "Dear Aunt," she said. "I shall be happy to express all the surprise you like when it is finished."

"Very well, then you may have it," Lady Euphemia said.

"Lady Cristina, I beg your pardon for intruding, but I thought you would want to know at once," the plump housekeeper said importantly as she bustled from the buttery onto the dais, a worried frown on her face.

"What is it, Alma?" Cristina asked.

"One o' the housemaids ha' spewed her breakfast all over the upper landing o' the east tower."

"Faith, I hope it is nothing serious," Cristina said.

"I'm thinking it be only summat she ate which she shouldn't have, but it may be worse. Or she may ha' taken summat t' make her sick, so she could have a holiday, but I'll say it as knows her, that our Tess dinna be the sort for that."

"I'll go to her at once," Cristina said.

Lady Euphemia protested. "You may catch whatever disease she has!"

"And give it to us," Mariota added.

"Don't be foolish," Cristina said. "Tess is part of the household, so I must see how sick she is. I doubt it will amount to more than Alma says, but we cannot have Tess passing some horrid sickness to everyone else at Lochbuie."

Without another word, she hurried in the housekeeper's wake, finding that the afflicted maidservant had descended to a chamber in the lower regions of the castle near the kitchen. The girl looked pale and drawn, but she was breathing easily and seemed upset only by the fact that Cristina had taken the time to visit her.

"Oh, my lady, I'm that sorry t' disturb ye. I'm sure it be nowt t' concern ye. I'm just thinking I must ha' eaten summat that disagreed wi' me stomach. It be a-roiling summat fierce, but the rest o' me seems well enough."

"You may be right, Tess, but I think you should rest quietly here this morning until we can be sure that no more is amiss than that. I do not want her working again until she can keep both food and water down, Alma."

"Aye, m'lady, I'll see she takes care. However, whilst ye're here, mayhap ye could just have a look at this storeroom. I were thinking . . ."

For the next twenty minutes Cristina listened to what Alma had been thinking, and approved several ideas the woman suggested that would improve their ability to keep an inventory of the stores throughout the year. Only as she bade her farewell did she remember that her sisters were still waiting in the hall for her, probably in a blistering fever of impatience.

Giving thanks that she had dressed for riding before breaking her own fast, she hurried to the great hall to find her husband entering through the stairway door, her aunt rolling up her embroidery and directing a young gillie to carry her tambour frame, and two gillies sweeping up crumbs. No one else was there.

"Where are Mariota and Isobel?" she asked.

Hector shrugged, glancing at Lady Euphemia, who frowned.

"Why, Mariota said they were going to find you, my dear, so that you could have your ride," she said. "Did they not do so?"

Fearing they had not really tried to do so, but reluctant to put her suspicions into words with Hector standing there, Cristina said, "No, they did not. I expect I shall have to go in search of them."

"Where were you?" Hector asked.

"One of the housemaids fell ill," she explained. "I'll wager Mariota and Isobel got tired of waiting for me and went ahead to the barn to visit the horses."

"Then let's go and find them," he said amiably.

She caught her lower lip between her teeth, realized that she had done so, and released it again. "I thought you had boats to careen," she said.

"My lads have begun laying out the logs to roll them onto the beach," he said. "I've plenty of time to bid your sisters good morning. In the barn, you say?"

Not for a moment could Cristina imagine Mariota doing anything so tame as to visit the barn merely to see which horse she was to ride. Still, if her impulsive sisters had done anything they ought not to do, they would just have to suffer the consequences. And consequences there would be, because Hector had been clear in his orders and she was sure he would enforce them.

They walked silently downstairs and out into the yard, from which they could easily see the barn. Noting at once that no horses stood outside, Cristina glanced obliquely up at Hector.

His lips formed a straight, hard line, and as if he felt her gaze, he said, "Do you suppose they are inside?"

"I hope so." But the suspicion had long since entered her mind that Mariota had taken advantage of Tess's indisposition to indulge a forbidden whim.

Looking at her now, he said, "Would they have gone without you?"

She sighed. "I did not tell the gillies that they should not. Did you?"

"Nay, lass. I trusted you to obey my commands."

The unfairness of that statement nearly undid her, but it was exactly the sort of thing that Macleod had said to her often, so she drew a deep breath and said, "I have obeyed you, sir. I told them that they must, too, and they have done so until now. In truth, I do not know how I could have stopped them today, since they left whilst I was with Alma and Tess." Suspicion stirred again as she heard the echo of her words, and then guilt. Mariota could have had nothing to do with Tess's illness.

Hector was frowning. Then, to her surprise, he shot her a rueful grin. "I'm a beast to scold you for their behavior, lass. Doubtless, if they are not accustomed to taking an armed escort, they just failed to understand the importance of doing so."

"Indeed, sir, I do not believe I understand it myself," she admitted, meeting his gaze easily enough now. "Everyone we have met hereabouts has been kind to me and to them, and most welcoming, too."

He nodded. "As long as you ride near Lochbuie, that will be true, but Clan Gillean does have enemies on the island, not the least of whom is your father's friend, the Green Abbot."

"Fingon Mackinnon?"

"Aye, he bears little liking for us."

"But why? He has always been courteous to me."

"You were a Macleod, lass. Now you are one of us . . . even if it be just for a short time." Although the pause made him seem less firm than he had been before when referring to his annulment, she was more interested in the Green Abbot.

"I am still the same person I was, and still my father's daughter, sir," she said. "Surely, Fingon would not harm me."

"He and his kinsmen would do nearly anything to harm me, however, and if he believes you to be the wife of my heart, as you say others do, then harm may well befall you. Moreover, if he believed he could cause trouble for me by abducting you or one of your sisters, he would certainly do so."

"But why? That would be to offend my father, too, would it not?"

"Perhaps, but we cannot trust Fingon Mackinnon to think of that."

"Faith, sir, but the sons of Gillean must have done something horrible to inspire such hatred in him. Will you tell me what it was?"

He met her gaze and seemed to search it for a long moment. Then, and again to her surprise, he nodded and said, 'He blames Lachlan and me for his brother Niall's death. The fact that the Mackinnons attacked us does not weigh with him. That Lachlan killed Niall is all that does."

"I did hear that his brother died violently," she said, remembering vaguely that her father had told her as much. Having never met Niall Mackinnon, she had paid little heed to the details, if Macleod had bothered to relate them to her. 'Niall Mackinnon was Chief of the Mackinnons, and also high steward of his grace's household before your brother assumed that position, was he not?"

"He was, and a right scoundrel as well," Hector said. "The first year that Lachlan and I served in our father's place at the Council of the Isles, he took umbrage at our representing such power without what he considered to be the proper age and experience to go with it. There is more to the story, of course, but now is not the time for it. Where the devil are your sisters?"

They had entered the barn and found only two gillies inside, tending ponies.

"Has either of you seen Lady Mariota or Lady Isobel?" Cristina asked.

"Ayc, mistress, we both did," the older of the two responded, glancing warily at his master. "The lady Mariota said ye were no going t' ride wi' them after all, and that if ye did come looking for them, t' tell ye they'd be back in an hour or two."

Hector said ominously, "Lady Mariota said that, did she?"

The lad swallowed visibly. "Aye, master."

"Henceforth, you are not to allow either of Lady Cristina's sisters to leave the castle without an armed escort," Hector said. "Do you understand me?"

"Aye, sir. We did say we should go along, but she said she didna want us."

"The lady Mariota?"

"Aye."

"Then henceforth," Hector said evenly, "you will not ask her. You will simply go with her. If she tries to stop you, you will unsaddle her horse."

"Begging your pardon, laird, but she didna want a saddle neither. Nor does the mistress ever want one, come to that."

Cristina bit her lip, but her husband said only, "We are not discussing your mistress's habits. You are not to allow

Lady Mariota or Lady Isobel to ride out alone again, or you will suffer my wrath. Is that clear?"

"Aye, sir."

"We shall want our horses at once."

"Aye, sir, yours be saddled yonder, because your man said ye might want him, but it will take a few moments for Lady Cristina's if ye want the saddle on."

"I don't want it," she said firmly.

Hector looked at her, but she met the look.

"A lady's saddle is most cumbersome, sir, and I can ride much faster without it," she said. "If we're to catch up with them, I must ride as they do. You need not worry," she added with a touch of asperity. "I won't fall off."

"I don't fear that, lass," he said. "I begin to think you capable of almost anything you attempt."

His tone was grim, even sardonic, but the words warmed her to her toes.

Chapter 9 ——————————

As Hector and Cristina rode west above the rugged southern cliffs of the island, she let him determine the course. She had no idea exactly where her sisters might have gone, although the lad had pointed west, but Hector seemed to have at least a strong notion. Except for the hour-long journey from Chalamine to Kyle Rhea, she had not ridden with him before, but he was an excellent horseman, an unusual skill in an Islesman, particularly such a large Islesman.

She knew that men of the Isles rarely traveled where they would need horses. When they traveled, they went in boats, so most of them were highly skilled boatmen, capable of handling any size craft from the smallest fishing coble to the largest galley or birlinn. But Hector Reaganach seemed as much at home on horseback as he did in his longboat.

His lips had tightened again into that formidable straight line, and his jaw was set. He did not seem to be anticipating the forthcoming meeting with Mariota with pleasure or eagerness. She opened her mouth to remind him that Isobel was only twelve and would have followed her elder sister's lead, but she shut it again. He most likely did not need reminding, and if he did, she could create some sort of diversion when the time came. It was enough that when he learned what they had done, he hadn't gone after them alone and sent her back inside the castle.

"You ride well, lass," he said a moment later.

"Thank you," she said. "I have ridden almost daily since I was a child."

"Is it true that Macleod allows you and your sisters to ride alone?"

She hesitated but answered honestly, "He did not like it when we did, sir, but the area around Chalamine is Macleod land for miles, and completely safe for us. Our neighbors are all clansmen and allies, so no one would molest us, and if we had trouble with a horse or broke a rein, we could easily find help."

He nodded. "Seil is like that, too, as is Morvern for Mac-Donald, but Mairi was nonetheless abducted once from the hillside behind Ardtornish."

"Faith, someone took a great chance in doing that!"

"And suffered the proper fate for his temerity, but my point is that nowhere is as safe as one tends to think it is."

"Mayhap not, but such a thing has never happened in Glenelg. Indeed, my father raises the issue only when others are around, and it is my belief that he does so because he wants to demonstrate that he has sufficient men to spare even to ride with his daughters, and thus increase his consequence."

"It is nonetheless your duty to obey him and not your business to determine if his judgment is sound," he said sternly. "I hope you do not intend to flout any orders that I give."

"I have not done so."

He looked at her, and she thought for a moment that she detected a twinkle in his eyes, but it vanished before she could be sure, and he said, "You would be wise not to do so in future either."

Casually, she said, "Lady Mairi told me that Isleswomen must be strong and able to do much of what their men do, because their men are so frequently away from home. My father was also frequently away."

"I'd not advise you to follow Mairi's lead," he said so gently as to send a shiver up her spine. "She is different, after all, being his grace's daughter."

"Indeed, I found her most knowledgeable and helpful. But what then do you expect of me when you are away?"

"I expect you to seek advice from my steward and from Alma Galbraith."

"Ah," she said, seeing nothing to gain by telling him that both his steward and housekeeper had already formed the habit of turning to her for direction. Deciding that diversionary tactics were in order, lest he press the point by telling her just what she should leave to which servants, she said, "You keep gazing at the ground, sir. Are we following their tracks?"

He smiled, and she found herself instantly wishing again that he would do so more often. "We're following someone's tracks," he said. "It looks as if two ponies are headed in the general direction the lad said they took, so I'm hopeful, although I cannot say I like this route. There were other tracks leading north, but if they've headed toward Duart, they'll encounter no danger. Most of the land between here and there is under our control or that of our kinsmen."

"But this way lies Mackinnon territory?" she guessed.

"Aye," he said. "And those two deserve to be put across my knee for this."

"Well, I hope you will do no such thing," Cristina said. "They are your guests, after all."

"Faith, lass, they are my sisters now as much as your own and deserve to be treated as I would treat any sister. If the only way to persuade them to obey my orders and keep them out of danger is to punish them, then that is what I must do."

She held her tongue. Knowing Mariota as she did, and his usual reaction to her, she did not believe he would carry out his threat. She understood his point, though, and feared that if she debated his decision with him, he would become more determined to carry it out.

"We'll go this way," he said, turning off the narrow path they had been following and urging his horse up the steep, rocky hillside. Scrubby, wind-battered trees fought with boulders for space there, but Cristina's pony was nimble, and she was easily able to follow the route Hector picked through the rocks and shrubbery.

The scents of the sea were strong, blowing in from the southwest. The sun shone brightly, and the air was warmer than it had been for months.

He was frowning again, his gaze fixed on a point ahead of them, but his expression showed growing concern rather than irritation.

"We should have come upon them by now, should we not?" she asked.

"I did expect to find them before now," he said. "But mayhap they ride faster than we expected or took a different track."

"Mayhap they knew we would follow," Cristina said. "Mariota did say she wanted to ride along the south coast, and although we have not taken this route before, I think she would keep her word, in case I did try to catch up with them. She might think that if she put distance between us, she might enjoy her ride longer."

He looked grim. "You should have said as much to me before now."

She shrugged. "To what point, sir? The lad said they had ridden west, but I knew as well as you that she might well have gone elsewhere."

"Does she do such things often?"

Cristina sighed. "She does not like constraints, sir, and I'm afraid she does her best to ignore them. My father has much indulged her."

"Sakes, if she flouts his commands with impunity, he has spoiled her beyond reason," he said roundly.

Cristina had thought as much from time to time herself, but Mariota was her sister. She said, "I doubt that he would agree with you, sir. She is so charming and sweet most of the time that one finds it hard to stay angry with her."

He grunted, but as he did, a sound reached them from a distance. Cristina thought it was a bird's cry until Hector gave spur to his horse and the powerful beast leaped forward. They had nearly reached the top of the hill, now shrouded in forestland, but the way was still steep, and although she followed him as swiftly as she dared, she knew better than to press her mount to the same speed as his.

Thus, he was some distance ahead of her by the time she crested the hill, and she still did not know what drove him to such speed. She could not hear the sound again over the pounding hoofbeats and rattling stones beneath her, but within the forest, the atmosphere altered, becoming shadowy and much cooler. Sunbeams pierced the canopy, shooting mote-filled rays to the leafy ground, which was so thick with leaves and mulch that it muffled the horses' hoofbeats.

The next cry that came was easily recognizable as a woman's scream and a recognizable one, too.

"That's Mariota!" Cristina cried to Hector.

He waved but did not turn or shout back. Indeed, his wave looked almost as if he meant her to stop and stay behind, but she could not do that, knowing that her sisters were in peril and that he might be as well.

They weaved their way among the trees, both riding faster than was safe, and she was thanking the fates that Hector had not insisted she use a lady's saddle, when Mariota screamed again.

Kicking her horse as hard as she could, Cristina leaned over its mane, urging it on. She had lost sight of Hector, but Mariota's cries drew her on until she came upon a clearing, saw her sisters, and wrenched her horse to a halt.

Both girls stood on the ground. Someone had torn Mariota's dress from her shoulder, baring it, and Isobel looked frightened and angry.

Three men faced Hector tensely, swords drawn. A fourth lay on the ground, motionless, with Hector's battle-axe buried to its pole in his chest.

∞⊃

He had come on the scene to find two louts manhandling Mariota, while a third held Isobel and a fourth surveyed the scene from horseback, smirking.

The smirk had vanished when Hector rode into the clearing at speed, and the man had foolishly drawn his sword and urged his horse toward him. In a single motion, Hector had drawn his battle-axe from its sling on his back and flung it, dispatching the rider. Then, flinging himself from the saddle, he faced the other three, his sword drawn, his dirk close at hand.

Mariota still screeched like a banshee, which was fine with him, because he knew it would distract the others more than himself. He was more concerned that one of them might try to ride off with Isobel.

Even as that thought darted through his mind, he saw Cristina gallop into the clearing, her pony's eyes wild, its mouth foaming. Her high speed made him think she had lost control of the animal, and fear surged through him. But when she turned her mount deftly and raced toward the other horses, he realized that she intended to scatter them.

Apparently noting his momentary distraction and intending to take advantage of it, one of the men facing him leaped forward. Hector spitted him with a single stroke and turned to meet the other two, close behind the first.

Deftly parrying a thrust from one, he swung his huge sword two-handed toward the other, making him step awkwardly back. Returning his attention to the first, he said, "Drop your— What the devil!"

Two other men ran out of the forest, waving small swords and shouting the Clan Gillean war cry. Recognizing both of them, Hector instantly returned his full attention to his attackers. Those two immediately dropped their swords, and the newcomers hastily divested them of their dirks as well.

"We'll take them with us, lads," Hector said. "Truss their hands behind them, then mount them and tie their feet beneath their ponies' bellies. I don't know exactly what happened here, but we'll take them back to Lochbuie to sort it out, since 'tis clear enough to all of us that this was no friendly meeting."

"They tried to abduct us," Mariota exclaimed. "Oh, sir, you saved our lives! How very brave you are!" And with that, she flung herself into his arms.

"There now," he said, patting her shoulder as he tried to extricate himself. "You are perfectly safe now. Isobel, did they harm you?"

"That loutish one there pulled me from my pony," she said, pointing to one of the two who stood before him. "And that other one tore Mariota's dress, trying to make her kiss him."

Hector turned his stern gaze on the second man she pointed out.

"Ye've nae authority over us," the man declared with clear bravado. "We're nae men o' yours."

"I have all the authority I need right here," he said, hefting his sword. "You assaulted these young women, and you'll answer for your crime at Lochbuie. Or, if you prefer, I'll arrange for you to stand trial before his grace's court at Ardtornish."

The older of the two grimaced. "We were just funning wi' the lasses, sir. We didna realize they be noblewomen, as how could we, when they was out riding all alone like they was?"

"Do you mean to tell me you would treat our common women so?"

"Nay, then, I dinna mean nowt o' the sort," the man protested. "I was no thinking at all, and that be plain fact."

As he finished speaking, Cristina rode into the group, flung herself from her horse, and ran to hug Isobel.

Watching her, Hector released himself gently from the still-clinging Mariota. "How frightened you must have been, my love!" Cristina exclaimed to the child. "What a dreadful thing to happen!"

"It certainly was," Mariota agreed, pushing back a strand of hair that had escaped her caul before she, too, hugged Cristina. "We were thankful to see Hector riding to our rescue before they could murder us, I promise you."

She beamed at him with approval, her smile dazzling even in the shadows of the small clearing, her eyes as green

as the shrubbery around her. He felt a strong sense of gratitude that she had avoided harm, and his voice was gentler
than he had intended when he said, "You should not have
ridden out alone, lass."

"But I didn't, sir," she said with a teasing smile. "I rode
with Isobel."

He wondered then if he had merely said they should not
go alone, or if perhaps that might have been the way Cristina
had relayed his orders. It was possible, he supposed, and if
Mariota had misunderstood, he should not scold her. Doubtless, the frightening incident would impress upon her the necessity of taking armed men with her in the future.

He glanced at Cristina, met her steady gaze, and felt a
glimmer of doubt.

"We would have been safe enough if those other men had
come to our aid when Mariota screamed," Isobel said.

"What other men?" he asked.

"Why, those ones there," she said, pointing to the two
who had run from the forest at the end to help him.

"I warrant they came when they heard her screams, just
as I did," he said.

"Aye, sure, but we saw them before. We asked them if
they knew any splendid views hereabouts, and Mariota
flirted with them. They said they would come with us, but
Mariota said they could not, and so they ran after us. That's
when we encountered those men. I thought the first ones
would help us, but they didn't."

Hector turned his gaze to the two men in question. "What
have you to say to the lass's description of events?"

"There be nowt we can say, laird, but that there were four
o' them and nobbut the two of us," the taller of the two said.

"You spoke to these ladies?"

"Aye, we did." The man hung his head.

"You knew they were gently born?"

"Aye, but when she—"

"I do not want to hear about what she did, only what you did," Hector said grimly. "You are men of Lochbuie, are you not?"

"Aye, sir."

"And you would like to remain men of Lochbuie?"

"Aye."

The other nodded. Both men looked frightened.

Cristina was astonished at how quickly the focus shifted to the two lads who had rushed in to help Hector. He looked angrier with them than with the two who had assaulted Mariota and Isobel. She stood quietly and felt profound relief when he said, "I'll attend to you two when we get home. For now, you can lead these two on their ponies. Later you will come back here and bury the two dead men."

"The abbot will want t' say words over them first," one of the captives said. "They be his kinsmen."

"Then you may tell him where they are buried if I don't hang you," Hector said. "You'd do well to hold your tongue now, however. Your chatter annoys me."

Cristina felt another shiver at his tone and was not surprised when none of the others said a word.

Hector lifted her onto her horse, then moved to do the same for Mariota and Isobel. To the two Lochbuie men, he said, "I'll expect you to bring those two villains home without incident, but we'll reach home before you do, so I'll send men to meet you, in case of trouble. You should be safe enough, though, if you follow the south shore."

"Aye, sir. We'll ha' nae trouble wi' them."

Cristina guided her mount up next to Isobel. "Are you all right, love?"

"Oh, yes, but it was frightening when it happened, Cristina. I did not like it when the first two tried to come with us, but you know how Mariota flirts."

Cristina nodded. She did know.

When Hector and Mariota joined them, they rode back the way they had come. In the silence of the forest, Hector said, "I thought I had made my wishes plain before, but since you two seem not to have understood them, I will make them plain now. You are not to leave the castle without an armed escort. Neither of your two encounters today would have occurred had you obeyed me."

Isobel said, "Cristina told us that, to be sure, but Mariota said she only said so because she was afraid to ride out alone herself, not knowing the countryside yet and all. And Mariota also said—"

"I don't need to hear what everyone said," Hector said evenly. "I'm telling you both now that you will obey me or you will not ride at all. I will not tolerate defiance, so do not try my patience any further."

"No, sir," Isobel said. "I'll remember."

When Mariota did not say a word, Cristina gave her a pointed look, but if she noticed, she gave no sign. With a sigh, Cristina turned her attention to Isobel, wondering if Hector would say more to Mariota or leave well enough alone.

❧❧❧

Hector let Cristina and Isobel ride a little ahead before he said, "I hope you don't mean to defy me, lass. It would not be wise."

"Dear me, sir, I would never do such a thing. Indeed, whatever Isobel may have thought, I did no such thing today. It is surely not my fault if Cristina led me to believe that she was merely suggesting we take an escort. Nor is it my fault that she dallied so long that we assumed she had changed her mind about going with us. Your lads said naught of armed escorts, nor did they hesitate to provide us with horses, so you can scarcely blame me for thinking I did nothing wrong."

"Perhaps, but only until that first pair took liberties with you," he said dryly.

She shrugged. "They are young men, sir. Young men always flirt with me, and I try not to be unkind, no matter how others may behave toward me."

"Did they do aught else?"

She sighed. "I should not have said that. I was not speaking of anyone I met today, and indeed, I hope you will not be too harsh with those men of yours."

"They deserve flogging, and I believe in giving men— and women, too—what they deserve. Had they gone farther than they did, I'd hang them."

"Dear me, you sound very fierce. I hope you do not mean to give me what I deserve. I have already suffered dreadfully." She sighed again, more heavily.

"Is your life so unbearable then?" he asked with a teasing smile.

"Well, you should know, sir. My own father and sister tricked the man who wanted to marry me into giving me up."

"I thought you bore some part in that, too."

"Goodness me, no. They locked me in my room until it was all over. I have never felt so betrayed, I promise you, for it was the most dreadful thing anyone has ever done to me.

I'm sure I would have adored being Lady Maclean and mistress of Lochbuie, for it is a comfortable castle, albeit not as comfortable as Chalamine."

"Would you enjoy managing a large household?" he asked.

"Oh, I expect I should if I had enough servants," she said naively. "Cristina did all that at Chalamine until she left, and Adela does most of it now because she enjoys it and I do not like to deny her that pleasure. Still, it seems simple enough. One just tells the servants what one wants them to do and they do it."

Hector thought she was probably right. That was generally what he did, after all, but he had never thought to ask his people to do a good many of the things they seemed to do now that Cristina had taken up the reins of his household.

He enjoyed his conversation with Mariota, and wished the ride home might have lasted longer. He found her charming and delightfully flirtatious, if a trifle overfond of herself, and he believed that she had suffered a good deal through the trick her father had served them. It seemed, too, that her family did not appreciate her as they should.

Only when he recalled that he had now to deal with four miscreants and see to the burial of two others did he remember that he had meant to scold her severely for her disobedience. By then, however, she had ridden into the barn with Cristina and Isobel, and he was reluctant to follow them merely to issue his rebuke.

❧

Cristina slid down from her horse and told the lad who looked after it to rub it down well. Then, turning to her sisters, she said, "Go directly inside now, for I want to speak to both of you."

Isobel looked self-conscious, but Mariota nodded and turned with a smile to the lad taking her horse. "Thank you for looking after him so well," she said. "I like him very much and would like to ride him again soon, mayhap tomorrow."

"Mariota, go on ahead with Isobel and wait for me in the hall, if you please," Cristina said. "I must have a word with Hector before I join you."

Mariota did not reply but told Isobel to hurry.

Satisfied that they would obey, Cristina found Hector in the yard rubbing down his horse and looking bemused. "What will you do with those men?" she asked.

"Doubtless hang one pair and flog the second," he said. "Why?"

"If the ones you mean to hang are Mackinnons, will that not exacerbate the problems you already face with the Green Abbot?"

"It may," he replied. "But I cannot allow them to assault my kinswomen with impunity. They'll have a chance to state their case at the next laird's court. Until then, they can enjoy the hospitality of my pit."

"And the other two are our own men?"

"They are. I mean to flog them both myself."

"That is harsh punishment," she said with a frown.

"It is what they expect and what they deserve, however, and I don't mean to disappoint them or to debate my decision with you, madam."

She frowned. "Of course not, sir, although from the sound of it, Mariota led them to believe she was a light-skirt of some sort. It hardly seems fair to punish them if they believed they were merely engaging in a flirtation."

"Sakes, lass, they admitted they realized the moment she spoke to them that she and Isobel were wellborn. And you'll not persuade me that you think those two were merely flirting with Isobel as well. They must have frightened her witless."

She sighed. "My sisters both behaved badly, sir. I understand why you did not scold them, for Mariota is an expert at avoiding reprimands. Doubtless, she flirted with you, too, because that is her way with all men. All the same, to punish our men when the fault lies equally with Mariota and Isobel for disobeying seems unduly harsh to me. Doubtless you know best, however, so I shall say no more."

"Go inside, lass, and if you are concerned about your sisters' part in this, tell them so. Tell them also that I shall not be as lenient if they are unwise enough to do such a thing again."

Nodding, understanding that although she felt sorry for the men he would flog, they did deserve their fate, she went to find her sisters.

⏤⏥⏤

Hector watched her go, admiring her dignity and the gentle sway of her hips but feeling oddly uncertain of himself. He knew she was right, that it was unfair to blame only the lads when her sisters were at fault, too.

Sakes, but he had not even said that much to Mariota. Instead, he had enjoyed her flirtation, perhaps even flirted a bit back. Nevertheless, he would do himself no favors if he were lenient with his men. The two expected flogging, and he had a reputation to maintain.

He sent lads to meet the prisoners and their escort and busied himself in the yard and the barn until they returned.

Then, ordering the Mackinnon pair relegated to his pit-dungeon, in the cellar of the main tower, until he could take the time to hold a laird's court, he ordered the two Lochbuie miscreants into the barn.

Facing them, his countenance as stern as he could make it, he said, "What have the pair of you to say for yourselves?"

"We didna ken at first that they was noblewomen, laird, but we should ha' minded our manners better after they spoke to us. We deserve whatever ye decide t' do wi' us, and that's plain enough," the older one said miserably.

"Do you agree with that?" Hector demanded of the younger man, a lad scarcely out of his teens.

Looking wretched, the youngster glanced at his compatriot and then nodded. "Aye, laird. I'd be wroth m'self did the like happen t' me sister just 'cause two dunderclunks what ought t' ha' known better chased her into the arms o' that filthy Mackinnon lot."

Hector nodded. "You know that you deserve a round dozen for this, but since it is clear to me that you have learned a lesson, I'll give you only three each," he said. "However, I'll also demand a fine of five merks from each of you, and I'll expect to have no more trouble from you. You'll become two of the best men at Lochbuie if you want to avoid my wrath in the future, for I promise you that if I have to speak this way to either of you again, you will be sorrier than you know."

"Aye, laird, thank ye kindly. We'll be nae more trouble t' ye at all," the older one said, grabbing the younger one's arm and giving it a shake. "Ye'll be thanking the laird yourself, Jem, and be earnest about it, lad."

Reluctantly, as if he were not so sure the lesser sentence

was any more to his liking than what the laird had said he deserved, the lad obeyed.

"Pull off your shirts then and take a post," Hector said.

When he had finished, the two went to help tend the horses, the older one stoic, the younger sobbing, although he had not screamed; and Hector strolled back to the castle, wondering if he had done the right thing or was a fool.

His unwanted wife seemed to be exerting an expected influence, and he told himself that it would be ironic, not to mention damned annoying, if the mistake in his marriage resulted in his becoming known as Hector the Mild, or worse.

Chapter 10 ⎯⎯⎯⎯⎯⎯⎯⎯⎯⎯

Cristina found herself listening for men's screams from the barn. Her father had ordered two men flogged once, and although he had not done the flogging himself, she remembered the men's screams as clearly as if the incident had happened recently instead of five or six years before. But she reached the hall without hearing anything other than the normal sounds of a busy castle.

A cow mooed, chickens clucked, and horses whinnied or stamped feet. Two men honing their swordplay in the yard provided ringing clashes of steel against steel that punctuated the steady bleating of a flock of sheep moving to a meadow on the hillside above the castle. The tongue clicks, whistles, and occasional words of their shepherd accompanied them. A blacksmith forging something in the smithy added the heavy clanging of his hammer on the red-hot iron as secondary percussion to the symphony of sounds. Not a single discordant note interrupted.

Entering the hall, she found her sisters chatting with Lady Euphemia as if nothing out of the ordinary had occurred.

"I am displeased with you both," she said without

preamble. "I told you plainly what Hector's orders were, and you ignored them as if I had never spoken."

"We're sorry, Cristina," Isobel said contritely.

"Faith, child, speak for yourself," Mariota said. "I do not know why you should take us to task," she added to Cristina. "Hector said naught to me of displeasure, his own or anyone else's. He understands that it was not our responsibility to provide a proper escort but yours as our hostess. We expected you to ride with us, after all, and to deal with such details if necessary. But you chose not to do so. To blame us for your failing is dreadfully unfair, and I do not intend to stand for it, so do not be trying to censure me, Cristina. What did you expect us to do when you decided not to accompany us and did not even bother to send us word? You could scarcely have been surprised that we rode on without you."

"You told the gillies to put my horse away," Cristina reminded her.

"I did no such thing. It is no business of mine to deal with your horse."

"You did tell them that Cristina had changed her mind," Isobel pointed out.

Mariota shrugged. "We thought she *had* changed her mind. Even so, it certainly is not my fault that they chose to take that belief to mean they should put her horse away. Nor can she blame them for thinking they should, however."

"Well, but—"

"That will do, Isobel," Cristina said, knowing from experience that debating such points with Mariota was useless. She saw only what she wanted to see and ignored everything else. Trying to argue with her was like trying to pick up water in a sieve. One could never persuade her that she was wrong, so it was no use trying.

Isobel persisted nonetheless. "I told her we should wait

for you, but she said as soon as you left that you were not coming. That is what she told the gillies, too."

"I said that will do," Cristina said more firmly. "I want you to go to your bedchamber now and choose what you will wear to eat your midday meal. I know you will not want to sit down in that dress. It is much too rumpled and untidy."

Isobel gave a shrug much like Mariota's. "I couldn't help that," she said. "When I tried to keep that man from tearing Mariota's dress, he pushed me down."

Feeling her temper stir again, but knowing that the man responsible for assaulting the child was probably already dead, Cristina was about to insist that Isobel do as she was bid when the command came instead from behind her.

"Do as your sister bade you, lassie," Hector said curtly. "You have already tried my patience—and doubtless hers as well—far beyond what I will tolerate. You run along and change your gown, too, Lady Mariota. I know you do not want to appear at dinner looking as if you'd been dragged through a bush backward."

"Bless me, sir, is that how you think I look?"

Lady Euphemia said, "Dear me, my love, you should never ask a gentleman if he thinks you look a sight, particularly when you must know that you do. Instead, you must thank him prettily for the compliment he has paid you by assuming that you wish to tidy yourself, for I am persuaded that you can want nothing more, looking as untidy as you do. And indeed, if I am not mistaken, we have scarcely enough time as it is, without your standing there chattering instead of obeying Cristina as you should. You come with me now, the pair of you, for I must certainly refresh myself as well, and I warrant that Lord Hector desires to have a private word with Cristina. So, come now, do, and quickly."

She reminded Cristina of one of the shepherds' dogs,

darting to and fro, nipping at the heels of its charges. She nearly smiled before she realized that Hector's stern gaze had shifted to her.

"Did you wish to speak with me, sir?"

"Aye, I do, but I think we'll seek a more private place," he said, drawing her right hand into the crook of his arm and holding it there.

Trying to ignore the fluttering in her stomach as she strove to imagine what could have happened in the past ten minutes to make him speak so abruptly to her, she let him take her from the hall and upstairs to his chamber.

"What is it?" she asked. "Have I done something more to vex you?"

"Nay," he said. "I know that you were concerned about those two men, and I wanted to set your mind at rest."

"Indeed, sir, in what way?"

"You were right about that. To blame them, and only them, for what occurred with your sisters would have been unfair. The Mackinnons are another matter, of course, and because I was angry about what they did, I think I laid more responsibility than I should have on my lads."

She looked up at him hopefully. "So you did not flog them after all?"

He grimaced. "They expected flogging, lass, and I do not want my men imagining that I will no longer punish them severely for wrongdoing. They showed disrespect to my guests—indeed, to my kinswomen—and they knew well what they deserved. Had your sisters' disobedience not initiated the entire affair, they'd have suffered a dozen strokes for their behavior."

She remained silent, seeing naught to gain by wondering aloud what he thought Mariota and Isobel deserved.

"I gave them each three stripes and laid them on lightly,"

he said. "I also fined them both and put the fear of God into them. They recognize my leniency, Cristina. I hope you will agree that I was not too harsh."

The thought of a heavy whip against bare skin made her shudder, but she knew the punishment was common and realized that he had indeed been merciful. "I think you did the right thing, sir. It is my belief that one should reserve harsh punishment for grave misdeeds, and they did redeem themselves considerably by flying to your aid. I own, though, I wanted to slap Mariota. I think she—"

"Sakes, then I think you are being overly harsh with her," he interjected. "She seems honestly to have thought you'd changed your mind about going with them, and we cannot expect her to have ordered her own escort."

Relief changed to irritation as Cristina tried to think of how to explain Mariota to him. But knowing that he was disposed to believe everything her lovely sister said, all she could think to say was, "I know her better than you do, sir."

"Aye, well, I know you both well enough now to understand that you are envious of her beauty and the admiration she draws from every man she meets."

An indignant snort outside the doorway turned instantly into muffled coughs.

Cristina clapped a hand to her mouth, but Hector strode to the half-open door and jerked it wide to reveal Isobel just outside, her face cherry red from coughing.

"What the devil are you doing here?" he demanded furiously.

Looking scared, she said, "I was afraid you would scold Cristina, or worse, and indeed, sir, she is not jealous, and it was not her fault, no matter what Mariota told you. Cristina did tell us never to ride out alone, but Mariota—"

"Enough!" he roared. "If you do not want to feel my hand

on your backside, my lass, you will take yourself straight to your bedchamber and change your dress, as your sister told you to do. I warned you before that I do not tolerate defiant women, so let me see no more of this disobedience."

"But—"

Grabbing her by a shoulder, he spun her around and gave her a hard smack on her backside. When she shrieked, he snapped, "If you do not want more of that, don't say another word. After we dine, you will put on a dress that you do not mind mussing and hie yourself to the kitchen, where I warrant Alma Galbraith can tell you which of the lads can use someone to help them stack the wood they are chopping now for the ovens. Do you understand me, Isobel?"

"You want me to stack wood?"

"Do you mean to tell me you do not know how?"

"Of course I know how, for I have often helped Cristina, but—"

"Then there is no more to be said about it," he interjected. "And if I ever catch you listening at doors again, I will put you straight across my knee and give you what you truly deserve without offering you an alternative. Is that clear?"

"Aye, sir," she said hastily. "I'm sorry."

"I do not want your sorrow; I want your obedience. Now, go!"

Redder of face than ever, Isobel fled.

Cristina said, "You should not take out your frustration on her, sir. She is only a child."

"By heaven, do not lecture me, lass, or Isobel will not be the only one who goes across my knee. I have put up with too much today already. I do not intend to put up with any more, so if you don't want to find yourself stacking wood alongside your little sister, I'd suggest you keep your tongue firmly behind your teeth."

Cristina said no more, excusing herself instead to change for dinner.

The meal proved a relatively quiet one at the high table, although Mariota kept up a stream of conversation by asking Hector questions about Lochbuie and Mull. In this endeavor she was ably assisted by Lady Euphemia, although the latter's contributions tended to be wandering memories of her own childhood and the differences between her family home and Hector's descriptions of Lochbuie.

Cristina, looking from one to another as if she were listening but feeling disconnected from the conversation, decided that Hector was not listening either, but was only watching Mariota when she talked. He heeded her words enough to answer questions or make polite comments, but his attention seemed riveted to her face rather than to her thought processes. That was just as well, Cristina decided, since Mariota seemed not to notice when she contradicted things she herself had said, in order to agree with nearly everything that Hector said.

The phenomenon was one that Cristina had noted before in her, and one that made it impossible to have an ordinary disagreement with her, let alone a full-blown argument. If one pressed Mariota, pointing out that she had just said the opposite thing to something she had said only moments before, she would insist firmly that she had never said any such thing.

Cristina's thoughtful gaze rested for a few moments on Hector. A ray of sun beaming down on the table near him made his eyes seem more startlingly blue than ever. His lips parted slightly as he watched Mariota, and he seemed oblivious to the others at the table.

Mariota, she knew, was perfectly aware of the impact she was having on him and delighted in it. She leaned forward so that her plump bosom was nearly spilling from her low-cut bodice, met his gaze boldly, and ran her little pink tongue over her lower lip as if she were inviting him to kiss her.

Cristina's stomach clenched, and she was aware that her hands had curled to claws. She wished she could order her sister from the table, scold her as Hector had scolded Isobel. Instead, she felt obliged to sit quietly and conceal her frustration. He had never wanted to marry her, so she could not accuse him of anything other than thoughtless, rather cruel behavior. But with his comments about just desserts still ringing in her ears, she could not help wondering if she deserved any less for her part in the marriage that her father had foisted on him.

But as sad as such thoughtlessness made her, the thought that she would eventually have to leave Lochbuie was becoming unbearable to contemplate.

"How can you say your favorite color is scarlet when you just said a few moments ago, when he was talking about heather, that it was purple?" Isobel demanded, breaking the spell of Mariota's flirtation and drawing instant censure.

"Don't interrupt," Mariota said. "Little girls should hold their tongues when they are allowed to dine with grown-ups. Moreover, I'm sure I never said any such thing. Did I, sir?" she said, smiling brilliantly at Hector.

"Well, you did," Isobel said. "Didn't she, Aunt?"

Visibly startled at being drawn into the discussion in such an abrupt way, Lady Euphemia looked warily from one to the other. "Oh, my dear, I'm sure Mariota may have said such a thing, talking of wildflowers, you know, and mayhap purple is her favorite color for a flower, but now I warrant she is talking of something altogether different and did not mean it as you apparently thought she did. I have noticed that I cannot always follow her thoughts exactly either."

"That's just what happens, I'm sure," Mariota said. "Not that it matters, Isobel. No one was speaking to you, as I recall, so hold your tongue, lest you get us in trouble again. I'm sure I do not want to enrage our dearest Hector more than we enraged him this morning. That was all Cristina's fault, of course, although I shan't say another word about it, for I'm sure she never meant to get us into trouble, and merely failed to explain his orders so that I could understand them. Still and all, though, I am never one to hold a grudge. I believe in letting such things go and never referring to them *ever* again."

"Like now," Isobel said dryly. "Oh, don't scold me anymore. I'm mum," she added, hastily applying her attention to her plate.

Hector had fixed a thoughtful gaze on her, but he said nothing.

The tightening sensation in Cristina's stomach increased. Catching Hector's gaze on her next, she wished she could excuse herself from the table, fearing that if she sat there much longer listening to Mariota, her anger would overwhelm her and she would say exactly what she thought of what Mariota had done and was doing. But a lady could not speak her mind so openly or walk away and leave her guests—not without censure. She was their hostess, although presently she did not feel as if she even belonged at Lochbuie, let alone sitting in the lady's chair at the high table.

Lady Euphemia sat at her left with Isobel just beyond. Mariota, however, sat at Hector's right in the place of honor. Had other gentlemen been present, his primary male guest would sit there, but in the informal family setting, Mariota had simply taken that place the day after his return from Finlaggan and no one had told her that she must not. So there she sat, monopolizing his attention as if she were some grand visitor and not merely the lady of Lochbuie's sister.

Truly, Cristina thought, life at Lochbuie had not been what she had expected married life to be. Although she had believed she could be happy as Hector's wife if he would simply accept her in that position and not puzzle his mind for ways to acquire an annulment, she was no longer certain of that. He did not want her, and as things stood, she feared that a life with him would be trying at best.

The meal ended at last, and uttering a vague excuse that she was certain no one else heeded, she escaped to the kitchen. Her first inclination was to pass through that chamber and out to the yard, but spying Alma in obvious disagreement with the cook, she could not bring herself simply to pass them by.

"What's amiss here?" she inquired, wrapping herself in her usual calm.

"Only that Calum has neglected t' send anyone out fishing and the salmon be all but gone," Alma said, glowering at the cook. "I told him ye'd want a proper fish course for your supper this evening, but he insists the master doesna care if he ever eats fish."

"Nor he don't neither," the cook said testily.

Cristina held up a hand, silencing him. "You mentioned that once before, Calum, but your master desires his guests to be well served, does he not?"

"Aye, I expect so."

Cristina waited for him to add the usual "m'lady," but when he did not, she drew a steadying breath and said, "His guests expect fish, so Alma is right, and you will have to send someone to catch a salmon or some fresh trout. Whoever goes will have plenty of time for it and will likely enjoy the expedition. If you do not have time to send someone, I will ask the laird's steward to do so."

"I'll see to it if ye insist," he said grudgingly.

"Alma, you may go now," Cristina said quietly, noting that Isobel stood hesitantly nearby in the doorway. "I believe Lady Isobel needs to speak to you."

"Aye, sure, m'lady, straightaway."

Cristina noted with approval that the woman gave no sign of the victory she must feel she had just scored over the cook. Turning back to him, she said evenly, "I thought you liked your position here, Calum."

"I do," he said. "I ha' been cook here since the laird came t' Lochbuie."

"Have you? Then doubtless in that time you have learned the proper way to address a lady."

"Aye, but they do be saying as ye willna be here long, so I'm thinking me manners willna come into it."

"I am here now, however," she reminded him.

"Aye, sure, but I work for the laird."

"Then, mayhap you should think of how he will react if I complain to him of your bad manners. Have you had cause yet to believe he will not support me in your dismissal as strongly as he has supported the other changes I have made here?"

"As to that—"

"Perhaps you should likewise consider that his steward will support such a dismissal," she said. "As I understand it, you and he do not get on well, and the laird has great respect for his steward." When he paled, she added gently, "You and I, on the other hand, have got along well until now, so I am at a loss to understand your behavior today."

"I'll mend me ways straightaway, m'lady. In truth, I ha'

nowt agin ye. Ye've made many a suggestion that I ha' appreciated, particularly since the laird come down t' me kitchen yestereve t' say he likes me new way o' doing things."

Gratified but still bewildered, she said, "Then why were you so rude to me?"

The man grimaced. "I canna tell ye, and that be plain fact. I shouldna ha' done it, but ye've enemies about who would see ye gone, mistress. Dinna turn your back on no one, I'm thinking."

"But who would do me harm?"

He shook his head. "Nay, nay, 'twould be as much as me life be worth."

Telling him to get on with his work and not to forget the fish, Cristina went in search of Alma again and found her in the yard, introducing Isobel to two lads only a year or so older than she was, who had been chopping wood for most of the morning, with a huge scatter of oven-sized quarter logs to show for it.

Isobel surveyed these fruits of their labor with narrowed eyes. She had done no more than tie a long apron over her gown, but Cristina did not say anything about that. "That's a lot of wood," Isobel said.

The shorter of the two woodchoppers looked at Cristina. "This lass says she is t' help us stack yon wood. Be that true, me lady?"

"It is," Cristina told him, drawing a heavy sigh from her little sister. "Lady Isobel has wanted something more energetic than needlework to do, so we thought you might like some help with the wood."

"We would that," he agreed, grinning. "Wi' three o' us, we can be finished in half the time." Glancing at Isobel, he added, "Well, mayhap no half the time, but less anyways. Then, mayhap they'll let us off t' do a bit o' fishing."

"Mayhap they will at that," Cristina said, glancing at Alma. "Calum needs fish for supper."

"'Tis true," Alma said. "I'll speak t' him. Doubtless he'll want t' send more than one lad just t' make sure o' the fish."

"I'll linger here for a bit," Cristina said. "I want to be sure Isobel knows just how we like the wood stacked at Lochbuie."

With a wry smile that said she knew young ladies did not usually help gillies stack wood, Alma turned on her heel and hurried back into the kitchen.

"Why don't you begin over here, Isobel?" Cristina suggested. "I'll lend you a hand for a short time."

Isobel looked disbelieving, but when Cristina said nothing more, she went with her to the far side of the woodpile and began selecting logs to stack. "You don't have to show me, you know," she said. "I've done it often enough at home to know exactly how you like it done."

"I know, love," Cristina said. "I just want an excuse not to go back inside yet a while. I'm not feeling very sociable, and I don't think I could endure another conversation with Aunt Euphemia or Mariota, let alone with both of them, until I've enjoyed a few minutes of peace."

"So you went to the kitchen and walked into the war betwixt Alma and Calum."

"Is there a war?"

"Aye, because Alma is a Bethune and Calum is a Mackinney."

"The Mackinneys are connected to the Mackinnons, are they not?"

"Aye, they are," Isobel said as she carefully squared her

logs on the stack. "And the Bethunes are members of Clan Gillean."

"I see. And doubtless Hector's steward is of Clan Gillean. I wonder why his cook is not."

Isobel said, "Calum had served him before, although he would not tell me in what capacity. He said it were nowt for a bairn's ears, that."

"You seem to have learned a great deal," Cristina said.

"I ask questions," Isobel said. "May I ask you one?"

"Of course you may," Cristina assured her.

"Are you angry with me, too?"

"Too? Oh, you mean because Hector was."

"And Mariota, but I displease her whenever I tell her she is contradicting herself. Really, Cristina, it is as if she sometimes gets a picture of things in her head that only she can see, and that picture changes whenever it pleases her to change it."

Cristina chuckled. It was an apt description of Mariota's more complex conversations. Nevertheless, she recognized Isobel's tactics and brought the conversation back to the point. "Hector had good cause to be angry with you," she said. "Eavesdropping is very rude."

"I only wanted to be sure you were all right," Isobel said.

"I can take care of myself, but I thank you for the thought."

"Do you like him?"

"Of course I do. He is my husband, and more than that he is . . . at least, he can be . . . a most charming gentleman."

"I've seen that for myself," Isobel said. "I like him, but I was thinking that he had eyes only for Mariota. Now I am not so sure, but he keeps his thoughts to himself, does he not?"

"Aye, he does."

"Is that why you are angry then?"

"Faith, I am not angry, not with him. Not with anyone," she added conscientiously.

"But you are," Isobel said. "You are always angry. Even when you laugh, you are angry—just as Mariota is always lying, even when she tells the truth."

"Isobel, what a thing to say about your own sister!"

"But she does, Cristina. She never tells the plain truth. She exaggerates everything so much that even when she is telling the truth, she lies."

Cristina opened her mouth to say "Nonsense," but she shut it again. Isobel was right. Mariota did tend to exaggerate everything she said.

The child gazed at her, patiently waiting, her blue eyes clear, her rosy lips slightly parted, clearly expecting Cristina to see her point.

Cristina did. "Am I really angry *all* the time?" she asked.

Isobel nodded, then added with a half smile, "Perhaps that is also an exaggeration, but you seem angry so often that I had to stop and think about it. Why are you so angry, Cristina?"

"I cannot answer you," Cristina said honestly. "I did not know that I seemed that way, but if it seems so to you, I suppose it must be so. I think you are very wise for your years, Isobel. You see things so clearly. I wonder how that came to be."

"I just watch people," Isobel said. "I learn by watching."

"And by listening," Cristina said with a twinkle.

Isobel grimaced. "Aye," she said, "and listening."

"We might all do better by listening more," Cristina said.

Isobel smiled and returned to stacking the wood, but a moment later, she said, "If you want solitude, why not escape to your tower for a while."

Deciding that that was an excellent notion, particularly as she wanted to think, Cristina went there directly but found herself recalling not the events of the past few days but her little sister's words.

Anger? How odd that she had not thought of herself as angry, whilst Isobel apparently believed that she was. She certainly got upset sometimes—frustrated, overwhelmed perhaps—but anger seemed too strong a word to describe her feelings except for the times that angry words flew around in her mind or those extremely rare occasions when she seemed to lose control and say dreadful things that she was sorry afterward for saying.

A sudden poignant memory struck her of a sunny morning in the garden at Chalamine when her mother had scolded her for an unseemly display of temper.

"Ladies do not make a gift of their emotions to all the world," Lady Macleod had said sternly. "Ladies set good examples for lesser persons to emulate. Courtesy and good behavior are duties, Cristina, and we Macleods never shirk our duty."

Lady Macleod's image was suddenly so strong that it was as if she were right there in the tower chamber speaking those words. And Lady Macleod always knew just what one should do in any situation.

Cristina had never seen any circumstance defeat her mother except her death. But death had taken her much too soon, long before she had been able to impart all the so-important things she knew to her daughter, abandoning her to a cruel world, barely half-armed to meet its challenges and burdens.

Cristina did not realize that tears had begun coursing down her cheeks until she dashed an impatient hand across one cheek to brush them away. But the gesture, startling her, released a torrent.

Before she knew what was happening, gusty sobs overwhelmed her. Gasping with them, too overcome to remain upright or to seek a chair or stool, she crumpled to the floor, hugging herself. Her sides heaved, aching as the sobs racked her body. Then uncontrollable, hiccupping cries came, heard by no one, because no one was there—ever, not for Cristina—although heaven knew that she did her best to soothe everyone else's tears, to soothe everyone else's woes, to solve everyone else's problems. But no one else cared enough, apparently, to be there for poor Cristina.

The flood stopped as abruptly as it had begun on the realization that her sorrow had twisted itself right around to self-pity—the very self-pity that she despised in anyone else. Had she no pride, no dignity, no self-control?

Using her sleeve, she wiped her face, her gestures jerky, hasty, and impatient. She was pushing wet strands of hair off her cheeks when the door opened without warning.

Hector stood on the threshold, gazing at her in astonishment.

Chapter 11

He saw at once that Cristina had been crying, and he felt a surge of guilt, knowing that he had behaved badly. Isobel's comments and Mariota's rather naïve prattle made it clear that they had ignored his command, and he could blame neither Isobel nor Cristina for that. He winced as he remembered accusing the latter of jealousy when she had disagreed with him about Mariota's guilt.

In truth he had not seen any sign of envy, but Mariota had said something of the sort at one time or another and in his annoyance with Cristina for questioning his judgment, he had flung the accusation at her.

Remorse sent him swiftly to her now, catching her by the upper arms and pulling her gently to her feet.

"What is it, lass? What has distressed you so? Was it what I said?"

She would not meet his gaze at first, staring instead at his chest. He wanted to see her eyes, not only to see how distressed she was but also to see if they were as golden when she was upset as they had been the first time he had noted their color. He wanted to pull her close, to hold her so she would know she was safe, and that feeling surprised him.

He told himself he would do as much for anyone in such apparent misery, but he realized he was nervous, afraid she would push him away if he did try to embrace her. She was usually so capable and serene. It occurred to him then that when she had made him feel as if he should mind his manners, he had thought her motherly, which was absurd. Although she was protective, loving, and kind, he had never in his life thought of qualities such as alluring golden eyes and skin like silk as motherly. Gripping her shoulders now, and feeling her tremble, he remembered that silken skin and how soft and inviting her lips always looked, and he wanted to see them again.

"Look at me, Cristina," he said, his tone brusquer than he had intended.

The tone had the desired effect though, because she looked up at him, her eyes widening as she did. They were as golden as he remembered them, but now he saw green flecks as well, doubtless because her gown was green.

She did not speak, but her lower lip quivered as if she might cry again, and he did not want her to cry.

Speaking more gently, he said, "What is it, lass? Was it what I said before about jealousy? I was wrong. I know you harbor no ill will toward your sister."

She shook her head and looked at his chest again. "It was not that."

"Then what? You can tell me. I do not like to see you like this."

She drew a breath, a deep one, as if to steady herself, and he waited with more patience than usual. At last, gathering herself and looking up at him, she said in a low tone, "Forgive me, sir. I am behaving badly. I—"

"Don't be daft," he said more in his usual way. "Something has distressed you, and I want to know what it is. Tell me now, and do not make me ask you again." So much, he thought, for patience.

To his surprise, she gave a watery smile. "You will think me even more foolish when I tell you," she said, her voice steadier. "I came here, seeking quiet and a place to think without interruption. Instead, for some reason I cannot fathom, my thoughts turned to my mother, to how she used to give me such sound advice. And then it was as if she were here, only she wasn't, and I missed her dreadfully, and so you found me awash in a sea of tears."

He brushed a damp curl from her cheek. She seemed so small and vulnerable that again he wanted to pull her into his arms, but he was still afraid she would dislike it. Although he was her husband, he had done little since their wedding night to assert his rights in that regard, and so doubtless, any such gesture would spoil the present mood. Accordingly, he said, "How long ago did she die?"

"Years ago, when I was eleven. So you see how foolish it is suddenly to feel her loss now so overwhelmingly."

"Nay, lass. I was fifteen when I lost my mother, and I have felt her loss nearly every day since. A simple cloud formation may remind me that she used to point out animals in the clouds and tell us stories about them. Or someone will look a certain way or use a particular phrase that will bring her face or voice into my head. It is not so strange, I think, and if you were close to yours, even less strange."

"Were you not close to your mother?"

"Oh, aye, I suppose as close as any lad, especially since neither Lachlan nor I fostered elsewhere. Our father kept us under his guidance, hoping that both of us would take to learning as he had. Lachlan did more so than I, but after she died, Ian Dubh sent us both to France to learn more of the world and to study with a friend there. The friend soon saw that I was disinterested in history and such, so he turned me over to a master swordsman to learn weaponry. Lachlan took lessons in weaponry as well, but although his skill is adequate, it does not equal his skill at politics and strategy. Nevertheless, we make a good partnership between us."

"Mairi said he could not get on without you. She told me that he has a gift for making plans and knowing whenever something is in the wind, because he has developed a network of informants throughout Scotland and beyond that makes him the best-informed man in the Highlands and Isles. But, without you to expedite his dreams and plans, she said, he would never have acquired the power and position that he holds now."

"Mairi should not say such things," he said, but he straightened, unable to resist the pride the words afforded him. Lachlan had often said as much, but Lachlan was as likely to tell him he was a dunderclunk as to pay him compliments. Brothers rarely complimented each other. It seemed more natural to compete against each other or to tease, criticize, or otherwise torment each other. "I hope you do not say such things to her about me," he added.

"What, tell her that you could never get on without Lachlan?" She smiled, clearly teasing him, but then added soberly, "I think you would succeed as well without him as you do with him, sir. You seem eminently capable of doing whatever needs doing. Your partnership does seem to be an excellent one, although I suspect that his grace is the one who profits most from it."

"Was it just the sudden, unexpected memory of your mother?" he asked, recalling a certain tension during the midday meal and unable to believe that the morning's events and his conversation with her after the meal did not contribute to her present mood. "Was that all it was, Cristina?"

She looked into his eyes again, searchingly, as if she sought reassurance or something else. He was not sure if she saw what she looked for or not, but she said, "I would be lying if I said that nothing else had upset me, sir, but it was nothing of importance. At least, I do not think so."

"Will you tell me?" Suddenly, it was of great importance that she should. "I truly want to know, lass. Was it aught that I did or said?"

She nibbled her lower lip, and he could not take his eyes from it. So soft, so plump, so kissable. Even when she stopped nibbling and spoke, he watched the movements of her lips, imagining how they would feel against his own.

"Are you listening, sir?"

He realized that he had not heard a word she had said. "Of course I was listening. Don't be daft." He felt heat in his cheeks and guilt at the lie. "Nay, lassie," he admitted. "I own, I was thinking of something else just then."

She frowned, saying more tartly, "Doubtless, you have more important things to do, sir. Indeed, I do not know why you came here."

Cristina fought to regain her calm, but the disappointment of realizing that although he had asked the question, he had not listened to the answer made her want to slap him. She could not do so, of course. For all she knew, he would slap her back, and a blow from a man as large as Hector might well knock her off her feet. Even as the thought crossed her mind, however, she knew she did not fear him. And despite her anger, so ingrained was her habit of peace-making that she had all she could do not to apologize at once for her sharp tone.

His was easily as sharp when he said, "I came here to find out why my wife had disappeared without a word to anyone."

"I did not know that you expected me to report my every movement," she replied. "I will do so in future, however, if that is your wish."

"Don't be insolent," he snapped.

"Faith, sir, is it now insolence for a wife to comply with her husband's wishes?"

He was visibly fighting to control his temper, and she wanted to reach up and smooth the frown away, to tell him she hadn't meant to be insolent and did not really think she had been. One moment she wanted to scold him for behaving like a thoughtless boy, for flirting so openly with Mariota, and for making his lawful wife feel as if she had no place at his table. The next, she wanted to apologize for worrying him, to fling herself into his arms and cry until she could cry no more.

She had only been trying to tell him she had been feeling invisible, as if no one had noticed that she was at the table, but even as she struggled for the words to say as much without explicitly blaming him for responding to Mariota's flirtation, she had realized he was not listening. Instantly, anger and disappointment had swept through her, and she had experienced a strong desire to break or smash something.

His lips tightened into a straight line, and she wondered if she had gone too far by standing up to him. If she had, nothing she could say was likely to assuage his anger—if he was even angry. A frown creased his handsome face, to be sure, but she suspected that his anger rarely resulted in silence. Perhaps he was merely thinking how best to punish her for her acid tongue. She recalled then that she had reminded him she was his wife. He certainly did not think of her so, and who could blame him?

On that thought, she felt the prickling of tears again, and to her horror, one spilled over and ran down her cheek.

Instantly, he caught her shoulders again and pulled her hard against him. "Please don't cry, lassie. I am truly a beast to add to your sorrow. I should not have said that, or any of it. I came to find you because I could not find the spurs I wore earlier and thought you must have put them somewhere. Lady Euphemia told me you had taken this chamber for your own, so I came here to find you. That's all. 'Tis a most comfortable-looking chamber, I think," he added, glancing around at the cushioned benches and the basket of needlework beside the back stool.

"I have not seen your spurs," she said, ignoring his compliment, certain that he had offered it merely to divert her thoughts. "Did you go anywhere after we returned—to supervise the careening of your boats perhaps?"

"Aye, but nowhere else, and I did not have— Nay, I stopped in the steward's chamber," he said. "Sakes, I remember now. I took them off whilst he was showing me some accounts. I can't think why I did that, but I'd better go and fetch them. Will you be all right here whilst I do so?"

"Aye," she said.

He continued to hold her as he said quietly, "I mean to ride with the lads when they go to bury those two louts who attacked your sisters, but we should talk more of this. To that end, I want you to share my chamber tonight. Will you do so?"

"Aye, sir, of course," she said, wondering at the emotions that instantly filled her. Doubtless, he wanted only to exert his husband's right to share a bed with his wife when the mood struck him to do so. That the mood had struck at last should not, she thought, fill her with such eager delight.

Reminding herself that, in her experience, delight usually presaged disaster, she decided she would be wiser not to read more into his request than he intended.

❦

The afternoon passed swiftly. Isobel came to find Cristina at last, dusty but smiling widely. "Stacking wood proved not to be such a tedious penance as I thought it would be," she announced.

Astonished to see that the child's gown was soaked to her knees, Cristina said, "How did your skirt get wet?"

"I waded into the water to help Fin land his salmon."

"You went fishing with him?"

"Aye, with him and Hugo. They said I could, so I did."

"Isobel, did you not understand that Hector does not want us to leave the castle without armed men to guard us? I thought he'd made his orders clear to you."

"But Fin took his dirk," Isobel said. "That is a weapon, so he *was* armed."

Cristina shook her head. "I don't know what to do with you. Surely, you must know that Hector would not consider two boys only a bit older than you are capable of protecting you against danger."

Isobel cocked her head. "Do you really think anyone would harm me? Fin said it was daft to think anyone would, since no one would even guess I'm a lady."

"Well, that much is true," Cristina agreed dryly. "Anyone seeing you now would take you for a common child of no sense or dignity, and a filthy one at that."

"But don't you see that if that is true, I was in no danger?"

"Do you remember what Hector said about defiant women?"

Isobel looked down. "Aye."

"What do you think he would say to that last remark?"

Isobel grimaced. "Must you tell him?"

"I don't know," Cristina said. "I don't want him to punish you again, because I'm afraid he'd be more severe this time. You know what he said he'd do to you."

"That was if he caught me listening at doors again."

Cristina sighed. "Go and change now. It will soon be time for supper."

Looking utterly unchastened, Isobel skipped away, and with a sigh, Cristina went to tidy herself for dinner. The slender, middle-aged maidservant Mairi had found awaited her in her bedchamber, and as the woman was smoothing her hair before replacing her caul, Cristina said, "I should like a bath after supper, Brona. Pray have the lads bring up a tub and hot water."

"Aye, m'lady, I'll see to it, though I'd no bathe m'self in the evening," Brona said, clearly surprised at the request. "It dinna be healthy."

"I helped my little sister stack wood today," Cristina said glibly. "I think I must have wood dust in every crevice of my body, but I've no time to bathe now."

Brona clicked her tongue. "Bless me, me lady," she said, "there be folks aplenty t' tend t' such chores. Ye do too much."

Perhaps that was all it was, Cristina thought. Perhaps she took on too much and should practice being a proper lady, the sort that appeared in bard's tales, dining on strawberries and cream, the sort that did no chores. The life such ladies led usually sounded boring, but perhaps they were happy and contented.

❧

Supper seemed to Hector to be a repeat of the midday dinner, but although Mariota flirted as much as she had earlier, he found the repetition childish and annoying rather than blood-stirring.

Isobel kept glancing at him with a wariness that told him she had been up to mischief again, and he found himself repressing a smile as he wondered what she had done. He thought the child more amusing than Mariota. She would never be as beautiful, but her conversation nearly always entertained him. Mariota had a lovely, feminine voice, and he enjoyed listening to her talk, just as he enjoyed flirting with her, but Isobel said things that made him think. She also reminded him of his more mischievous boyhood friends. He had always been ripe for adventure, but their father had more often than not declared such activities mischief or plain disobedience, so he and Lachlan had nearly always suffered for their "adventures."

Isobel turned her attention to Cristina, and following her gaze, he saw his wife give a slight shake of her head. Instantly the child relaxed, fixing her attention on her supper. So whatever she had done, Cristina knew about it and did not mean to tell him. The evening might grow interesting, he thought, although in the interest of pursuing his own plan, he might let Isobel keep her secret until morning.

Having learned that Cristina's woman had ordered a tub and hot water to her chamber after supper, he countermanded the order, telling the lads to carry the tub and water into his chamber instead. He would assist his lady wife with her bath.

Ordering claret with supper, he filled Cristina's goblet with the rich red wine. When she had taken a few sips, he signed to a gillie to refill it.

"Art trying to make me drunk, sir?"

"It seems a fair tactic to employ, considering our history," he said.

She wrinkled her nose at him. "On the contrary, it would be unfair, since I do not need to be ape-drunk to obey your wishes."

"We'll see," he said, grinning at her and wondering how she would react to finding her bathtub in his bedchamber. He felt an eagerness he had not felt since his earliest experiences with the fair sex, an anticipation of pleasure or pure fun. That he was experiencing such feelings with regard to a wife he still insisted he did not want struck him as odd, but not so odd that he intended to deny himself.

That sense of eager anticipation suffered a setback when a messenger arrived as they were finishing their meal. Recognizing the lad as one of Lachlan's from Duart, Hector took him aside at once, since most of Lachlan's messages were private ones. However, the message came not from his twin but from their father.

As he read Ian Dubh's brief, even curt command that he present himself forthwith to discuss a certain matter that had come to his attention, Hector's imagination carried him instantly back to his boyhood, when such commands were nearly always harbingers of most unpleasant, often painful interludes.

He sighed, realizing it would be nonsensical to sail to Duart and back just four days before he had meant to leave for Ardtornish. His plan had been to sail to Duart then and stay two or three days to discuss in detail Lachlan's plans for the arrival of Robert the Steward.

The Steward's safety was primary, of course. His journey to Ardtornish and his stay there had been a matter of concern from the day he announced his intention, and comments made during the Council of the Isles had made Lachlan suspect that certain clans who did not approve of Robert as heir to the throne might make difficulties during his visit. As Lord Admiral, he was determined that his grace's Shrove Tuesday celebration would involve no mischief, and thus he and Hector had decided to meet beforehand to discuss various ways to foil any enemy plots and, if still necessary, to dispose of the petrel-oil problem that seemed to have spread to several isles. Now it looked as if Hector would be arriving at Duart even earlier.

He would have to leave orders with his steward to have a longboat and oarsmen ready for the morning, and make arrangements for the lads to finish careening his other boats and for them and Cristina to follow him to Ardtornish in due course. But for now, he turned his thoughts to the evening ahead with his wife.

"Have you a moment to spare for me, sir?" Mariota asked, coming up to him with a charming smile and laying a graceful hand on his arm.

"Indeed, lass. What may I do for you?"

"You may entertain me," she said. "One thing my sister has sadly neglected at Lochbuie is evening entertainment for her guests. We've not seen a single player or heard a single minstrel. Surely, you do not treat all your guests so shabbily."

"Do you not have needlework or some other such thing to occupy you?"

She wrinkled her nose. "Oh, certainly, but such tasks by

themselves are boring, sir. I would much rather converse with you. We were meant to be married after all, and I find that I am desperately in love with you." She fluttered her lashes and leaned closer. A cloud of her musky perfume enveloped him.

"You must not say such things," he told her gently. "I am lawfully married to your sister and am therefore now your brother according to both the Kirk and the laws of Scotland. You should behave to me as you would to any other brother."

"But I have no brothers, and although I know you are married to Cristina, that is not my fault any more than my lack of brothers is, for all that my father once told me that had I been a son instead of another daughter, my mother might still be alive. They kept trying to get a son, you see, until it killed her."

"Sakes, what a thing to say to you!" he exclaimed, shocked by her matter-of-fact tone as much as by what Macleod had told her.

With a shrug, she said, "It was what he believes, that's all, but I do not wish to talk about that, because he did something much, much worse to us, he and Cristina. Were we both not victims of their foul plot?"

"We can do nothing about that now," he said, curbing growing impatience because he knew that she had been as upset by Macleod's trickery as he was.

"Well, but of course we can," she said indignantly. "Neither of us owes a thing to anyone else. Ireland is quite near the Isle of Mull, I'm told, so can we not just take one of your boats and go there? I know you mean to annul that stupid marriage to Cristina, because nearly everyone hereabouts knows that. Indeed, Isobel said that because of it, your cook rather insolently told Cristina he did not expect her to remain at Lochbuie longer than another sennight or so."

"My cook will soon learn the wisdom of civility," Hector promised grimly, realizing that that incident had probably figured among the events Cristina thought not important enough to complain of to him. "My life is here, Mariota, and I do not intend to leave Lochbuie or the Isle of Mull."

"Well, I own I shall find it more comfortable to stay here than to have to make a new life in Ireland. I'm told the Irish are not at all like we are, although the few I have met seemed ordinary enough," she added musingly. "But although being with Irishmen would not be as good as being with my own people, I'm sure they would like me once they came to know me."

"I'm sure they would," he said, trying to conceal his distaste for the conversation. "Nevertheless—"

"Oh, aye, it must be as you say," she said airily. "And if we must stay at Lochbuie, I expect we must bide our time until you can gain a proper annulment. Doubtless, Abbot Mackinnon will aid you with that. Indeed, had you not interrupted our ride this morning, I meant to ask him to do so for you."

Only her obvious naïveté kept him from losing his temper. Retaining rigid control, he said, "Mariota, do you not realize that the men who assaulted you and Isobel this morning were the Green Abbot's men? They were, I assure you. You must not try to make a friend of him whilst you are here. Indeed, I forbid you to have any contact with him at all. Do you understand me?"

"Oh, very well," she said. "Although you are wrong, you know. Fingon Mackinnon has been a particular friend of my father's and mine for years and years. He would never do me harm."

"You will obey me nonetheless, or by heaven, I'll send you home."

"Do you know that when you get angry, you get two straight little creases right between your eyebrows? They make you look very fierce, but as the years pass, they may engrave permanent marks there, which I will not like so much."

"Mariota!"

She squeezed his arm and smiled brilliantly at him. "Oh, don't be cross with me, sir. I shan't do anything you do not like. Did I not just tell you that I have fallen quite madly in love with you?"

"Aye, you did say that," he said with a smile, finding himself unable to withstand her smile. Nevertheless, as he went to give his orders to his steward before meeting Cristina upstairs, he found himself breathing a deep sigh of relief. At least, Cristina would not enact any dramatics for him.

❦

Still feeling tipsy from the wine at dinner, Cristina faced her maidservant in dismay. "What do you mean they will not bring my tub in here?"

Brona looked wretched. "'Tis that sorry I am, m'lady, but the lads did say the laird ordered them t' carry the tub and hot water t' his bedchamber. He said, too," she added with a blush, "that he'd take pleasure in aiding ye wi' your bath."

"Oh, he did, did he?"

"Aye." Brona's voice was small. "I couldna make them bring it in here."

"No, of course you could not," Cristina agreed. Even she

could not countermand Hector's order. "Help me remove my caul, will you?"

"Aye, mistress, straightaway."

Cristina sat in bodice and shift on the stool near her looking glass and tried to relax as the woman began to pull the pins out and free her hair.

"Shall I brush it, m'lady?"

"No, thank you. Just twist it into a knot atop my head, and pin it so it will stay up whilst I bathe. Then you may fetch my blue robe for me."

"Will I help ye off wi' your bodice and shift then?"

"I'll keep my shift on for now," Cristina said, knowing she would feel too vulnerable walking across the landing and into the wretched man's room with nothing on but a thin robe. She felt less so in her shift, although not by much.

After Brona had brought her robe and helped her slip it on, Cristina drew a deep breath, took her brush in hand, and stepped out onto the landing that separated her bedchamber from Hector's.

His chamber door stood a few inches ajar.

Pushing gently on it, hoping to find the room empty, she jumped when she caught movement ahead of her, and then relaxed when she heard a splash and saw one of the gillies pouring a pail of hot water into the tub. The tub was nearly full, the water hot enough to send curls of steam into the air.

The lad smiled at her. "Be this tub full enough for ye, m'lady?"

"Aye, thank you," Cristina said.

"That pail alongside be cold water an ye need t' cool the water some," the boy said. "Shall I fetch ye more hot water t' keep near?"

"Nay, for I mean to be quick," she said. "You may leave now, and I'll just bar the door behind you."

The voice she least wanted to hear just then said with a chuckle from the landing, "Nay, lass, you will not bar the door. No one would be so rude as to walk into my chamber without rapping first and gaining permission. 'Tis the very reason I thought you'd enjoy your bath more in here," he added as he stepped into the room. He was grinning.

Grimacing, she said, "I wonder how it is that I never noticed before now how devilish your smile is."

The gillie chuckled as he slipped past his master out of the room, and Hector shut the door firmly behind him.

Cristina said ruefully, "Doubtless, the entire castle will be made a gift now of his version of what just occurred in here."

"Nay, lass," he said as he moved nearer, looming over her and making her more conscious than ever of their sadly unequal sizes. He reached out to tuck an errant strand of her hair up into her topknot as he added, "My lads know better than to repeat aught they hear or see of my private affairs, unlike my thickheaded cook."

Feeling flames in her cheeks, Cristina said awkwardly, "Your cook?"

"You should have told me," he said, tucking a finger under her chin and tilting it up so that she had to look him in the eye. "I should not have to learn of my cook's impertinence from Mariota by way of Isobel. God only knows how much truth was in Mariota's version, though, so before I deal with him, I want to hear the tale from your own lips. Now."

"It was nothing," she said, wishing her voice were stronger, firmer, and that he would take his finger away. When he had touched her hair, he had sent shivers all through her, delicious ones. And now, with but one finger touching her chin, he was causing waves of heat to flow through her body, stirring feelings where she had never known such feelings before.

She could not think. "I pray you, sir," she said, "do not punish him for his impertinence. I reprimanded him, and he apologized. When he did so, I made it clear that his apology was sufficient to mend matters. If you punish him now, he will think I asked you to do so because I need the reinforcement of your authority to manage this household properly. That would undermine my own authority."

He did not reply at once, but his finger released her chin. She could scarcely breathe for wondering if he would touch her again, and if so, where?

He rested that hand on her shoulder and reached with the other one to take her brush from her and toss it onto his bed. Then he rested that hand on her other shoulder and looked deeply into her eyes. She gazed steadily back at him.

"Very well," he said. "I will not make a point of punishing him, as I had certainly intended to do. Is it true, though, that he told you that he did not need to obey you because our marriage would soon be annulled?"

"Aye, more or less. I was afraid at the time that Isobel had heard everything, but you say it was Mariota who told you?"

"Isobel told her, she said."

"Then I'm thinking it must be all over the Isle of Mull by now."

Instead of denying it, he looked thoughtful again.

She watched him warily, and meeting that look, he smiled apologetically and said, "You may well be right, lass. In any event, I begin to believe that getting our marriage annulled may not be the simple matter I once thought it would be."

She looked down, but that finger came at once to her chin

again. As her gaze met his, she said, "I'm sorry, sir. I don't know what more I can say."

"You have already said too much," he said. "We will deal with whatever comes, because we cannot undo what has already been done. I can, however, help you take off this robe, and I think I should do so as speedily as possible, lest the water in your tub turn ice-cold."

As he reached to untie her robe, the back of his hand brushed her belly and the shivers began again, but she did not feel chilled. Instead, her body tingled, and she found she was not at all fearful but only curious to see what would happen next.

Chapter 12 ————————

Her robe felt astonishingly soft in Hector's hands as he gently eased it open and gazed appreciatively at her full, plump breasts beneath the thin cambric material of her low-cut shift. Why, he wondered, did he not remember those beauties from their wedding night? Why in the name of all that was holy had he taken so long to gaze upon their bounty again?

The firelight set shadows dancing on nearby walls, but the light outside had gone, and the lad had lighted only two of the wall cressets. They would want more light soon, to see while she bathed, but candles could wait a few moments longer.

He wanted to unpin her hair and see how long it was. He could not remember that either. Indeed, he mused, for a man of his experience not to recall a thing about his wedding night seemed an abomination, especially since he believed he had married the homely sister rather than the beauty. He should remember astonishment if nothing else, for as any idiot could see, Cristina was anything but homely. Only by comparison with the glorious Mariota could one think such a thing for even a moment.

He knew that if she was going to get her bath, he dared not touch her with intent or purpose, but her very gentleness and calm enticed him. Deciding he could control himself, he took his time easing her robe from her body until she stood in just the thin shift that covered her from her breasts to below her knees, and the flimsy silk slippers she had worn to supper. Casting the robe aside, he untied the blue silk bow at the top of the shift's lacing and, using both hands, spread the opening wide. Only then did he let his fingers caress the pillow-soft, silken skin of her breasts.

He heard her breath catch in her throat, and the sound stirred a sharp response in his body.

"Faith, lass, art sure you want a bath?"

"I'm sure," she said, a note of laughter in her voice. "If you had let me bathe in my own chamber, sir, I warrant I would be finished by now."

"I wanted to see you," he said, attempting to push the shift off her shoulders and down her body. "Sakes, I want to see you now!"

"It comes off more easily over my head," she said demurely.

He needed no further invitation, whisking the shift off, then standing silently to gaze at her as she stood motionless before him.

The firelight turned her skin golden and set highlights dancing in the curls piled atop her head. He reached out to touch one breast but drew back his hand with a grin, watching her watch his hand, knowing he was teasing her and that her body yearned for his touch. His own body stirred then, reminding him that she was by no means the only one eager for pleasuring.

With a near groan, he caught hold of her with both hands, drawing her close, wrapping his arms around her and holding her the way he had wanted to hold her earlier. "I hope you no longer feel like weeping," he murmured into her curls.

"No, sir, but the water is growing cold."

"So you would rather bathe than learn ways to please your husband, would you?" he said.

"I thought my bathing in here was meant to please you."

"And so it is," he announced, ignoring her shriek as he scooped her into his arms and turned toward the bath.

"For pity's sake, sir, test the water first. It still shoots steam into the air."

"You test it," he said, dipping her bare backside near enough to sense the water's warmth. "Kick off your slippers, lass, unless you want them washed, too."

She pushed them off at once with her toes and dipped her hand into the water. "It is still warm and not too warm," she said. "But I forgot my soap."

"I have soap," he said. "Fancy French soap that smells of lavender."

"Do you indeed? And do you bathe ladies often in your chamber?"

"Nay, lass, but a man likes to be prepared." With that, he plopped her into the tub, splashing himself in the process. "Now see what you've done," he said.

"Aye, your shirt and doublet are wet, so you had better take them off. And don't forget the soap," she reminded him as he began to unfasten his doublet.

"I won't," he promised. "Although if you get saucy, I may let you chew on it rather than wash with it."

She chuckled, slipping lower in the water and leaning against the high back of the tub. In the firelight, her wet breasts gleamed, tantalizing him.

He yanked off his doublet and shirt without thought of

any damage he might do them by treating them so cava-
lierly, snatched up the soap from the washstand where he
had put it earlier, and strode back to kneel beside the tub.
"Now," he said, "where shall I begin?"

◦◦◦

Realizing that for once it did not matter a whit to him
that he had married the wrong Macleod sister, Cristina decided to enjoy her bath and his company, since common
sense warned her that such an evening might never come
again.

His hands hovered above the tub, one holding the soap
near her breasts, the other near the foot of the tub, but she
said, "I can soap myself, sir. I'm sure it would make the
bath go faster."

"Ah, but I've decided that I do not want it to go faster,
because you deserve a little special treatment, I think, after
your long, wearisome day. You also deserve just a little
punishment for keeping secrets from your lord and master,"
he added, touching the soap lightly to her right breast. "Sit
up a bit more if you please. I cannot wash them properly
whilst they are submerged."

Her body tingled everywhere, and her breasts seemed to
swell, their nipples leaping to attention. As she obeyed his
command, slowly sitting straighter in the tub, her body
fairly hummed in anticipation of what he might do next.

"Don't nibble that lip," he warned her. "I mean to taste
it myself later, and I shan't be happy if you shred it before
then."

Surprised, for she had not realized that she was chewing
her lip again, she stopped, and when he chuckled, she
looked up at him.

He kissed her lips lightly. "Just a taste," he said as he pulled back again.

She nearly protested, but before she could do so, he rubbed the soap across the nipple of her right breast. Then, lathering his two hands, he handed the soap to her and said, "Hold this now, and don't let it fall into the water. It's damned expensive stuff." As she held it obediently above the water, he said, "Hold it with both hands, lass. If you drop it, I'll be most displeased."

Holding it away from the water with both hands, she was helpless to protect herself as his soapy hands roamed freely over her breasts and arms, and then lower, where they were soapy no longer, to caress other parts of her body at will. When one intruded between her legs, tickling the curls at the juncture of her thighs, and a finger darted into the opening there, she nearly came up out of the tub, but he pressed her back with his other hand, saying gently, "Not yet, lassie, not yet."

Her body felt as if the fire had leaped from the fireplace into the tub and had invaded her. Her breasts tingled so much they ached, and she wanted him to hold her so that she could press herself against him. Never had she had such thoughts before, but they seemed natural now.

He seemed to have forgotten about the soap, as his hands made free with her body. One had settled between her legs as if it meant to stay there, while the other cupped and caressed her breasts until she began to fear she would go mad.

As he slowly trickled water over one breast, rinsing soap from it, she said, "Please, sir, I would . . ." But she finished the sentence with a moan as he lowered his head and took the nipple into his mouth, sucking hard on it, and nibbling it gently with his teeth, sending waves of pleasure throughout her body and making her moan louder.

Shifting his attention to the other breast, he sucked long and hard there, too, and she continued to hold the bar of soap, forgotten now as her attention focused on his lips, tongue, and teeth, and the wondrous sensations they created.

"Stand up, lassie," he said at last, his voice a near groan.

Thinking that he meant to let her out of the bath at last, she obeyed at once. Handing him the soap when he asked her for it, she began to step out of the tub.

"Nay, nay, we're far from finished," he said. "Stand still now, whilst I finish soaping you."

"I'll freeze."

"I promise you won't," he said, and proceeded to prove his point by drawing the soap over her breasts and belly to the fork of her legs and between them, then down over her thighs and knees and up the back of first one leg and then the other to her bottom and the cleft between its cheeks. His fingers tickled her there, too, and she gave a cry of passion mixed with dismay.

"Be still now, or I'll have to exact a penance," he warned.

To her shock, she found herself wondering if the penance might be as delightful as everything else had been.

⊂⊇⊃

Hector was thoroughly enjoying himself, but he knew his body would betray him soon if he did not speed things up. The mere motion of passing the soap over her body, of caressing her skin and hearing her moans, was stirring him in ways he could not remember any woman stirring him before. Teasing her was pure delight.

He had expected her to be timid, because her experience

was small, but instead she seemed eager for his touch and fascinated by the sensations erupting in her body. Her reactions stirred him to try new things just to see what she would do.

But his own time was swiftly coming, and he did not want to spend himself before he had even got her into bed. So at last, he dropped the soap onto a nearby stool and reached for the pail beside it.

"Not that one," she exclaimed. "That's cold water!"

He put a finger into it. "So it is," he said. "Let me see now, how much penance do you deserve to pay?"

"You'd better not," she warned.

"Stand quietly, lass. Remember, I am still your lord." He grinned at her and then got to his feet and went to fetch the ewer from the washstand. "You should have asked the lads to fetch a pail of hot water for rinsing, but I suppose this will have to do," he said as he scooped soapy water into it from the tub and poured it over her from her shoulders to rinse her off. A few moments later, he reached for the towel from the washstand and wrapped her in it.

"I haven't told you to go anywhere yet," he said as she stepped out of the tub. "You must be properly dried first, so stand here by the fire."

He took the same care drying her that he had taken soaping her, and enjoyed it nearly as much, but his body was not accommodating his desire to linger over such simple pleasures, and was demanding instead that he get on with the main business of the night. Accordingly, he soon cast the towel aside and carried her to the bed, laying her atop it and moving to deal with the rest of his clothing.

When he had taken off his breeks, hose, and shoes, he saw that she had pulled back the coverlet and slipped beneath it. He took time only to light a few more candles before joining her there.

He was so big, she thought, bigger lying next to her than she remembered. How could anyone as small as she was ever satisfy such a man? Not that Mariota was much more than a couple of inches taller and a few pounds heavier. But she would not think of Mariota tonight. She had promised herself she would not.

He reached for her and drew her closer. His hands felt rough against her skin, and his cheek against hers was rough, too, with the beginnings of a beard. But she forgot the roughness when he rose on one elbow, leaned close, and kissed her hard on the lips. His forearm slipped beneath her, and his lips eased their pressure as his kisses grew softer and more teasing. Then his lips parted, and his tongue touched her lips, pressing itself between them into her mouth. It seemed odd for him to kiss her so, but she did not mind in the least and moved her tongue to meet his, tasting it. It seemed to fill her mouth, but she did not mind that either.

His free hand moved to cup her left breast, and his thumb teased the nipple, bringing it to aching attention again. She wanted him to kiss it again, to suckle it as he had before, as a bairn would. The thought made her smile.

"What?" he murmured against her lips.

"I was just thinking that you are too big to count as a bairn," she said. Then, realizing that she must sound daft, she smiled again, but he shifted as she did and captured her nipple between his teeth, his tongue teasing it as his thumb had done before, but warmer, softer, more stimulating. That he had apparently understood her cryptic remark made her feel warm in a different way, and she tugged on his ear until he raised his head and looked at her. Then she kissed him on the lips and pressed her tongue hard between them as he had done to her.

With a groan, he pulled her tight against him, kissing her possessively. His hands began to play with abandon up and down her body until she moaned and wanted to cry out. But then one moved between her legs, opening her to him, and then it was no longer his hand but another part of him that pressed for entrance.

"Faith, but you are too large," she exclaimed against his lips. "Take care!"

"Don't be foolish," he said gently, though she could hear amusement in his voice. "'Tis naught we have not done before."

"But—" The protest ended in a gasp as his mouth claimed hers again and he plunged into her, filling her as she had not known that one body could fill another. The ache was nearly unbearable, making her want to cry, and she felt tears trickling down her cheeks.

"Oh, please, sir," she begged, barely able to get out the words when at last his mouth released hers.

⸎

Hearing her moans and her plea, Hector felt a surge of pleasure, believing that her passion matched his own. The way she had squirmed under his soapy hands earlier was as nothing to her writhing now, and his body seemed to have gone mad with the passion she stirred in him. As if it had taken on a mind of its own, it plunged into her harder and harder until it spent itself at last, and with a gasp of release, he collapsed atop her, breathing hard.

"Sorry, lass," he murmured as he eased some of his weight off her. "That was magnificent! Left me limp as a rope though, so I hope I've not suffocated you."

She did not reply, and at last, he raised himself up and peered carefully into her face, astonished to see tearstains. "Cristina? Sakes, did I hurt you, lass?"

"I think so," she said, sounding a little breathless still. "I did not know, you see, did not imagine what you were doing. I mean I do know about such things, but obviously not as much as I should."

Frowning now, he eased out of her and rolled aside, pushing back the coverlet as he did.

"Sakes," he exclaimed, staring at the crimson stains on her lower body and his own in stunned amazement, "you were still a maiden!"

"Aye, of course," she said.

"But you said we had lain together as man and wife!"

Eyes widening with evident bewilderment, she said, "We did."

"Not if you are still a maiden, we didn't," he retorted. "You lied to me!"

"I don't lie," she said. "We were married, sir. How could we lie together *except* as man and wife?"

⬿⬾

The ache between her legs was easing, but his angry expression caused a greater ache in her heart. The evening had been going so well. She had been enjoying herself more than at any other time since leaving Chalamine for Lochbuie. Indeed, she could not remember a more pleasant occasion, right up to the moment he had unexpectedly plunged into her. She realized now that she ought to have expected some such thing, for she knew how animals mated and had suspected that humans did something similar. But that was one of the many things her mother had failed to explain before her death, and Lady Euphemia, being a maiden herself, had never thought to explain it either, if she knew.

It had not occurred to her that the phrase "lying together as husband and wife" might mean more than a couple's sleeping in the same bed after they married. That it did mean more was certainly clear now.

"I didn't know," she said as he sat up and swung his legs to the side of the bed. "Does it matter so much?"

"Aye, well, it matters enough," he said, his voice a near growl that sent a new sort of shiver up her spine. "Had I known when I woke up that fatal morning, I could simply have handed you back to your father and demanded an annulment on the spot. Since we had not yet consummated our marriage, I should easily have acquired one, and you need never have come to Lochbuie."

His anger seemed to cool as he spoke, and she was glad. In truth, she was also glad that she had not known the details of consummation before that night, especially if knowing would have kept her from coming to Lochbuie. "I'm sorry I've angered you," she said. "I just didn't know. No one ever told me."

"I'd like to believe you," he said, adding with a sigh, "Sakes, lass, I do believe you, for other than your part in our wedding in submission to your father's will, you have never given me cause to believe you have lied to me or that you would. Still, I must think on this. I cannot take you with me tomorrow, but I'd meant—"

"Tomorrow?"

"Aye," he said. "The message I received after supper came from Duart, from my father—a command to present myself at once. That he's unwilling to wait even four days until I go to talk with Lachlan before we go on to Ardtornish leads me to believe that he has heard rumors from Lochbuie that displease him."

"About wanting an annulment?"

"I don't know that. It could as well be the assault on your sisters, for a belief that I had failed to protect my guests would certainly displease him. I'll know what it is only when I speak with him, but if it has thrown him into a temper, I'm guessing I'll not enjoy the conversation. I was thinking I might take you with me in the hope that your presence might soothe him. Now, however—"

"Faith, sir, I could not be ready to go tomorrow in any event," she said. "I still have things I must do to prepare for the court at Ardtornish, and what of my sisters? My aunt? And what of the guests you invited here to Finlaggan?"

"None of that matters now," he said grimly. "No guest will trouble you if I am not here, and I mean to go to Duart alone. As for Ardtornish, I think it will be easier if I go there alone, too. If rumors are flying about, as they seem to be, I'd as lief we not provide grist for new ones. Nor will I want to leave you alone there if Lachlan has other duties for me. Someone has to lead the flotilla that goes to fetch the Steward. I think Lachlan will go, but he may send me."

"Do you mean to leave me here then, and not let me take part at all?"

"Aye, at least until I decide what course I mean to take—about us."

Disappointment, and fear of what his course would likely be, brought tears to her eyes, but she blinked them away, trying to think. He had apparently been willing to forgive her for her part in the horrid wedding, and even to share his bed. Then, upon discovering that she was still a maiden, he had grown angry again, had apparently felt betrayed all over again. And, fair or not, it was all her fault, again.

So why did she feel so angry, and why did his decision to leave her at Lochbuie seem so unfair? Why did she want to rail at him and call him names, to fly into a rage as loud and violent as any Mariota had ever created?

Her fingers curled when he stood up. "Where are you going?" she asked.

"I don't know. I must think."

"Then think in here, my lord. It is your bed, after all, not mine." Gathering her dignity, she slipped past him out of the bed, picked up her robe from the stool over which he had cast it, donned it hastily, and left the room.

She paused on the stone landing, hoping he would come after her. When he did not, she pushed open her bedchamber door. By the time she had shut it behind her, tears flowed freely down her cheeks, but she recalled that her thighs were bloody, and she did not want Brona to find her so in the morning.

By the time she had cleaned herself and climbed into bed, she had regained most of her composure, but her thoughts still refused to order themselves. Although she told herself she was only disappointed that he would not take her to Ardtornish to meet Robert the Steward and enjoy the Shrove Tuesday festivities, she knew that the deeper sadness she felt derived from more than that.

She had begun to hope that he would not send her back to her father.

Having raised her to the greatest height of pleasure and delight that she had ever known, he had dropped her from that height to crash on the rocks of her own creation. Just as she had begun to believe he might decide to keep her as his wife, Fate had intervened again to smash her hopes to splinters.

"Will I never learn?" she muttered. "I'd be wiser not to care at all about anyone, because the people I love most always seem to slip away just as I realize how much they matter to me."

It was too late where Hector was concerned though. Despite the short time they had been married, she had moved beyond thinking of him as merely a kind and charming man. She knew now that he could be as cruel as his nickname suggested—thoughtless, irritable, and impatient—but none of that mattered, because she was swiftly coming to suspect that she had fallen in love with the wretched man.

Hector had watched with an ache in his throat as Cristina left his room. He wanted to leap after her, to stand between her and the door and forbid her to leave. But believing the urge stemmed from no more than childish anger and frustration, he had successfully resisted it.

He told himself that she had now twice betrayed him, that he had no sooner forgiven her for the first time than she had betrayed him again. Nay, it was worse, because he had forgiven her for the one without even knowing about the other.

How could anyone blame him for his fury? Kirk law was clear enough on the subject. If a couple failed to consummate their marriage, annulment was no more than a formality. If consummated, it became more difficult, requiring powerful connections and considerable money. Had he known himself eligible to apply on the strongest grounds, he would have done so at once. He might have had to go outside the Isles, since the Green Abbot was the only cleric within them wielding sufficient power to grant a simple annulment, but Clan Gillean had powerful friends in Stirling and Edinburgh, and in Paris if need be.

However, in the case of a consummated marriage, only the Pope could grant an annulment, and their marriage was certainly a consummated one now.

The twin voice in the back of his head muttered that he was no worse off than he had been, since he now stood in exactly the same situation as he had before, but he did not want to hear it. He did not feel as if he were no worse off.

The twin voice murmured again, reminding him that had all gone as he believed it should have, he would now be married to Mariota.

Oddly, that thought steadied him as none before it had.

Instinct and common sense told him that marriage to Mariota would not have been what he had dreamed it would be. Recalling that he had thought he would enjoy gazing on her beauty for the rest of his life, he called himself a brainless fool. The lass never had a thought in her head that did not concern herself. She was childish, disobedient, and annoying in her chatter. But knowing he was well out of that marriage did not reconcile him to the one Macleod had forced upon him.

As he got back into bed, knowing he must sleep if he was to hold his own against Ian Dubh, he decided that one thing was certain. For once in his life, he was going to make his own decisions and follow his own course. He was not going to do what Lachlan would do. Nor was he merely going to bow to his father's decree if, as he suspected, Ian

Dubh meant to dip an oar into his personal affairs. His marriage was a sham, but it was *his* marriage, and only he would decide what to do about it.

Accordingly, the next morning, after a nearly sleepless night in a bed that seemed strangely uncomfortable, he left Lochbuie before sunrise without a word of farewell to anyone other than his steward, boarded his lead longboat, shorn overnight of its barnacles and manned by thirty oarsmen, and set out for Duart. He told himself that leaving in such a way was a kindness to Cristina, because she could tell her sisters and her aunt whatever she thought it best to tell them.

His sense of having managed things as well as possible increased with the sun's appearance in a cloudless sky of cerulean blue. The tide was coming in, giving the oarsmen all the aid they needed for a speedy journey, and well before midday they were gliding oars up to beach on the shingle below Duart Castle.

Noting that his twin's favorite longboat was not at its usual mooring in the little harbor, Hector felt the first hint of unease. He had counted on Lachlan's support in whatever confrontation he faced with Ian Dubh.

Leaving his captain to see to the housing of the men with the castle steward, and his manservant to see his personal effects conveyed to the chamber he occupied during his visits, Hector strode off ahead of the others, climbing the hill to the castle entrance on the north side of the curtain wall.

The great timber door opened as he approached, and his brother's porter welcomed him, adding, "Himself be waiting for ye, sir."

"In the hall?"

"Nay, sir, in my lord's chamber."

Duart boasted a small inner chamber that his twin used

as a place of business, where he met his informants and conferred with friends and allies of MacDonald of the Isles. Since MacDonald had doubtless already removed from Finlaggan to Ardtornish, Hector suspected that Lachlan had gone there as well, but since Hector had told him he would stop at Duart, he found it odd that even Mairi was absent. Had she been there, she would have come seeking him the moment the first guardsman on the ramparts spied his banner and shouted the news, but he saw no sign of her as he made his way through the great hall to the inner chamber.

He entered without ceremony to find Ian Dubh at Lachlan's great table, a pile of documents and other such paraphernalia spread before him. He was writing on a sheet of foolscap, but he looked up when Hector entered.

"You made better time than I anticipated," he said.

"Your message indicated that I'd be unwise to tarry."

"Indeed, but wisdom does not seem to be your guiding precept these days, so perhaps it is not odd that I did not expect you to come with all speed."

"Where is Lachlan?"

"Ardtornish, or mayhap elsewhere," Ian Dubh said. "Boats for his flotilla have been arriving daily in Loch Aline, and that business of the petrel oil has grown unseemly again. His grace sent here to ask him to look into it, because apparently a few mischief-makers have begun spreading the trouble to other isles."

"Mischief-makers?"

"Aye, but Lachlan will attend to them, and to the boats, so they need not trouble us now. I thought we should have a private talk about your activities."

"Where is Mairi?"

"I asked her to let me speak to you alone. She is in her

parlor and will doubtless be overjoyed to see you when you present yourself to her later."

The atmosphere in the room chilled as Hector met his father's stern gaze, and Ian Dubh let the silence lengthen before he said crisply, "You will abandon this notion of an annulment at once. I won't have scandal, and since you got yourself into this marriage, you will make the most of it or suffer my extreme displeasure."

Chapter 13 ———————

Hector gazed steadily back at his angry father, striving to give no indication of his feelings. Indeed, those feelings, as near the surface as they were, were unfamiliar to him, except the one that made him feel twelve years old again, facing punishment for some misdeed or other.

Those misdeeds, now that he came to think of it, had usually been committed at Lachlan's instigation and the punishments usually shared. This time he was on his own, just as he had told himself he wanted to be.

He considered reminding Ian Dubh that the problem had resulted from Macleod's chicanery, not his own, but he dismissed the thought as soon as it stirred. He had made his own choices. Had he not forced the issue at the outset, he would not have married Cristina, so in truth, he could blame no one but himself.

"Have you nothing to say for yourself?" Ian Dubh demanded.

"No, sir," Hector said.

"Then you will set aside this notion of seeking an annulment."

Oddly, the idea of spending the years ahead married to

Cristina did not disturb him as much as it had, but the thought of submitting tamely to such a decree did. Perhaps it was that Lachlan's words, then Ian Dubh's, reminded him that the decision did not lie wholly with him, because he owed them both his obedience.

The reminder did not work. He simply could not knuckle under this time. He would make his own decision in this matter if no other.

With a slight smile, he said, "I have not yet decided exactly what I will do, sir, but I will certainly ponder your concerns, and Lachlan's."

"If annulment was appropriate, lad, you should have said so at once and not after you'd consummated the marriage. 'Twould be no better than rape to gain an annulment after taking advantage of the lass."

Stunned at the course his father's thoughts had taken, Hector opened his mouth to tell him they had not lain together until the previous night, but he shut it again without saying a word. He believed that Cristina had misunderstood the matter just as she said she had, and he would not have anyone accusing her of a greater part in the conspiracy than she had played. That tale would remain strictly between them. Still, if his father opposed the very notion of annulment, and Lachlan did as well, any chance of successfully applying to Rome would be small.

He could tell the Pope the truth, that this wife had mistakenly made him think they had consummated the union on their wedding night, but to do so would be to appear a great fool, and it would embarrass Cristina. He found that thought as distasteful to him as the thought that others might come to view her as pitiable, a woman who had lost her maidenhood and whose husband had then cast her off.

"I must tell you," Ian Dubh said, "I had little interest in

your marriage to a younger daughter, but this with the elder is not without merit. She will doubtless bring a decent tocher, and Macleod will find himself in sad straits if he refuses to pay it. I have told Lachlan that I would have him speak to Macleod about that."

Hector had not thought of a tocher for Cristina, but it was customary for a father to provide one for any daughter that married, and one from a man with Macleod's wealth and standing should be considerable. But he did not care about that. He wanted nothing from Macleod.

Still, acquiring a tocher would give Ian Dubh something else to think about.

"Is there aught else that you want to discuss with me, sir?" he asked.

"You are mighty reticent, my lad."

"I have not been disrespectful, Father, nor disobedient. But I would lead my own life, and with respect, sir, I will decide what is best for me and for my wife."

"Where is she?"

"At Lochbuie."

"I cannot think why you did not bring her with you," Ian Dubh said. "You still have not properly presented her to me as you should."

"Again, with respect, sir, I invited you to my wedding, where you might easily have met her. You elected not to attend."

"True, but I have been busy with these documents. I told you, did I not, that they pertain to events that occurred whilst Bruce was attempting to unite Scotland?"

"Aye, you did."

"One of them apparently pertains to financial or military aid promised him by someone fleeing from King Philip of France—the fourth one, that would be."

"Indeed, sir. Very intriguing, to be sure. Did you say that Mairi is somewhere about? I do want to pay my respects."

"Aye, you should. She will be pleased to see you and will doubtless scold you for not bringing your Cristina with you. She would have liked to see her."

"Does Lachlan return in time to sail with us to Ardtornish?"

"Nay, he will sail into Loch Aline and go straight to confer with his grace. He would have you join them there as soon as you can. Mairi says she will go to Ardtornish for the festivities but prefers to remain here with the bairns until then."

"And you, sir, do you go to Ardtornish to pay your respects to the Steward?"

"Perhaps," Ian Dubh said vaguely, his attention already drifting back to the documents on the table before him. "I believe he is a good choice to succeed David, but only because he will not stir passions on either side. The whole country can benefit from a few peaceful years, I'm thinking—if he does actually take the throne, that is. Things do not always progress as one expects, although the mendicant friars do say that David has been ailing of late. Still, there are those who hope not to follow the Bruce's will."

"You refer to clans that do not support the Steward?"

"Aye, who else? Some of them are most warlike in their dissatisfaction, I'm told. The Mackinnons, certainly, even your Macleod and his ilk."

"The Mackinnons seem to find joy in mischief," Hector said. "But Macleod told me that he has no real objection to Robert, that he would merely prefer someone of more ancient lineage. Moreover, Robert has acted ably as steward of the realm. Why would anyone fear he'd be a bad king?"

"Faith, lad, they don't fear him. They think themselves

superior to him. Surely, you understand that. Mackinnons and many others have been on this earth a far longer time than the upstart Steward has. Even Clan Gillean, for all that many call us babes, can document our history further back than the Steward. He derives his primarily from his grand-sire's position with the MacDonald of his time, and from his own maternal kinship with the Bruce's sister. Historically, the man is a fledgling. 'Tis no wonder that clans with thousand-year histories dislike him."

Hector could not disagree. He barely knew Robert the Steward, but what he did know did not encourage him to think the man would make a great king of Scots. Robert had been an able administrator in his younger days, but his greatest achievement was the production of innumerable sons and daughters, legitimate and not, whom he had married into most of the great clans.

Because of those connections, Hector doubted that Robert would encounter too much opposition when the time came to take the throne. Few would attempt to displace a man with whom they felt familial connection. The Macleods might rant about the unfairness of Parliament's overlooking their ancient heritage, but Hector doubted that they would actively oppose him. The Mackinnons, on the other hand, could prove dangerous. And if mischief was brewing over petrel oil, he would not be surprised to learn that they had at least a finger in that as well.

He would have to mention the possibility to Lachlan. He would not put it past Fingon Mackinnon to be making mis-chief there merely to divert the attention of the Admiral of the Isles from affairs closer to home.

All in all, he thought, as he left Ian Dubh with his docu-ments, the meeting had gone well. As often happened, an-ticipation had been worse than reality. He was a grown man now, after all, no longer a lad to tremble at the thought of displeasing him. Yet his father's generally soft-spoken displeasure had always been enough in the past to make him quake in his boots. In truth, he had frequently been answering for both Lachlan and himself, because as he recalled now, his wily brother had all too often managed to avoid such confrontations altogether.

He went in search of Mairi and his naughty nephews, seeking entertainment of a lighter nature, but found his sister-in-law alone in her parlor.

"Sit down, sir, if you are still able to," she said with a sympathetic smile.

He grimaced. "I'm a wee bit old for flogging, lass, but he is unhappy with me, not least because I've not yet arranged for him to meet my wife."

"That must be nonsense, because he met Cristina right here at Duart."

"The devil you say!"

"Surely he did not say he had not yet met her."

He thought back to that part of their conversation. "Nay, he said only that I had not yet properly presented her to him, and when I reminded him that I had invited him to the wedding, he changed the subject to his precious documents."

She grinned. "I think he likes her."

"I should have guessed that he'd met her, simply by the fact that he seems to approve of her."

"Aye, well he disapproves of annulment, I know. Lachlan does, too."

Hector sighed, and when his nephews chose that moment to fling open the door and dash into the room, he greeted their noisy welcome with unmixed relief.

"Cristina, Soot is missing! I cannot find her anywhere," Isobel exclaimed, rushing up to Cristina as she was taking inventory of the castle linens. She had already listed everything in the cellars and storage kists.

"Kittens often disappear, but I'm sure she'll pop up when she gets hungry," Cristina said. "Help me fold this sheet. Then perhaps you will be kind enough to carry it up to my tower chamber for me. I want to mend that tattered hem."

"You have scarcely sat still since Hector left," Isobel said as she took one end of the sheet and gave it a shake as she moved away from Cristina. "Even Mariota has noticed that you seem never to light anywhere long enough to talk."

"He has been gone only two days," Cristina said with a smile. "Moreover, it takes many hands to make a household run smoothly, and I warrant you will not suggest that Mariota has been much help."

"No, for she does not think they are her responsibility. I like to help though, and I'll be glad to take this sheet up for you. I could mend it for you as well, if you like." When Cristina hesitated, Isobel added indignantly, "You won't say you cannot trust me to do so. You know I can stitch every bit as finely as you do."

"I know, love. You set a very pretty seam, and even your embroidery is above reproach. I expect it is just a matter of wanting to see to things myself."

"More likely, it is a matter of not wanting to depend on anyone else," Isobel said roundly. "You never have."

"Oh, not 'never,' surely!"

"Well, in my experience, you rarely can bring yourself to ask anyone for help, so I suppose it is a good sign that you will let me take this thing to your tower chamber," Isobel said with the air of wisdom she wore so lightly. "I did not think you would allow me to go there. It has become your private retreat, after all."

Cristina shook her head. "You shame me, my love. I do not want you to feel as if you cannot enter a chamber of mine, any chamber, nor do I want you to think I don't trust you, for I do. If you like, you may mend that sheet. Indeed, I must have quite a pile of mending by now, and I will gladly welcome your help with it."

"Excellent," Isobel said, grinning. "I make progress. Perhaps I can now trick Mariota into offering to help, too. Aunt will, certainly."

"Aye, she will," Cristina said, "but I think we will ask one of the gillies to carry the basket down to the parlor for us. It will be more comfortable there for the four of us than my wee tower chamber."

Isobel did not argue that point, and Cristina was grateful. She did not want her sanctuary invaded. She would not mind spending time there quietly with Isobel, and the kittens often shared it with her, but the thought of Lady Euphemia talking nonstop or Mariota complaining to her there made her wince.

She finished the inventory and took the stairway to the landing between her bedchamber and Hector's, thinking about how quiet the castle was without him and how much she noticed his absence. Memories of the night before his departure ambushed her thoughts if she did not fill her mind with household chores, so she kept as busy as she knew how to be. She did not want to think about that night, or how stupid she had been, or how she had inadvertently tricked him again.

He had said he believed her, and perhaps he did, but how could he not believe that she had witlessly betrayed him again nonetheless? How could she have been so stupid? She had not even questioned Macleod about what he had meant when he threatened to stay and see that she did lie with Hector as his wife. She had simply assumed he meant that she had to sleep with the man.

Since then, she had wanted to please Hector, to make him glad he had married her and not Mariota, but she had known she could not simply seek his approval; nor could she now. She could be no more than what she was, and he plainly wanted a wifc whose beauty would stun everyone who looked at her.

That woman she could never be, and now that others knew he wanted an annulment, surely there could be no reason for him not to seek it openly. Perhaps she should offer to help. She could even approach the Green Abbot. Surely, if she explained what had happened and confessed her role in it, she might persuade him to add his support to Hector's application.

She sighed, knowing she could do no such thing. Not only had Hector forbidden her to approach the abbot, but she did not want to aid the annulment.

She was entering her bedchamber, trying to persuade herself that if she just did what needed doing and did not fret over things she could not change, she would do well enough, when she heard Isobel shouting from the next landing.

"Cristina, Soot nearly drowned! Oh, hurry! I don't know if I can save her!"

Casting the fresh linens she had carried up with her onto the bed, she ran up the stairs and found Isobel on the landing, tenderly cradling the black kitten, which was soaked to the skin and shivering miserably.

"Only look at the poor wee thing! Who could have done it?"

"Done what? How did she get like this?" Cristina demanded as she took the kitten and wrapped it in her skirt, carrying it downstairs as she talked.

"She was trapped in a pail of water in your tower room," Isobel said. "The pail was too deep for her to climb out, and she was nearly exhausted. Had I not gone in when I did, she would have drowned. Where are you going?" she added.

"To the kitchen," Cristina said. "'Tis the warmest room in the castle."

They met Mariota on the way. "What is all the fuss?" she demanded.

"Hector's kitten nearly drowned in a pail of water," Cristina said. "She's shivering and weak. I just hope she doesn't sicken and die."

"Well, it would hardly be a tragedy if it did," Mariota said. "Many people drown kittens at birth. Indeed, I warrant this one and the gray would have suffered that fate had Isobel not given them to you as wedding gifts. I told her Lochbuie probably already had more cats than you'd need, but she would not heed me."

"Hector likes Soot. He'd be upset if anything happened to her."

"Don't be a noddy," Mariota said. "If he wants a kitten, he'd simply get another. When do you mean to go to Ardtornish, Cristina?"

"I don't know that I'm going at all," Cristina said, stepping past her. "Hector went to Duart and means to travel straight on from there to Ardtornish. He said nothing about my going, but I expect that when he wants me, he will send for me."

"Well, I would not stand for such treatment," Mariota said, following as Cristina and Isobel continued on to the kitchen. "It is to be a grand occasion, after all, and you are his wife. You should be there. If I were his wife, I would be."

"I'm sure you would," Cristina said. "Isobel, get that basket yonder and move it near the fire. Calum, I'm going to put this kitten by the fire to warm her. She nearly drowned in a pail of water."

"Aye, m'lady. Mayhap she'll be a good mouser one day."

"Such a fuss over a kitten," Mariota said, chuckling. "Now it will doubtless turn the kitchen upside down. You should not be leaving pails of water around in your chamber for kittens to fall into, Cristina."

"I didn't," Cristina said, frowning, "I cannot imagine how it got there."

"Doubtless, one of the maids or lads simply thought you'd like fresh water in your tower room, just as you do in your bedchamber," Mariota said airily.

Cristina nodded, thinking it a reasonable answer. It was not until just before she fell asleep that night that it occurred to her to wonder how Mariota had known the kitten's accident had occurred in the tower chamber. The wee thing seemed to have recovered from its ordeal with no ill effects, but she was sure she had not mentioned the room in describing its ordeal to Mariota. There must be an innocent explanation, she decided. She would ask her about it in the morning.

However, the arrival of Macleod of Glenelg shortly after Cristina had broken her fast the next morning put all thought of questioning Mariota out of her head.

"Sir," she exclaimed, "what brings you to Lochbuie?"

"Why, I've come to take Mariota to Ardtornish wi' me to meet the next King o' Scots," Macleod said. "'Tis time and all I found the lass a husband, after all. I'd thought ye'd be on your own way there by now, lass."

"No, sir, nor did I expect you, so I'd not have gone whilst my aunt and sisters remained here. My husband has gone, however, to confer with his brother at Duart. He'll go on to Ardtornish from there," she added glibly. "I knew you would be going, of course, but I did not know that you meant to stop here and take Mariota with you. Do you mean to take Isobel and Aunt Euphemia as well?"

"Nay, nay, what would I want wi' a hoyden and a jabber-woman? Ye'll keep them here, and if you go to Ardtornish, you can decide what to do with them then. So he didna want ye wi' him, eh?" he added abruptly. "How did ye come to vex the man this time?"

Although he had guessed a portion of the truth, she did not intend to tell him more, so she drew herself up to her full height instead and looked him straight in the eye. "What can you mean by that, I wonder," she said, ruthlessly repressing the much angrier words she yearned to fling at him.

He had the grace to redden, but he said bluntly, "Ye should be wi' your husband. To deny ye your rightful place at his side be to offend all Macleods. Moreover, the Steward will wonder where ye are."

"Then he must wonder, I expect. Will you want a meal before you depart?"

"Aye, sure, and why not? I'm no planning to leave till I've had me dinner. Would ye ha' me believe your sister can be ready to leave in less time?"

Cristina sent word to the kitchen that he would join them for the midday meal, then went in search of Mariota to tell her to pack her things.

"Ardtornish?" Mariota's eyebrows soared upward, and then she smiled with delight. "I am to go to his grace's court with Father?"

"Aye, and straightaway after we dine," Cristina said.

"Shall I help you with anything, or can you manage on your own?"

"What of Isobel?"

"She is to stay here with me."

"Good," Mariota said. "A little girl like that one would just be in the way at such an affair as his grace intends to hold."

"The reception for the Steward is still days away," Cristina reminded her.

"That gives me plenty of time to meet people," Mariota said, flinging open one of her chests and beginning to pull clothing from it. "If you can spare me Tess or your Brona for an hour or so, I shall manage easily, I think. I just hope I don't look like a dowdy compared to all the grand ladies who will be there."

"You could not look dowdy if you tried," Cristina reassured her, wishing she could command her to stay away from Hector.

As if Mariota had read her thoughts, she looked up with a sly smile and said, "Don't you wish you could be there to keep an eye on that handsome husband of yours? I shall enjoy flirting with him, I can tell you. After all, once he gets his annulment, nothing will stand in our way."

With a sigh, Cristina said, "I'll send Tess to help you."

Noting that her fingers were curling again, she hurried away, and sent a gillie to relay the message to Tess.

Then, without a word to anyone else, she hurried up to the tower chamber and shut the door, wishing she had ordered a bolt or bar installed on it that she could throw to lock herself in. She would attend to that when Mariota had gone. That thought, in that room, reminded her of the kitten's near-fatal mishap, and she looked for the pail it had fallen into. Someone had tidied the chamber, sweeping and opening the curtain over the one narrow window, but she found the pail, empty now, standing in the corner behind the door.

Her thoughts shifted again to Mariota. Surely, her usually lighthearted sister would never do anything so cruel. In a rage, as Cristina knew only too well, Mariota was capable of nearly anything, because she thought only of her anger and her determination to get even with whoever had caused it. But she had shown no sign of anger at Lochbuie. On the contrary, she had seemed very happy.

Even when she had disobeyed Hector's edict, she had suffered no consequences, clearly having charmed him into believing she had had good reason for her behavior, just as she had charmed Macleod over the years—and anyone else who might have had cause to be annoyed with her. In any case, Soot could not have angered her. Doubtless, the whole thing had been an accident, the kitten having climbed or fallen into a pail left by a careless housemaid, and Mariota's knowledge had come, as most knowledge in the Isles came, from swiftly flying word of mouth.

❧

Having no wish to endure more of his father's company without the mitigating influence of Lachlan's presence, Hector had gone on to Ardtornish the next day, finding his twin in conference with the Lord of the Isles.

"Faith, but I did not expect you so soon," Lachlan said.

"You said you'd intended to get the flotilla organized," Hector said. "I went to Duart, expecting to find you there, but Mairi said you had come here. When do you fetch the Steward?"

"Ranald is going to fetch his grandfather," Lachlan said,

referring to one of MacDonald's elder sons. "It was his own notion, and I think it an excellent one."

MacDonald said, "Robert will reach Oban on Saturday. Meeting him there means the shortest sea journey, so Ranald will take my royal galley to fetch him, and the flotilla will escort them. We have more than fifty boats, with more arriving each day," he added with satisfaction.

"We've so many that I mean to send half of them to make a show of strength in the west," Lachlan said. "There have been more accounts of trouble there, and I want to stop it. I'm thinking a small navy of longboats will deter them."

"I've been wondering about this matter of petrels," Hector said. "'Tis a dangerous business, collecting the wee birds from precipitous cliff tops, but 'tis one that Islesmen have practiced for years without much trouble. The oil goes abroad, and the gelt for it comes back to his grace, who divides it and its benefits among the Islesmen. In fact, except for the one argument you settled weeks ago, we seem to hear only rumors of this violence and disruption. We've had none at all on Mull."

"What are you thinking? What reason could anyone have to stir rumors?"

"Mayhap to divert fully half of your flotilla away from Oban."

"Faith, even if you're wrong, we dare not chance it. We must ponder this."

Hector nodded, very glad that he had not let Cristina come with him, and glad, too, that the rest of his boats would arrive that day or the next from Lochbuie.

In the days that followed Mariota's departure, Cristina missed her almost as much as she missed Hector. For the most part, she had enjoyed her company and her merry comments. Lady Euphemia was kind and meant well, but she was not as cheerful as Mariota. Even so, Cristina rejoiced to see how comfortable her aunt was at Lochbuie. The hesitant manner so natural to her at Chalamine had disappeared, replaced by a distinct if somewhat vaguely expressed interest in everything that took place at the castle. One afternoon, Cristina had found her sitting with a group of the servants' children, telling them bards' tales, to their great delight.

Lady Euphemia asked if she wanted her for any particular purpose, and when Cristina said she did not, her aunt had happily returned to her storytelling.

Isobel, too, seemed happy at Lochbuie, and Cristina was coming to value her little sister's company. The child was bright and considerate, if a little prone to impulsive behavior. She had shown no disappointment at either Mariota's departure or Macleod's refusal to take her with them to Ardtornish.

"I'm not old enough yet to marry," she said matter-of-factly. "In fact, I do not think I want a husband. I wish that women could live by themselves if they wished to do so, because I think I'd like above all things to live in a tower on one of the smaller isles, where I could do exactly as I pleased."

"Some of the isles are quite small," Cristina pointed out with a smile. "You would want enough room to ride your pony."

"You are teasing me," Isobel said. "But don't you think life would be more peaceful if men were not continually fighting each other? Women's lives certainly would be, without men constantly making demands upon them, wanting their dinner and clean shirts, and all. Let them cook and wash for themselves, I say."

Cristina laughed. "They'd all soon be filthy and would starve."

"No, they wouldn't. Most of them manage well without women when they go off to war, or go off in ships to puff off their consequence along some coast."

"True enough," Cristina agreed. "Sometimes they can be useful to have around though," she added, thinking of the pleasure she had enjoyed at Hector's hands before the awful moment that anger had replaced his passion. Whatever happened between them in the future, she hoped that somehow they could be friends. Not that such a thought eased her mind. She wanted much more than that.

"What?" Isobel said, watching her. "Your face changed just then. It softened, then looked sad. What were you thinking?"

"Private thoughts, my love, not for bairns' ears."

"You sound like Calum now, but whatever those thoughts were, they must have been about some man I haven't met, because all the ones I have met want to tell you what to do and how to do it. Not that Hector is an ogre or anything like that, because I do like him mostly, and I'm glad you married him instead of Mariota."

"People would have thought it odd indeed if I had married Mariota."

Isobel chuckled. "You know what I mean. Do not pretend you do not."

"I know."

"And I think you are glad you did, too."

Cristina could not deny it, although her heart ached when she thought of the likely trials that lay ahead of her. She could not help but be frustrated and resentful that Mariota was at Ardtornish, doubtless with Hector and doubtless flirting outrageously with him as she had from the day they'd first met.

And he, villain that he was, was doubtless flirting right back.

⊱❦⊰

Time passed slowly, but welcome diversion came two days later, when a gillie announced visitors just as the ladies were finishing their midday meal.

"Ian Dubh, Chief of Clan Gillean, and her ladyship, Mairi of the Isles," the lad intoned in a manner more suited to the lord chamberlain Cristina had seen at Stirling when Macleod had taken her to court in hopes of finding her a husband.

She jumped up to greet her guests, making a low curtsy to Ian Dubh and bidding him welcome to Lochbuie.

"I am pleased to see you again, sir," she said, as he drew her to her feet and kissed her cheek.

Instead of answering her directly, he smiled as he looked around. "Do I detect your hand in this hall, madam? I vow my son never made a room look as comfortable as this."

"Cristina has wrought wonders here, sir," Mairi said, grinning at her. "But we should explain our mission to her immediately, do you not agree? I warrant she will want some time to prepare."

"Yes, indeed," he said. "You are right to remind me, my dear. The plain truth is, madam, that I have taken the decision to attend this party his grace means to arrange to show the Steward how much support he has in the Isles, and I should take it as a great favor if you will do me the honor to accompany me."

Cristina looked from one to the other in astonishment. "Me?"

"To be sure," Ian Dubh said. "I cannot imagine what my son was thinking, leaving you to follow him on your own. Most inconsiderate of him, I think."

"In fairness, sir, he did not leave me to follow him. He told me I was to stay here at Lochbuie, that he would likely have duties and so forth, and so would not have the time to look after me."

"Just so, and very typical, I must say, when he has a beautiful new wife to show off to everyone, to be spending his time thinking only of matters of business and doubtless planning to be at hand for any mission his brother might choose to assign to him. But he is newly married, and one of his solemn duties is to present his lady to MacDonald. Since that has apparently slipped his mind, we must do all in our power to make sure his lapse does not offend his grace or the Macleods. Therefore, I would take it kindly if you can be prepared to depart after we break our fast in the morning. I presume you can accommodate us both here for the night."

"Oh, but are you sure? That is, yes, sir, of course we can," Cristina said when her first words were met with a glacial look that reminded her instantly of Hector and made her wonder how she had ever thought his father was less intimidating.

"I'll go upstairs with you," Mairi said, adding with a teasing grin, "Doubtless, you will want my sage advice as you choose what gowns you will wear."

"Oh, yes, do come with me," Cristina said, already thinking about what she would need. As they hurried upstairs to her bedchamber, her heart was singing.

Chapter 14

Well," Mairi said as they entered Cristina's chamber, "are you angry with me for sticking my oar into your affairs?"

"Is this your doing then?"

"Mostly, but I cannot take all the credit—or blame, if that is your feeling."

"Nay, for I'll admit I've been wishing I could go to Ardtornish."

"Aye, well, Hector was a villain not to make arrangements for you to follow him, especially since he had boats aplenty to carry you, but I do understand why he did not insist that you accompany him to Duart. He must have expected to find his father in a rare taking after receiving such a curt command to present himself. And, indeed, when word reached Ian Dubh that he meant to seek an annulment, he was angry enough to flay him, but in the end, I don't think he handed him his head, although he did make his feelings plain."

"Are you sure?"

"Aye, for after Hector left for Ardtornish, his father became thoughtful, and then he set aside his beloved documents and said he would have to take a hand in things.

Seizing my opportunity, I told him that when I'd asked about you, Hector had said you were not going to Ardtornish. I said I thought that a pity, because I knew my father would want to meet my new sister. So here we are."

"I'm very glad. I hadn't realized how sorry I was not to be included in the festivities, because I did not mind staying here whilst he went to Finlaggan. Oh, but mercy, what am I to do with Isobel and Aunt Euphemia?"

"Bring them along, of course. Two more will make no difference to our oarsmen, and Ardtornish has plenty of room. If Hector forbids you to share his room, you may share mine—at least, until Lachlan returns from wherever he is, which he is sure to do before his grace's reception for my grandfather. But I doubt that your husband will order you to sleep elsewhere."

"He will not be pleased to see me," Cristina said with a grimace.

"Bless the man, he cannot eat you," Mairi said, laughing. "Nor will he blame you when he sees that you have come with his father. He may be a trifle cool to you at first though, particularly if he strictly forbade your going."

"He didn't forbid it exactly," Cristina said, remembering. "He just said that I was to stay here."

"Well, that's all right then," Mairi said comfortably. "But where is Mariota? You have not mentioned her."

"My father came and took her with him to Ardtornish," Cristina said.

"Without offering to take you or Isobel or even Lady Euphemia?"

"He did not mention me, but he did say he would not take a hoyden or a jabber-woman with him," Cristina said, making Mairi grin.

The grin faded quickly as Mairi said, "You know, I can

perhaps understand his leaving your other sisters with Adela to look after them, because she seemed quite competent to me, but he ought to have taken Lady Euphemia with him, even if he did not want Isobel. Mariota should not be at my father's court without a reliable woman to act as her chaperone."

"You have met my aunt several times now," Cristina said. "Do you think she could keep Mariota out of mischief?"

"Faith, I doubt that anyone could influence that young woman sufficiently for that, but it would certainly look better to others if she were with them."

Cristina agreed but refrained from pointing out that she had had nothing to say in the matter and changed the subject to the important matter of her clothing.

Brona entered a few minutes later, and after asking her to send someone to tell Isobel and Lady Euphemia of the treat in store for them, the two young women turned their attention to Cristina's packing.

～～～

The next day dawned gray and cool, and the air against Cristina's face felt soft with a hint of rain. But lack of sunshine had done nothing to dampen her spirits as she boarded Ian Dubh's longboat for the journey up the island's east coast to the Sound of Mull. Intermittent sunlight emerged shortly before they stopped at Duart to enjoy a late midday meal, and they wasted no time thereafter before boarding the longboat again and sailing the remaining five miles to Ardtornish Bay.

Ardtornish Castle, principal residence of the Lord of the Isles, sat sixty feet above them on a rocky promontory that jutted into the Sound at the west end of the bay. One of eight castles guarding the Sound, its brownish black basalt-block walls loomed dark and formidable against the shadowy afternoon sun. Just as formidable were the towering, sheer basalt cliffs that formed the bay.

"The Morvern Witches' skirts are flying up today," Mairi said, gesturing toward misty spills of water billowing out from the cliff walls as the oarsmen rowed them into Ardtornish Bay. "You can see *Creag na Corps* from here, too."

"I know that rock," Cristina said, staring at the highest cliff. "That's the one from which they throw felons to their deaths on the rocks below, is it not?"

"Aye," Mairi said soberly. "But we'll see none of that on this visit. This is a festive occasion, and everyone will be here, mayhap even my sister Marjory."

"If so many are here," Isobel said as the oarsmen deftly turned the longboat and swept it up to the landing in grand style, "where are the boats they promised?"

"Most likely in Loch Aline, yonder to the west, if they have not already sailed to meet my grandfather," Mairi explained. "'Tis a safer harbor, because the longboats and galleys are less exposed to the weather there, and to mischief as well."

"Sakes," Isobel said, "who would dare make mischief against a man as powerful as the Lord of the Isles?"

"You'd be surprised," Mairi said. "Sometimes the ones you least suspect prove to be great villains, and men of power are always targets."

"Truly?"

"Trust is often a sometime thing," Mairi said soberly. "Feuds can stir amidst even the greatest of friends, and a man in my father's position often finds himself surrounded by as many enemies as allies. However, for the next few days, everyone will be smiling. Just don't trust every smile,

Isobel," she added. "Pay attention to actions, too. A wise woman heeds the whole demeanor of a person, and his actions, not just his smiles and bows and flattering words."

Cristina was amused to see how seriously the little girl took Mairi's advice. But she knew that it was sage advice and that she'd do well to heed it herself.

They retired to Mairi's chambers for an hour to refresh and tidy themselves before she led them to the great chamber of the main tower, where her father greeted his guests and where Cristina saw at once that the Lord of the Isles' court might hold more pitfalls than she had feared.

Directly to MacDonald's right stood the Green Abbot of Iona, a tall, willowy man, garbed in the knee-length black robe and fine trunk hose of a courtier. And standing next to him, smiling flirtatiously as they chatted, was Mariota. Until then, although Cristina had known Fingon since her childhood, she had never noticed how foxlike his narrowed eyes, long nose, and sharp chin could make him look.

Mariota had not yet seen her, and as Cristina waited for her to do so, a slight prickling at the nape of her neck caused her to glance behind her. As she did, her husband entered the chamber with his twin at his side.

The pair of them made an impressive appearance, for not only did they wear the splendid French finery that many of the Isles nobility preferred for court dress—and which their command of the seas allowed them to procure—but as tall as they were, and as broad-shouldered, they caused many a head to turn their way.

Lachlan was speaking to Hector, but Cristina knew her husband was not listening, for his gaze had riveted on her. His eyes blazed, and his jaw was set hard.

A shiver shot up her spine, but she fought to ignore it as

she turned away with as much calm as she could muster to make her curtsy to the Lord of the Isles.

Hector could hardly believe his eyes, but there she was, the wife he had supposed safe at Lochbuie, curtsying low before MacDonald. As she smiled up at his grace, he drew her to her feet and spoke to her. Then she vanished from Hector's view when a man and two women insinuated themselves between them to speak to MacDonald. So intent was he on seeing her again that another moment passed before he realized that the man was his father and one of the two women was Mairi of the Isles. The other was her good friend Fiona MacDougall.

The sight of Ian Dubh gave him pause, and he muttered an epithet.

"What did you say?" Lachlan demanded. "I swear you've not heard one word I've said to you."

"I said, what the devil does he think he is doing?"

"You cannot be surprised that our august parent has decided to attend the festivities? He would not want to figure as one of the opposition to the Steward."

"I don't care one way or the other about his being here, although I'd expect him to have mentioned his intention when I saw him a few days ago," Hector said grimly. "I do object to his countermanding *my* orders to *my* own wife."

"I thought you wanted to *dis*own her," Lachlan said gently.

"Don't you start with me, my lad."

"Then control your temper before you draw every curious eye," his twin recommended. "Beat the lass for disobeying you if you dare, or tell our father to keep his fingers out of your marriage. But too many people are watching us now, including the wicked abbot, for you to indulge that temper of yours here."

"Never fear that," Hector said, scowling. "If so many are watching, they will merely think you and I have had a falling-out. And if you continue to offer me advice when I don't want it, that may well happen."

"Will it, indeed?" Lachlan asked, grinning impudently at him.

"Our audience may think so at least," Hector said, punching him on the shoulder playfully but with enough force to make him stagger.

Lachlan laughed aloud and clapped him hard on the back. "Our father is looking at us, and his grace, too," he said. "Do you want to continue this farce?"

"Nay, but I do have some few things to say to my lady wife."

"Then go and talk to her. Greetings, your grace," he added, stepping forward to make his bow and studiously ignoring the abbot. "I see that you have met my lovely sister-in-law."

"I have, indeed," MacDonald said, glancing from one twin to the other with a smile. To Hector he said, "You have done yourself proud, lad."

"Thank you, your grace," Hector said, looking directly at Cristina.

When he saw her eyes widen, he knew she had been fearful of his reaction to her presence, and that thought gave him pause, more so than anything his twin or his father had said to him. He realized in that moment that he did not want to frighten her or to fight with her. Knowing what he did want was another matter.

One moment he felt trapped with her in an unwanted

marriage, the next he wanted to protect and comfort her as his wife. Indeed, from one minute to the next, he did not seem to know if he was on his head or on his heels.

Lachlan and Mairi were watching them, a half smile on his face, a slight frown on hers, but Hector ignored them both as he held out a hand to Cristina. "Will you walk with me, madam, if his grace and my father will give us leave. I have missed you and would speak privately with you."

"His grace will certainly excuse you," MacDonald said, smiling.

Ian Dubh nodded, his expression stern.

"Then it must be as you wish, my lord," Cristina said with the calm that almost never seemed to fail her, as she placed a hand on his forearm.

He guided her away from the gathering around MacDonald, pausing only to see if his grace's wife, Lady Margaret, had come in. He was glad to see that she had not, for otherwise he might have hesitated to take Cristina from the room. No one would complain if he did so now, however.

He thought the mossy green silk gown she wore was especially becoming to her. Its low-cut bodice emphasized the soft plumpness of her creamy breasts, and its blond lace trimming matched the color of her hair, which she wore simply, pulled back and confined in a gilded net. "Have you visited the battlements?" he asked.

"No, sir."

"Then I'll take you up to admire the view," he said.

She went silently, preceding him gracefully up the narrow, twisting stairway and onto the ramparts of the castle. The view was breathtaking, because despite the gray sky, they could see for miles.

"See Duart there to the southeast," he said. "And that

castle west of us on the far promontory is Aros. Mingary lies even farther west, at the end of the Sound."

"You are angry with me for coming here," she said.

"Nay, lass, I ken fine who brought you."

"You were angry when you saw me."

"Aye, I was," he admitted. "I dislike having my orders countermanded."

"I know, but I did want to come, so I cannot pretend I tried to persuade your father that his decision was unlikely to please you."

"Much he would have cared," he said. "He knew his interference would displease me, so I'm guessing he fetched you himself from Lochbuie."

"Aye, he did."

"Then his mind was made up. You'd have had no chance to dissuade him and would likely have drawn his reproaches had you tried. Mairi was with him?"

She hesitated.

"I'm not going to bite her head off either," he said. "If the truth were known, I'm glad you came and sorry that I did not arrange for you to follow me here."

"Truly?"

"Aye."

She seemed to expect him to say more, and at last, ruefully, he said, "I've been busy, as I feared I'd be, but nonetheless, nearly everyone here has asked me about you. Only a few had known of our marriage before the Council meeting at Finlaggan. But thanks to your father, who surprised me by not gloating but spoke of our marriage often there, many more learned of it, and most of them seem to have told their wives and daughters."

"Aye, they would," she agreed. "Everyone thinks about marriages, you know, and a good many of the men at Finlaggan must have looked on you as an excellent prospect for one of their daughters."

"Perhaps, but if you think their lasses ignore me now that I'm married, you are wrong. They flirt just as openly as they did before, including your sister."

"You can scarcely blame Mariota, sir. You have made no secret—to her and others—that you would have preferred to marry her. She believes that after you get your annulment, you *will* marry her."

He grimaced. "About that annulment, lass—"

"You need not tell me, sir. You have already made your position clear."

"Nay, lassie, I have not, not if you still think I wish I had married your sister, because I don't want any such thing."

She looked searchingly into his eyes. "You don't?"

"Nay, though I don't deny I did wish it at Chalamine, even afterward, until I came home to find her at Lochbuie. I vow, I've never known a lass so full of herself as that one is. I doubt she ever thinks about anything except as it affects her."

He had thought she would be pleased or relieved to know he had abandoned the idea of marrying her sister. Instead, she looked surprised, even worried.

"Prithee, sir, whatever you do, do not say any of that to her."

"Sakes, lass, I'm not going to march up to the wench and tell her that I've come to my senses. 'Twould be bad manners for one thing, and unkind."

"You don't understand, sir. Mariota believes you love her and want to marry her. If you tell her you don't, she won't spare a thought for rudeness or unkindness. She simply won't believe you. In the best case, she may decide you don't mean it and will ignore all you say. But she is more

likely to blame me or someone else—anyone—for per-
suading you to reject her, and if she does . . . She . . . she
can fly into terrible rages when things do not go as she expects them to, and when that happens, she does not think before she acts. She might do anything."

"Well, she had better not try such a scene with me, or
with you," Hector said grimly. "She will swiftly discover
that my temper is more than equal to hers."

"But don't you see, sir? That is what I fear most."

∽∾∽

Cristina did not know what more she could say to him.
Mariota was difficult to explain to those who did not know
her well, who had seen only her kindness and charm. He had
certainly experienced that charm, but having never seen
Mariota in a rage, Cristina knew he could not possibly understand how dreadful they could be.

"She has already tried my temper today," he said.

"Indeed?"

"Aye, lass, and do not give me that innocent look. What
were you about to let her be so friendly with the Green
Abbot?"

"I did not let her. Your father, Mairi, and I had only just
arrived ourselves when you walked in. Mariota has been
here for days, and she was already standing with the abbot
and his grace. Then Fiona MacDougall came up to welcome
us, you and your brother came in, and Mariota and the abbot
left soon afterward."

"I saw them go," he said. "Cannot your aunt keep a closer
eye on the lass?"

"Aunt Euphemia and Isobel arrived with me, but although my aunt is here now, she is not firm enough to con-

trol Mariota," Cristina said. "Surely you have seen that she does as she pleases. Moreover, if you take her to task over her friendly ways with the abbot, she is likely to become more friendly rather than less so."

"Sakes, but your father should have beaten obedience into that lass."

Cristina pressed her lips firmly together and did not reply.

"I'll speak to your father," Hector said. "I still don't know if he truly supports the Steward, but he does support MacDonald, and he may not realize that the abbot and his lot of Mackinnons lack that same loyalty. He would not want his daughter to find herself in opposition to the Lord of the Isles."

Cristina was not so sure, but she did not want to quarrel with him. "I must go and find her, sir. Perhaps I can persuade her to avoid him, although we have known him since we were children. If he is truly an enemy of his grace as you say, then why does MacDonald make him welcome here?"

"Because MacDonald is a practical man. He treats his friends as if they might become his enemies and his enemies as if they might become his friends. And the abbot wields tremendous power hereabouts to use for good or evil."

"How can he if he is in such disrepute with Rome?"

"Sakes, lass, local folks don't care about his troubles with the Pope. All they care about is being able to marry and baptize their children, and Fingon is the most powerful cleric they know. If he should excommunicate anyone, other local clerics would refuse that person the sacraments whether the Pope agreed or no."

"Does the Pope truly dislike him so?"

"I don't know that he dislikes him, personally," Hector said. "But surely you know the Roman Kirk expects its priests to remain celibate and to follow other rules and practices that do not march with our ancient Celtic ways. Even the Celtic Kirk barely supports Fingon's longtime practice of fathering children with the lady of his choice. That practice finds no favor in Rome."

She nodded. She knew that most Roman priests did not marry, but she had not realized the Pope took such a dim view of the ancient practices. That seemed a trifle intolerant of His Holiness, since everyone knew the Celtic ways were far older than those of the Roman Kirk. Had God looked on the older ways with the same disfavor, surely He would long since have allowed them to fall into disuse.

"It will be time for supper soon," he said. "We'd better change our clothes."

"When will the Steward arrive?"

"Soon, but come along now. Where have they put your things?"

"I'm not sure," she admitted. "No one asked me, nor would I have known what to tell them."

"I'll wager Mairi had them carried to my chamber," he said. "I'll take you there, and then I'll seek out your father."

It was as he had expected, and Brona was waiting for her in his room. He left them to her ablutions and went to find Macleod but soon returned, shaking his head.

"You were right," he told her when she had dismissed Brona. "Your father said she ignores the men buzzing round her, because she believes that after I have our marriage annulled, I'll marry her. He told her he won't allow it, that you and I are legally married and will remain so, but he says it is as if she does not hear him. She also told him the Green Abbot has promised to support my application for annulment, so I expect we will encounter even more rumors about that here."

Cristina sighed. For a short time, before he had sought out her father, she had hoped again that he no longer meant to seek an annulment, but if the abbot would support him, perhaps he would get one after all.

His man entered to help him, and she sent Brona away and watched as he swiftly changed his doublet for a more splendid one of dark gray velvet trimmed with miniver and silver buttons, which made his eyes look bluer than ever.

Moving to a stool so that his gillie could brush his hair, he said, "I believe you said you had attended his grace's court before, did you not?"

Suppressing the irritation that stirred whenever he reminded her that he did not recall meeting her before arriving at Chalamine, she said, "Aye, sir, I have."

"Then you will know you must take care to avoid discussions of his grace's affairs or any other political matters," he said. "It is easy for someone who knows little of such things to offend someone who has a personal stake in them."

"But I generally talk only to other women," she protested.

"That matters not," he said. "Women parrot what their husbands say and are even more likely to take offense if one seems to speak in opposition to their views. This matter of the petrel oil is such a topic. You have not had much to do with that, because Glenelg and Skye do not harvest much of the stuff, although they benefit as we all do from its export and sale. But the outer Isles look upon it as a very valuable substance and guard their oil like birds of prey. It is best, I think, to avoid talk of such things, and of course, you must avoid talk about the succession to the throne."

"Indeed, sir," she said coolly. "Perhaps you have prepared a list for me of topics that I may safely discuss."

He glanced at her and at his man, just then selecting a jewel for his doublet. When he looked back at Cristina, she met his gaze steadily. "I think you are sensible enough to judge such matters for yourself," he said. "If someone broaches a subject that makes you uncomfortable, you can always say that you see your husband beckoning, and excuse yourself. Now, if you are quite ready, we can go downstairs," he added, as though she had been the one delaying them.

Since their chamber lay in the new wing of guest chambers adjoining the main building at the garderobe tower, they returned to the main building to descend the stairway in the north wall to the main entrance, and went out into the courtyard.

A strong wind blew through the Sound from the west, but the castle formed a solid protective barrier, and although the wind roared, the air in the courtyard barely stirred. They followed other guests across the yard to the great hall, which stood a short distance from the main castle and formed a third wall for the courtyard.

A wide walkway passed between the southwest corner of the hall and the guest wing of the castle, giving a clear view of the hillside beyond, because no curtain wall guarded the Morvern side. The Lord of the Isles feared no attack from that direction because Morvern had proved ever loyal. Indeed, the castle's greatest protection was that loyalty and its own easily defended position on the steep promontory approachable only from Loch Aline and the easily defended steep stairway hacked into the cliff's face from the landing in Ardtornish Bay.

The great hall was a vast chamber some seventy feet by thirty feet, presently teeming with his grace's guests, many of whom, as Cristina knew, traveled daily to Ardtornish from nearby castles to attend his court, and traveled back each night.

The company at Ardtornish was nearly always merry, the music entertaining, the food generous and well prepared. It was a welcome change for those whose winter larders provided only scanty stock by now, and especially welcome with the beginning of the long Lenten season only days away.

Hector escorted her to the high table on the dais opposite the main entrance, pausing briefly to present her to Lady Margaret before finding her place several seats to the left of her ladyship. As soon as Cristina had made herself known to the women on either side of her, Hector moved to the gentlemen's end of the table, at MacDonald's right, and took his place next to Lachlan.

MacDonald soon nodded to his chaplain to speak the grace before meat, and afterward, everyone sat down and the meal began with great fanfare, as six gillies preceded by his grace's piper bore in a whole roasted boar on a silver platter, surrounded by myriad other delicacies. They paraded their burden around the entire hall, coming to a halt before the Lord of the Isles, who smiled his approval before they took it aside to begin its carving. Other courses, beginning with six haunches of venison and two great salmon, followed with equal ceremony.

Cristina had hoped to sit beside Mairi, but Mairi occupied the place of honor beside her mother, and two other ladies separated her from Cristina. Nevertheless, Cristina's nearest neighbors proved amusing, and she enjoyed the food.

Minstrels played from the gallery throughout the meal, which his grace's butler and his minions continued to serve with splendid pomp and ceremony. Afterward, a troupe of players entertained the guests with miming, juggling, and other antics, and then the musicians began tuning their instruments for dancing.

The trestles in the lower hall were swiftly cleared away to make room, and a group of young people began to form a line for a ring dance. Cristina remained where she was at the high table, believing that Hector would come for her.

He did not do so right away, but other ladies also lingered at the high table, including Lady Margaret and Mairi, so she did not wonder at his absence. They all sat on the same side of the table, so she had been unable to see him after everyone sat down, and even now she could not do so without leaning forward and peering down the row of people between them. To do that would be unmannerly, so she contained her soul in patience but tapped her foot in time to the music.

Each of her near neighbors had departed, and she saw Mairi rising to accept an invitation to join the dancers. The handsome man who approached her had come from the gentlemen's end of the high table, and Cristina believed he was one of Mairi's half brothers from her father's marriage to his first wife, Amy Macruari.

She still saw no sign of Hector or his twin. When MacDonald caught her eye and smiled at her, she smiled back, hoping that her expression before then had not betrayed her annoyance with her husband, or her impatience.

"Cristina, do not sit here like a stone," Mariota said merrily from behind her, startling her. "Come with me and join the dancers."

"I'm waiting for Hector," Cristina explained.

"A pox on Hector," her sister said, laughing. "He and Lachlan Lubanach left the hall ten minutes ago with some other men. I warrant they have important matters to discuss, but that should not keep you from having fun. Come with me now, do. Our father has likewise disappeared, so mayhap the Council has business. There, see!" she added, gesturing. "His grace just got a message to leave, too."

MacDonald stood as Cristina looked at him, and then he bent to speak to Lady Margaret. She, too, arose and let him guide her from the dais.

"Where is Aunt Euphemia?" Cristina asked.

"Retired to her chamber, of course. The good thing is that she has taken Isobel with her. That child should not be dining or supping in such company."

"I know, but neither should we be demanding private service for her in her chamber," Cristina pointed out. "There can be naught amiss in her taking her meals with the court, as long as Aunt Euphemia stays with her. It is not as if you want our aunt hovering over you," she added with a teasing smile.

"No, I do not," Mariota replied with fervor. "But come, we may join the dancers now, may we not?"

Cristina agreed, deciding that with Macleod and Lady Euphemia absent, it behooved her to keep an eye on her impulsive sister.

Instead of joining the line of dancers at the end, Mariota brazenly headed toward the middle, breaking in between two handsome young gentlemen and announcing with a saucy grin that they would not mind.

Feeling fire in her cheeks, Cristina felt obliged to follow her and was grateful when both gentlemen seemed only charmed by her sister's impetuousness. To her surprise though, the man whose hand grasped her own flirted openly and most delightfully with her, ignoring Mariota and making Cristina laugh at his witty comments and blush at his brazen compliments.

"Please, sir," she said after one outrageous example of

the latter, "you should not say such things to me. I am a married lady."

"What did you say, lass?" he said, cocking his head toward her and raising his voice above the music and laughter. "I cannot hear you!"

Leaning closer to him to repeat her request, she raised her voice, too, but she barely got the first word out before her companion pulled her to him and kissed her heartily on the lips.

Shocked, Cristina stepped back, but he only grinned at her and pulled her from the line of dancers.

Bending nearer and still grinning, he said, "If you want to slap me, mistress, go ahead. It will be worth it, for you are far and away the most beautiful woman I've ever clapped eyes on. Indeed, I'd do it again in a minute."

Feeling dizzy with shock but flattered nonetheless, she said urgently, "Please, sir, my husband—"

"I did hear you say that you were cursed with a husband," he said with an exaggerated sigh. Then, clapping a hand to his chest, he added, "Show him to me that I might slay him and claim you for mine own."

"Don't be daft," Cristina said more sharply, looking swiftly around, fearing to find Hector swooping down on them. "I should not . . . Mercy!"

Her exclamation led her companion to follow her gaze to the main entrance.

MacDonald and his lady had returned, and standing with them near the door were Hector Reaganach, Lachlan Lubanach, Mairi of the Isles, and an older man.

The musicians in the gallery stopped playing at a signal from MacDonald, and his piper stepped forward. His lord chamberlain announced in stentorian tones, "His grace Robert the Steward, heir to the throne of Scotland!"

The piper began to play as Robert stepped forward, and everyone in the hall bowed or curtsied as he did.

As Cristina swept her skirts aside to make her curtsy, she saw her husband looking at her. His gaze shifted to the man beside her, then back again.

Hector Reaganach did not look pleased.

Chapter 15 ⎯⎯⎯⎯⎯⎯⎯

Cristina wanted to look almost anywhere but into her husband's eyes, and yet she could not seem to look away. It was as if he held her captive even with half the length of the great hall between them. She wondered if he had seen the impudent fellow kiss her, and realized that he must have, since she could imagine no other reason for him to look as if he wanted to throttle her.

A strong hand grasped her elbow, and a deep, mellifluous voice that she barely recognized as that of the man who had kissed her murmured close to her right ear, "Who the devil is that fellow yonder, the one glowering at you so rudely? I've a good mind to go and teach him some manners."

Cristina stared at him, wondering if he was mad.

The hall quieted down, but anyone who had hoped the heir to the Scottish throne would make a speech must have been disappointed, because the Steward only nodded in response to the deep show of respect and then turned back to talk to his daughter, the lady Margaret. The piper ended his tune, and MacDonald nodded to the minstrels to resume their play.

"Damn that fellow. He still glares at you. Bless me, but I *will* speak to him."

Terrified that he would but feeling at the same time an insane desire to laugh, Cristina caught his arm and said, "Do not, sir, unless you would sacrifice your life!"

"Sakes, lass, you do not know who I am. I promise you he is no match—"

"I may not know you, but I do know him," she interjected before he could make a promise she was sure he could not keep. "And although you may be an excellent swordsman, he is better."

"Faugh, my reputation is known throughout the Highlands, so I fancy I can handle that great lout. Indeed, he looks too large to be much good with any weapon. Doubtless, if he tried to draw his sword, he would trip over his own big feet."

"He is Hector Reaganach," Cristina said.

The man said nothing, but a muscle in his jaw tightened, his eyes narrowed, and his cheeks paled.

"He is also my husband," she added gently.

He swept her a low bow. "Forgive me, my lady, I did not know. In that case, I will stay my hand, but I'll not apologize for the kiss. I enjoyed it too much. That great gowk is a lucky man and a fool, too, to leave you unattended. If he continues to do so whilst I am at Ardtornish, I promise you, I will not be such a fool as to ignore opportunity." He winked at her, turned away, and vanished into the crowd.

Even as he disappeared, she was conscious of Hector's approach, although she had to turn her head to see him. He strode toward her, ignoring the people he passed, who parted to either side of him as though they avoided a passing storm.

A thrill stirred her nerves, bringing all her senses to attention. He looked ripe for murder, yet she waited calmly, and this time, she had no need to contrive or force that calm. That he had seen another man take interest in her and disliked it was plain. Could a man who still wanted his marriage annulled feel sufficient anger over such an incident that he could look as Hector did just then?

A voice in the back of her mind whispered that he was merely guarding that which was his, just as he would have guarded a cornfield or a Lochbuie cow. The thought depressed her, but then he stopped in front of her, his eyes alight with blue fire, his lips pressed into a straight line.

"Who was that infernal rogue who dared to kiss you?"

"You saw him?"

"Aye, of course I did. Who the devil is he?"

"I don't know."

He caught her hard by the shoulders. "What do you mean, you don't know? You must know if you allowed him to kiss you."

"Would you create scandal here, sir? Pray, release me." When he did so immediately, disappointment surged, but she said, "I did not 'allow' him to kiss me. He simply did so. Then the music stopped, and he left without mentioning his name. Indeed, if you don't know him, I do not know how you can imagine that I must."

"His name is Fergus Love," Mariota said cheerfully, appearing beside them, apparently unaware of any tension. "Is he not the handsomest gentleman you ever saw? I think he'd do very well for Cristina after the annulment, Hector, don't you?"

"Our affairs are none of yours, mistress," he said sternly. "Come, Cristina, I would have words with you. And as for you, Mariota, I suggest that since the hour is late, you should excuse yourself and go to bed."

"What, before the mummery begins? I won't do it. My

father is here now, in any event, sir, and 'tis he who commands me, not you."

"As if anyone commanded that chit," he muttered as he turned away and urged Cristina firmly toward the door leading out to the courtyard.

"People are watching us," she said. "Can you not at least pretend to be enjoying yourself?"

"Do you expect me to enjoy beating my wife?" he growled.

She held her tongue and tried to pretend no one was watching them, telling herself that he would do no such thing, and wishing her self would believe her.

Why was it, Hector asked himself, that even when the lass was solidly in the wrong she could make him feel as if he had somehow misbehaved and was the one marching toward punishment? As he ushered her toward the courtyard door, his gaze swept the room, but he did not see the scoundrel who had dared to kiss her.

Why had she not slapped him? It had not looked to him as if she had uttered one word of protest, but likewise she had not turned a hair when he had approached her to ask her, as it was his right and duty to ask her, what the devil she had thought she was doing, letting such a man take liberties with her. If he spoke a trifle curtly, was that any more than she had deserved? Certainly not.

Now she walked beside him, meek as a nun's hen, without a word to say for herself except to warn him not to make a scene. As if she had not provided the gossips with a month's worth of tattle with that one absurd kiss.

And what the devil had Mariota to do with it? Why was

she hovering about Cristina, and tattling to him of kisses and handsome men who might marry her if he annulled their marriage? From what he had seen of that wench, she spent every waking moment flirting with anything in a doublet and trunk hose and grew jealous if the poor lads as much as glanced at another female.

Cristina still had not said a word in her own defense. Had the wench no pride?

Cristina's confidence had fled, and she felt as if he were rushing her to her doom and she could do naught to prevent it. Not only was he twice her size, but he fairly crackled with his anger. She did not want to speak for fear that he would stop where they were and read her a scold that would reduce her to tears. Whatever happened between them, she did not want to figure as the main topic of conversation throughout the castle. Indeed, she feared that she had already provided the gossips with enough to keep their tongues wagging for weeks, and she knew Mariota well enough to suspect she would do her best to keep them wagging.

After all, she recalled, Mariota was the one who had broken into the line at that spot. She wondered if her sister had meant all along to bring the young man to her notice. All that gave her pause was that she found it hard to imagine Mariota encouraging such a handsome man to take interest in Cristina rather than in herself.

They entered the main tower, and Hector fairly pushed her ahead of him up the winding stairway to the next floor. Passing the inner chamber, they crossed the stone bridge in front of the garderobe tower to the guest wing, and soon came to the door to his bedchamber.

When he pushed it open and urged her inside, her heart was pounding, but whether it was from their journey's speed or her fear of what he meant to do, she could not have said. Her nerves tingled, but she was not afraid of him. If anything, she was annoyed that he had taken her from the hall before making her known to Robert the Steward. She would have liked to meet the man who would be King of Scots. She had never even seen him before, and the likelihood that he would spend a great deal of time in the Isles was small.

When the door shut behind her with a snap, Cristina drew a deep breath and turned to face her husband.

He looked grim, but in the next moment, the grim look faded, replaced by one that spoke of something other than anger. His eyes smoldered, his lips parted slightly, and his breathing quickened.

When her gaze met his, an answering chord within her responded instantly. It was as if he had touched her, as if he had caressed her the way he had when they had lain together at Lochbuie. She dampened suddenly dry lips, wondering what he expected of her.

"Come here," he said hoarsely.

"What are you going to do?"

"You deserve that I should put you across my knee, do you not?"

"Nay, sir, for I've done naught for which I should be punished."

"I told you to stay home, did I not?"

"Would you have had me disobey your father?"

"He kissed you, and you did naught to stop him."

"Your father?"

"Have a care, wife." He caught her by the back of the head and drew her closer. "If you mean to be free with your kisses, you had better keep the best ones for your lord, had you not?"

"If you command it, sir," she said demurely.

"Sakes, lassie, I do not know what spell it is that you cast over me. I swear I knew naught of such when first we met, so how is it . . . ?" But his words ended in a groan as he pulled her roughly to him and kissed her mouth hard, as if he would wipe all memory of the stranger's kiss from her.

She felt beyond control, as if she wholly lacked the ability to stop him. Nor did she want to stop him. His lips were bold against hers and demanding, taking all she could give. His tongue demanded entrance to her mouth, and as it plunged inside, his hands moved over her with the confidence of hands that knew her body and knew she would not deny them anything they sought.

"Take off your clothes," he commanded, stepping back and breathing hard.

"I must send for my woman," she said. "I cannot do it by myself."

"No matter," he said, gripping her bodice in both hands. "I'll maid you."

"Don't tear it," she warned, catching hold of his hands, though she knew she could not stop him if he insisted on ripping the gown from her. "I like this dress."

"I'll buy you a new one," he said.

"I don't want a new one." She looked straight into his eyes, her hands gently holding his, her gaze steady and direct.

He sighed. "Turn around then."

She obeyed, and his fingers worked swiftly.

"I warrant this is not the first time you have played lady's maid, sir."

"This is no time for impertinence, lass. You tread on thin ice as it is."

But she knew he was no longer angry with her. He was very likely still angry with Fergus Love, but not with her. Something had stirred his passion, and she did not mind that at all.

His hands were firm on her body, firm with the gown's fastenings, and firm when he pushed it from her shoulders to fall with silken whisper to the floor. Her underskirt followed, and she stood in her shift, his hands still firm on her shoulders.

"I'm thinking that I'll require maiding myself," he said, his deep, almost growling voice sending waves of heat into her cheeks and throughout her body.

"I'll do my best," she said. "But I warrant I am not as familiar with the ways of gentlemen's clothing as you are with the ways of ladies'."

"If you can prate only insolence, lass, don't speak at all. Just tend to your duties and obey your lord."

She smiled, wondering how it was that a woman could enjoy being commanded in such a way.

"Do I amuse you?"

"Aye, sir, a little," she said, looking up and smiling more broadly.

"Impertinent lass. You deserve whatever punishment I devise for you."

"Do I?"

"Aye, come here and kiss me, and see that you do it thoroughly."

"I do not know why I should. I doubt that the rules of annulment allow a man to command a wife that he intends to set aside."

She could hardly believe the words had passed her lips, but they had and hung now in the air between them.

He frowned. "Did I not make myself clear earlier?" he asked. "Unless you wish it, madam, I no longer mean to seek an annulment, and certainly not to marry your sister. Do you not think we can make a success of this marriage of ours?"

"Aye, if you wish it, sir." Her pulse had quickened, but instinctively she contained her reaction, saying as calmly as she could, "Until God or the Kirk wills it otherwise, I've sworn to act as your wife in every way."

"Good lass," he said, taking her in his arms again. "Now, I suggest that you begin with the ties of my doublet. Since you are so ignorant in the ways of masculine clothing, I will instruct you at every step."

"Aye, sir, but I would beg a boon of you first."

"You would dare to set conditions? Have you forgotten that this is by way of being punishment for a forward wife?"

Ignoring that question in the belief that it was but more of his teasing, she said seriously, "I do not think you understood me earlier with regard to Mariota, sir. If you truly mean to honor our marriage, I beg that you will not tell her so. Let her see for herself and grow accustomed to it slowly."

"Sakes, lass, I do not know why you fret about Mariota. She draws so much attention from the lads here that I warrant she'll not give me a second thought. Don't bother your head about her. Instead, you may unlace my shirt."

With a sigh, certain that he did not understand at all, she turned her attention to his shirt, finding it harder to deal with the laces when he chose that moment to whisk her shift over her head and begin teasing her breasts. Moments later, he scooped her up in his arms and strode with her to the bed.

Laying her gently upon it, he pulled off the rest of his clothes in a trice and got under the covers beside her, slipping an arm beneath her and drawing her close. Then, raising himself on one elbow, he claimed her lips again in a long, thorough kiss as his hands roamed freely over her body, stirring heated responses wherever they touched her until she writhed beneath him, moaning her desire for him. When he possessed her, he did so swiftly, bringing her to a peak but then pounding to his own release, leaving her hungry for more.

"Sorry, lass," he murmured sleepily as he snuggled her close. "I guess I missed you more than I knew."

Within moments, he was asleep, but Cristina lay for an hour, wondering why she felt as if he had abandoned her again. It was not as if she had expected more, because her experience was so limited that she did not know what to expect. But he seemed sated. Indeed, he had groaned at the end and collapsed atop her as if he had fallen unconscious. Yet she felt as if she had only begun a climb toward nearly unbearable passion. Nothing in her experience matched what he seemed to feel, yet the promise had been there, promise that she would have liked him to fulfill.

In time she forced her thoughts to Mariota. Could Hector be right? Could the attention her self-centered sister was receiving from every suitable young man attending his grace's court satisfy her? Cristina's experience told her that no amount of attention from lads who wanted Mariota would satisfy her. If she had decided that she wanted Hector, she would not rest until she had him. But if he did not want her, if he had indeed decided to be content with the wife he had and that the Holy Kirk had ordained, what then? The possibilities did not bear thinking of, and inevitably exhaustion crept in, sending Cristina at last into restless slumber.

She awoke to find herself alone in her husband's bed. Not a sight or sound in the bedchamber suggested that he had slept there, leading her to believe that his man had crept about, first dressing him, then tidying the room without disturbing her. Very considerate, to be sure, but she would have been happier had Hector wakened her with a kiss and bade her good morrow.

Thus it was with jaundiced eye that she regarded the new day, which matched her mood, since it had dawned with scudding clouds and towering, distant thunderheads. As the morning progressed, the sky grew grayer and dipped lower, creating a look of hard, wet rain in the clearness of the foothills.

Nor did anything else about the morning improve Cristina's mood. No sooner did she walk into the hall to break her fast than Mariota greeted her with the cheerful news that Fergus Love had been looking for her.

"You have made a conquest, my dear," she said. "He waxed on and on about how beautiful you are until I vow I was bored with his chatter."

"Usually, when anyone compliments another woman in your hearing, you tell us how stupid he is," Cristina said.

"Well, if you are going to be rude about it, I shan't say any more," Mariota said, visibly annoyed.

Instead of coaxing her into a sunnier mood, Cristina said, "I do not care a whit about Fergus Love. I thought his behavior last evening was rude and foolish. To be kissing a woman he does not know in full view of her husband does not suggest that he uses his head for anything more useful than wearing his hat."

"Men are always foolish when they fall in love," Mariota said, taking no notice of Cristina's displeasure. "You would know that if you'd had as many suitors as I have. And you need suitors, Cristina, for you'll soon be without a husband."

"I know you have heard that Hector means to apply for an annulment," Cristina said, goaded into discussing the very topic she had warned Hector to be wary of. "But truly, my dear, that does not mean he will get one, or even that he may not change his mind about applying."

"Oh, I know about all that," Mariota said with a smirk. "Mairi explained the whole thing to me, and Father did, too, but I know what I know even so."

"But surely you understand that if he cannot get it, our marriage will stand."

"'Tis you who does not understand," Mariota said. "Just because his father and his stupid brother told him that he must not have your marriage annulled, you think he will heed them, but he will not. He loves me, as he has from the start."

A knot formed in Cristina's stomach as the meaning of Mariota's words struck her. If Hector had made his decision because his brother and father had commanded him, that decision meant none of what she had thought. She excused herself as deftly as she could from Mariota, intending to return to her bedchamber, but she did not get far before Isobel waylaid her, demanding to know how she was to entertain herself in a huge castle that apparently had no children her own age.

"Father says I am to stay away from the great hall, the cliffs, and the Sound, and to amuse myself without getting into trouble. I should like to know how I am to do that when I do not even have a pony to ride or anyone to walk with me."

"There must be children somewhere," Cristina said. "I'll ask Mairi."

"Well, what shall I do until then?"

"Where is Aunt Euphemia?"

Isobel grimaced. "Truly, Cristina, you cannot expect me to hang on her sleeve all day. She does not like it, and nor do I."

"There you are, Isobel. I have been searching everywhere for you," Lady Euphemia said, bustling up to them. "Really, Cristina, I wish you would speak to this naughty child. I do not know where she is from one moment to the next."

Cristina looked sternly at Isobel. "What have you to say to that?"

Indignantly, Isobel said, "I did tell you, Aunt Euphemia. I asked you to suggest something I might do, and you said it was up to me, that I should exert my imagination to devise some way of entertaining myself, and so I did. Only there isn't anything, and so I was asking Cristina."

"Well, you cannot just disappear like that," Lady Euphemia said. "It is too much to expect me to guess what you are doing and where you are from one minute to the next. Tell her, Cristina. I do not know why you brought her in the first place. This is no place for a gently nurtured child. You should have left her at Lochbuie."

Struggling to control her temper, knowing it would do no good to speak sharply to either one, Cristina said, "Isobel knows that she is at Ardtornish, Aunt Euphemia, and I doubt she will misbehave whilst she is a guest of the Lord of the Isles. Nor do I think you need bother your head about where she is every moment."

Turning to the visibly gratified child, she said crisply, "I shall try to find out what other children do to amuse themselves here, Isobel. His grace has numerous grandchildren, after all, so I'll ask Mairi at the first opportunity. For now though, I suggest that you apologize to Aunt Euphemia for worrying her and attend for an hour or so to the needlework pillow cover you wanted to finish before Easter."

Isobel made a face expressing her opinion of the needlework, but Cristina was unsympathetic. "You asked me," she said. "Now, go and do it."

"Very well, but I don't have to like it," Isobel said. Then, turning to Lady Euphemia, she said, "I'm truly sorry, Aunt. I did think I was doing as you asked."

"Then we'll say no more about it," Lady Euphemia said. "Go along now. I want to speak privately to Cristina."

With a sigh, Cristina waited, wondering what else her ladyship had to say.

"Mariota told me about that impudent young man last evening, Cristina. I'm surprised at you. Why, your father would be ... well, I don't know what he would be, but not happy, my dearest, not happy at all. You should keep young men like that one at a distance now that you are married. Mariota told me that Hector was angry, as well he should be. I know that she thinks you should be encouraging other young men, because she believes that he means to cast you off and to marry her, but I cannot think he would be so foolish. Such a wise young man, and sensible withal, but you mustn't encourage other men, dearling. Men never like that at all."

Wanting to scream, but forcing calm out of pure habit, Cristina said, "I did not encourage him, Aunt Euphemia. I do not know why everyone believes that."

"It is the way people are," Lady Euphemia said. "If a man approaches a woman, people assume that she encouraged him, that he would not approach if she did not seem willing to meet him halfway."

"Well, I didn't. But Hector believed that for a short time, certainly."

"He believed what he wanted to believe. All men do that."

"But he cannot want to believe that I would . . . would . . ."

"Make him a cuckold," Lady Euphemia suggested blandly when Cristina could not put the thought into words. "Of course he can believe it. I have heard that he was quite a rogue with the ladies before his marriage. I don't say that I heard of him cuckolding anyone, but still, there you are. The things men . . . people . . . dislike in others are usually the traits they dislike most in themselves, you know. Which is not to say that Hector encourages other women, merely that he knows that the flesh is weak, and that therefore the possibility for mischief always exists."

Cristina sighed. "I suppose that's it exactly, and yet I tend to react to things he does and says much more than to things anyone else does or says. There is no accounting for it. I cannot control my emotions anymore, Aunt. I have always been able to do that, you know, to stay calm whilst everyone around me was flying into a temper or flinging insults about, even when Father was at his worst."

"Oh, aye, you were a marvel, my dear, always resolving everyone else's troubles and arguments. But things are different now."

"But what's the matter with me?"

"If I told you, you wouldn't listen."

"But something's happened. I can feel it, and it's as if I don't know myself anymore. It's terrible."

"Nay, not terrible. You love him, that's all."

Cristina stared at her, wondering how a spinster like Lady Euphemia could be so certain of such a thing. "I own, Aunt, I have wondered if I do," she admitted, "but I have heard others talk of love, and nothing they have said sounds like what's happening to me. Nevertheless, I think that may be exactly what it is."

"Happens all the time," Lady Euphemia said. "Difference is, most women it happens to aren't married to the man in question. But do not encourage other men, my love, and beware, too, of Mariota. She insists that he means to get an annulment, but your father assures me that that is not the case."

"Mariota will accustom herself to that in time if we can be patient and let her enjoy her own view of things until it changes," Cristina said. "It does no good to tell her things she does not want to hear, but her interest will eventually shift to someone else and she will come to understand that Hector will never marry her. As long as no one succeeds in making her face that fact before she is ready, all will be well."

"I wish I could be sure of that," her aunt said with a sigh.

"Really, it is not like you to dramatize such a thing," Cristina said. "'Beware of Mariota,' indeed. Unless, of course, you fear that Hector may think his own flesh is weak and that she will seduce him."

"Faith, what a thing to say!" Lady Euphemia exclaimed. "I did not warn you to keep an eye on your husband, dearling, but on your unpredictable sister. Mariota is spoiled and accustomed to getting what she wants. She never recovered from your mother's death, and your father has indulged her beyond what is sensible. In a rage, she is capable of anything, so we must take care not to enrage her. Why, I believe she tried to drown that kitten at Lochbuie, merely because it is Hector's."

Shocked, but remembering that she had wondered about that herself, Cristina said only that she was sure that had been an accident. Lady Euphemia seemed ready to continue the discussion, but Cristina simply could not. She apologized again for Isobel's behavior and excused herself. Then, hurrying downstairs, wanting only to escape the crowded castle and find somewhere peaceful, she crossed the courtyard and headed for the walkway between the great hall and the guest wing. She had nearly made it when she heard her father's voice bellowing her name.

Closing her eyes, she halted in her tracks, drew a deep breath, and turned to face him. "Yes, sir, what is it?"

"What is it? That's what you ask me! I want to talk to you, daughter. What is this nonsense I hear about another man? Some upstart scoundrel that Mariota tells me is mad about you and that you encouraged just as any light-skirt would."

"I did not," Cristina said, keeping her tone even, but wanting to shout the words at him. She knew he was the last person she should allow to ignite her temper, since he would certainly slap her and not care that they stood in full view of the entire castle. By the same token, she reminded herself, he did not care that he was taking her to task in view of anyone who wanted to watch.

He did not heed her denial in any case, launching into a stern and angry lecture, demanding that she honor the courtesies of her position and remain chaste. Every word flying from his lips offended her, but she held her tongue, letting the insults flow over and around her as she had done in the past, putting her energy into withstanding the flood rather than making what would surely be a futile effort to stem its course. By the time he finished, she could feel prickling tears in her eyes, more from the effort of remaining silent than from anything specific that he had said. But her throat ached, and her soul withered under the onslaught.

In time, he ran out of things to say, ending with, "I don't

want to hear any more such accusations about you, lass, so mind your ways."

Her usual practice was to say "yes, sir" to anything he said in such a diatribe, but for once she remained silent, even when he stood grimly facing her, clearly waiting for her to show contrition or remorse.

At last, he said, "That's all then. You may go. Just heed my words."

She stood silently even then, looking him in the eye until he turned and strode back to the castle. Drawing a long breath, she let it out slowly, then turned and walked away toward the cliff tops above Ardtornish.

The air was heavy, clouds loomed to the west, and a chilly damp that might be fog by nightfall oozed from the ground and clung around her, but it was still better than being indoors.

Chapter 16

Hector was beginning to think Robert the Steward ought to have stayed in Stirling, where he was surely safer than in the Isles. Only by the sheerest luck and the success of a clever trap, had he and his entourage arrived safely at Ardtornish.

Lachlan had sent half the flotilla with Ranald of the Isles, as he had said he would, but sent the second half shortly afterward to follow and watch for trouble. The attack had come just as Ranald's boats were entering the harbor near the village of Oban, but when the rest of the boats had shown themselves, their attackers fled.

News of the event had swept through the castle after his arrival, and its aftermath—lengthy discussions of further security measures and plans to find and capture the attackers—had not only taken him and Lachlan from their supper the previous night but had deprived them both of a leisurely wakening that morning.

In the darkness before dawn, Hector's man had entered the bedchamber silently to waken him and tell him Mac-Donald demanded his presence forthwith. He had scrambled into his clothes without wakening Cristina, and had hurried to the great chamber, where he found his twin and Mac-Donald already waiting.

Lachlan was pacing, fairly twitching in uncharacteristic impatience.

"Faith, brother," he exclaimed, "did you intend to sleep the day away?"

MacDonald smiled at Hector. "Good morning, sir," he said. "I warrant you earned your rest, and I deeply apologize for disturbing it, but we've need of you."

"I came as soon as my man roused me," Hector said. "What's amiss now?"

Lachlan grimaced. "I'm certain we are harboring the instigator of the Steward's ills under this very roof, but I've not a scintilla of evidence against the man other than his known dislike of us."

"You speak of Fingon Mackinnon, of course."

"Aye, his eminence, the Green Abbot, who has been far too friendly with your new sister, sir, or whatever that lass is to you," Lachlan said with more curtness than he was wont to use with his twin.

Evenly, Hector said, "Mariota is naught to me other than my sister-in-law, as you ken fine, my lad, so let me hear no more such implications from you."

"I beg your pardon," Lachlan said. "But I'm at my wits' end and scrambling for answers. The plain fact is that the attacking fleet came from the west, straight at us, as if they knew our exact location."

"Doubtless they suspected Oban as the meeting place from the outset," Hector said. "But if they did not, it would have taken no great skill for one of the boats in the first half of your flotilla to fall back and get word to the attackers."

"But how would they guess his destination?" MacDonald asked.

"With respect, your grace, the Steward's intentions have been known all over the Isles for weeks now, and with travel by water being as unpredictable as it is this time of year, the most sensible place to meet him was Oban."

"Aye, that's true enough," MacDonald said.

"What we have yet to determine is their exact intention," Lachlan pointed out. "Had Hector not suspected the petrel business was a diversion, they might have triumphed. As it was, since our lads' primary duty is to protect the Steward, most of the enemy boats managed to escape, and none flew any identifying banner. The lads on the one we did catch are not talking, at least not yet," he added grimly.

"I'll have some of my men question them," Hector said.

Lachlan nodded. "Aye, that was my intent, but we must deal with this quickly and quietly. His grace does not want it known that the Steward faced danger from any Islesmen. And that's the rub, since the news has spread already."

"Say they were pirates," Hector suggested. "'Tis easy enough if they flew no clan banners, and his grace can order you to find and hang every last one of them."

MacDonald frowned. "Aye, that might work, and the suggestion of pirates would stir no coals with any feuding clans. I fear that some may take sides if it becomes known that organized opposition exists to Robert's taking the throne."

"Forgive me, your grace, but why should that matter now?" Hector asked.

"Because David is ailing," MacDonald said. "If his enemies fear he is dying, the fat will be in the fire, and if the opposition manages to organize itself swiftly and David does die, Robert could face massive rebellion before he wins his crown."

"But Parliament approved the succession laid out in the Bruce's will."

Lachlan shrugged. "Men do say that words written down forty years ago ought not to govern what happens now, particularly if the Steward proves too weak to hold what he claims is his. And as you know, many Islesmen believe that one of the more ancient clans deserves that crown more than the Steward does."

"'Tis the very reason my father-in-law's children began calling themselves Stewarts," MacDonald said. "I've counseled against it myself, fearing that such a change reinforces the opposition's belief that, nephew of the Bruce or not, the hereditary Steward of the Realm has no business to become King of Scots."

"He is safe enough at Ardtornish," Lachlan said. "I'll send out word to gather the fleet in the Sound, Loch Aline, Loch Linnhe, and the Firth. We can say that far more boats than expected turned out to pay their respects. Then, with nearby waters teeming with Isles' galleys and longboats, any enemy of his lordship's or yours, your grace, will certainly think twice before stirring up more mischief."

"Aye, I'll not argue against that," MacDonald said "I do not look for battle, but neither will we shy from it, and I think some folks need reminding that I strongly support the Bruce's will."

Hector spent the next several hours setting Lachlan's plans in motion, both to question the captured prisoners and get word to the Isles chiefs that MacDonald wanted their boats to patrol neighboring waterways. He knew that more would arrive before darkness and for days to come, as clan chiefs reluctant to show strong support but unwilling to offend MacDonald beyond forgiveness began arriving. So many men and boats should, he believed, deter further mischief while Robert remained a guest at Ardtornish, and would protect him during his return journey.

Having attended to the duties assigned him, he went in search of Cristina to warn her that he would likely be too busy to pay her proper heed until the Steward returned to Stirling. He did not mean to leave her to her own devices altogether, of course, certainly not before he made sure Fergus Love understood that he was to keep his distance. He had not had a chance yet to speak to the scoundrel, but he meant to make time to do so before either of them was much older.

He went to their bedchamber, but Cristina was not there. Nor was his man anywhere about, or her woman. Downstairs in the great chamber, he found Lady Margaret, Mairi, and a host of other ladies, but no Cristina.

"I haven't seen her since we broke our fast together this morning," Mairi said when he asked her. "She seemed tired and mayhap quieter than usual. I just assumed she'd not had much sleep," she added with a twinkle.

Running Lady Euphemia to earth in the hall, he learned that she had spoken sternly to Cristina about Isobel's behavior and her own, and much else that she had said to her, but she also assured him that Cristina had seemed her usual serene self.

"Do you know where she went, my lady?"

She looked astonished. "Goodness me, no. I am not her keeper, after all, and Cristina has always looked after herself perfectly well. Indeed, she is your wife, sir. I should think that if anyone should know her whereabouts, you should."

"I know where she went," Mariota said, coming up and tucking her hand into the crook of his arm and fluttering her lashes as she looked warmly up into his eyes. "Take me for a walk round the courtyard, sir, and I shall tell you all I know."

"Sakes, lass, if you ken what's good for you, you'll tell me at once."

She pouted. "If you mean to be cruel to me, Hector Reaganach, I vow I shall never marry you, seek you ever so many annulments."

Recalling Cristina's warning but feeling strongly that he should discourage Mariota's false belief as much as possible, he repressed his irritation with her enough to say evenly, "I become daily more contented with my marriage, lass."

"'Tis kind of you to say so, and I know Cristina must be grateful that you do not shout your intentions to all and sundry, but I do know your true intent, sir, and I support it, though mayhap I should not, since she is my sister. But this muddle in which we find ourselves is all her fault, after all, and none of mine."

"Where is she?"

Mariota shrugged prettily. "You are being unkind now, but I shall tell you, because I am not. She went to walk on the hilltop. I warrant that by the time you set out to find her, she will be back in the castle, hungering for her midday meal."

"Have you looked at the sky, lass? Storm clouds have been piling up just west of us these past few hours and more. Are you sure she left the castle?"

"Aye, sir, and why not? A little rain won't hurt her, and I vow, I can hardly bear the noise and bustle of this place, as crowded as it is. Moreover, Cristina actually likes solitary walks, so who can blame her for seeking peace?"

A clap of thunder startled them both.

"Who indeed?" he asked dryly. "Forgive me, but I must go and find her."

She pouted again but did not try to stop him.

He paced while a lad readied his horse but, as soon as the saddle was on, he mounted and gave spur. Beyond the shelter of the castle's walls, a wind bearing the metallic scent of impending rain huffed around him as if it would blow him off his horse. Lightning crackled in the distance, and thunder grumbled close upon its heels, shooting icy prickles of fear up his spine. Despite a responsive, shuddering twitch along the pony's withers, he spurred it on up the hill.

By the time he drew rein at the top, the sky was even lower, and blackening. Increasingly gusty winds had blown away ground fog and the wispy skirts of mist that had hovered earlier over the bay. Grumbling thunder rolled inexorably nearer and grew ominously louder as one flash of lightning after another stabbed the earth, stepping swiftly toward him—much too swiftly.

Surely, she was not such a little fool as to have come up here. No sensible woman—and Cristina had proven herself eminently sensible—would venture unnecessarily into the path of such a threatening storm. But since Mariota had said she was walking on the hilltop, he could not take the chance that he might be leaving her to the mercy of what was quickly developing into a howling, flaming fury.

He hesitated, trying to think, realizing that she might have taken any path, even wandered aimlessly through the woods, and that the vast area of Morvern lay before him. A fresh crackling in the air followed a scant second later by a searing flash of light and a deafening crash of thunder made him duck his head reflexively.

"As if ducking could save me," he muttered, feeling stupid but flinching when another bolt stabbed a promontory just across the Sound. Glancing about, he half expected to see her laughing at him from the tree line that bordered the clearing, where dense bramble-ridden forestland stretched away across much of the landscape.

But he did not see her there. Had she taken another route back to the castle?

Forcing himself to think calmly, he remembered his earlier appraisal of his sensible wife, surely too sensible to wander off into unknown countryside alone. Moreover, he had warned her and her sisters never to do such a thing, and she was not defiant by nature. Had Mariota been the one he sought, he would have had more cause to worry about that.

Instinctively, he turned toward the cliff tops, deciding that Cristina would have sought a panoramic view, a place to think where she could see the landscape spread before her. She might even be watching the approaching storm. He had noted that she had no fear of the elements, and it occurred to him that she might be unaware of the danger lightning posed to humans. He certainly had said nothing to her about its terrors, fearing that she might deduce, as she so often did, exactly what was in his mind as he warned her.

She would realize then that he was neither ferocious nor formidable but a common coward. The lass barely heeded his wishes now, for all that she pretended to do so. What would life be like if she lost all respect for him?

As that thought formed in his mind, he grimaced, knowing he did not want to lose Cristina's respect. Then he saw her, and another chill shot through him, for she was sitting on the rock, on *Creag na Corps,* the great judgment rock from which the Lord of the Isles ordered convicted felons flung to their deaths. Wrapped in a thick, dark cloak, tightly hugging bent knees with her chin resting on one, she gazed intently out over the bay and the Sound toward Duart, as if she could see all the way to Lochbuie or even Finlaggan. She was paying no heed to the threatening storm. Indeed, sitting as she was, she made a perfect target for an errant lightning bolt.

At the next flash and the crackling onset of its accompanying roar of thunder, he flung himself from his horse, not daring to shout lest he startle her or frighten her into jumping up and trying to run from him. In truth, the way the thunder rolled and reverberated around them, he doubted she would hear him if he did shout.

He ran as if the furies of the storm chased him, his pulse pounding in his ears, terrified that fate would hurl the next lightning bolt at her before he could reach her. The thunder faded to brief silence, and a scrape of his boot on the rock startled her just as he leaped onto the rock behind her. Giving her no time to act, he clapped an arm across her shoulders, slipped his other under her knees, swept her off the rock, and dashed back from the cliff's edge toward the sheltering woodland.

Raindrops sprinkled them as he ran, quickened before he reached the trees, then spattered and danced on the thickening spring canopy above. When he had her safe from the lightning, his terror changed to fury. Setting her on her feet with a thump, he grabbed her by both shoulders and shook her hard.

"What did you think you were doing, sitting out in the open like that?" he shouted. "You might have been killed!"

"Nonsense," she retorted. "You may have saved me from a wetting, for I did not realize the rain was nearly upon me, but that is all, and you frightened me witless when you grabbed me as you did. Moreover, if you want to snarl at me, sir, I suggest you wait until we find shelter. Most of these trees bear only new spring leaves, and we'll soon be soaked through if we linger here."

He shook her again. "By heaven, lass, if I startled you, it was as nothing to the fright you gave me. Do you not know anything about lightning?"

"Aye, sure, I do," she said. "It generally strikes mountain peaks and trees, I believe, so we cannot be any safer here in the woods than I was out in the open."

"You know little about it then. Lightning strikes where it likes, but rarely hits thick groves of trees, because it seeks high points—treetops or ridgelines. *Creag na Corps,* where you were sitting, is just such a place." He pointed, and as he did, a deafening crack of thunder engulfed them and a bolt struck the cliff not far from the rock. "Did you see that?" he demanded, giving her another rough shake. "Have you no sense, that you would risk your life in such a foolish way? Are you daft?"

"Perhaps I am," she snapped. "What difference can it make to you?"

"By heaven," he said furiously, giving her yet another shake, "do not try my patience any further, because I'm as near as I've ever been to putting you across my knee. You deserve it for wandering up here alone, for risking your life as you did by making a target of yourself for the lightning, for deceiving me from the outset of this marriage of ours, for daring to flirt with a scoundrel like Fergus Love, and for coming to Ardtornish when I told you to stay at home. Sakes, but I ought to send you straight home since you have no more sense than a . . . Are you listening to me?" he demanded when he noticed that she was staring stonily at him. "You'd better be listening, by God, because whether either of us likes it or not, I am your husband, my lass, and you will listen with respect when I—"

"Let go of me," she cried, jerking away from him.

The sound and fury—both his and the storm's—overwhelmed Cristina until she could not think. She tried to tell herself that he was reacting as he was because she had frightened him, but it was as if his shaking her and ranting at her snapped something inside.

"What difference would it make to *you* if lightning struck me down?" she went on angrily while he gaped at her. "Why should you care when you never wanted anything to do with me in the first place?"

"Be sensible, Cristina," he shouted over the storm as he gave her another shake, albeit not as roughly as before. "Of course I'd care if lightning struck you."

"You don't care a whit about me, Hector Reaganach. If I died, you could have Mariota, and say what you will, she is the one you have always wanted, and she wants you, so my death would merely put things right."

"I don't want Mariota," he said. He was not holding her as tightly, and he sounded calmer, but he clearly spoke with half his attention on the weather, so the conversation was not of primary importance to him, which angered her even more.

"I wish you would listen to me," she said. "I know you think I'm a female of little brain, but still you expect much of me, sir. Indeed, everyone expects me to resolve every problem, and I'm tired of it. Doubtless, you will think me selfish, but I've begun to feel as if my only purpose on this earth is to look after everyone else. If Isobel cannot find entertainment for herself, she expects me to provide it."

"Now, lass," he began.

But she ignored him. "When you couldn't find your spurs, you assumed that I'd put them somewhere, even though you'd mislaid them yourself. And when I successfully pressed you to think where you might have left them, did you thank me? No, you wondered why you had left them there, as if I could tell you why. The responsibility is always mine. When Mariota takes the bit between her teeth, it's my fault. The world thinks Aunt Euphemia looks after the Macleod sisters, when in fact, I look after Aunt Euphemia. As for Father . . . well, the fact is that everyone expects me to look after them, and no one looks after me!"

"Poor Cristina," he said, reaching for her.

Sounding like pity, his words provided the last straw. Before he could touch her, she slapped him across the face as hard as she could. "Don't you dare touch me," she shrieked. "You have not that right. I know I said I would obey you, but you do not *want* to be my husband. The only reason you have not applied for an annulment is that your father and brother forbade it, not because *you* decided not to, and thus you have no rights where I am concerned. I don't want a husband who keeps me only through his obedience and sense of duty!"

He stopped still and looked at her, and for a long moment, silence loomed between them. Even the noise of the storm faded away. She glowered at him, still furious, but when he said nothing, it slowly dawned on her what she had done.

Even in the dim light of the storm-drenched woodland, she saw that his left cheek was as red as fire. She could almost see the imprint of her hand on it.

Her breath caught in her throat, and her heart began to pound.

She stepped back carefully, as if the ground right beneath her feet had threatened to open up and swallow her.

His eyes narrowed, a muscle high in his cheek twitched, and he visibly gathered himself. "You go too far, lass," he said, his voice grim, as he shifted his weight to step toward her. "No one—"

The air crackled, the hair on her neck tingled, and the woodland turned white around them as the heavens crashed, deafening her, and Hector threw himself at her, carrying her beneath him to the ground.

She landed with less force than she had expected and realized that he had cupped her head tightly against his chest and somehow had managed to cushion her fall as well as he could with his left forearm and leg while keeping the bulk of himself protectively atop her. The ground was soft, too, padded with inches of leaf mulch covering loose dirt. Nonetheless, she could scarcely breathe under his weight, and when the noise stopped and silence fell upon the woods again, he did not move.

"Please, sir," she muttered, gasping.

He seemed to tremble, and then he drew a deep, shuddering breath.

She tried to shift from underneath him but could not. He still gripped her tightly, and his tremors were stronger, so she knew the lightning had only stunned him if indeed it had done anything more than startle them both out of their skins.

He seemed to realize that he was crushing her with his weight, because he rolled a little to one side, but still he held her tight, her face half-buried against his chest in the thick velvet doublet he wore. She felt him heave a great sigh, and as he did, she tried again to free herself.

"Keep still, lass," he said, his voice low and containing an uncertain note that she had not heard before. "I want to hold you a little longer."

A bubble of laughter surprised her at the thought that he could find comfort in smashing her lips and nose into his chest, but she suppressed the laughter, understanding that he meant much more than that by his request. At last, though, she managed to turn her head enough to draw a full breath.

He was still shaking.

"Are you hurt?" she asked.

"I might have lost you," he said, and again that uncertain note struck her.

"But you didn't," she said. "And even if you had—"

"Don't say that again," he muttered gruffly. "I *would* care, and I did *not* decide about the damned annulment because of my brother or my father. I decided because of you, lass, only you."

Memory of what she had said and done flooded over her, but as she tried to think of something to say, a drop of water struck her cheek, trickling down her neck and under her cloak, making her shiver. Another followed it, and another.

"Did I hurt you?" he asked.

"Nay, although I did think for a moment that I'd be crushed."

"The lightning . . ." His voice shook, and he said no more.

She lay quietly, still thinking about all that had happened, ignoring drops that fell from the tree branches with more frequency. If Hector noticed them, he gave no sign. "Could the woods be on fire?" she asked. "Does lightning not start fires?"

"Aye, but with the rain pelting down on these woods as it is, we are safe," he said. "I knew that, and yet . . ."

"And yet the lightning still terrified you," she said.

"You know then."

"Know what?"

"That I'm a coward."

"Don't be ridiculous."

"How can it be ridiculous? Only think of what my

enemies—or worse, my own men—would say if they should learn that the man they call Hector the Ferocious is afraid of a little lightning."

"You're not a coward," she said firmly. "No coward, least of all one terrified of lightning, would risk his life as you did to snatch me off that rock. You simply have a healthy respect for its power, based on your extensive experience with it."

"That's true enough," he said. "Lightning struck down a servant of ours when I was a child. I saw it happen."

"Mercy."

"One minute he was in the field, herding a stubborn cow toward the barn to milk, the next he was dead and the cow as well, both smelling of roasted meat."

Her stomach curled at the image his words evoked. She said, "How horrible for you! I never knew anyone struck by lightning, although I have heard tales, of course. I never paid them much heed, because the walls of Chalamine are thick and we always felt safe inside. Today, I expect I cared more about being away from the castle alone, and watching the storm, than I did about my safety. But truly, I did not realize I was in such danger. I will take better care in future."

"You'd damned well better," he said.

"You are still angry with me."

"Me? What about you?" he demanded, pulling back to look down at her. "You were like a spitting, clawing cat, hurling accusations at me, at everyone."

"Feeling sorry for myself," she said with disgust. "Horrid."

"Not so," he said. "Much of what you said was true. You are so kind to everyone that we take advantage." He winced.

"You *are* hurt!"

That made him grin. "Nay, lass, only wet. An icy rain-drop went right down my back. We need to find shelter."

"I said that long ago," she pointed out. "Should we not just go back?"

"We'd be soaked through," he said. "At least here, although we'll be damp, the trees afford us some protection. Besides, I know of a croft nearby where we can even make a fire to warm ourselves if we can find dry wood."

"Won't the crofter have some?"

"Last time I looked, no one lived there," he said. "It's part of his grace's Kinlochaline holdings. My grandfather, Ewan Maclean, was constable there when his grace's father was Lord of the Isles. Lachlan and I used to play in these woods."

He got to his feet as he spoke and extended a hand to her.

Cristina took it willingly and let him draw her to her feet, but she could still see the imprint of her hand from the slap, and she watched him warily. It seemed a lifetime ago that she had vented her anger, but it had been only a few minutes.

He reached toward her, and she stiffened, but he just brushed a strand of hair from her cheek. His touch sent a jolt through her, as if the very blood coursing through her, making her heart pound again, were liquid fire. She could not seem to move, only to watch him and wonder how he would punish her for striking him. That he would let such an insolence pass was impossible to believe.

Her mouth was dry. She licked her lips.

A little hoarsely, he said, "Come, lass. Stop gaping at me as if I were going to murder you, and let's find that croft."

"You looked as if you wanted to murder me," she said as he put an arm around her shoulders and urged her farther into the woods. "I'm sorry I hit you."

"Not as sorry as you were about to be when Nature intervened," he said.

She swallowed hard, but his arm was warm across her shoulders and he was urging her to a faster pace. She had taken off her caul when she sat down on the rock, and had left it behind when Hector grabbed her, so her hair was wet and untidy. She must, she thought, look a sight. Doubtless, he would have more to say to her, too. She was not looking forward to finding that croft.

⤜⤛⤜

Hector tried to imagine what she was thinking. Could she really have meant it when she said he should not think himself a coward despite his fear of lightning? For that one dreadful moment when the lightning flash had turned the woods to white light, he had thought her lost to him, had thought them both lost. At least one tree had suffered from the blast, for he had heard its branches shatter and smelled charred wood, but the odor had dispersed quickly, and now he could detect only the herbal scents of damp woodland.

The croft lay in a clearing just ahead, and although ominous rumbles still sounded from time to time, the worst of the storm had passed, and they grew distant. Only the rain remained, pelting down heavily. They would have to make a dash across the clearing to the croft, or they would be soaked to the skin.

Cristina had not spoken and kept nibbling her lower lip. He knew what she was thinking as well as if she had told him, but it was good that she worried. A wife should never strike her husband and should certainly never think she could do so with impunity. His anger had vanished, but he would exact a penance for her insolence. He expected to enjoy it, and mayhap she would, too.

Inside the croft, the dirt floor lay a foot or two below the level of the ground outside, down stone steps from the door-way. The air inside was as chilly and damp as it was outside, but Cristina helped Hector gather nearly dry kindling and logs, and, with the tinderbox he carried, he started a small fire on the stone hearth.

Rain came through the single small window, but he found a broken shutter outside and managed to block most of it by jamming a branch between it and the wooden frame and tucking leaves and small branches into the remaining cracks. By the time the fire began crackling, the croft was as cozy as they could make it.

The floor was dry enough for him to spread his cloak, and he drew her down on it beside him. "Your cloak is wet," he said as he lifted it from her shoulders and spread it over a broken settle near the hearth to dry. "Snuggle close to me, lass. The heat of our bodies will keep us warm until the fire burns off the chill in here."

Her skin prickled at the thought that he would soon say all he wanted to say to her, but she obeyed without comment. After they had sat quietly staring into the fire for a few moments, she said, "I have been thinking about what you said."

"About the annulment?"

"Nay, about the lightning."

"Oh."

"You are like your ships in that you just fear fire more than water; that's all."

"Aye, perhaps, but about the annulment, lass. Do you be-lieve me?"

"I do," she said, looking directly at him. "You don't tell me lies, sir."

"You're a sweet lassie," he said, bending nearer to kiss her.

She leaned away. "You barely heeded what I said about the lightning."

"It was enough before when you said you don't think me a coward."

"Well, don't kiss me just because you think I'm sweet."

"Faith, lass, I don't just want to kiss you," he said, pressing her back onto his cloak and leaning over her to look into her eyes. "I want to make love to you, but if you're still going to insist that I have no right to do so, I can just take a nap until the rain stops." He leaned closer, his lips less than an inch from hers, his breath warm, his body tensely appealing beside hers. "What do you say, sweetheart?"

Chapter 17 ————————

Her face was flushed, Hector noted, either from reaction to his question or from the heat of the fire, and she had lost her caul somewhere, because her hair was loose and tangled, clinging in damp, honey-colored strands to her temples and cheeks. Her bodice ties had come loose so that it gaped, revealing her slim throat and the lacy edge of her shift, as well as an enticing reminder of the rounded curves below.

Her lips were but an inch away, and she looked up at him with wide eyes. When he put his hand on her breast, she gasped, and her breathing quickened. His body stirred strongly, and he said, "Well, sweetheart?"

"Are you still angry?" she asked.

"Nay, but you do deserve to pay a penance."

"What sort of penance?"

"Kiss me."

She licked her lips, and he waited no longer, claiming them with a groan and tasting them thoroughly. Her response was all that he had hoped it would be. When her lips parted, he thrust his tongue into her mouth, savoring its velvety warmth.

Pulling her laces free, he opened her bodice, nearly

groaning again when his hand met the lacy cambric of her shift.

"You have too many clothes on," he said, sitting up and pulling her with him. He dealt swiftly with her skirts and shift, tossing them aside and moving to embrace her again.

"Wait," she said. "I'll freeze."

"You won't, for I'll put another log on the fire."

"But what of your clothing?"

"Sakes, but you're an impatient wench," he said, smiling. But he stood, built the fire up, and then stripped off his clothing without more ado, tossing doublet, shirt, trunk hose, shoes, and netherstocks wherever they might fall, his awareness that she was watching stimulating him considerably.

He turned to face her, naked, and saw her blush again. Lying next to her on his side, elbow crooked, his head on one hand, he said, "Now, where was I?"

Taking his free hand, she placed it on her breast. "Here," she said.

Needing no further encouragement, he bent nearer and kissed her, tasting her mouth again briefly before moving to taste first her right breast, then the left one. Her soft skin tasted salty, and when he took a nipple in his mouth to suckle it, she moaned and began to press her body against his. His hand lay on her belly, but when she moved, he eased it lower, to the soft curls at juncture between her legs.

She moaned again. "I want to hold you," she said.

"Touch me first," he said. "Touch me as intimately as I touch you."

He heard her quick indrawn breath, but she did not protest. Nor did she obey him at once, touching only his chest and caressing his sides. Then, lightly, she put a finger to one of his nipples, rubbing it gently before she gripped it between forefinger and thumb.

Although she seemed barely to be touching him, the blood roared in his ears, and he was throbbing below. His body was urgent for hers. He slipped two fingers into the opening between her legs and delighted in her sharp gasp.

"Grip me harder, sweetheart, and caress me lower, as I hold you."

Obediently, she shifted her free hand and gripped his throbbing penis hard enough to make him cry out, "Nay then, harder above, but gently there, lass, lest you would unman me!"

A sudden twinkle leaped to her eyes, and she said, "Have I discovered a means by which to make you obey me, Hector Reaganach?"

In response, he rolled atop her, his right knee between her legs. Having already ascertained that she was ready to receive him, he eased her hand away and entered her, plunging deep. When her body leaped to meet his, he moaned in his pleasure and captured her mouth with his.

For the next several minutes, both of them lost themselves in passion until his claimed him and he pounded into her and gained his release. When he stopped moving, she moaned, and he knew that she had not reached hers.

Relaxing, he lay for some moments beside her, listening as her quick breathing eased itself. The rain outside had eased, too, but it still beat a steady patter on the croft's thatched roof. After some moments, he leaned up on his elbow again and looked into her eyes. She stared straight up at the ceiling.

"Smile at me, sweetheart," he said.

Her smile was soft, but her body moved impatiently,

squirming in her frustration. He let her squirm for a moment or two, and then moved his hand to tease her a little more.

She gasped.

"Now, who is in control?" he said, grinning at her.

"You are," she said, gasping again.

"Recall that I am a musician, sweetheart. If I want to exact a penance, I can strum you like my lute."

She moaned, and taking that for encouragement, he moved lower down to tease her with his tongue where his fingers played.

To his delight, she made no objection, clearly savoring his attention until he brought her to release. Afterward, she lay quietly, staring at him in wonder. "I didn't know," she said. "I never knew anyone could feel like this."

Lying beside her again, holding her close with her head on his shoulder, he drew a deep breath and let himself relax, feeling much of the same wonder that she had expressed and wishing they could linger. But the rain had stopped.

"We should get back," she said a few moments later. "People will worry."

"Let them," he said, thinking that even with her hair in a tangle, she looked beautiful. "Not that anyone *will* worry," he added. "Those who might do so must know that I came in search of you, and they also know that had I not found you by now, I'd have roused the entire castle to look for you."

"Would you?"

"Aye, lass, so remember that, because if you ever give me cause to do that, I'll have something to say when I find you that you won't want to hear."

"Like this, today?"

He grinned. "I admit this turned out better than I'd expected. I think you can safely expect to see me at Lochbuie soon after your own arrival there. I'm greedy to taste your treasures again as soon as possible."

"Faith, sir, you can savor them all you like right here at Ardtornish," she said, giving him a wary look.

He met it soberly. "I still mean to send you home, sweetheart. I spoke in anger before, but the plain fact is that my duties here will consume my time until the Steward departs, and afterward for mayhap a sennight or so until things settle down again. You'll find peace at Lochbuie, and I'll worry about you less if I know you're safe there, well away from the likes of Fergus Love and your sister Mariota's mischief. I'll send Isobel and your aunt along with you, if you like."

"I won't be sent back like a misbehaving wife," she said, sitting up and pushing strands of hair off her cheeks. "I've done nothing to warrant that, sir, and well do you know it. Nor will Isobel or Aunt Euphemia jump to your command. You would have to gain my father's permission first, I think."

He frowned, knowing she was right, that he could not order Macleod's sister or young daughter back to Lochbuie. But where Cristina was concerned, either he would be master of his household or he would not.

Sternly, he said, "You'll go, my lass, if I have to sling you over my shoulder and carry you down to the longboat. And if you think my men will dance to your piping after I've given them their orders, you'll find you are much mistaken."

She got up, put on her clothes without asking for help, shook the dust from her skirt, and felt her cloak to see if it was dry. He watched, wondering why he had never noticed before how gracefully she moved, how each movement and gesture conveyed a serenity and elegance that made just watching her such a pleasure.

When she looked pointedly at him, then at his clothing scattered across the dirt floor, he took the hint and dressed quickly.

He wanted to say more, to be sure she understood that he would brook no defiance—even that he would miss her—but both instinct and logic told him he would do better to keep silent. He doubted that she would defy him now that he had issued a command, because she was obedient and tended to avoid confrontation. She would not like it, but she would pack her things and return on tomorrow's afternoon tide.

∽∝∾

Cristina was grateful for his silence. The passion he had shown during their coupling had given her sufficient confidence to tell him she would not go, because she had been nearly certain that, sexually sated as he was, he would not fly into a temper with her. But either she had not chosen her moment as well as she had hoped or his decision to send her home was stronger than she had realized.

She would not press the point now, but perhaps later, after supper and the reception for Robert the Steward, she would find a way to influence his decision, or at least to delay her departure for a day or so, until others would also be leaving. She had heard other women talk of using feminine wiles, in bed especially, to persuade their husbands to a certain course. She had a feeling that Hector would not be easily persuaded now that he had made his decision, but she could certainly try.

The silence between them lasted until they reached the

clearing at the top of the cliffs and he whistled for his horse. When it did not respond, he whistled again, a louder, more piercing sound that made Cristina want to cover her ears, but still there was no sign of the horse.

"Spooked by the storm and already in the barn, I'll warrant," he muttered. "Sorry, lass, I should have tied him. I guess we're walking."

She did not mind in the least. The last thing she wanted to do was to ride pillion with him, or worse, to ride in front of him on his saddlebow with his arm around her. A brisk, bracing walk in the rain-washed air would suit her just fine.

He took her by the shoulders, startling her and making her realize that his grip there before had bruised her, but he only gazed into her face this time and gently brushed a few errant strands of her still-damp hair from her cheeks as he said, "What happened to your caul?"

"I pulled it off whilst I sat on the rock, because I wanted to feel the wind in my hair. I expect it blew away after you snatched me up."

He smiled wryly, saying, "Looking as we do, I'm thinking it will be as well for us both if we can manage to slip inside and upstairs without meeting Lady Margaret or his grace."

Grateful as she was for his light tone, aware that he was trying to ease the tension between them, she did not respond. She did not care whom they met.

The clouds were breaking up as they scudded eastward, and sunbeams spilled through the openings, like shining pathways from heaven to earth. Their golden light sparkled on the waters of the Sound and the bay, and made the raindrops on the grass and shrubbery glitter like brilliants on formal court costumes.

As Cristina and Hector approached the walkway between the hall and the guest wing, he said, "We'll just have time to change for supper if we don't dawdle, so we have excellent reason to slip in through the kitchen instead of the main entrance. We'll tell anyone we meet that we're in a hurry, not wanting to be late."

She nodded and let him lead the way. No one moved to stop him, nor had she expected that anyone would, although the kitchen stairway was for servants' use, and guests rarely used any but the main entrance to the castle.

When they reached the guest wing, he paused, saying, "Now that you're safely inside, I want to make certain my horse did return to the barn, lass, so I'll leave you here. You'll get your clothing changed quicker if Brona does not think she has to guard your modesty from me. But I'll be back in a twinkling."

Brona was waiting for her, making Cristina glad—and not for the first time—that she had not taken a maid of her own with her from Chalamine to Lochbuie. To have had to endure just then the strictures of one who had known her from the cradle would have irritated her beyond endurance. But although she had come in looking as if someone had tried to launder her clothes while she wore them, Brona simply began with her usual quiet air of dignity to assist her.

"I was caught in the storm and lost my caul," Cristina said as the woman began gently to comb out the tangles in her hair.

"I can see that, m'lady," the woman said. "I think we'd best sit ye down by yon fire, so your hair will dry. It would no do t' be sending ye down t' pay your respects t' the next King o' Scots wi' a wet head."

Cristina moved obediently nearer the hearth, and Mariota walked in.

"Faith, but where have you been, Cristina?" she exclaimed. "I thought you'd got lost, or were still vexed with me."

"You should not walk into this room without rapping first, my love," Cristina said with a smile as she imagined her sister's shock had she walked in on Hector as he was changing his clothing. "You forget that I share it with my husband."

"Nay, I did not, but I saw him crossing the courtyard, and I knew you would not mind if I interrupted you."

"Then come in and shut the door," Cristina said. "I'm just getting warm."

"But where were you? I thought you just went for a short walk."

"We got caught in the storm on the cliff, near a rock on the highest point. I think it is the one Mairi called the judgment rock."

Mariota nodded. "*Creag na Corps.* What on earth were you doing there?"

"I wanted some peace, so I went up alone to see the view, but don't start scolding me, for I promise you, I have already heard all I want to hear about it."

"From Hector? I told him I thought perhaps you'd gone up there."

"Yes, he found me just as the lightning caught up with us, and seeing me exposed to it as I was frightened him witless, so naturally he lost his temper and said horrid things to me."

Mariota said complacently, "Aye, well he won't be doing that much longer. I talked with the abbot today, and he faithfully promised—"

"Mariota, you didn't!"

"Well, of course I did," Mariota said. "He likes me,

Cristina, and he sees the bigger picture, just as I do. He says we can sort it all out in a trice, so you need not fret about Hector's temper. I can tell you, it won't worry me in the least, because I know exactly how to keep a man's mind on something other than scolding me."

"Aye, you do," Cristina agreed. "But Hector is not a man you can manipulate so easily. Indeed, he means to send me home tomorrow," she added with a sigh.

"He does?" Mariota's expression lightened, but then, as if she realized that joy was not the proper emotion to display, it altered ludicrously to sympathy. "I'm desperately sorry that you'll have to go," she said. "You must be so disappointed."

"I'm not exactly delighted," Cristina said dryly, aware of Brona's presence. Hoping the woman's discretion was as trustworthy as it seemed to be, she added, "I'm afraid most folks will think he's punishing his wife for misbehavior."

"Mayhap a few," Mariota said. "But recall that nearly everyone will leave by week's end. Doubtless Hector will be busy till then looking after the Steward."

"Aye, but he'll be back here at any moment," Cristina said, standing and asking Brona to fill the washbasin so she could wash her hands and face before donning her gown and sitting down again to have her hair arranged.

Eyes atwinkle, Mariota said, "I know you have to hurry, so I'd better go. If he is in a temper, I don't want to see him now, anyway," she added, chuckling.

Cristina fixed her attention on her appearance for the next twenty minutes before she realized that more than enough time had passed for Hector to go to the barn and back. By the time Brona had finished arranging her hair, she was wondering if she ought to send a gillie to find him, but before she had made up her mind, the latch clicked and he hurried in, looking both worried and harried.

"Did your pony not return?"

"Oh, aye, he did, but he managed to strain a hock somehow. I'm guessing the lightning frightened him and he stumbled, or he stepped into a rabbit hole."

Guilt surged through her. "Mercy, and it's my fault. If I hadn't—"

"Enough, lass," he said firmly. "It was no one's fault. I should have tied him or at least looped the rein over a bush before I ran to get you."

Discretion or none, Cristina decided that she would prefer Brona's absence now more than her presence. "That will be all, Brona," she said. "I'm quite ready to go downstairs, and you can tidy up in here after the laird has dressed."

"Aye, m'lady," she said, bobbing a curtsy and departing.

"You should go ahead, lass. Your father will be down by now, and you can make my excuses to his grace if he looks for me—or if Lachlan does. Be tactful."

She nodded. "I'll do my best, sir, but hurry."

As she walked briskly toward the stairway, Fergus Love stepped out of a shadowy alcove ahead of her, smiling broadly. "There you are," he said. "I wondered if you had managed to leave your chamber before I could run up here."

Pausing, she said with a touch of annoyance, "But you should not approach me this way, sir. You must know that such behavior is inappropriate."

"My lady, I cannot stay away," he said, spreading his hands. "I am helpless against the power of your attraction. I came at once when I heard that your husband had lingered elsewhere, leaving you in need of an escort to make your appearance below. No such beautiful lady should go unprotected at his grace's court."

As if he had known her all his life, he took her hand and placed it in the crook of his arm. "Think of me as your protector, lass. I'll look after you well."

"Please, sir, you must not," Cristina said in dismay as she tried to pull free.

"Ah, lassie, do not tease me," he said, catching her other hand, pulling her hard against him and holding her there with an arm around her waist. "There now, you feel the evidence of my desire for you," he said, leering at her.

"Oh, for mercy's sake," she snapped, disgusted. "If you do not release me at once, I shall scream."

"I cannot allow that," he said, capturing her mouth in a hard kiss and raising a hand to cup the back of her head so she could not pull away.

Furious, Cristina raised a foot and stomped down as hard as she could. Although she could not see her target, she felt it and heard him cry out in pain.

Jerking back his head, he gaped at her in astonishment. "How dare you!" he snapped. "By heaven, when you are mine—"

But Cristina did not hear the rest because a large hand grabbed his shoulder and spun him around as another gripped her arm and pulled her away from him. Before Fergus Love could protest the rough treatment, a cracking blow from Hector's right fist sent him crashing full length to the stone floor.

Standing over him, Hector growled, "Do not lay hands on my wife again."

"Mercy, sir," Cristina exclaimed, looking at her would-be suitor in shock. "What if you've killed him?"

"What if I have?" Hector demanded. "You stay away

from him, my lass, or you'll suffer the consequences of my temper, too."

"If you think for one moment that I—"

"I don't, or we'd be heading back to our bedchamber right now for some plain talk, instead of going down with dignity to join his grace's honored guests."

"Are we just going to leave him there?"

"We are. Have you an objection to that?"

She hesitated, but his grim scowl told her she would win no debate with him over the likes of Fergus Love. "No, sir," she said.

"Good. You may precede me. These steps are too narrow to go two abreast."

As they passed the first turn in the spiral stairway, Love's voice sounded from above: "I don't know why you're so wroth with me, lass. Your own sister said you were that taken with me and would soon be free, seeking a husband. 'Tis shameful to serve the one man willing to wed you with such wicked treatment."

Cristina gasped.

"If Mariota sent that scoundrel to waylay you outside your bedchamber door, I'll have something to say to her that will make her hair curl," Hector snarled.

"Please, sir, do not," Cristina said, feeling a shiver of fear at the thought of what might ensue from such a scene.

"Your sister badly wants skelping," he said. "Everyone may blame you when she takes the bit between her teeth, but you cannot control her alone, so I'll help. I expect I'd better wait till after his grace's reception before taking her to task though."

However, to Cristina's further dismay, Mariota was standing just outside in the courtyard, and she grinned as soon as she saw her step through the doorway. "I see

Fergus found—" She broke off, apparently seeing then that the man following Cristina was not Fergus. Her mouth fell open.

Cristina exclaimed, "Mariota, what were you thinking, to send that man upstairs like that! Do you realize he believed I would welcome his attentions?"

"Never mind, lass, I'll deal with this," Hector said grimly.

"I don't know what you think you must deal with, sir," Mariota said, smiling. "If the stupid man took liberties, I'm sure it is not my fault. Fingon told me Fergus wanted to extend his acquaintance with Cristina, and reminded me that after the annulment she will need another husband. I hoped his interest would comfort her after you were so mean and said you were sending her home. I was just being kind."

"The devil you were! If you were my daughter, by heaven, I'd—"

"Daughter! Faith, I've no wish to be your daughter. I mean to be your wife, and if you think you will bully me then, you had better think again."

Before he could finish telling her what he wanted to do to her, Cristina said, "For shame, Mariota! Keep your voice down lest others out here hear you. Do you not realize that that horrid man tried to kiss me right outside our bedchamber?"

"Even if he did, I—"

"We left him lying on the floor," Cristina interjected curtly. "It was dreadful, Mariota, and if you sent him up there, the whole thing *was* your fault!"

Mariota looked from one to the other, and as her wide-eyed gaze met Hector's furious one, her expression altered. "I didn't know," she said. "I do apologize if anything I might have said led him to believe he could behave so dreadfully, but you must have done something to make him think he could kiss you, Cristina, because I certainly never told him to. Please, you must believe me, sir. I'm most dreadfully sorry. Truly, I am, but it was not my fault. Cristina is always so friendly, and doubtless her natural, rather flirtatious nature led him to believe—"

"Be silent," Hector snapped. "I do not want to hear another word from you. I mean to tell your father of this new mischief you have stirred. You have behaved disgracefully, and if you think for one moment that I'd want to marry you, ever, you were never more mistaken. I'd as lief marry a she-badger!"

"You don't mean that," Mariota said, her eyes welling with tears.

"I have never meant anything more," he declared, ignoring them. "Now, leave us before I tell you—no matter who can hear it—exactly what I think of you."

Gathering her dignity, she turned on her heel and walked quickly away.

"Oh, sir, you do not know what you have done," Cristina said, wondering what she could possibly do to ease the pain Mariota must be feeling.

"I know what I've done," he said. "I've emptied your idiot sister's head of the twaddle with which she, unaided by anyone else, has stuffed it, and I see what a miraculous escape I had. Had I followed my own course, I'd have married her and been duty-bound to honor the marriage, which terrifies me. That woman is mad."

"Nay, sir, not mad," Cristina said, although she had often thought as much herself. Mariota's tears had stirred her as little as they had stirred him, because from early childhood, she had watched her produce tears at will. Still, Cristina knew that her sister was suffering, because that was always the case when she felt slighted, and she would react to Hector's anger even more than to anyone else's, if only because she had persuaded herself that she loved him.

"Mariota does not feel things the way other people do, so she doesn't always understand the results of her actions," she added. "She would tell you that she thinks with her emotions and thus more creatively or just differently than others do. After explaining that to you, she would expect you to accept her view."

"Then you had better be sure she understands that I meant every word I said to her," he retorted. "Because if she ever plays such tricks with us again, I won't be so lenient. And lest you wonder, I mean to tell your father about this straightaway."

Cristina nodded, knowing that nothing she could say would dissuade him. She also knew, though, that nothing he could say to Macleod would persuade him that Mariota had done anything horrid. If Mariota was ever to understand that she could not control Hector, Cristina knew she would have to have a long and difficult talk with her, and at least try to make her understand why he was so angry with her.

In the meantime, they joined the others in the great hall and had taken their places on the dais before she found an opportunity to speak to Mariota. Fortune, or more likely Mairi's influence, had put Cristina two places away from her on the ladies' end of the table with Mariota at her left and Lady Euphemia just beyond.

Cristina did not know the woman to her right but deduced that she must be of importance, because she sat next to Mairi of the Isles, who was, as usual, in the place of honor beside Lady Margaret Stewart.

Everyone still stood, waiting for the grace before meat,

and she was glad to see, for Mariota's sake, that Hector and Macleod were not next to each other.

Robert the Steward took the place of honor at MacDonald's right, with Lachlan Lubanach next to him. Hector and a string of Isles chiefs that included Macleod followed, and since the Steward had not traveled with his lady wife, Cristina assumed that the woman next to her must be a chief's wife.

As everyone sat down, Mariota leaned close and hissed, "I do think you might have stopped him from speaking to me so rudely."

Glancing right to be sure her neighbor was safely engaged in conversation with Mairi, Cristina said quietly, "Mariota, keep your voice down. When you sent that man up to waylay me, you precipitated a most unpleasant scene. I am not surprised that Hector is angry, only that you cannot see that you were in the wrong."

"But I apologized," she muttered. "You heard me."

"You said you were sorry," Cristina said. "After you do something dreadful, you always say you are sorry, over and over, but you never mean it, and people can tell that you don't. Even as you were apologizing, you cast blame on me for what had happened. Don't you see how that turns your apology into an accusation?"

"Don't be daft, Cristina. You simply fail to see everything as clearly as I do. You let minor details and stupid logic distract you, such as what others might think and so forth. I *never* do that."

Cristina gritted her teeth. "That's true enough," she said. "You don't."

"Because I always know just where I'm going," Mariota declared, "and I never let such trifles get in my way. Hector doesn't understand that about me yet, and you are mean not to explain it to him. I think you are just manipulating him for your own selfish purpose, because you're afraid you'll never find another husband after you lose him. But you're a fool if you think I'm the only one you need worry about, because he is enormously popular at this court. The women adore him, and he flirts with them all. Only consider Fiona MacDougall. They say she's been mad about him for years, and she can always make him laugh. And, for his part, Hector is always most attentive to her. You've seen as much for yourself. Why, I shouldn't be surprised to learn that he beds her whenever he likes."

Cristina gasped. "How dare you—" Conscious of the always-curious crowd below the dais and the gillie at her shoulder about to pour claret into her goblet, she broke off, forced a smile, and nodded for the lad to proceed. When he had done so and moved on, she leaned near Mariota to say fiercely into her ear, "If I ever even suspect that you have repeated that piece of vulgarity to anyone else, Mariota, I will see to it that everyone learns what a liar you are."

"But—"

"Not another word," Cristina snapped. "That was a horrid thing to say to me, and it is untrue as well. Fiona MacDougall is one of the kindest women I know, and I will not allow you to tarnish her reputation merely to achieve your own ends."

"But—"

"Silence," Cristina hissed, hoping the constant din of conversation in the hall would make it impossible for anyone else to hear her. "You heed me well, Mariota. If I hear from anyone that you are spreading such scandal, I will not only tell Father but also Mairi, who is one of Fiona's closest friends. She will undoubtedly tell his grace, who is quite fond of Fiona and likely will banish you from his court.

Now, do not speak to me again tonight. I am far too angry with you to say anything kind."

Mariota's eyes instantly filled with tears, but Cristina felt no remorse. She knew that Mariota was not crying because she was sorry for what she had said, but only because her words had not had the effect she had intended them to have.

Knowing that the tears would disappear the moment something else attracted her sister's attention, and noting that the lady on her right had stopped chatting with Mairi, Cristina turned her attention in that direction and introduced herself.

Discovering the woman to be the wife of a chief from one of the isles involved in the upset over the collection and sale of petrel oil, she put everything else out of her mind to draw the woman out on less controversial topics. They discussed her children and the fact that Cristina had newly married. As they chatted amiably of difficulties inherent in trying to turn a hitherto masculine household into a comfortable home, the woman said, "I cannot tell you, madam, how pleasant it is to talk of things other than petrel oil. It seems as if everyone else is determined to debate that topic, and what with trying to remember from one moment to the next what I am supposed to say and absolutely must not say, I grow quite befuddled, so I'd as lief not discuss it at all, lest I find myself deep in the suds."

"But what could you possibly say that you should not?"

"Faith, one never can be sure. Why, I merely suggested that his grace might like to know how important the oil is to the Holy Isle, and my husband barked like an angry seal. He is MacFadyen of Coll, you see, where much of the oil is collected."

"But everyone knows the oil is used for sacramental use everywhere."

"Aye, but the Green Abbot wants us to donate a vast amount of it—years' worth—directly to his abbey, saying MacDonald should not make the abbey pay. But there, I should *not* be talking of that, so pray let us discuss something else."

Chapter 18 _____

Cristina was happy to indulge so good-natured a neighbor as Lady MacFadyen, and although she could not in good conscience ignore Mariota, thanks to her ladyship, she was able to maintain a courteous demeanor toward her. Nevertheless, she felt only relief when the meal was over and the evening's entertainment began.

MacDonald had arranged for minstrels and a troupe of players to amuse his guests, and a number of the men joined in a sword-dancing competition. Lachlan Lubanach was one of them, showing himself to be nimble and quick. Hector remained seated, although he watched the dancers with interest.

When Cristina looked to see if he would join them, Mairi caught her eye and grinned. Speaking across Lady Mac-Fadyen, she said, "Don't look for your husband to dance tonight, madam. For as long as Lachlan serves as master of my father's household and high admiral of his navy, he has strictly forbidden Hector to do so."

"But why?"

Mairi chuckled. "Because the last time the two of them entered such a competition together, Hector nearly lopped off another man's head as they picked up their swords. Only Lachlan's swift parry saved the poor lad."

Mairi's amusement was contagious, and Cristina laughed with her. When the dancing was over, however, she was delighted to see Hector take a lute from one of the minstrels and begin gently to pluck its strings. His musical skill was what had first attracted her to him. Before she had heard him sing, she had thought him just another self-important member of his grace's court, albeit a handsome one. But the first time she had heard him take lute in hand, it had been as if he sang to her alone.

His touch was light and skillful, and conversation faded to silence as he played. When he had everyone's attention, he began to sing, and Cristina watched and listened with much the same awe she had felt the first time. He had chosen a ballad about the conquests of Somerled, and although nearly everyone there must have known the story of that great leader's victories over the Vikings, they listened intently. She had forgotten the impact Hector's voice had on his listeners.

When he finished, silence fell, but then he began a livelier song that soon had his audience laughing. When it ended, someone called out for another favorite, and someone else yet another, because many of his grace's guests had enjoyed Hector's music before. In his large hands, the lute looked like a toy, but he played with the deft touch of an expert, and his deep voice was vibrant and pleasing. Minutes later, he encouraged members of his audience to join him in singing the chorus of a popular ballad, and her clear treble soared above the others. She saw him watching her, and when he smiled, she felt a rush of pleasure, as if he had touched her.

Hector wondered why he had not known that Cristina possessed such a clear, lovely voice. Indeed, he wondered why he had not noticed her at his grace's court before, since several people had mentioned that it was a pleasure to see her there again and had congratulated him on his marriage. Because she did not wear the bright colors and extreme fashions that had become so popular amongst Islesmen and their women, he had feared that she might feel out of place. But although she did not try to achieve the sartorial splendor in which her sister Mariota delighted, he had soon realized that Cristina's quiet elegance pleased him more.

Mariota's necklines plunged too low, and her bodices fitted so tightly that he wondered how she could breathe. Moreover, she seemed always to be preening herself, and flirted with any man who looked her way. He would not envy the man who won her, but they flocked to her like cattle to a salt lick.

As he finished the song, he saw Lachlan motioning to him from the rear of the hall. A number of people were calling out more tunes for him to play or sing, but he shook his head with a smile, stood, and handed the lute to the minstrel from whom he had borrowed it.

Catching his twin's eye, he jerked his head slightly in Cristina's direction and turned toward her, knowing Lachlan would understand that he meant to see his lady safe in her bedchamber before joining him. He had told him about the incident with Fergus Love while they ate, and they had discussed it at length. But before he could deal with Fergus, he had to deal with the captives.

Cristina saw him moving purposefully toward her. The minstrels had begun playing a tune for a ring dance, so she wondered briefly if he wanted her to join the dancers with him or just to talk. But although he was smiling, she had seen the exchange of nods with his brother and suspected that something was in the wind.

When he reached her, he extended a hand and said, "Come, my lady. The hour grows late, and Lachlan and I have matters to discuss with his grace as soon as the Steward retires. I would see you safely abed before I must go."

Unwilling to accuse him of not trusting her to stay there, even with her father and her aunt still present—not where anyone might hear, at all events—she said only, "Would it not be disrespectful for me to leave before the Steward does, sir?"

"I'll make your excuses," he said, taking her hand and placing it on his arm.

"Has there been more trouble then?" she asked.

"My lads have been questioning the men we captured after the attack," he said. "We mean to discuss what they have learned, and decide what to do about it."

She frowned, and as they moved toward the courtyard door at a pace quick enough to discourage anyone who might want to speak to them, she said, "So, it is not more trouble over petrel oil this time?"

He glanced at her. "Nay. At least, I do not think that business enters into it, since this last was an open attack on the heir to the throne."

She hesitated, then said, "I think perhaps I should tell you what I learned at supper, anyway."

"Wait until we are outside," he said.

Accordingly, minutes later, as they crossed the courtyard, she said quietly, "Lady MacFadyen of Coll told me the abbot approached her husband to demand that he contribute a large amount of oil directly to the abbey on the Holy Isle."

"The devil he did! Coll is Maclean land—Lachlan's, in fact—so what that damned interfering scoundrel thinks he is about, I should very much like to know."

"He told MacFadyen that his grace should not be profiting from sales of oil to the abbey," Cristina said.

Hector's response was a distinct snort. "MacDonald holds no brief for the abbey, the abbot, or for the Pope's authority, come to that," he said. "Doubtless, Fingon thinks we should give the oil away to any kirk in Christendom that wants it. But stay," he added. "Iona's petrels provide barrels of the stuff, and both the abbey and the Holy Isle's inhabitants benefit to the same degree that everyone else in the Isles does from the sales. Why would he demand donations from other Isles when he could just keep a portion of his own, and the result would be the same?"

"I don't know," Cristina said.

"Nor do I," he said. "But I mean to find out. I'm glad you told me of this, lass. We've suspected that he's up to mischief, but what it is, we cannot fathom."

They did not talk as they went upstairs to their bedchamber, and once inside, finding Brona waiting patiently, Hector kissed Cristina lightly and told her not to wait up for him.

"I've no idea how long I'll be," he said. "But you have much to do tomorrow to get ready to leave, sweetheart, so you should go straight to sleep."

She held his gaze, wishing she could tell him what she thought of his ordering her to bed, but she knew that if she tried to dismiss Brona, he would tell the woman to stay, and

Brona would not disobey him. With a sigh, she watched him leave, promising herself she would tell him during the next private moment she had with him. The afternoon's incident had relieved her of any fear that the earth would swallow her if she spoke sharply to him—or even slapped him, for that matter.

The plain fact was that Hector made her feel safe, and he would soon come to rue that fact if he thought he could ride roughshod over her wishes and opinions. The thought made her smile, and nerve endings throughout her body tingled at the thought of challenging him again.

⊗⊗

Finding his twin in the hall, only to learn that they would remain there until the guest of honor had departed for his bed, Hector contained his impatience for another half hour. At last, though, Robert stood up. His entourage moved to attend him, and after a ceremonial farewell to their host and hostess, they left the hall.

The minstrels continued playing, and folks returned to their dancing as Lachlan said, "His grace would have us meet him in the great chamber straightaway. Have you had any news from your lads yet?"

"Aye," Hector said. "Although I cannot say that they have found out much to aid us yet. They claim that someone—a stranger—paid them to attack the flotilla. One of them has remained devilishly quiet though," he added. "'Tis my belief that he knows more but fears to speak. The men are still questioning him."

Lachlan nodded. "Keep at it then," he said.

"There is another thing," Hector said, and went on to tell him what Cristina had learned from Lady MacFadyen.

"MacFadyen's as loyal as they come," Lachlan said, frowning. "I must not keep his grace waiting, but I want you to go back and see if perchance MacFadyen is still in the hall. If he is, ask him about this business. I would ken more of it."

Hector found MacFadyen, but the man could tell him no more than his lady had told Cristina.

"She ought not to ha' spoken o' that business, because I told her she ought not, but I'm thinking females ha' their tongues hinged in the middle," he said, shaking his head. When asked why he had not told Lachlan of the inquiry, he said, "I said nowt of it t' him 'cause 'twas only some Mackinnon saying he spoke for the abbot and no the abbot himself. I thought it were nobbut mischief-making."

"A reasonable attitude, that," Lachlan said when Hector reported it to him soon after joining him and MacDonald in the great chamber on the second floor of the castle. "Still," Lachlan added, "I would know more."

"I, too," MacDonald agreed. "Did you get the man's name, the Mackinnon?"

Hector nodded. "I did, your grace, someone called Kinven, MacFadyen said. He is not here, however, and MacFadyen did not know where I might seek him."

Lachlan said with a rueful smile, "Then you are bound for Coll on the morning tide, my lad. I cannot say why I feel urgency over this, since it seems to have naught to do with the puzzle at hand, but I do, and I trust such feelings."

Hector nodded. He trusted them, too.

The conversation turned then to the matter of the captives and what little information they had gleaned from them. Hector's instincts had been twitching since the attack on the Steward's galley, and despite all the precautions they were taking and planned to take when they returned him to Oban, he could not help thinking they were missing something important.

When he said as much, Lachlan and MacDonald agreed, and their discussion lasted into the small hours.

Cristina awoke shortly after sunrise the next morning in an otherwise empty bed. She had a vague memory of her husband joining her in it at some point, and a slightly clearer one of him kissing her and bidding her farewell. It had still been dark though, so she could not be sure that he had done any such a thing.

Learning a short time later from Brona that he had taken a large contingent of men, his favorite longboat, and an escort of four others, and was on his way to the Isle of Coll for an unknown time and purpose stirred her curiosity and no small measure of annoyance. That he had told Brona he'd left a longboat for his wife, with several others to escort her to Lochbuie, only irritated her more.

"The least he could have done was to waken me properly and tell me himself," she muttered to herself when Brona left her and went to fetch the gown she wanted to wear. She wondered if his trip to Coll had aught to do with what Lady MacFadyen had said, decided it did, and cursed all gossips, and petrels in general.

Brona returned to the chamber then with the moss green gown Cristina had requested, laid it carefully on the bed, and said, "We'll ha' t' bustle about, m'lady. You ought t' ha' told me yestereve that we'd be leaving today."

Guiltily, Cristina apologized for the oversight, not mentioning that she had hoped to change Hector's mind but that first the captives and then the apparently ubiquitous petrel oil problem had intervened. The temptation to inform Brona that they were not leaving after all was strong, but although Cristina had assured herself only the previous night that Hector held no more fears for her, she realized that she did not have the nerve to defy him. Indeed, she thought with a rueful smile, she would not put it past him to have asked Lachlan to make sure that she obeyed.

Since she was in no hurry, tide or no tide, and still hoped Hector would return in time for her to try her feminine wiles on him, she told Brona they would leave as late as possible on the afternoon tide, certainly not before the midday meal. And when the captain of her longboat approached as she was leaving the hall after the meal to tell her they might miss the tide if they did not leave by three, she told him airily that she would do her best but that four would be more convenient for her, and then obligingly sent gillies to fetch what baggage Brona had ready.

She had not seen Mariota at the table, and Lady Euphemia had seemed a bit worried about her. Macleod told them he had no idea where the lass had gone and was clearly not worried in the least. Nonetheless, Cristina knew she could not leave Ardtornish without bidding her good-bye and at least trying to soothe her injured feelings. She wanted to find Isobel, too.

Accordingly, she went upstairs to the room Mariota and Isobel shared with their aunt, only to find it empty. Realizing then that her sisters might be searching for her, she went to her bedchamber but found only Brona there. The room was empty of Cristina's belongings except for the cloak and gloves she would wear.

"Have you seen Lady Mariota or Lady Isobel?" she asked.

"Nay, my—"

She stopped, mouth agape, when the bedchamber door crashed back on its hinges and Isobel ran in, red-faced and nearly out of breath.

"Thank God I've found you, Cristina," the child exclaimed. "Mariota said she's beside herself with remorse over the mischief she's caused, and to prove it to you and Hector, she's going to throw herself off one of the cliffs!"

"Isobel, are you sure that is what she said?" Cristina demanded, catching the little girl by both shoulders and looking directly into her eyes.

"I'd never make up such a thing," Isobel said indignantly. "I knew I had to tell you at once, especially as one of the gillies said you are leaving today, but you know how Mariota is. I warrant she's only trying to make herself important."

"Perhaps," Cristina said doubtfully, remembering how distraught Mariota had been and how impulsive she could be in such a state.

"You *know* how she is," Isobel insisted.

"I suspect you are right, dearling, but surely you can see that I dare not risk the possibility that this once she may have meant exactly what she said."

Isobel's smooth brow furrowed. "But what will you do? You aren't really leaving, are you? If you tell Hector Reaganach, mayhap he—"

"I'm going nowhere until I find Mariota," Cristina said, adding more sharply, "And we must tell no one."

"But surely Hector or Father, or even Aunt Euphemia might—"

"Might what?" Cristina demanded. "What do you imagine any of them could do if she stands on the edge of a cliff and threatens to throw herself over the edge?"

"They could order her to come to her senses." But Isobel's tone lacked conviction, and Cristina knew she was having the same difficulty that she herself was having in imagining Mariota submitting meekly to any such order.

"Just so," she said when Isobel gaped at her helplessly. "If ordering her to be sensible had ever proved useful, I'd be happy to issue that order myself. Mariota is as likely to heed my orders as anyone else's, don't you agree?"

Isobel grimaced and said with a sigh, "She is more likely to do the very thing one commands her *not* to do."

"Just so," Cristina said. "Persuasion is necessary, and I've years of experience, so heed me, Isobel. Until I know the truth, you must promise me you won't say a word to anyone about Mariota's threat. Only think what a scandal it would cause that she had threatened such a thing, especially with the Steward here! Father would ... Faith, I do not know what he would do to her, but I do *not* want to find out."

Isobel paled at the thought but said sturdily, "If she kills herself, will that not create an even greater scandal?"

"Aye, so you must not delay me. But I want your word that you will say nothing to Hector or to anyone else until I give you leave."

Isobel hesitated.

"Come now, you know that I shall do much better with her on my own, because neither Hector nor Father would attempt to contain his displeasure with her. If one of them should begin bellowing at her, it could well mean disaster."

"That's true," Isobel said with a sigh.

"Will you promise me?"

The child nodded.

"Good," Cristina said, gently squeezing her shoulder. "You can safely leave this to me, dearling, but mayhap you should stay out of sight until I return. Hector is away, but I warrant he'll be back soon. If he or if Father should chance to miss me and demand to know my whereabouts, you would have to reveal them."

"They won't find me," Isobel said firmly.

"Thank you," Cristina said. "Brona, I'll take my gloves, but keep my cloak for me. Isobel, run out to the barn and bid them ready a horse for me, one that I can ride without a saddle. I've no time to lose."

Isobel ran to do her bidding, and knowing the gillies would take a few moments to prepare the horse, and that Mariota was likely waiting impatiently for someone to come look for her, Cristina glanced at the frowning Brona, then took a moment to tuck errant curls beneath her caul. To stir curiosity by seeming to be in a demented rush would serve no purpose, and what little time she lost she would regain by not having to walk to the cliffs.

"Brona," she said gently, "I cannot ask you to deceive the laird or my father, but if you could manage to avoid them for a short time . . ." She paused hopefully.

"Go, m'lady," she said. "I'll no betray ye an I can help it."

Cristina hurried, but Isobel had already disappeared by the time she reached the barn, and a silent gillie gave her a leg up. Grateful for his lack of curiosity, but wondering why he said nothing about her riding off when every servant in the place must know by now that she was supposed to be leaving Ardtornish in less than an hour, she said, "I shan't be long. I mean only to ride to the cliffs for some fresh air. Should anyone ask after my whereabouts, pray tell him I will return shortly."

"Aye, my lady," the lad said with a nod.

Turning her mount toward the cliffs, she urged it to a gentle lope as she rode alongside the castle, sending up a prayer that the pace would not arouse anyone's curiosity. At present, the area seemed deserted except for two gillies crossing the yard from the steps that led down to the bay landing, and she decided that people must already be beginning to dress for the evening festivities.

As soon as she thought it safe to do so, she dug her heels into the palfrey, urging it to a faster pace. If Hector saw her, he would doubtless scold her for riding too fast up the hill, but she would tell him the palfrey needed more exercise if it couldn't manage such a gentle slope.

The thought of what he would likely say then drew a smile, and she realized that she enjoyed their verbal jousting except when he was truly angry. That he might be that angry, if only because she was missing her tide, did not deter her.

He would surely understand that Mariota's safety mattered more than returning to Lochbuie on any particular tide. He had proven himself astonishingly reasonable in most matters, and although he certainly had a temper, and could certainly be stern and unyielding when he believed himself in the right, he had also shown that he had common sense and a strong sense of humor. Not that the situation held any of the latter, and what he would say to Mariota when he learned of this latest start, as doubtless he would, she did not want to imagine.

She saw no sign of her on the way up the hill, and since she could see *Creag na Corps* from the slope, she wondered if her unpredictable sister had merely been teasing Isobel. The lads she had seen at the top of the stairs—doubtless the ones who had carried down her baggage—should also have seen Mariota had she stood poised on the rock to leap, and they would certainly have raised an alarm.

But if Mariota was enjoying one of her dramas, she would not show herself until the scene had played out as she intended it to. Moreover, if she truly intended to do away with herself, she would not care how many people saw her.

"The more, the better," Cristina muttered, relaxing. Doubtless, Isobel was right, and their sister was indulging herself in one of the impulsive, dramatic scenes to which she was prone. Such events, enjoyed by Mariota and feared by the rest of her family, had followed upon nearly every incident in which she had felt slighted or had not had her own way. The scenes had grown rarer as she grew older, not because she no longer enjoyed them but because everyone else tried to avoid them.

"Hector was right," Cristina told herself. "We have spoiled her, but I don't know how we could have avoided it, when the consequences of stirring her rage were always so dreadful. He doesn't yet know her as we do."

She reached the hilltop, but it was another five minutes before *Creag na Corps* came into view and she saw Mariota sitting on the edge of the great rock.

As soon as she saw Cristina, she jumped to her feet.

"Mariota, I'm glad I found you," Cristina said, drawing rein, her voice just loud enough for her sister to hear. "I know supper won't be served until after Vespers, but everyone is already beginning to dress, and I—"

"I shan't be hungry."

"Nevertheless, my dear, you must come now. You know Father will be angry if we are late, and his grace will be annoyed, too, if you create a scene."

"I shall not create a scene at supper," Mariota said mildly, "for I shall not be there at all. Is that what you call what I'm doing?" she asked before Cristina could speak again. "Creating a scene?" As she spoke, she stepped onto the great flat rock and held her arms wide as if she were spreading wings.

"Will it be just another scene if I step off this rock and plunge to my death?"

"Do not even speak of such a terrible thing," Cristina begged. "You make my blood run cold. Come now, where is your horse?"

"I walked," Mariota said curtly. "You see, Cristina, I do occasionally think of things other than myself, for all that you think I do not. I did not want some poor horse to wander off or starve waiting for someone to think of looking for it. Besides," she added, "I knew you would bring one."

These revealing words allowed Cristina to relax again for the first time since she had seen Mariota on the rock. "Then come with me now," she said coaxingly. "I'll pull you up behind me. It will be easy, standing on that rock as you are," she added as she touched the palfrey with her knee.

"Stop where you are," Mariota said as the palfrey stepped forward. "I'm not going to ride with you, Cristina."

"This one is not as spirited as we like," Cristina said, choosing to misunderstand her. "But she can easily carry us both, I promise you."

"Don't try to cozen me, for I know exactly how it is with you," Mariota snapped. "You think you will walk into the hall and tell them all that I tried to kill myself but that you—the wonderful, capable Cristina—talked me out of it."

"That is not at all what I would do, and you should know it."

"I do know. I expect you told everyone you were coming to save me."

"I told no one."

"Then what is Isobel doing here?" Mariota demanded, pointing dramatically.

Startled as much by the sweeping gesture as by Mariota's

words, Cristina turned and saw her little sister just riding into view.

"You told Isobel yourself what you meant to do," she reminded Mariota.

"I did no such thing," Mariota said flatly. "As if I would make a gift of my intentions to a mere child."

"Faith, then how do you suppose I knew to look for you up here?"

"I warrant you followed me," Mariota said, tossing her head.

"Mariota, not a moment ago you accused me of telling everyone what you meant to do. If I knew to tell them, surely you must realize that I knew where to look for you before I came to find you."

"Do not quibble, Cristina! You knew because you are always watching and spying on me, keeping note of my every movement and thought."

"You know that is not true, my love," Cristina said, striving for patience.

"I know naught of the sort. I know you would like me to believe otherwise, whilst you, in your evil way, persuade others to believe I am capable of doing quite utterly dreadful things. I cannot help it if men want to please me. They just do!"

"No, Mariota—please, my dear, you must be ill to say such things. Do you not recall that only a short time ago you were apologizing for causing that dreadful incident between Hector and Fergus Love? I should not have spoken so hastily or so angrily to you then, I know, and I beg your pardon for that. I know you meant no real harm. You are my sister, and I love you dearly."

"I doubt that you even understand the meaning of love, Cristina. You are nothing but a mouse, uneducated in true emotion. You always think so logically, so coldly. I am not like you, thank heaven, so although you frequently insist that you understand me better than anyone else does, you do not know me at all."

"But I do."

"You don't! You don't understand anyone who thinks with her feelings rather than with her brain. I tell you and tell you, and you just say no one can do that, because you cannot. But I can, Cristina, and I do. You think you are superior to me and that I should be like you, but I don't want to be like you, because Hector loves me as I am, and I love him. That's why I'm sorry, Cristina, because you tricked yourself into a loveless marriage, and for as long as I live, that is all it will be. That is the true picture, the one you refuse to allow your logical mind to see."

"That is *not* true," Isobel declared loudly.

Cristina jumped at the sound of the child's voice so near. So intently had she been watching and listening to Mariota, and fighting the unhappily familiar sense of her brain spinning in her head, that she had not heard Isobel dismount and approach.

Chapter 19 ————————————

Isobel, you should not have followed me," Cristina said quietly. "I am quite vexed with you, and I want you to leave now before you upset her further."

"Aunt Euphemia said I should keep my eye on you," Isobel said.

"She did not mean you should follow me everywhere I go, and even if you suppose she did mean that, you will do as I bid now and go back at once."

"I'll strive to hold my tongue, but I won't leave," Isobel said firmly.

Cristina sighed. Arguing with her little sister would do nothing to aid the situation and could do much to worsen it if Mariota took further offense.

Turing her back on Isobel, she gently urged the palfrey nearer, encouraged when Mariota made no objection. Behind her, Isobel remained mercifully silent.

"Stop there," Mariota commanded. "I do not know what you hope to accomplish, Cristina, because I won't go back with you. If I did, people would say I didn't mean what I said, and I won't have that. They'll see how things are after I fling myself to the wind and they see how desolated Hector Reaganach is. I can hardly wait to hear what they say to you then!"

"Dear heart, how do you imagine you will hear anything if you throw yourself off this dreadful cliff?"

"I'll know," Mariota said confidently. "I know just how it will be, too. People who are jealous of me now will pretend to be sad, and people who never liked me will pretend to have been my dearest friends."

"I cannot think why you would imagine such things," Cristina said sadly.

"Because it is how she would behave if someone she didn't like jumped off a cliff," Isobel said. "She would display only the emotions she wanted other people to see, the ones she believes would make them think how thoughtful and kind she is."

"That will do, Isobel," Cristina said, suppressing her realization that the child had undoubtedly described Mariota's state of mind exactly.

"Sorry," Isobel muttered.

Mariota shot her younger sister a look of dislike. "I expect you think you are wiser than Solomon, but you do not know the first thing about anything, and I wish you would leave. No one wants you here."

"I warrant *you* do not, but I am staying."

"I'm sure I don't care what you do, but if Cristina means to try to persuade me to go back down to Ardtornish, I'd as lief she get down and talk to me privately without any more impertinence from you."

"Don't do it, Cristina," Isobel warned. "Stay on your horse."

"Hush, Isobel. You are not helping."

"Oh, but she is," Mariota said almost merrily. "I am quite

amused by her, I promise you. You foolish child, do you imagine that I would hurt Cristina?"

"She does not imagine anything of the kind," Cristina said before Isobel could speak her thoughts aloud. Slipping down from the palfrey, she kept a firm grasp on its reins so it could not wander off.

"Why don't you let Isobel hold your horse," Mariota suggested. "If she is going to stay, she might as well be useful."

"Very well," Cristina said, turning to hand the reins to the child. Giving her a minatory look as she did, she said quietly, "I don't want to hear another word from you, or by heaven, I will ask Father to lock you in your bedchamber for a month."

Grimacing, Isobel nodded.

Cristina turned back toward the great rock, feeling more relaxed, certain now that Mariota had no intention of ending her life. Although she would have liked to shake her for her wickedness in scaring them as she had, and half hoped that Hector would scold her or worse, she wanted to do nothing more now to upset her.

"You gave me such a scare," she said gently as she approached her. "Truly, my dear, you deserve that I should be angry with you."

"Just look at the view from here, Cristina," Mariota said as she turned with another sweeping gesture to face the bay and the Sound beyond it. "See how the sun sparkles on the water. It looks like molten gold. And the clouds drifting yonder," she added with a further sweep to the west. "See how white they are."

"It is a beautiful afternoon," Cristina agreed. "But it will be dusk before too long, and everyone will wonder where we are. We must return straightaway."

"In a few minutes." Her voice was more subdued. "Come

up here with me. It feels as if I'm on top of the word, standing here. I want you to know how it feels."

Ignoring a prickling sensation at the back of her neck at
the thought of standing so near the edge, determined not to
give Mariota the satisfaction of knowing that the great
height frightened her, Cristina stepped onto the rock. She
expected to hear Isobel shout to stay where she was, but the
child remained silent.

The edge was too close, but Cristina knew that she must
not show her fear, because Mariota delighted in proving herself braver than anyone else and might well do something
even more dangerous.

"Isn't it glorious?" Mariota said, gazing out at the view.
"You can see Duart Castle from here."

Cristina swallowed hard. Her knees felt weak, even with
Mariota standing between her and the edge. She wanted to
tell her to step back, but she was afraid her voice would not
work properly.

A gust of wind stirred leaves and grass, making them rus-
tle behind her.

"That breeze is growing stronger," she said, hoping she
sounded calmer than she felt. "We really should go."

"In a moment we will, but come closer first and look
down," Mariota said, turning slightly to take hold of her
right arm. "Don't be afraid. I'm not." Her grasp was gentle,
her voice likewise.

When Cristina stiffened, the grip on her arm tightened.
"You're afraid, I can tell you are," Mariota said.

"No, I just—"

"Why, you're as tense as can be, but you must put your
fears aside lest everyone know you for a coward. Here,
come right to the edge. I promise, if you fall, I'll tell everyone you did so trying to save me," she added with a chuckle.

"What a thing to say!" Cristina exclaimed, trying to free her arm from Mariota's grip.

"Silly, I was just teasing. Just come a tiny bit closer."

"No, Mariota, please. You are much braver than I am, and so I will tell anyone you like, but I do *not* want to stand any nearer to the edge."

"I said, come!" She pulled hard.

Cristina dug in her heels. "Let go," she said. "I don't like this game."

"It is no game," Mariota said, and her tone was no longer cheerful or teasing. It held a grim, threatening note, and fear swept through Cristina as she struggled to free herself.

"Please let go, Mariota." Striving for calm, Cristina found herself fighting terror instead. "What can you possibly prove by forcing me to the edge?"

"I have nothing to prove, Cristina, but likewise 'tis not I who should fling herself to the wind. You are the one trapped in the loveless marriage."

"That's not so!"

"Think how neatly everything will resolve itself if you just step off this rock," Mariota went on as if Cristina had not spoken. "Then Hector will marry me, and we'll live happily ever after."

"Hector does not love you, Mariota, nor do you love him. You just want him because he married me. You did not want him at all until then."

"I did not see until then how you and Father had tricked me," Mariota said.

"Let go!" Cristina cried, trying again to wrench free of the viselike grip.

"Just step over the edge, and everything will be as it should be," Mariota said, her matter-of-fact tone more terrifying than her bruising grip.

"*No!*" Isobel shrieked.

Suddenly she was beside them, pulling Cristina back and kicking Mariota.

"Get back from the edge!" Cristina screamed.

"Let her go, Mariota!" Isobel shouted. "What are you thinking? Would you have everyone know you for a murderess?"

"Go away, Isobel," Mariota said in that strange, unemotional tone as she dragged Cristina inexorably nearer the edge. "I told you, no one wants you here."

Gathering all her strength, Cristina yanked hard, freeing her arm just as Isobel shoved Mariota.

Stumbling, Mariota grabbed the child, and before Cristina's helpless, horrified gaze, they went over the edge together.

Hector strode from the castle toward the barn. Having expected to find Cristina in his bedchamber preparing to depart on the afternoon tide, he had discovered an empty room instead. Even her clothing and maid were gone, but he knew the longboat had not left, because his captain had told him as much, and the tide would soon be on the turn.

Fearing that she might have gone off alone again, might even have decided to defy his orders and stay, he decided to find her and bring her back. She would leave Ardtornish if only as far as Duart, even if his oarsmen had to row her there against the tide. And he would go with her, at least overnight, if only to tell her that the business at Coll had proved as much a mystery as ever, that he had found the man Kinven, only to learn that he'd merely repeated what he had heard from someone else. That Mackinnon had stirred rumors to make mischief, he was sure, but short of tracking down every man who had repeated them, the chance of proving it was nil. As to why, he could not guess, unless for another diversion.

The barn was empty. Shouting for a gillie, and recalling that his own horse was lame, he chose the first one he came to, which happened to be a prized young bay of Lachlan's. As a gillie came running in response to his shout, he pressed a bit firmly into the horse's mouth and slipped the bridle on.

"I'm taking this one," he said unnecessarily, as he flung the reins over the horse's head and leaped to its back.

The lad looked at him in dismay. "D'ye no want a saddle, laird?"

"Nay," he said. "Have you seen my lady?"

"Aye, sir," said a second lad, stepping into the barn behind the first one. "Lady Cristina rode out twenty minutes ago, mayhap a bit longer. Told one o' the other lads she were riding t' yon cliffs."

Recognizing him as Mairi's gillie, he said curtly, "East or west, Ian?"

"That I dinna ken, sir," Ian said, adding as Hector wrenched the bay's head toward the wide doorway, "Ye should ken, laird, that the lady Isobel followed straightaway afterward, saying she meant t' catch up wi' her."

Hector gave Ian a direct look, feeling instant irritation when the lad bit his lower lip. "What else?" he demanded. "Don't try telling me it is your normal custom to allow that child to ride off alone, for I won't believe you."

"Nay, sir, but she did say she meant to catch Lady Cristina. The lady Isobel is not known for telling untruths."

When Hector continued to glower, Ian said, "I canna say aught were amiss, laird, but Lady Isobel did seem . . . She looked gey fierce!" he added bluntly.

"Angry?"

"Nay, no so much angry as determined . . . mayhap concerned. I did shout at her t' tell me if aught were amiss, but she just waved and rode on."

"Anyone else?" Hector asked dryly.

"Nay, laird."

"Did the lady Cristina appear to be in a hurry?"

"Well, she did take her horse without a saddle, but so did Lady Isobel. They, both o' them, ride like the wind and dinna care for ladies' saddles."

"Aye, that means naught," Hector agreed.

Feeling a sudden if inexplicable sense of urgency, he urged the bay to a lope past the castle and onto the grassy slope above. He was nearing the hilltop when a flurry of distant movement to his right drew his notice. Squinting into the distance, with increasing wind, and sunlight casting dancing shadows and bits of golden glare, it was a moment before he realized that someone—more than one person— seemed to be dancing on *Creag na Corps*. Then he realized with shock that they were not dancing but struggling, and by their flying skirts, they were women.

"Are they mad?" he muttered to himself, already spurring the bay to a faster pace. It occurred to him that by ordering his lass home, he might have upset her so much that she had attempted to take her own life.

Spurring harder, he prayed that the good Lord would not allow her to do anything so foolhardy. He had never imagined she could be so impulsive, or so foolish, and did not want to believe it now, but if anything happened to her . . .

He could not finish the thought. He hoped that Mariota was one of the women with her, and would be strong enough to hold her until he could reach them and tell Cristina that he wanted only to keep her safe, that his temper never meant anything, and his strongest flashes burned out as surely as lightning bolts did. Even as that thought crossed his mind, he saw two of the strugglers fall over the cliff.

Crying out in anguish, he kicked the galloping horse as hard as he could.

Chapter 20 ─────────

Unable at first to make herself look over the edge, Cristina stood in abject horror for a long moment before she heard voices calling to her from below. Hope surging, she stepped carefully near the overhanging edge of rock and looked down.

The cliff did not, as she had supposed, slant inward at that point, although the rock overhung the edge by at least a foot. Below it, the cliff wall bulged out like a middle-aged man who had for years drunk more ale than was good for him. But like that same man, below the bulge, the rest of the wall plunged straight and sheer.

A few feet below her, Isobel clung to a terrifyingly scrawny shrub jutting from the bulge, and below her, Mariota clutched a fist-sized rock poking out from the wall with one hand and a slightly larger shrub than Isobel's with the other.

"I think this plant is tearing loose," Isobel said, sounding far calmer, Cristina knew, than she would sound under similar circumstances.

"Let me see if I can reach you," she said. Lowering herself to all fours, she stretched out flat on the rock, inched forward, and reached a hand toward the child. The distance was much more than she could manage. "Can you pull yourself up to grab my hand?" she asked, knowing the answer but hoping Isobel might see a way.

"I'm afraid if I let go with either hand I'll fall, and I dare not pull harder on this wee shrub," Isobel said. "My feet are just dangling free, Cristina. I can't find anything to rest them on, and I'm afraid to move them about any more."

"What are you waiting for, Cristina?" Mariota demanded. "Do something!"

"Can you help Isobel find purchase for at least one foot?" Cristina asked her.

"I dare not move! I nearly didn't catch hold of anything as it was, and this is all your fault, Cristina—yours and Isobel's. You should never have come up here, and having done so, you should have moved away from the cliff when I told you to."

Seeing nothing to gain by attempting to persuade Mariota that she had done nothing of the sort, Cristina inched forward until her torso hung perilously over the edge. Focusing on Isobel, so she could avoid looking at the plunging drop below her, she gripped the rough edge of the great rock as best she could with one hand and reached again toward her little sister with the other.

"I cannot move any nearer without toppling over, myself," she said.

"But I can't possibly reach you," Isobel said, visibly struggling now to control her fear. "Oh, Cristina, what are we going to do?"

"We are going to get you both back to the castle safely," Cristina said firmly as she scrambled to her feet. "Don't move. I'll be right back."

"You say that as if we could go somewhere," Mariota snapped. "Where are *you* going?"

"Just wait," Cristina said, snatching up her skirts and running back to the palfrey, which stood patiently waiting with its reins dangling to the ground.

Isobel's pony was nowhere in sight and, cursing its obvious defection but knowing she had no time to look for it, she snatched up the palfrey's reins, slipped off its bridle, and ran back to the rock.

Twisting the leather lines into a single strong cord and knotting it in two places, she said, "See if you can catch this line, Isobel."

"Even if she can," Mariota protested, "it will not reach this far, so how will you get me up? I'm holding nearly all of my weight on a rock that is too small to grip with both hands, and this stupid shrub is going to rip out at any moment."

"I don't know how," Cristina admitted. "Perhaps, if Isobel can grab this line and wrap it around her wrist, you can hold her foot with the hand you are now using to hold the shrub. Then perhaps I can at least hold you both until help arrives."

" 'Perhaps' does not reassure me, and what help?" Mariota demanded. "We are the only ones here, and you said you told no one else you were coming."

"Someone will see us," Cristina said, confident that Hector must have returned by now and would come after her, as he had before, as soon as he discovered that she had not yet left and was not in their bedchamber.

Dropping to her hands and knees again, she lay flat and wrapped the twisted leather line tightly around her wrist and hand. As she dangled the other end toward Isobel, she glanced toward the castle.

"Can you see anyone?" Isobel asked, still tightly clutching her shrub and making no move toward the makeshift rescue line.

"I see men on the boat landing and a small group near the castle entrance, and at least some of them seem to be looking this way. Oh, thank heaven," she added, as movement caught her eye some distance to the right and new hope surged through her. "A horseman is galloping up the hill. I think it may be Hector."

Even as she narrowed her eyes to be sure, Mariota said, "Grab those reins, Isobel, for mercy's sake. I'm slipping. We cannot wait for anyone else to help us."

Cristina heard Mariota scrabbling for a foothold, but Isobel remained still, scarcely breathing, staring wretchedly at the leather line but too terrified now to let go with even one hand long enough to reach for it.

"Grab it, Isobel," Mariota commanded. "We'll both die if you don't."

"Look at me, Isobel," Cristina said calmly. When the child obediently shifted her gaze, she said, "You can do this, my love. You know you can. The line is just inches above your right hand."

"I'm so afraid," the little girl said with a shuddering sob.

"I know you are, but I want you to take a deep breath. Forget your feet. Forget everything but the line just above you. I tied a fat knot near the end of it, as you will see when you look again. You need only grab it above the knot, and your hand will not slip. Don't look down," she warned when Isobel began to turn her head. "There is nothing for you to see down there, and Hector will soon be here."

"But what if—?"

"Think only about what you must do. You are looking into my eyes. I want you to shift your gaze down to my hand, to the line I am holding. Then follow that line to the knot. When you see the knot, fix your eye on it. Think about which hand you will use. When you have decided how you will do it, do it quickly. I promise that if you grab it, I will not let you fall."

"But what about me?" Mariota repeated, breaking the calm that Cristina had tried to instill with her voice.

"One thing at a time," Cristina said, adding a touch of asperity to her tone and willing Mariota to be silent long enough for Isobel to obey.

"You don't care about me. You believe that I—"

"Be silent, Mariota. Isobel needs to—"

"Oh, yes, of course, think only about what Isobel needs! She is the only one you care about, isn't she? I don't count."

"Please, Mari—"

The line jerked hard in Cristina's hand, nearly pulling her over, for in the instant that she shifted her attention to Mariota, Isobel let go of her shrub and lurched to grab the line. Then it jerked again as she grabbed it with both hands, and Cristina held her little sister's full weight with one hand.

Knowing she could not do so much longer, she quickly moved the hand she had pressed against the rock to keep from slipping and grabbed the line instead.

Fighting to hold tight, shutting her eyes to concentrate, and praying that she would not slide right off the rock, Cristina realized that from such a position she could not pull the child up by herself. As it was, she could barely move or think of anything other than her desperate need to hold on to Isobel and not fall.

As the latter thought crossed her mind, the weight on the line increased sharply and Isobel screamed.

Cristina's eyes snapped open to see that Mariota had

grabbed Isobel's leg and was apparently trying to climb up the side of the cliff, right over the child.

"Mariota, no!"

Hector heard the screams but could see only trees from where he was. Lashing the poor bay to an even faster pace, he felt as if he were in the dreadful nightmare he had often endured at fifteen, after his mother's death. In the dream, he had believed he could keep her from dying if he could get to her in time and warn her, but his feet had always seemed mired in mud or sand. No matter how hard he tried, he always knew he would be too late, and he feared that he would be now.

The screams stopped as he reached the hilltop and turned toward the cliffs. Only a wee bit farther, he thought, through the trees to the clearing.

"Please, God," he muttered, dreading what he would find, "let her be safe."

Still at full speed as he crossed the clearing, and seeing only a female form stretched flat and slowly sliding over the edge, he wrenched the bay to a plunging standstill by the great rock and flung himself off the horse.

"Mariota, what are you doing?" Cristina shrieked. "Let go of Isobel!"

"I can't," Mariota shouted over Isobel's screams. "I meant just to give her a boost so she could grab the line, but that shrub I was holding came free."

"No, it didn't. I can see it," Cristina said.

"That's not the same one," Mariota replied. "That one would never hold me."

"Please, let go of Isobel," Cristina cried, digging with her toes, fighting to stop sliding, knowing she was much too far over the edge for safety. "I can't hold you, Mariota. I'm slipping, and all three of us will fall if you don't let go."

"Just hold on to us, Cristina. Hector will be here soon. You said he would."

As Mariota spoke his name, Cristina heard hoofbeats behind her but feared he would be too late. Her hands, arms, and shoulders throbbed with pain, and she felt certain that to slide even an inch or two more would mean the end of them all.

Isobel screamed again, yelling shrilly at Mariota to let go of her, but Cristina barely heeded her cries. She had shut her eyes again, and so firmly had she fixed her mind on praying that they would not all fall before Hector could reach her, that she had no energy left for anything else. She barely heard the scraping footsteps.

Suddenly, the line was lighter.

As relief flooded her mind, a paralyzing scream drowned out Isobel's cries, and Cristina's eyes flashed open to see Mariota plunge to the rocks below.

Despite her shock, she held tight to the line, as Hector threw himself on her and reached out to help her hold Isobel.

❧

Holding himself off Cristina with one hand, Hector grabbed the makeshift line just below her grip with the other and eased the child's weight from her.

"Let go now, lass," he said. "I've got her."

"We must pull her up together," Cristina said, her voice choked with tears. "Mariota gave her life trying to push her to safety. We must not let her fall now."

"We won't, but trying to pull together is too dangerous. We'd get in each other's way, so I'll roll to my left and you ease back from the edge and get up."

She did not reply, but when he raised up to let her scoot out from under him, she moved to obey him, trying at the same time to retain her hold on the line.

"Let go," he said. "I've got her."

She hesitated. Then, with a stifled sob, she let go. That sob, however, reminded him that she had just seen one sister plunge to her death and must be terrified for Isobel's safety. That she struggled for her usual control made him want to weep for her, but he could not deal with her until Isobel was safe.

Gently, he said, "Move back farther from the edge, sweetheart."

"But you may still need my help."

"No, I won't. Truly, lass, you can trust me to do this, but I need you out of my way so I have room to move. I don't want to worry about your safety, too."

When she still hesitated, he said more sharply, "Get off the rock *now,* Cristina. I cannot pull her up until you are out of my way."

When she moved back at last, albeit only a few steps, he focused his attention on Isobel. "Hold on as tight as you can, lassie, because I'm going to pull you up now. Take care that you don't swing into the cliff wall as I do. Use your feet to hold yourself away, and don't worry if your foot slips. I won't let go of you."

"My hands are sweating, and my fingers feel numb," Isobel said.

His heart clenched with cold fear at these words, and he heard a hastily stifled squeak of terror from Cristina. Fighting a nearly overwhelming urge to snatch the child to safety, he kept his movements slow and steady, knowing that even the smallest jerk could loosen numbed fingers from their grip.

When he could reach her hands, he grasped the nearest slender wrist firmly, and slowly stood up.

Sensibly, Isobel retained her hold on the leather line with both hands until her feet were near the rock. Then, with a sudden tug, she raised both feet the last inch and planted them solidly on it.

Putting his arms around her, Hector held her close. "You were very brave," he murmured against her curls as tears pricked his eyes. "I'm proud of you."

"Bring her back away from the edge," Cristina snapped.

Knowing she still feared for their safety, he said soothingly, "We're safe, lass. Give Isobel a moment to collect herself."

"We don't have moments to spare," Cristina protested, "We must get to Mariota as quickly as we can."

"We cannot help her," he said.

"You do not know that! She may still be alive, and she will need me."

Knowing that in the unlikely event that Mariota had survived the long fall, she would be suffering agonies of pain and unlikely to survive long, he said calmly, "I saw lads running from the landing, Cristina. They will get to her quicker than we could. You and I must look after Isobel, because she may have injured herself when she fell over the edge, or by supporting her own weight for so long afterward."

"You look after her," Cristina retorted. "I'm going to Mariota."

Isobel tugged his sleeve, muttering urgently, "Don't let her go, sir."

"I won't," he assured her as he drew her away from the edge to solid ground, watching as Cristina strode purposefully toward the nearby palfrey, and wondering when she would realize that he and Isobel still held its bridle and reins.

He noted at the same time that Lachlan's bay was not where he'd left it but had moved a short distance away to a point nearer the tree line.

"Can you wait here for a moment or two?" he asked Isobel.

"Of course, but please, sir, don't let her make you angry."

"I will strive to control my temper," he said, still watching Cristina, "but I will not allow her to race down that hill in the state she's in."

She had reached the palfrey and stood gazing blankly at it for a moment. Then she glanced over her shoulder at him. She had remembered the bridle.

"Please, sir," Isobel begged. "She loved Mariota, despite all her faults."

"I know she did," he said, watching Cristina look about for a place from which she could mount. When she grabbed the palfrey's mane and began to coax it toward a boulder of suitable height, he added brusquely, "Stay here. Oh, and lass—" He waited until Isobel looked at him. "You might try trusting me, too," he said.

She twinkled. "I do," she said. "I trust you to lose your temper the minute she defies you again. I remember, sir, that you don't tolerate defiant women."

Hearing the echo of his own words from the child's lips nearly made him smile, but Cristina had persuaded the reluctant palfrey to move to her boulder and would soon be able to mount.

"Wait, Cristina," he yelled, breaking into a run.

Had the palfrey been used to such treatment, or Cristina's skirts less cumbersome, she might well have mounted and ridden off before he reached her. As it was, when she saw him running toward her, she abandoned the palfrey and ran to Lachlan's bay, catching up its reins, grabbing a handful of its mane, and flinging herself over its back.

Before she could right herself and find her seat, the half-trained horse reared and screamed in protest, sending her flying.

Hector leaped toward her, managing to break her fall but letting her slip to the ground as he grabbed the bay's bridle and forced it down, smacking it away from Cristina and doing his best to avoid its flailing front hooves. Then, looping the reins around a branch, he turned purposefully toward his wife.

"Don't touch me," she snapped at him as she scrambled to her feet. "She is my sister, and I am going to her. She will need me."

"She does not need you, and you are not going anywhere," he said grimly, fighting to keep from grabbing her and shaking her until her teeth flew from her head. "Have you not risked your life enough today that you would do so foolish a thing as to try riding a half-trained horse, without a saddle and in skirts?"

She did not respond, standing with her face turned so that she need not look at him, staring into space, jaw clenched, her lips pressed tightly together as if she fought to keep the words she yearned to shout at him from flying off her tongue.

After enduring the silence as long as he could, he put a hand at the small of her back, meaning to go back to her palfrey and bridle it for her but wanting to keep her near him lest she dash off again, as he feared she might in her present state.

However, the moment he touched her, she whirled with an unearthly screech and began pounding him as hard as she could with her fists.

He stood still, hands at his sides, making no effort to restrain her, ruthlessly suppressing his increasing urge to grab her and shake sense into her.

"Do something!" she screamed, still hitting him. "Why don't you *do* something? Why didn't you come sooner if you were going to come at all? Why couldn't you save her? You said I need not do it all, that you would help, so where were you? You did nothing to help me prevent what happened!"

He remained silent, and when she had exhausted herself, her pummeling fists pressed together against his chest as she bent her head to them with a gasping sob.

Putting his hands gently on her shoulders, he said, "What happened to Mariota was not my doing, sweetheart."

"I know it wasn't," she said with another gusty sob.

"Nor yours."

She burst into tears then, and he drew her close and held her, letting her cry. As she did, he glanced at Isobel, meeting her solemn gaze over Cristina's head. But seeing her sitting patiently, he returned his attention to his wife, and even after her sobs eased to sniffles, he waited until they stopped and she gave a deep sigh.

When she made no attempt to free herself but slid her arms around him, he experienced an unexpected deep sense of peace, as if the world, having tilted, had righted itself again. Warmth spread through him as he held her, and he knew in that moment not only what he wanted most of all in life but that he had found it. He knew, too, that he wanted more than anything to free her from her burdensome sense of responsibility for everyone else in her world.

When she finally looked up at him, her face tear-stained and smudged, strands of her hair straying untidily from her caul, her eyes red and swollen, he wondered how he could ever have thought she was not as beautiful as Mariota when she was so much more so. Cristina's beauty radiated even now from within, from her very soul. Whatever happened between them after this, he could not let her destroy herself in the belief that she bore responsibility for Mariota's death.

Steeling himself and keeping his hands on her shoulders, he looked down at her. "You don't really believe any of the fault for her death lies with you, do you?"

"Of course I do," she said with a sigh. "How could it be otherwise? I should have seen her distress and explained things better to her."

"What things? No, don't try to answer that," he added grimly. "She would not have listened to you. You know that. She never listened to anyone."

"But if I just had been kinder, more understanding—"

"You were always kind to her, Cristina," he said, realizing only when she winced that his hands had tightened on her shoulders. Easing his grip, he added, "Faith, lass, you are kind to everyone. But I'm thinking it is not kindness that stirs you to assume blame for her death but pure arrogance."

She stiffened as if he had slapped her, which in a way, he supposed he had.

"How can you say such a horrid thing?" she demanded.

He was relieved to see her anger. The unnatural stillness she had displayed until then had frightened him.

"I say it because it is true," he said.

She glowered at him. "It is *not* true!"

"Believing that you wield sufficient power to control the

lives of everyone around you, and protect them from their own faults and folly, can be nothing *but* arrogance," he said. "Do you honestly believe that any mortal possesses such power?"

"But—"

"Nay, sweetheart," he said, putting a finger to her lips to silence her. "We can talk more about this later, but we must return now before an army of the curious engulfs us. Since Isobel's pony appears to have fled to the barn or wandered elsewhere, I'll take her up with me."

"I want her with me," Cristina said. "I need to feel her close to me."

"Nay," he said again, his tone still gentle. "You're exhausted. You'll both be safer if I take her, so not another word," he added when she opened her mouth again. "I've more to say to you before this day is over, but not now. Come, I'll put you on your palfrey."

She looked at him as if to protest again, but he met her gaze steadily and she did not. Without realizing it, he had dropped the palfrey's bridle when he had taken her in his arms, so he picked it up and walked with her to the waiting horse. Slipping its bridle on, he looped the reins over its head, then gripped Cristina around the waist and lifted her to its back.

"Do you feel steady enough?" he asked.

"Aye, of course I do. Truly, sir, I could—"

Shaking his head, he waved to Isobel, who picked up her skirts and ran to him. "You're going to ride with me, lassie," he said. "I'll mount first, and then—"

He stopped, realizing that he could not pull her up without risking further injury to her arms.

Cristina saw the problem at once, saying, "You cannot do it, sir, nor can you risk leaving her on that raw young horse alone even for the short time it would take you to mount. You'll have to let her ride with me. This palfrey is used to skirts."

"I'll put her up with you until I've mounted," he said. "But then I'm taking her from you. And no more backchat, lass. I've only so much patience."

So saying, he lifted Isobel up to her, mounted the gelding, and got it under control before taking the child back again. Then he helped Isobel settle herself in front of him so that he could hold her safely and still control the horse.

"You follow me," he said to Cristina. "That way I won't have to worry about you urging that poor animal to a gallop down the hill."

Not only did she not argue but she did not say another word. Her expression revealed that her thoughts had turned inward, and he did not know whether to be glad or sorry. Either she was thinking about what he had said to her, which would be good, or she was back to blaming herself for Mariota's fall, which would not be.

"How are your arms?" he asked Isobel.

"Not so bad," she said. "I didn't even realize I'd hurt them until you started pulling me up that wall, but it was hard then to hold on." Her voice trembled.

Matter-of-factly, he said, "I warrant it was, but you are safe now."

Glancing over his shoulder, he saw that Cristina was obediently following. He had half feared that she would try to ride to where she could look down at the rocks along the shore and see who was tending to Mariota's body.

"Sir, I think you should know—" Isobel broke off whatever she had been about to say and leaned away to look behind him.

"She won't hear, little one. What is it?"

"Do you remember that Cristina said Mariota sacrificed her own life trying to help push me to safety?"

"I do," he said. "If it's true, I'm glad she showed such courage, but I did think it sounded a bit out of character."

"It isn't true," Isobel muttered.

"Tell me then."

"She . . . she was trying to climb up me."

Stifling an urge to swear, he said, "I don't think she realized how much such an action imperiled you, little one. As I see it, the one constant thing was that she thought of no one but herself. She rarely seemed to have the slightest awareness that her actions might have consequences to others."

"Is that why she never seemed really sorry, even when she said over and over again that she was?"

"I believe so. Something was not quite right with her, I think."

"She wasn't mad," Isobel said stoutly.

"Nay, not mad, just not the same as normal people."

"You won't say that to Cristina, will you?"

"I think she knows," Hector said.

"But she doesn't! And . . . and I think she needs to go on believing Mariota did something good in her last moments, sir. To believe that may ease her pain."

"I've noted before that you are wise beyond your years, Isobel, and so you are—wiser than most grown folk, I think."

"Not so wise, sir, but I do watch people and try to learn from them."

Hector chuckled at the memory of her eavesdropping, and realized it was the first time his sense of humor had stirred since seeing the two figures fall off the rock. Giving her shoulder a gentle, affectionate squeeze as they came into sight of the great-hall courtyard, he saw that a reception committee awaited them.

∽∾∽

Cristina, too, had observed the small but growing crowd gathered on the east side of the great hall, but lost in her thoughts as she was, she could not stir any interest in them. Only after she and Hector rode into the yard and people rushed to meet them did she try to focus her mind, but her thoughts refused to cooperate until she recognized the Green Abbot striding angrily toward her.

"There she is," he exclaimed, angrily pointing a finger at her. "Murderess! She killed her sister, as I saw with my own eyes. Clap her into irons, I say!"

Cristina stared blindly at him. "I . . . I . . ." But she could not continue, could not deny that Mariota's death, although not murder and despite what Hector had said, was somehow, in some way, her fault.

As she gaped at the abbot, her father appeared beside her, his face red with fury. "What ha' ye done?" he demanded, reaching for her and pulling her off the palfrey. Giving her a shake, he added, "'Twas a wicked, wicked thing you did!"

"She didn't!" Isobel cried as Hector dismounted and set her on the ground.

Then Hector was beside Cristina, his strong hand reassuringly gripping her shoulder as he snapped, "She did nothing of the sort, Macleod, and you know it. And so do you," he added, turning to the abbot. "What you saw was my lady wife nearly sacrificing her own life to save her beloved sisters, and 'tis an abomination for you to accuse her as you did. By heaven, if you were not a man of the cloth—"

"But I am a man of the cloth," Mackinnon said. "What is

more, I wield more power in these parts than even Mac-Donald does."

"I'll challenge that," MacDonald said, moving to stand near Hector.

"I'd challenge it, too, if I were you," another voice said, and Cristina saw Robert the Steward step up beside Mac-Donald.

"Would you, sir?" Mackinnon said, raising his chin. "Would you also question my word when I tell you that you have won support from a man who takes gelt from his abbey kirk to fill his own coffers, a man who cheats his own people?"

"Are you now hurling vile accusations at your liege lord?" MacDonald asked in a gentle voice that nonetheless shot shivers through Cristina and made her tremble. But Hector's hand did not twitch at MacDonald's icy tone, and she was certain that steady hand on her shoulder was all that kept her upright.

"My only liege is my Lord God," the Green Abbot said piously, not intimidated. "You have defied His laws, Mac-Donald of the Isles," he declared. "You have taken from your own people, even forced your own kirks to give good gelt for the holy oil you should be giving to them freely."

As Cristina watched and listened, Lady MacFadyen's words echoed in her mind, and without a thought for consequence, she heard herself using Hector's favorite word as she said, "Sakes, Fingon Mackinnon, but you demanded that the people of Coll donate years' worth of oil to you. And if you demanded it on Coll, I'll wager you demanded it from other isles as well."

Mackinnon turned to her again, his eyes blazing with anger, and that reassuring hand dropped from her shoulder as Hector stepped in front of her.

"My lady wife speaks the truth," he said for all to hear. "I warrant that you are responsible for even more mischief than that if the truth were known."

Mackinnon stepped toward him. "Why, you heathenish upstart, how dare you speak so to me! Do you know what I can do to you? Excommunication is no mere word to me, Hector Reaganach, but a power that will send you to hell!"

"Hold there," MacDonald commanded. "For all you say, Fingon, you do not hold sway on these grounds. Indeed, if I had my way, I'd hang you for your misdeeds, because I believe we know less than half of what you've done. You've long had a reputation for wickedness, and should be ashamed of yourself."

Mackinnon whirled toward him, but Hector caught his arm as it went up.

"Sakes, man, don't be daft," he said. "Be you cleric or madman, my duty is to my liege. If you take another step or raise that hand again, I'll smite you down."

"You dare!"

Silence fell as the two glowered at each other, until Robert said, "You know, MacDonald, I advise you to confine this mischief-maker to his Holy Isle. Indeed, as soon as I properly wear the crown of Scotland, I may issue such an order myself."

Looking from man to man, Cristina noted furtive movement not far behind Robert and MacDonald. To her annoyance, she saw Fergus Love easing his way toward her through the onlookers there.

He was watching her, and when her gaze met his, he winked impudently.

That he could approach her, even flirt with her, with her husband beside her and her sister having just plunged to her death, appalled her. She turned haughtily away, but curiosity being stronger than willpower, only a moment passed before she looked back again.

Fergus was still coming toward her, nearing a point behind and between Robert and MacDonald. Was the man mad?

As the thought crossed her mind, she saw him reach inside his doublet and begin to take something out. Even as mesmerized by his daring as she was, she recognized a dagger hilt when she saw one.

Crying a warning, she thrust herself between MacDonald and the Steward, shoving both aside as hard as she could, and saw the dagger flash toward her.

Chapter 21 ————————————

Hector's attention had riveted itself to Fingon Mackinnon, and as he waited tensely for the man to stand down, something pricked him into wondering why Fingon was behaving so oddly. The man had clearly wanted to stir trouble from the moment they had returned, and it was unusual for him to make mischief at court.

Suddenly, with a discernible gleam of triumph, his gaze darted sideways.

Hector heard Cristina cry out and felt her leap away from him toward MacDonald and the Steward. Instantly, he kicked the smirking abbot solidly in the stomach and knocked him flat. Without waiting to see him land, certain he would not soon get up, Hector whirled as Cristina pushed between MacDonald and the Steward, and saw the dagger flash up to meet her.

With thought for nothing but that dagger, he flung himself after her, reaching for her as he did. When his hand touched fabric at the back of her gown, he grabbed it hard and wrenched her toward him, lifting her off her feet and swinging her toward his left hand, as he kept moving toward the flashing dagger.

She screamed again, this time in frustrated fury as much as fear, he knew, but she was safely behind him and the man who would have killed her, and Robert as well, stood in front of him. Having not taken sword or axe to search for his errant bride, and with his dirk thrust as usual into his boot, he held no weapon of his own as he lunged at Fergus Love. He did not need one.

The dagger went flying as one powerful forearm knocked Love's right hand up, and the man screamed in such a way that Hector was sure he had broken his arm. But to make sure Love would cause no more trouble, he shot a heavy fist to the man's chin, felling him to the ground. Standing over him, wishing he would get up so he could hit him again, Hector fought to control his fury. It was MacDonald's right, or Robert's—but not his—to determine Fergus Love's fate.

Reaching down, he hauled him up and thrust him into the waiting hands of two men-at-arms who had plunged through the crowd to aid him as soon as they realized trouble had erupted.

As they hustled Love away under strong guard, Hector turned to Cristina.

She eyed him angrily, and he nearly smiled, because she looked like his Cristina again. Evidently, she had fallen when he thrust her behind him, because she was dusting her skirt off with Isobel's help and glowering like an angry child. He wanted to take her in his arms.

She said tartly, "I think you ripped my gown, and he would not have harmed me. He had already recognized me and was turning the blade aside."

"Cristina, he nearly killed you," Isobel said, touching her arm as if she would soothe her temper away.

"He was threatening the next King of Scots and Mac-Donald, who is my liege lord," Hector said sternly, adding in a quieter tone, "And before you take me to task in front of them and everyone else here, my lass, you might pause to think about the penalty for striking the Lord of the Isles *and* the heir to the kingdom of Scotland."

Her face paled, and she glanced from MacDonald to Robert and back.

"What *is* the penalty?" Isobel asked, wide-eyed.

Hector was already wishing that he had not mentioned penalties, because it had occurred to him that the one for striking MacDonald was death from *Creag na Corps*. In order that the same thought not occur to Cristina, he added, "Never mind, Isobel. You had better apologize at once, lass, and hope the Steward does not order you back to Stirling to stand trial for what you did."

MacDonald smiled at her and said, "Don't frighten your lady wife, sir. She undoubtedly saved his life and perhaps my own as well. That villain is clearly deranged to have attempted such violence here before so many."

"He had help, your grace," Hector said, moving to stand over Mackinnon, who was struggling to rise with the help of one of his minions. "I realized in the midst of it all that something was amiss. 'Tis my belief that the Green Abbot stirred things up a-purpose to divert attention from Fergus Love just as he diverted ships away from the flotilla protecting Robert. He knew what Love meant to do here."

"Prove it," Mackinnon snarled. "Just try to prove any of that."

"Do you think Love will not talk to us?" Hector asked. "He will."

"Nay, then, he will not," Mackinnon said. "He has naught to say."

"We'll see," Hector said.

Noting two men near the stairs to the boat landing, and

realizing that others below must have recovered Mariota's body by now and would soon be carrying it up, he caught MacDonald's eye and gave a slight nod in that direction.

MacDonald gave no sign of noticing but turned to Cristina and said soberly, "We are exceedingly grateful for your quick action, my lady. Your bravery—"

"Please, your grace," she said. "I did naught for which you should thank me. I did not even think. I just acted."

"It is by their actions that we know our friends, Lady Cristina," Robert said. "And I count you from this moment my very good friend, indeed."

She curtsied low, and when she arose, Hector took her hand and tucked it into the crook of his arm, holding it there firmly.

"I hope you'll both forgive us," he said. "My lady wife has endured a trying day, and I would see her rest. With your permission, we'll forgo taking supper with everyone in the great hall this evening."

"You have our permission, sir," MacDonald said. "Take good care of her."

"You come with us, Isobel," Hector said, and the child nodded.

"But why should we . . . ?" Cristina began.

Hector squeezed her hand harder, and to his surprise, she fell silent.

With Isobel following at their heels, he urged Cristina through the crowd and across the courtyard. When she tried again to speak, he said, "We'll talk all you like when we reach our bedchamber, but not now, sweetheart."

They were nearing the main entrance to the castle when he heard his twin shout his name from behind. Pausing, hoping Lachlan had no new orders for him, he turned and saw with relief that Mairi was with him.

Mairi caught Cristina in a warm hug and said, "What a horrible thing!"

"Aye," Lachlan agreed quietly. "We're sorry for your loss, my lady, and will do whatever we can to help ease your pain."

She looked up at Hector. Sadness had returned to her eyes, but she no longer had the blind look that had frightened him so, and he was grateful. "We cannot go in yet," she said. "They'll be bringing her body up soon, and I must be there."

"Nay, lass," he said gently. "You'll come with me and give me no more argument. Lachlan will see to her care, and Mairi will help. You can see her later."

Mairi said, "Aye, he's right, Cristina. You must rest. I'll order supper sent to your chamber, and I'll find Lady Euphemia, for I know she will want to help prepare Mariota's body. You need not worry about Isobel either, because I'll look after her, too. You'll let me do that, won't you, Isobel?"

"Aye," Isobel said. "But only if Hector promises to keep his temper."

Mairi laughed and looked at him with a teasing twinkle.

"I'll say what I said before, lass," he told Isobel. "I can only do my best."

She smiled at him, nodded, and turned away with Mairi. Before Lachlan could follow, Hector said, "One moment, my lad, I want another word with you."

~~~

When he stepped aside to speak to Lachlan, Mairi turned back to Cristina, saying, "Don't fret. I have already told my husband that on no account is he to send Hector anywhere for at least a sennight. His place until then should be with you."

Cristina nodded, remembering that Hector had said he still had much to say to her, and uncertain if she should thank Mairi for interceding. Nevertheless, she felt herself warm within at the thought of Hector staying near.

He spoke only moments with his twin before returning to her side. "We'll go in now, sweetheart," he said.

She made no further objection, knowing she could depend on Mairi to see that Mariota was attended as she should be. As the realization settled into her mind, she felt the warm place inside her grow larger. For almost as long as she could remember, she had been able to depend only on herself, because with the exception of a servant or two, everyone around her, in his or her own fashion, had proven either patently unreliable or too young to depend on. Now, in the space of little more than a month, she had found several people she could trust.

Mairi was one, Lachlan another, and Isobel . . . Isobel was wonderful, and she would miss her dreadfully when the child returned to Chalamine. And then, of course, there was Hector. She glanced up at him as she moved to pass him and go up the spiral stone stairway. He was frowning, but when her gaze met his, he smiled and put an arm around her, giving her a hug.

It was a solid arm, a reliable arm, and he was a man who looked after his own. She had known the moment she had seen his arms go around Isobel that the child was safe, and had known, too, that Isobel truly felt safe, because who would not? She herself had certainly felt so, facing the abbot with Hector's hand on her shoulder.

Her spirits thus felt lighter by the time they passed the garderobe tower and entered the guest wing. As she stepped into their bedchamber, she was conscious only of Hector behind her. Hearing the door snap to, she turned to face him.

"I don't want to go to bed yet," she said firmly.

"We're not going back downstairs, sweetheart. You might as well rest."

"I'll rest if I must, but I won't sleep, sir. My head would simply fill with images again, and I don't want that. I want to remember Mariota as she was when she was laughing and merry, not as she was when she . . ."

"I understand, sweetheart. We can talk if you like."

"Not if you mean to scold me."

"Nay, lass, I'll not do that, although you frightened me witless when you rushed at that knife. I had all I could do not to throttle the bastard."

She nearly told him again that she did not think Fergus Love had meant to harm her, but she knew it would be a waste of breath, since Fergus might not have been able to stop himself in time. Moreover, defending him might stir Hector to anger again, and she did not want him angry with her, not tonight.

He had taken off his doublet and was kneeling on the hearth, tucking spills beneath logs and kindling already arranged for them and ready to light.

"Won't you have to be present when they question Fergus?" she asked.

"Nay, for I've told Lachlan I'll be taking leave of him for at least a month," he said as he took out his tinderbox. "I want time with my bride and time to finish putting Lochbuie in order. He has plenty of men to do his bidding. He can get along without me for a time."

Having lighted the small fire, he stood and walked toward her, his expression sober and searching. "We should talk more, lass, about what happened today. I fear you are still blaming yourself."

She sighed. "Mayhap I am somewhat, but I understand what you meant about the arrogance of doing that. Still, I keep thinking 'if only this' or 'if only that.'"

"Everyone does that, and you took care of them all for a long time."

"Aye, but that is certainly no reason to have blamed you as I did, nor in truth, do I blame you at all."

"Never mind about that now," he said, moving to put his arm around her.

"Something was wrong with her, Hector."

"I know," he said. "Come and sit with me by the fire. I want to hold you."

"She always said she was not like everyone else," Cristina said as she sat beside him on the settle and leaned her head against his shoulder. "But I never thought she could be capable of what she did today."

"No one did, sweetheart. I didn't see anything at all amiss with her until I found her with you at Lochbuie and came to realize that she thought only of herself. Even then I saw naught but selfishness in her behavior. Later I realized that talking with her, trying to understand what she was saying, was like trying to grab smoke. I could see wisps and curls of the way she saw the world, but if I tried to pin it down and see the clear picture, I couldn't do it. No one could."

"I'm glad others did not see her like that," Cristina said.

"Aye," he agreed. "Oddness in one's family is better hidden."

Narrowing her eyes at him, she said, "So it is good that she died?"

"I did not say that, nor would I," he said. "Mariota's death was a tragedy, sweetheart, but she will be remembered as young and beautiful, even noble. Troubadours may even sing ballads about her, and bards will repeat the tale of her courageous sacrifice forevermore. How she would have loved to know that!"

Cristina was silent. She had not thought of such a possibility. She did not want to think about it, but she could not bear that he did not know the truth.

Glancing up at him, she said, "There is something you should know."

When he did not reply, she drew a breath and said, "I do not think Mariota was really behaving nobly. I think—" Saying the words proved exceedingly difficult, but she forced herself. "I think she thought only of herself again today, because I'm nearly sure she was not trying to help Isobel. She was trying to climb right up her, sir, and I nearly dropped them both. If she hadn't fallen—"

"We need not think about that now," he said, drawing her closer against his solid, warm body. "You will remember her as merry and laughing. Most everyone else can remember her as they please, too."

"You won't tell Isobel what I told you, will you?" she said. "'Tis better for her to believe that Mariota tried to save her, I think."

"I won't tell her," he said solemnly, but a note of laughter in his voice made her look up at him again.

"It isn't funny," she said.

"Nay, lass, but you should know by now that Isobel knows more about some things than the rest of us all together, and your sister Mariota was one of them."

"Isobel knows?"

"Of course she does. She's the one Mariota tried to climb. She told me not to tell you though. She said *you* needed to believe in Mariota's sacrifice."

"I should have known," she said, snuggling closer. "She told me once that I never want to depend on anyone else. She was right, too, because I never believed I could do so before, and I suppose I'm still not used to trusting other people completely. But thanks to you and Mairi and Isobel, I'm learning."

"I know how hard it was for you to let me pull Isobel up alone," he said.

"Aye, but I knew she was safer in your hands than mine. I think seeing Mariota fall must have disordered my senses, but in truth, I knew Isobel and I were both safe the moment you fell on top of me. I just couldn't . . . the shock . . ."

When he remained silent, she drew a breath and went on, "But then you pulled her up, and when you put your arms around her, I knew she felt as safe as I feel whenever you put them around me. Anyone would."

"I'm glad *you* do," he murmured.

The fire crackled comfortably, and the air in the chamber had warmed. So, too, had Cristina. Her left hand rested lightly on Hector's muscular thigh, and her head leaned against his solid chest. His arm around her felt good and right. She could hear his heart beating, slowly and powerfully. She was content.

He, too, seemed to feel no need to talk. One of his fingers toyed with a curl that had escaped her caul. As he did, it tickled her neck, and she turned her face up toward his, invitingly.

Obligingly, he kissed her, but although she responded at once, the kiss was light and most unsatisfactory. His eyes gleamed, and she knew he felt the same stirrings that she did, that he was restraining himself out of respect for her loss.

Still looking into his eyes, she murmured, "Is it wrong of me to feel like this with Mariota lying dead below?"

"Nay, sweetheart, 'tis but a natural urge that many feel at such a time. Death often makes folks yearn to create new life."

"Then will you make love to me?"

He smiled. "If you want me to, I will, and gladly. Shall I send for Brona to help you prepare for bed?"

The thought sent heat to her cheeks. "I don't want Brona, but mayhap we should send for enough hot water to wash our faces and hands. Indeed," she added unhappily, "mayhap we should wait until they bring our supper."

"And mayhap we should not wait at all," he said. "I can serve adequately as a maidservant, can I not?"

She smiled. "Aye, you can."

"Don't move," he commanded, releasing her and standing. "I'll be back."

With that, he strode to the door, flung it open, and shouted for a gillie. When one came, she heard Hector ordering him to arrange to keep their supper hot for at least an hour and to have whoever brought it up rap on the door before he entered.

Then, shutting and barring the door, he faced her with intent.

"Come here to me," he said.

"It is warmer by the fire," she said. Her voice sounded strange to her, low and husky, deep down in her throat. Her lips suddenly felt dry. She licked them.

Without taking his eyes off her, he walked slowly back to her. Standing close enough to make her body sing, he stopped, looked down at her, and said, "A good wife obeys her husband."

"Aye, but it is warmer here by the fire."

He pulled her to her feet. "Turn around," he said.

She turned, trembling when she felt his fingers lightly touching her back.

"I did rip this gown," he said. "But 'tis only a small tear. You can mend it."

"My mending basket is overflowing," she said.

"Then I'll get you another gown," he said, slipping his finger through the rip in the gown and making her tremble again as it caressed bare skin above her shift. He kissed her neck and kissed it again, laying a trail of soft kisses from just under her left ear around to her throat. And then her caul was off, pulled without ceremony from her head and tossed aside, and he began to seek the pins in her hair, kissing her as he dropped them to the floor one by one until she could stand no more. She turned abruptly, throwing her arms around him and holding him tight.

Moments later, her bodice and skirt were off and her shift pulled over her head and cast aside. He picked her up then and carried her to the bed, laying her on it, then standing over her, gazing down at her with visible pleasure.

"Are you just going to stand there?" she asked.

In reply, he began to take off the rest of his clothing, slowly this time as if he taunted her, and her desire for him increased as she watched. He was a splendid-looking man, and she never tired of watching him move.

He lay down beside her, took her in his arms, and kissed her, saying, "I think we'll invite Isobel and your aunt to live with us. They amuse me and will make good company for you whenever I'm away. Do you think your father will object?"

"No," she said. "Adela is competent, and the others are growing up fast. He won't miss either of them, and I'd love to have them with us."

"Good," he said, kissing her again. Then, to her delight, he eased lower, teasing her with kisses all down her body until she squirmed as she had on the floor of the croft with the rain beating down. He brought her to near release, then took her swiftly, his own passion clearly more than he could contain and more than enough to ignite hers. She felt as if she were on fire one moment, soaring the next.

As they lay sated in each other's arms afterward, she murmured drowsily, "You do make me feel so safe." Then, when he hugged her in response, she added, "I will miss her, though."

"I know."

"I'm just sorry for your sake that I'm not as beautiful as she was."

He chuckled, turning to face her as he said, "When I first saw your sister, I was foolish enough to think I would value her for her beauty and her charm. I have since learned that I did not know the meaning of those words."

"Their meanings are scarcely obscure, sir. She was stunningly beautiful."

With a wry smile, he said, "Aye, well, in my foolish ignorance, I actually thought I could be happy gazing at her for the rest of my days, as if her looks would never fade. As to her charm, I recognized only the sort that made no secret of admiring me. I was a most despicable fellow then, I'm afraid."

"Never," she murmured.

"Sweetheart, the woman I thought I wanted was not, fortunately for me, the woman I won. The woman I married is much, much more valuable to me and will be so to the end of our days. I have been more fortunate than I deserve, because you have taught me that true beauty only *begins* with flawless skin, golden eyes, and a smile that lights any room—and that charm is but one facet of timeless beauty, the sort that radiates from within. I love you, Cristina, with all my heart."

"I love you, too," she said. "But I have loved you much longer."

"Wise lass," he said, kissing her gently. "I owe your devious parent a far greater debt than he will ever know."

She arched her eyebrows. "You do not mean to tell him?"

"Sakes, no. The man is insufferable enough. Only think what he would be like if I were to admit to him that you and I belong together and always will!"

Dear Reader,

The germ for *Lord of the Isles,* like that for *Highland Princess,* sprouted from a collection of bards' tales [*West Highland Tales* by Fitzroy Maclean, Edinburgh, 1985]. When I discovered that the progenitors of the two clans were possibly twins, and their names were Lachlan Lubanach ("the Wily") and Hector Reaganach ("the Ferocious"), I was hooked. Further research revealed that although Hector was likely the elder of the two, Lachlan became chief of Clan Gillean because his father thought the clan needed a leader with brains rather than brawn. When I learned that Lachlan had employed questionable methods to marry the daughter of the Lord of the Isles and greatly increase the clan's power, I knew I had at least one good story. The problem arose in finding (or creating) Hector's story.

Other than his famous battle-axe, his ability to expedite his brother's plans, his skill with weapons, his marriage to Cristina Macleod, the name of the son who succeeded him at Lochbuie, and the line that succeeded him, we know practically nothing about Hector Reaganach. His story springs from my own imagination augmented by a bard's tale about a superstitious man with too many daughters.

The real Cristina Macleod may well have had seven sisters. We'll never know, because unless women married very prominent men, their names and antecedents rarely appear in ancient genealogies (or less-than-ancient ones, for that matter). We do know that her father was Murdoch Macleod of Glenelg and believe that her mother was a MacNichol. We also are nearly sure that Cristina had at least one brother, Torquil Macleod, who deserves mention because he became Chief of the Macleods of Lewis, but I decided to dispense with him in *Lord of the Isles.* I rarely take such license when

I have the facts, but some question does exist as to whether they were brother and sister or of entirely different generations, so rather than try to fit him in without cluttering up the story, I just left him out.

Petrel oil did provide a lucrative income for the Islesmen from the time of Angus Og, the father of MacDonald of the Isles. At first, Norse poachers collected oil only in the Orkneys. Angus decided to collect it on other isles, too, and export it, but it was his son who ultimately sought the help of the Hanseatic League and others for its transport. Under MacDonald, with the Isles united at last, business boomed, and the number of petrels diminished accordingly, although not for long, since petrels produce their chicks, called fulmars, in abundance.

Since Hector the Ferocious was the progenitor of the Maclaines of Lochbuie, some readers may wonder why I've spelled his name as "Maclean" in this book. The reason is that the change in spelling, according to the present Chief of the Maclaines of Lochbuie, did not come about until after 1746. Until then, the two branches were simply Macleans of Duart and Lochbuie.

I should also repeat two points I made at the end of *Highland Princess,* to clarify them for readers who have not yet read that story. The first is that in the fourteenth century, only one Mac Donald (sic) existed, and he was Lord of the Isles. Mac Donald was not yet a surname but a title, meaning *the* son of Donald, and so there could be only one at a time. Eventually, the name evolved into the various spellings used today. I used the modern spelling, MacDonald, to avoid both reader and proofreader confusion.

The second point I'll repeat is for those readers who have visited the nearly treeless Western Isles of Scotland and who may be wondering about all the forests in *Lord of the Isles.*

Until the sixteenth century, the Isles boasted mo[...]
thousand acres of trees that later vanished throug[...]
unfortunate habit of denuding forests to provide [...]
building materials, while doing little until the present day to
replenish them.

For readers interested in learning more about Maclean-
Maclaine history, the best of many sources I have found is
Warriors & Priests by Nicholas Maclean-Bristol (Tuckwell,
1995). For those interested in Macleod history, I'd recommend *The MacLeods: The History of a Clan* (Edinburgh,
1981); and *The Macleods of Dunvegan* (Clan MacLeod Society, 1927). Numerous online sources also exist.

For those who want to know more about the Lords of the
Isles, I suggest the following sources: *House of Islay* by
Donald Grumach (Argyll, 1967); *The Clan Donald* by Rev-
erend A. MacDonald (Inverness, 1896); *History of the
Macdonalds and Lords of the Isles* (with genealogies) by
Alexander Mackenzie (Inverness, 1881); *The Lords of the
Isles* by Raymond Campbell Paterson (Edinburgh, 2001);
and *The Islesman* by Nigel Tranter (London, 2003, Frances
May Baker).

If you enjoyed *Lord of the Isles,* please watch for *Prince
of Danger,* coming from Warner Books in November 2005.

Sincerely,

Amanda Scott

http://home.att.net/~amandascott/

About the Author

AMANDA SCOTT, best-selling author and winner of the Romance Writers of America's RITA/Golden Medallion and *Romantic Times*'s awards for Best Regency Author and Best Sensual Regency, began writing on a dare from her husband. She has sold every manuscript she has written. She sold her first novel, *The Fugitive Heiress*—written on a battered Smith-Corona—in 1980. Since then, she has sold many more, but since the second one, she has used a word processor. More than twenty-five of her books are set in the English Regency period (1810–20), others are set in fifteenth-century England and sixteenth- and eighteenth-century Scotland. Three are contemporary romances.

Amanda is a fourth-generation Californian who was born and raised in Salinas and graduated with a bachelor's degree in history from Mills College in Oakland. She did graduate work at the University of North Carolina at Chapel Hill, specializing in British history, before obtaining her master's in History from San Jose State University. She is a Fellow of the Society of Antiquaries of Scotland. After graduate school, she taught for the Salinas City School District for three years before marrying her husband, who was then a captain in the Air Force. They lived in Honolulu for a year, then in Nebraska for seven years, where their son was born. Amanda now lives with her husband in northern California.

Prologue ————————————————

West Loch Tarbert, Scotland, October 1307

Fingers of a thick Scottish night mist crept in from the sea, shrouding the dark forests and glens of Knapdale and Kintyre in ragged cloaks of gray and veiling the stars and the slender crescent of moon overhead, as four ships, barely visible, passed one by one through the passageway into Loch Tarbert. Although their sails had been furled for lack of wind to fill them, the ships moved silently on the inflowing tide, like hulking black ghosts.

The small watcher on the hillside, having successfully escaped the confines of his bedchamber to breathe the damp air of freedom, began to fear that if the mist rose much higher off the loch, he would not find his bedchamber again that night. The consequences of that might be severe, but freedom from authority, even for an hour, was worth the risk, especially with ghost ships for entertainment.

Curious to learn how such large galleys could move so silently without wind to drive them or any splashing of oars, he moved quietly down the hill, nearer to the shore. General visibility was even worse near the water, but he could still perceive the moving black shapes through the mist.

Now, faintly, came the occasional splash of an oar, although not the heavy, rhythmic splat and splash one associated with galleys as their great banks of oars flashed in and out of the water to the beat of a helmsman's ringing gong. Nor did these ships' gliding progress resemble that of such greyhounds of the sea.

A moment later, the curtain of mist parted slightly, and he saw that the one directly in front of him followed a smaller longboat, the oars of which made little sound as they dipped carefully in and out of the water. And if the mist was not distorting other sounds he now heard, a second such longboat moved between him and the bulk of that ship. Smaller boats were towing the galleys into the loch.

The child frowned. Should he run and warn someone? Had the men-at-arms that usually guarded the passageway all fallen asleep? He could not imagine such a thing happening, not when the penalty for such dereliction was a hangman's noose and a speedily dug grave. But perhaps witches had cast a spell over the guards.

He would face punishment if he told anyone, because his father would surely find out then that he had disobeyed him. But curiosity rather than fear of punishment drove him to decide to follow the boats farther up the loch. Even longboats required up to thirty oarsmen, and galleys held many more, possibly men-at-arms, too. He should acquire more information, if he could, before he told.

As he paused moments later after scrambling around a boulder in his path, a rattling of stones behind him nearly stopped his breathing. Standing absolutely still, he fought to calm his pounding heart as his ears strained to hear more.

Another rattle, a scraping sound as if someone had

slipped, and a small, hastily suppressed cry brought a sigh of irritation when he recognized the voice.

He waited grimly where he was to block the way as the follower scrambled around the boulder. The result was a startled, louder cry when they met.

"Shut your mug or by the Rood, I'll shut it for ye," he hissed.

"Ye scairt me near t' death!"

"I'll do worse than that if ye dinna hush up. D'ye no see them ships?"

"Aye, o' course. Who are they?"

"I dinna ken," he muttered. "But if any man wi' them sees us or hears us, they'll likely murder us so we canna tell anyone else."

"Faith, why should they, when our own da's wi' them?"

The lad frowned. "He is?"

"Aye, for I near ran into him when I followed ye through the hall. I had t' hide whilst he rousted out some o' the men t' go wi' him t' meet the strangers."

"We'll ha' to get back quick then," he decided, suppressing disappointment. "Someone will catch us sure if we don't, and our da will skelp us sure for this. I warrant we'll learn all about them ships come morning, anyhow."

But the next morning, when the sun shone brightly again on the loch, the ships were gone. Not a ripple remained to bear witness of their passage.

Chapter 1 —————————

Macleod land in Glenelg, Scotland, Summer 1378

Nineteen-year-old Lady Isobel Macleod, having escaped the confines of Castle Chalamine and her father's harping criticism, rode her pony bareback and with abandon over the hill and down the track toward Glen Shiel. The day was gloriously fine with a warm salty breeze blowing in from the sea. Wildflowers bloomed in huge, colorful splashes, and not another human being was in sight.

Glen Shiel was not the lonely isle of her dreams, with the solitary tower she had often told her sisters she intended to remove to just as soon as she found the means to do so, but it would do for an hour or two. She had only one more sennight to go before she could return to the Isle of Mull and Castle Lochbuie, which had been her home for the past seven years. She missed the Laird of Lochbuie and his wife, her sister Cristina, and she missed their bairns and her cats, as well.

Chalamine, although it had been the home of her childhood, no longer felt homelike with only three of her seven sisters still living there. Adela was rapidly turning into an old maid, burdened with the responsibility of managing the household, while Sidony and Sorcha were fairly champing at the bit to find husbands and marry so they, too, could leave. Isobel intended never to marry.

At least her father had given up insisting that each sister wait until her elder ones had done so. That superstition had died with her sister Mariota seven years before, along with Murdoch Macleod's dreams of a grand future for them all.

Putting Mariota firmly out of her mind, Isobel considered her options for the next hour or two. She could ride on to Loch Duich or back toward Loch Shiel, or she could stay off the worn tracks and look for someplace new.

As she pondered the possibilities, movement on the hillside opposite her caught her eye. Thanks to the steepness of Glen Shiel, the distance was not great, and she easily discerned two horsemen. Just then, they seemed to disappear into the shrubbery, and she realized they must have followed some track or other than she had not known was there.

Curious now, she touched her pony lightly with her whip to urge it to a faster pace. At the bottom of the hill, she forded the merry burn that tumbled through the glen toward Loch Duich and made her way up the other hillside. She was no longer certain she would be able to find the exact place the two had vanished, but that did not really matter. She had a purpose of sorts now, more than just an escape.

A few moments later, she came to a thick grove of trees that she remembered having seen just to the right of the men, and discovered that a merry stream wove its bubbling way downhill through the trees. Riding into the shady woods, she drew rein and listened. She did not want to meet anyone, and it had occurred to her that the two men, having vanished nearby, might reappear at any moment.

She felt no fear, because anyone in the neighborhood would know her, and she had only to tell any stranger that she was Macleod's daughter. The other clans in the vicinity were friendly ones.

Hearing no sound above the water's bubbling other than the usual forest tweets and chatters, she urged her mount on and soon found the track she had been seeking. It was no wonder that she had not come upon it before, because it began at a narrow cleft between two boulders and looked as if it might lead into a crevice rather than into another glen. But the passage widened soon afterward, and shortly after that she came upon a grassy clearing surrounded by more woods against a near backdrop of steep granite walls and peaks.

Finding no sign of the two riders she had followed, she rode across the clearing to see if the glen continued much farther. Entering the woodland, she savored its utter silence until a man's scream suddenly shattered it.

The scream seemed to come from only a short distance ahead of her and was not repeated, so although she urged her pony at once toward the sound, she did so with care, listening for any other sound that might tell her what had occurred.

The darkness in the woods lessened, and when she saw sunlight ahead and heard male voices, one in particular talking calmly but sternly, as if there had been no sound to disturb the peace, she drew rein. She could not make out their words.

"Doubtless we should leave," she murmured to the pony. "Whatever is going on is no business of ours, I'm sure, but curiosity has always been my besetting sin, and I suppose it always will be." With that, she slipped off the horse, landed lightly on the soft ground, and looped the reins over a tree branch.

Patting the pony's nose, she said, "No noise now. I'm depending on you."

Knowing she could not depend on the horse, and recalling the many times she had been punished for eavesdropping, she sent a prayer aloft that no one would catch her this time, and moved swiftly but quietly through the trees toward the voices, carrying only her riding whip.

She stopped behind a large chestnut tree near the edge of the woods and peeked cautiously into the clearing ahead, then gaped at the sight she beheld.

Six men had gathered around a seventh, who hung by his tautly stretched arms, tied to branches of two great oak trees. He was dark-haired and wore only breeks and boots. His muscular back and arms were bare, and blood oozed from two stripes across his broad shoulders. As she realized what she was witnessing, one of the six raised a heavy whip and said loudly, "You'll tell us eventually, Sinclair. It might as well be now whilst you can still talk clearly."

"Demons will be roasting you in hell first," his victim said in a deep, vibrant voice that easily carried to Isobel's ears.

"You know my skill," the other said. "Faith, man, you screamed at only the second stripe. Do you really want to test me?"

When his victim remained silent, he raised the whip again.

"Well now, what have we here?"

Isobel whirled, bringing up her riding whip, but a large hand clamped hard on her forearm. "Nay, now, lassie," the man holding her growled. "Drop it, and be grateful you did not strike me. You lads hold your whisst now," he called in a louder tone. "We've a lovely lass here, come to amuse us!"

Isobel sighed, but it was certainly not the first time that God had failed to answer her prayers.

She did not protest while her burly captor hustled her across the clearing to the others, but when he jerked her to a halt in front of the one with the whip, she said fiercely, "I don't know who you are, but I am Macleod of Glenelg's daughter, and you have no business here, certainly not to be doing what you are doing. If this man has broken a law, he should be hailed before the laird's court and given fair trial."

"Aye, sure, but that depends upon whose law he's broken, does it not?"

"You talk in riddles," she said, but even as she said the words, she realized that she had misjudged the men gathered there. Judging by their clothing, they were not common ruffians. Two wore swords that any of her father's men-at-arms or those at Lochbuie would have cherished, and the leader wore a black doublet and trunk hose of excellent cut. A chill of fear crept up her spine, but she ignored it and glared at the leader. "A law is a law," she said. "Cut him down at once."

"Faith, lass, but you're full of orders for one who has no army behind her," one of the men said with a chuckle. "I warrant she'd be a rare one in bed."

"Let her go," the man tied to the trees snapped. "She knows naught of what she sees here, but if she goes missing, men will come looking for her. She may even have an escort out there somewhere. Heaven knows, she should have one."

Isobel could see his face now and thought him one of the handsomest men she had ever seen. But as his gaze met hers, another thrill shot up her spine. He was tied and helpless, but the look he gave her reminded her of the formidable Laird of Lochbuie when he was angry with her.

The leader had been watching her narrowly, but he jerked his head now toward the man who had captured her. "Take a look," he said.

"She's alone. I saw no one with her."

"Look anyway. Sinclair is right. One like that is bound to have keepers." Motioning to two of the others, he said, "Cut him down for now and tie both of them in the cavern until we sort this out. I don't want any surprises."

A short time later, despite her protests, the men forced her to go with them toward a granite wall a short distance away, and through an opening in that wall. Beyond lay the pitch blackness of an underground cavern. Moments later, she was tied hand and foot, as was her sole companion, the one they had called Sinclair.

"I'm surprised they did not gag us," she muttered when the others had gone.

"No one would hear us in here if we shouted, and you're mighty cool for a lass in such a predicament," he said. "Do you have keepers somewhere nearby?"

She sighed. "No, I'm alone. No one will even think to look for me for hours, but when they realize that I'm missing, that will change."

"Is your father so powerful then?"

"Aye, he's powerful enough, for he's a member of the Council of the Isles," she said. "But my sister's husband is more so, and I've lived with them these past seven years. Most likely he'll come looking for me soon, if they haven't killed me."

"How is it that he's more powerful than a member of the Council of the Isles?" he asked, and she thought she detected amusement in his voice.

"He is Hector the Ferocious," she said simply.

Silence greeted that reply, and the amusement was gone

when he said, "I see. I think you will survive longer if you do not mention that to our hosts."

"But why not? Hector terrifies most men."

"Just so," he said. "But these are not 'most men.'"

"Then we had better start thinking of a way to escape from them," she said matter-of-factly.

Her companion chuckled, then laughed aloud, the sound reverberating from the cavern walls.

"I do not know why you laugh," she said. "Once one recognizes that a necessity has arisen, one should greet it with resolution and a plan."

"Well, you'd best plan quickly then, because I think they're coming back."

THE EDITOR'S DIARY

Dear Reader,

Ever notice that the best-laid plans have a funny way of crumbling like blue cheese, especially when you throw love into the mix? Come see what a ferocious man and a flirtacious lady do about it in our two Warner Forever titles this May.

Romantic Times BOOKClub Magazine calls **Amanda Scott's** previous book "a dynamic story," and they couldn't be more right. But her next book is even better, so prepare to be dazzled by **LORD OF THE ISLES**. Lady Cristina Macleod, eldest daughter of a Highland chieftain, is smitten with Hector "the Ferocious" Maclean. As a warrior fearsome enough to earn every man's respect and a man rakishly handsome enough to win any woman's affection, Hector is the perfect match for Cristina. The only problem is that he has just asked for her younger sister's hand in marriage. However, Cristina's father has a secret plan to fix everything. For throughout the western Highlands, marrying off one's younger daughters before the eldest is considered unlucky, and Macleod hates to be unlucky. So as guests arrive for the wedding, Macleod plies everyone, especially Hector, with a powerful Scottish whiskey. But what will "the Ferocious" do when he discovers he's married to the wrong sister? And can Cristina win his heart?

Much like Hector "the Ferocious" Maclean, Cassie Cooper in **Lori Wilde's MISSION: IRRESISTIBLE** knows all about plans going awry. Entrusted with planning a ball that honors the reunification of two halves of a priceless Egyptian amulet, Cassie Cooper knows her job is on the line. But really—how hard is it to plan a party for scientists? So when the lights cut out, half the amulet goes missing, and a mummy collapses with a knife in his back, Cassie knows she's in trouble. Desperate to save her job and find the artifact, she turns to her nemesis: Dr. Harrison Standish—or Standoffish as she calls him. So now this man who doesn't believe in romance and this woman who's in love with love must unravel the secrets behind this magic amulet while dodging bad guys and racing against the clock. But will love catch them first? Grab a copy and find out why *Rendezvous* raves Ms. Wilde "has a unique voice that will soar her to publishing heights."

To find out more about Warner Forever, these titles, and the authors, visit us at www.warnerforever.com.

With warmest wishes,

Karen Kosztolnyik, Senior Editor

P.S. Are you hungry for more? Pick up these two treats that never fail to satisfy: Lani Diane Rich tells the witty and hilarious story of a woman whose mother is kidnapped with only an ugly parrot for ransom and a sexy ex-fiancé for help in MAYBE BABY; and Marliss Melton delivers an intriguing new romantic suspense about a Navy SEAL who uncovers the truth behind a stunning DIA agent's disappearance only to fall head over heels for her in IN THE DARK.